morning wondering whether you'd go to sleep hungry again that night. His test was supposed to put an end to all of that.

Three days prior they'd been down at the riverside, slinging rocks into the river for nothing more than fun. It was their usual hangout on the off hours, when Traders Way was too bare to bother with its pickings, or when they'd had a good score the night before and could afford to spend time just being boys again.

Wilt had a natural affinity with the sling; it was the first and only weapon he'd learned to use. The only one he'd ever felt comfortable wielding. Some of the other thieves had daggers and knives, but Wilt knew better than to carry that sort of hardware. If a guard caught you with one of those, you were sent straight to the dungeons for a week at least, and who knew what you'd look like when you came out. If you ever came out. A sling could quickly become a scarf or a belt when the guards caught up with you.

Of course, if they never caught up with you, that was something else entirely.

He'd been trying to impress Higgs with the advantages of the sling. All he'd needed was a length of cloth, or even better a belt or strap of soft leather. Then whatever he could find for ammunition: rocks in this case, rotten fruit more often than not inside the city walls.

He'd been pleasantly surprised by Higgs's ability to find good slinging stones, but when it came to being able to wield the sling itself, Higgs was taking some time to learn the basics.

'Argh!' Higgs screamed in frustration as his third stone went flying straight up into the sky.

Wilt kept his eye on it as it arced above them. The last two had landed a little too close for comfort. 'You're loosing them too late.'

Higgs muttered something under his breath and bent down to grab another perfect stone.

'What was that?'

'Nothing.' Higgs spun his sling quickly and loosed his stone, this one splashing straight down into the water at his feet.

'Too early.'

'Thanks, genius, I hadn't noticed.'

'Don't get angry with me. Just focus on what you're doing. You'll get it eventually.'

Higgs muttered some more insults under his breath and bent down for another stone.

Wilt smiled to himself and gazed out over the river, toward the far bank where the Tangle waited, its green depths silently swaying. Beckoning to him. A shiver ran up his spine as he stared into it. The Tangle. Wild and unknown. Growing ever closer to the walls each year, waiting to consume the city.

Another splash, this time a few metres out into the river, pulled his thoughts away and told him Higgs was beginning to find his range.

'Better.'

He turned away from the river and looked up at the high walls behind them. Guards patrolled the ramparts, their attentions focused in rather than out. In a strange way they knew the Tangle provided more protection than they ever could. Nothing was coming from out there; at least, nothing they could ever be expected to guard against.

Another splash, far out in the centre of the river, grabbed his attention again.

'That's great, Higgs. Almost as far as mine.'

'Almost?' A new voice answered, its tone tinged with amusement.

Wilt spun around and stood quickly as he saw Lodan standing next to Higgs, the sling dangling from his hands.

Wilt stumbled over his words. 'I— I mean.'

'Come then, show me your skill.' Lodan held the sling out, a grin twisted on his face. Behind him, Higgs was bent over, trying to mask his laughter.

'I didn't—'

'Come.' Lodan cut him off gently but in a tone that brooked no argument. Lodan was known to all the thieves in Greystone, and most of the regular folk as well. He was a tall, dark-haired man, gentle of face but with a coldness in his eyes that spoke of years spent in the shadows. He was the public face of the Grey Guild, the closest anyone ever got to the guild's mysterious leader, a figure known only as the Hand.

Wilt scuttled over the river rocks to where Lodan and Higgs stood and grasped the offered sling.

'Let's see how far you can sling it then, boy.' Lodan's face was serious, but there was a twinkle in his eyes as he watched Wilt pick up a rock and begin to spin the sling up to speed.

With a grunt, Wilt snapped the sling loose. At the last second he flicked his wrist, sending every last ounce of force from the sling to the rock. It flew out over the river, arcing high in the air and easily clearing the distance Lodan's rock had gone.

'Told you.' Higgs's voice was quiet and sure, with a hint of a grin in his words.

Wilt turned back to Lodan, who was still staring at where the rock had disappeared into the river.

'Huh.' He turned back to look at Wilt appraisingly. 'Not bad at all.'

'That's nothing, you should see his aim. He can—'

'That's enough, Higgs,' Wilt interrupted, his cheeks beginning to flush red.

'He can what?' Lodan's voice was calm and deep, and he seemed genuinely interested.

'If you throw a rock out there, he can hit it before it lands,' Higgs blurted before Wilt could stop him.

'Can he now? I think I'd like to see that.' Lodan bent over to grab a rock.

'Higgs is just boasting, I'm not that—'

Lodan silenced him with a look and bounced the stone in his hand. 'Show me.'

Wilt didn't argue; he simply reached down to grab a rock of his own and started to spin the sling.

'Tell me when,' Lodan said, his arm cocked and ready.

Wilt began to spin his sling. 'Whenever you're ready.'

Wilt heard his own quiet tone as though he was listening to someone else. The world seemed to have shut down, all outside noise and movement slowing into a low murmur beneath him. All that he was aware of was the sling moving in his hand, his senses stretched and waiting.

Then there was something more. It was as though he could feel the green of the Tangle waiting for him to act, the breath of the trees held in the silence of the moment, holding the world still for him.

Suddenly Lodan drew back and threw his stone high out over the river. Wilt watched it move in slow motion, its arc clear. It was almost like he read it; no thoughts—stones couldn't have thoughts, could they?—but the action itself. As though each movement was preordained and therefore obvious. All he had to do was play his part.

For a long moment he waited, enjoying the sense of the world around him slowing, the universe pausing for him, only him—a taut drum waiting to be struck.

He loosed his stone with another low grunt and the world sped back into life. The sounds of the river, the birds high above and the wind in the trees where the Tangle waited—it all came back in a rush as his rock speared toward the one Lodan had thrown. It met the other with a crack and shattered it in mid-air, bits of rock showering down into the river.

Higgs let out a yell of triumph and jumped in the air. Wilt studied the ripples in the water where the rocks had landed, a strange calm having settled around his shoulders. Eventually he turned back to see Lodan studying him.

Wilt shrugged and dropped his head, embarrassed.

'Great shot,' Lodan said, holding his hand out to clasp Wilt by the shoulder. 'You may be just the one we're looking for.'

The gathering was in a large disused warehouse situated between the markets and the south gate of the town. In happier times, merchants would travel along the Traders Way, the main street that ran from one end of Greystone to the other, stopping off at the markets in the centre of town to buy and sell their goods. And if a few barrel-loads of ale, or a chest or two of cloth, or even a stray wagon of grain were to go missing on the short trek from the gate to the market, well, a smart merchant knew this was the price to pay for the privilege of trading in a place like Greystone. Merchants who weren't smart, who raised a hue and cry over their missing goods, soon learned the error of their ways. They were bustled straight to the southern gate guardhouse to make a formal complaint. Only once they had left the town altogether did they realise that what had been one missing chest was now five. Any wagons they still had with them were decidedly lighter than they were before.

Now that the times had turned and traffic along the Traders Way had slowed, the Grey Guild too had shrunk in size, their shadows dwarfed in the vastness of the warehouse space they met in. They could also afford to be picky when it came to prospective new members, and so they had come up with the tasks.

Anyone who wanted to join the Grey Guild could, but first they would be tested. In a town the size of Greystone, everyone knew everyone else anyway, so one's reputation and skills were generally common knowledge by the time they presented to the Fingers as a prospective recruit. This knowledge in turn helped the Grey Guild leaders shape each individual challenge to suit. The tasks were designed to push each thief to the limit, and many had failed to complete theirs. As times got harder and the need for new thieves lessened, the tasks had become harder still.

In fact, no one had been successful in completing their given task in well over a year, since Lodan had come to the fore and introduced harsher restrictions. Word was that the last person to try—and fail—had been Red Charley.

Now it was Wilt's turn, and it looked like he too had failed.

Wilt stood in the vast warehouse and gazed up at the cracked beams and broken windows that lined the high walls, letting a little light from the grey sky seep into the warehouse. A circle of torches lit the middle of the room where he stood, and the flames marked out various shadows that stood just outside his view. The Fingers. Wilt knew many more faces studied him than he could make out in the dullness.

'Wilt. You stand before us, yet you have delivered no prize. Explain yourself.' The voice was Lodan's, and Wilt recognised the tall silhouette standing to his side.

Wilt stood mute before them and held out his empty hands. 'I cannot. I—'

'I can.'

A new voice, all too familiar to Wilt, called out confidently. Red Charley stepped forward into the light, the bundle of rags held triumphantly before him.

'I knew about your little test for this boy. He did not have the necessary skills to complete it. I did.' Red Charley unwrapped the bundle and held up the small dagger, grey now in this light.

Lodan's shadow inclined its head. 'Is this true, Wilt?'

Red Charley interrupted before Wilt could answer, his voice louder now. 'I hold the evidence in my hand!' He raised the dagger higher still and stepped forward, his voice dropping in a low threat. 'I challenge any who doubt me to speak now.'

Wilt remained mute. Red Charley glared at him, daring him to speak. The silence stretched as Wilt's mouth moved, but no sound came from his lips.

'I thought not.' Red Charley smiled, and turned to the shadows.

'I challenge.' Wilt only whispered the words, but they rang out in the silence of the great hall.

'What?' Red Charley wheeled around and pointed the dagger at Wilt's chest.

'I challenge,' Wilt repeated, more confidently now, staring into Red Charley's eyes.

'As you should, boy. As you should.'

The new voice boomed from the front of the hall and the room fell silent as a large round figure made its way toward them. Finally it entered the circle of light, and Wilt froze as he recognised the face of the blacksmith he had stolen the dagger from.

The blacksmith held out one enormous hand and clapped Wilt on the shoulder, almost knocking him over. 'After all, you stole it fair and square.'

Lodan's voice rang out in the silence. 'Remove this charlatan.'

A scuffle broke out as rough hands seized Red Charley and threw him to the ground. The dagger was jerked from his hands and a gloved hand cuffed his mouth as he was dragged away.

Lodan stepped forward into the circle of light as Red Charley's feet disappeared into the shadows. 'Some people never change.'

The blacksmith shook his head as he watched the scene, then slowly turned to Wilt. 'Now, boy, I believe this is yours.' The dagger had been handed back to the blacksmith, who now held it out to Wilt.

The young thief studied him warily.

'It's all right lad, take it.'

Wilt reached out slowly and took the blade. As soon as his hands touched the hilt, the dagger shone a bright blue, filling the hall with a strange glow.

'Ah. Good to see that crafter knew what he was doing. Red Charley is just the sort of fool who would try to take credit for the theft of a prize. Each one of them is enchanted—they remember the first hand to touch them and respond again whenever they're back in that hand's grasp. Helps avoid just this sort of situation. There now. I think that removes all doubt, don't you, Lodan?'

'Yes sir.'

'A good theft it was too. Didn't sense this one at all. Read me like a book, didn't you, boy?'

Wilt stood completely still, hypnotised by the blue glow of the blade in his hand.

'The glow marks a prize fairly taken by your hand. Lodan, if you would.'

A long thin arm reached out to Wilt. He only hesitated a moment before handing his prize over to Lodan. As soon as it left his hand, the blue glow faded and the blade became a dull uniform grey.

'Yes. That crafter did know what he was doing.'

Wilt turned toward the blacksmith then, a hundred questions on his tongue.

'You have questions, lad. Lodan will answer them for you. Congratulations. You are now a member of the Grey Guild.' The blacksmith turned on his heel and walked into the darkness.

'But, who are you?' Wilt called after the retreating shadow.

Lodan's hand fell on his shoulder. 'That was Master Turner, boy. You know him as the blacksmith. We know him as the Hand—leader of the Greystone Guild of Thieves.'

Chapter 3

The next few weeks were a blur to Wilt. He was now a member of the Grey Guild, and as far as Higgs was concerned that meant they both were. In exchange for the guild's protection and associated comforts, they were expected to pull their weight. They moved out of the small abandoned shop they'd been living in and into a much cleaner building off Traders Way, one of a multitude of haunts the Fingers claimed as their own. These days there were more than enough disused buildings for them to pick from.

There was also plenty of work to keep them busy. Wilt started at the bottom as a simple pickpocket, and began to make his name immediately. He'd been lifting purses from the careless along Traders Way since he could walk. Higgs was even better at it, helping him reach his quota in record time each week. Eventually he had to rein Higgs in; they were making the other pickpockets look bad in comparison.

Though trade had faded, there were still more than enough merchants and customers wandering the markets to support the thieves. Under the command of Lodan, they moved in and out of the crowds, lightening purses and pockets as they went, careful to never take too much or attract the attention of the guards. They would put up with only so much.

Wilt found it all incredibly easy. Wander the market and pick a target. Then watch them. Let them meander through the curving lanes and stalls, let them feel comfortable in their environment. Let them drop their guard. Then watch some more. Then read them.

He spotted one quickly: a fat man, wealthy. Wary too, by the way he held his coat tight around his belt. That was where the goods were. Wilt could simply walk past and cut his purse, but he was one of the Fingers now, above such clumsiness. No, he would work this properly, like a professional.

Wilt relaxed his mind completely, draining it to an empty pool. Suddenly he was inside the man's mind, every thought as clear as his own.

Not this one. Looks too cheap for Mary. She'd know the price to the copper. Maybe a shawl instead. The ones piled under the table. Purse always getting in the way. Damn this back of mine.

Wilt stepped forward then and stood close behind the soon to be less wealthy man. A few gentle tugs on the purse and it was loose. His fingers sorted quickly through the coins to identify the silver and take a few. Leave the copper for the cut-purses, leave the gold for the guard if he raised the alarm.

Wilt melted away into the crowd and allowed himself a small smile. It was becoming easier every time, calling upon his strange ability. He no longer questioned it, or doubted it would respond. At times it was almost impatient to be used, pushing out at him, urging him to call on it, to let it out into the world.

It didn't take the Fingers long to recognise Wilt's particular aptitude for the tasks he was set. After only a couple of weeks, Lodan recommended Wilt be allowed to work outside the market, anywhere he thought the best targets would be. Lodan was trusted by the Grey Guild and, his advice heeded, he passed the good news onto Wilt with only a small warning. He should stay away from the south of the market. Red Charley still controlled those streets, and he had a long memory.

'Tell me again about the prize, Wilt.'

They sat huddled by the small fireplace in the room that was now their own. No one was going to roust them from this place, but old habits died hard and they kept their fires small and their belongings packed. Wilt didn't think they'd ever grow out of that. They'd never known anything else.

Wilt looked at his small companion sitting by the flames. They were well fed these days but Higgs was still skin and bones, his cheekbones prominent and his face falling away into a small pointed chin. If Wilt was honest with himself, he looked almost like a ferret, though he'd never tell Higgs that.

'It was a dagger.'

'A blue dagger.'

'That's right, a blue dagger. Though it was only blue when the one who had rightfully stolen it held it in his hands.'

'And that was you.'

'That's right, that was me.'

'And so when Red Charley took it from you it wasn't blue anymore, so everyone knew he hadn't stolen it properly at all.'

'Who's telling this story, Higgs?'

'You are.'

They both stared at the flames some more, Wilt enjoying the feeling of them clearing his mind.

'Wilt?'

'Yes, Higgs.'

'How did the crafter make the dagger turn blue?'

'I don't know. I expect you'd have to be a crafter to know that.'

'How do you get to be a crafter?'

'It's one of the skills they teach in Redmondis. You know that story.'

'The mountain fortress, where they teach all the skilled ones. If you get chosen to be a student, you get sent to Redmondis, and you get tested by the Prefects there, and if you pass their test you get given one of the skills.'

'You know more about it than I do.'

Higgs began counting them off on his fingers. 'There's crafting, there's healing, there's soldiering, there's apotha ... apothec ... apotaca ...'

'Apothecary.'

'There's potions, there's foreseeing.' Higgs ran out of fingers and stopped. 'There's lots of them.'

'There are lots of them. Too many to count. I doubt anyone knows them all.'

Higgs lay back down on his bed and closed his eyes. 'Wilt?'

'Yes, Higgs.'

'If you were chosen, what skill would you choose?'

'I don't know.' Wilt's eyes became heavy as he looked into the flames. 'I don't think it works like that. I don't think you get to choose. I think the skill chooses you.'

'I'd choose to be a crafter.'

'Okay, Higgs. Go to sleep.'

'Then I could make a blue dagger as well. Or maybe a green one. Or a red one!'

'Higgs.'

'Yes, Wilt?'

'Go to sleep.'

Wilt was beginning to get comfortable in his new life. He was excelling in the Grey Guild, and even Higgs had managed to make himself more useful lately, helping to organise the younger street urchins under Lodan's control. Most merchants ignored the urchins completely, never thinking of minding their tongues around the ever-present street rats. As a result, the Grey Guild was better informed now than it had ever been, with eyes and ears in every alley.

Things were finally beginning to look up for Wilt, so much so he actually began to relax and enjoy life. He really should have known better.

It had started off as a simple job. He'd been handed the message by one of the tavern wenches at the Thirsty Captain, the largest and busiest of the taverns lining the docks on the eastern side of the city. It was a favourite haunt of the merchant sailors who shipped in and out of Greystone on a daily basis. A tavern that offered hot meals and cold ale, and knew better than to charge full price for the workers who kept the trade of Greystone flowing. And for those looking for other entertainment, well, that could be found easily enough as well.

Wilt didn't look closely at the girl who handed him the message. That was his first mistake.

He had heard that some of the girls working here offered other services for those willing to pay, and he hadn't wanted to send any wrong signals. Not that he wasn't curious. He had been lost in the roaring fire burning in the main room, letting his ears work for him, scanning the random conversations that slipped in and out of hearing. Suddenly someone grabbed his hand and wrapped his fingers around a small slip of paper. Her hand had been warm, and she'd squeezed his fingers lightly before disappearing into the crowd. Knowing better than to react, he hadn't even glanced up at the girl before she moved away.

The note was from Lodan. Wilt recognised the thin, slanted scrawl immediately. *The blacksmith requests your company.* He downed the rest of his drink in a gulp and stood up immediately. The Hand had asked for him specifically. That meant something important. A rush of excitement washed over him and he no longer paid any attention to the crowd.

That was his second mistake.

More than one pair of eyes watched him stride quickly across the tavern floor and push out into the darkness of the streets, and more than one pair of feet moved to follow him.

Wilt had never been summoned specifically by the Hand before, had never even heard of it happening to someone else. Messages were usually passed through Lodan or one of the other more experienced thieves, but Wilt decided not to question it. He hurried down the east road toward the markets in the centre of town. Perhaps the Hand had heard about his progress with the Grey Guild; perhaps he'd been impressed. Perhaps he wanted to reward him.

The blacksmith requests your company. The wording suggested the meeting place was at the forge itself, rather than the warehouse where they'd met earlier. That made sense. One-to-one meetings were probably less formal. Maybe they'd sit in the back room and the Hand would get him to tell the story of how Wilt took the prize from under his nose. He'd been impressed by that.

Wilt smiled as he trotted down the road, oblivious to the shadows that flitted from rooftop to rooftop beside him.

Maybe they'd share a drink. Higgs would be so jealous.

The forge was shuttered when he got there, but there was a glow from the back room so Wilt strode in confidently. Heat still emanated from behind the heavy iron gate of the fire as he passed it, and the blacksmith's tools were set out on the anvil in front of it. Wilt paused in his step as he noticed the thin knife laying amongst the tools, its surface straight and sharp. It was free of blemishes, except for a heavy dent halfway up the blade, almost a chip, as if the blacksmith had lost control mid swing and struck one blow too many on the shining blade. He slowed to a stop as he stared at the imperfect work, his mind finally beginning to catch up. There was something wrong.

Wilt reached out slowly to let his fingers brush the flaw in the blade, and a vision whipped across his eyes.

Red Charley, standing beside the forge, a cruel smirk on his face. Staring at the flawless knife on the anvil, weighing the heavy hammer in his hand, unable to resist this small mischief.

It was a trap.

Wilt spun on his heel and started toward the door, but two shadows seemed to fall out of the darkness to block his way.

'So. Not completely stupid then.' Red Charley's voice came from behind him. 'Turn around, Meat.'

Wilt froze and let his senses flow out from him.

'Boys, it seems young Meat here has lost the use of his limbs. Loosen him up for me, would you?'

The shadows moved toward Wilt, and he forced his body to relax as they fell on him. No use running now, there was no way out. Not yet. The larger of the two figures dropped Wilt to his knees with a punch to the stomach. He gasped theatrically, though the blow seemed unimportant as he kept searching around the room for a way out. The other one kicked him and rolled him over to face Red Charley.

'Not so smart now, are you, Meat? Lodan's scrawl isn't the easiest to master, but given time and the right talents—' Red Charley interrupted himself with a heavy kick into Wilt's guts. 'Anything is possible.'

Wilt looked past Red Charley to the anvil and the set of tools sitting beside the forge. A heavy hammer, some tongs, and something that looked like a large hook glowed briefly in the darkness.

'Your little stunt cost me face in the guild. Did you think I would let that go? Boys, bring him to his feet.'

Wilt glanced from the tools to Red Charley as he was lifted up off the dirt. Red Charley paced back and forth, his eyes bright with anger. Wilt swallowed and focused his mind. Red Charley was mad and capable of anything. He had to escape.

'Open the forge.'

Wilt heard the heavy gate open and felt the heat of the fire kiss his skin as it flared up with a rush of air. He closed his eyes. *Forget the fire. Forget the fear. Focus. Focus on their minds.*

'I knew you were a coward the first time I saw you, Meat.'

Wilt's sense scrambled over the surface of Red Charley's mind, but it was closed, a blank wall of nothingness, with no way for him to get in. *Look to the others.*

With a silent effort he switched his attention to the other two men.

Charley's really gonna to do it. Gonna burn him. Gonna cook his pretty flesh.

Wilt's mind retreated quickly from the excited darkness of that mind. Samson. He was just as mad as Red Charley. He then focused on the other man.

Hold the boy and keep your mouth shut. They're just gonna scare him.

He was the one. If he could just get him to loosen his grip …

'Open your eyes, Meat.'

Wilt opened his eyes and lost contact with the other man's mind. Harken, that was his name.

Red Charley stood in front of him, holding up a single glowing coal in the pair of tongs. The other tools were within reach behind him.

Wilt closed his eyes again and reached out for Harken's mind.

Don't let him loose, even if they do burn him. Don't show any weakness.

Wilt could feel the heat from the coal tighten his skin as Red Charley held it up to his cheek.

'Can't even face this, can you, Meat? Closing your eyes won't help you.'

Wilt clawed desperately for purchase on the other man's mind. His fear lent his sense a panicked strength.

Red Charley let out a small sigh of pleasure as he pushed the glowing coal against Wilt's cheek, pain screaming through Wilt's mind—through his mind and into Harken's, wiping out everything in its path.

Harken stiffened and fell backward as the shock overwhelmed him. Wilt felt him falling and jerked his arm free, throwing the limp man straight into Samson. Samson stumbled and fell onto the hot gate of the forge, shrieking with pain, holding his smouldering hands up in front of his face.

Red Charley was only beginning to react as Wilt dashed behind him, grabbing the hook from the anvil as he ran into the back room.

'No!' Red Charley's scream echoed around the forge as he spun and charged after his prey.

Wilt rushed through the door into the small room without hesitating. Leaping on to the desk he jumped again, holding the hook above his head to catch the roof beam directly above. He pulled his arms tight as it bit, crunching his legs into his chest and letting his body's momentum swing him up and over, releasing the hook at the top of the arc, flipping full circle in mid-air to come back around just as Red Charley charged into the room. Wilt thrust out his feet in a two-footed kick that landed in the centre of Red Charley's chest. His bodyweight did the rest, crushing his attacker backward into the ground. Wilt heard a deep crack as Red Charley landed and knew he'd done some damage to the man, but he didn't stop to check.

Wilt pushed himself to his feet and ran out into the cold darkness, only looking back when he was sure he heard no sounds of pursuit. The door of the hut glowed in the darkness, and a single shadow emerged and limped away. Wilt ran on, the cool air soothing the deep burn on his cheek.

Chapter 4

The red burn on Wilt's cheek didn't fade with time. The wound closed and healed, and the skin became smooth again, but the angry red colour stayed, permanently marking his cheek. He was reminded of it each time he caught his reflection. Higgs knew better than to ask about it, as it only seemed to make Wilt angry.

They had been working hard for the Grey Guild, Wilt as one of the Fingers and Higgs with his new role of overseeing the street urchins—the Rats, they called themselves with pride—and had been given the day to spend as they wished. Wilt had mentioned the overabundance of river pebbles he'd seen lining the eastern wall of the city, and Higgs had grabbed their slings without further prompting. Once at the city wall, they took turns flinging the small stones hard and flat across the width of the wide grey river and into the trees lining the far bank.

'I know something you don't know,' Higgs said with a grin. He spun his sling quickly over his head and flung his rock in a high arc over the swiftly moving water. It fell just short of the far bank, landing in the dark water with a plonk. His skill with the sling had improved in leaps and bounds.

'Do you now?' Wilt took his time picking his stone from the pile at his feet. The vagaries of the river tides had washed up a good pile of ammunition at this spot, so he could afford to be fussy. Higgs continued to blindly pick out his stones, but Wilt preferred to take his time.

'Even Lodan doesn't know about it yet.'

'I doubt that.' Wilt finally decided on a perfectly sized, round, shiny black stone.

'It's true.' Higgs had let another rock fly, which fell into the water again. He was getting closer.

'This something your Rats told you? What does that make you anyway? Chief Rat?'

Higgs ignored him. 'Something one of them heard. Know where she works?'

'What, you mean you're not all vagrants?'

'She's a cook's helper. In the duke's kitchen.'

Wilt placed his rock in the pocket of his sling and gave it a few experimental spins over his head. Good. Not too heavy. 'A dish pig.'

'A helper. And she heard word that some special guests are coming to town. The kitchen will have to prepare meals for them.'

'Dignitaries.'

'Something like that.'

Wilt stepped to the water's edge, set his feet, and began to spin his sling.

'Funny thing about the food though. No meat.'

Wilt had the sling spinning in a blur over his head now. 'No meat?'

Just a few more, then release. Follow through.

'No meat. Know who don't eat meat, Wilt?'

Three two one. 'Who?'

'Prefects.'

Wilt slipped and fell backward as he let go and the stone flung out in a great high arc over the water, easily clearing it to the other bank. Wilt didn't notice, though; he hadn't watched the stone's flight at all. His eyes were locked on Higgs's grinning face.

'A Prefect? Coming here? To Greystone?'

Higgs's grin widened as he nodded his head.

Wilt rolled onto his side and sat up. 'You need to tell—'

'Already done. You don't think you're the Rats' first port of call, do you?' Higgs turned back to the pile of stones and picked out another, whistling happily.

'Sit down, Wilt.'

Wilt sat down in the small booth across from Lodan and looked around the tavern. Harvest festival was the busiest time of the year, and crowds were up. Business was unusually good for the tavern keepers of Greystone, and they were making the most of it, raising prices across the board. They couldn't be sure of such a crowd next year, or the year after, and they knew well enough to strike while the iron was hot.

A young waiter wandered past their table and Lodan signalled to him for drinks. He included a three-fingered tap on his shoulder to ensure the tavern staff knew it was for serving members of the Grey Guild. No watered down or overpriced ale for them.

Wilt scanned over the various rich targets in the room until his gaze came to rest on Lodan.

He was openly studying Wilt's face. 'See anything you like?'

'Oh yes.' Wilt grinned and Lodan allowed a small smile to brighten his cold features.

'Yes, these are rich times for all of us. Too rich for some.'

Lodan's eyes darkened, and Wilt found himself sitting straighter in his chair. There was something about Lodan that demanded immediate respect from his men. A quiet strength in his words. He knew exactly what he asked of his crew and would only have done so if he had faith in their ability to complete the task. He was a born leader; some said he was the obvious next in line for the position of the Hand, though none would dare put such thoughts into words around Lodan.

'Let me guess.' Wilt's smile had faded.

'Red Charley. He's been getting more active in recent months. No longer feels it necessary to follow the guidelines. Been taxing the merchants on the southern side of town a little too heavily of late.'

'The guard?'

'The guard won't step in until they have to. Which will be soon if nothing is done, but we could all do without a total lockdown. No, best to try and sort these things out ourselves.'

'So?'

'So the decision has been made to remove Red Charley from his position. Permanently.'

Wilt sat back against the bench and let out a slow breath. There was certainly no love lost between him and Red Charley, but this? Even he wasn't so sure. The scar on his cheek throbbed with a sudden heat.

'Relax, Wilt, we're not talking about killing him.'

'But you said—'

'You can remove players from the game without violence, so long as you know the right moves to make.'

The knot in Wilt's stomach loosened. The waiter returned with two brimming tankards of ale and Wilt took a long draught.

Lodan smiled at him. 'You didn't really think we'd just kill him, did you?'

'No, but—'

'But you weren't sure. And you weren't sure whether you liked the idea. You are still young, Wilt, and there are far larger stakes being played for than you can yet see. Trust in the Hand, Wilt. He is a good man. A smart man. A man not known for the obvious.'

Wilt put his drink down and looked at Lodan. 'So what do you need me to do?'

'There's a special guest coming to town. Not many people know of it yet, but everyone will soon enough. One of the Prefects of Redmondis is passing through …'

Wilt crouched by the high window and watched the crowds pass along Traders Way. Lodan had said the caravan from Redmondis was due today, and they had never been known to be late for anything. Some said it was yet another one of the skills, the ability to pass untroubled through the trails and forests that surrounded Greystone, even through the Tangle itself. Wilt thought it had more to do with the threat of the skills than any actual ability held by the members of the entourage. Even the dumbest highwaymen knew better than to risk the wrath of Redmondis.

Wilt let his mind clear as the people walked below him and sent his sense skimming over their thoughts.

Carol should be here. Always gives the best price for silk.

Two more months of this and I'm for the south. Damn the forests—I'll take them over this 'Greystone tax' any day.

And five more is twenty-three silvers. That's almost a gold. Wait till the Master hears about this day.

'Wilt?'

Wilt snapped his head around and saw Higgs standing behind him in the shadows.

'Higgs. You snuck up on me again. You're getting good at that.'

'You were doing it again, weren't you?'

'Huh? Doing what?'

'That thing you do sometimes. You do it when you want to know what someone else is thinking.'

'And what would you know about that?'

'I can tell. I can feel it, hear it almost. Like a distant song, or like the wind. Besides, your eyes go funny.'

Wilt turned away from the window and dropped down from the ledge back into the empty storeroom. 'Funny how?'

'I don't know. They go all grey. I don't like it.'

'What are you doing here, Higgs?'

Higgs dropped his gaze to his toes. 'Lodan asked you to do something, didn't he? Today? I thought maybe—'

'No, Higgs.'

'But I could help you! I can keep an eye on things, make sure no one sneaks up on you when you're doing that thing.'

'Higgs, go home.'

'You know Red Charley is still looking for you.'

'Higgs, enough. Go home.' Wilt glared at Higgs until he turned away. 'Don't let me catch you out here later. I'll be back soon enough.'

'Okay,' Higgs squeaked as he walked away.

Wilt felt a sudden rush of guilt and regret at speaking to him so bluntly. He almost called him back, then remembered he had more important things to worry about. He turned to the window and leaped lightly up to the ledge.

The crowd below had thickened, but there was still no way of picking out who he was looking for by sight alone. Wilt sent his mind out again.

Damn those guards. Too busy drinking and gambling to watch out for common thieves.

If his nibs thinks that he'll be getting a hot dinner tonight after sending me in here to deal with this crowd then he has another thing coming.

What the Prefect asks, you do. One does not question the Prefect. There.

Wilt snapped his eyes open and saw the small group of men pushing through the crowds. They were unremarkable, three men all shrouded in long, hooded red cloaks. The man he had read was at the rear of the group; two larger men walked closely in front of him. Must be some sort of servant or valet. Now, which of the others was the Prefect?

He watched them push past more people; the one on the right always seemed to reach out and push people out of the way for them both. Not him then. He was the bodyguard. Probably very well trained.

Wilt turned his eyes to the other man now, the one who had to be the Prefect. He sent his mind out quickly to try to read him but came back blank. It was as though his sense couldn't get a grasp on anything, as though the other man's mind was a cold glass wall.

Yes, he was the one.

Wilt hurried through the storehouse into a back alley and looped around to stand just in front of the group on Traders Way. He pretended to browse one of the many stalls lining the street, hoping to pick up more information as they overtook him.

The general hum and chatter of the crowd faded as he concentrated his attention, but the three men passed him silently and continued up the road toward the market in the centre of town.

Wilt knew he had to work quickly. If they got to the market they could go anywhere. Lodan's information only went so far, and he didn't fancy trying to follow them all the way to their destination. Especially if they headed into Red Charley's territory.

He turned away from the stall and moved up the Traders Way, letting the crowd shield him from the men he was following. He had to come up with something quickly. They were only a few blocks from the market now.

The servant, the shorter man trailing the others. You can read him. Perhaps he can show you the way.

He let his mind go as he walked, trusting his body to make its way quietly through the crowd.

One does not question the Prefect. Still. This is perhaps not the best use of our time. The talisman should be entering this town as part of a formal procession, not snuck in through the back door like some sort of cheap harlot.

There. Wilt smiled. The talisman was his target. Now to find out exactly where …

And these two. The Prefect with his airs. Not sure enough to hold the talisman himself, trusting his bodyguard to protect it. A man whose only skill is with the fist and the sword. Not worthy of even laying his eyes on the talisman, let alone carrying it against his breast.

So. The bodyguard, the man on the right of the Prefect. He was the one. Must be holding it in his coat pocket. Now, how to …

Idiot doesn't even know what he is holding. Stopping every few blocks to stretch himself 'from the long ride'. He rode in the carriage, not outside in the rain like me. At least he has the sense to step into the shadows before doing it, not inviting every thief with eyes to target him.

Wilt closed on the group, closer than was sensible. He felt safe with the link he had established, and it was providing him such good information. All he had to do was follow them into the shadows, then move in while their guard was down.

Sure enough, the three men moved toward the next alley exit. Wilt knew a shortcut and could beat them there.

He ducked into the nearest doorway and pushed to the back of the store. The owner only glanced up at him as he passed, knowing better than to question a member of the Grey Guild. Wilt opened the rear door leading into the storeroom and then swung open the window into the small alley behind the store. He vaulted out and hurried along the damp stone path toward the alley where his target would be. He felt so light on his feet, so confident, as though nothing in the world could hold him back from his task. He was the best thief in Greystone, and would be in and out before the Prefect's bodyguard even knew what had happened.

'Wilt.'

The man probably wouldn't even notice the theft until they were blocks away.

'Wilt, stop.'

The best thief in Greystone.

'Wilt!'

Wilt stopped and shook his head, feeling the strange fog clouding his thoughts lift suddenly.

'Over here.'

Wilt looked up and saw Higgs waving at him from a small window on the first floor.

'Quickly. They're coming.'

He knew better than to argue. Wilt scaled the stone walls

quickly and slipped through the window. He turned and saw that he now had a view of the larger alley he had been heading for. Three shadows, two large and one smaller, were entering the alley from the Traders Way.

'This better be good, Higgs. You're not supposed to be here.'

'It's a trap, Wilt. I could feel it. He was reading you.'

'What do you mean? I was reading him.'

'But you were reading what he wanted you to read. He was leading you here. I could almost hear it, like I was telling you before. And I saw his eyes, under his hood I could see them when he did it. They were like yours.'

'Like mine? How?'

'They were grey. They were all grey.'

Chapter 5

Wilt and Higgs crouched in the shadow of the window and watched the three figures as they entered the alley. The two larger men stopped and turned to the shorter man. He gestured angrily at them. Wilt relaxed his mind and sent his senses out.

'Be careful, Wilt.'

He's not here.

But I thought you could lead him.

He must be stronger than we thought. Forget it. Move on. If he's that developed he can probably hear us even now.

Without our sensing?

Of course.

Wilt flinched then as a single thought sang out, impossibly loud, as though an entire choir of voices was yelling directly into his ear.

Next time, little thief.

Then all thought was abruptly cut off and Wilt was knocked onto his haunches.

'Wilt!' Higgs turned to help him up. But Wilt waved him back, his head spinning.

'I'm okay. Watch them! Watch where they go.'

They both turned to the window just in time to see the last figure disappear into the rush of the Traders Way.

'Follow them!'

Wilt pulled himself to his feet and stood dazed for a second as a wave of dizziness washed over him. Higgs was already out the window, scuttling quickly down the wall and hitting the stone floor of the alley at a run. Wilt shook his head clear and followed him.

They pushed into the rush of the Traders Way and hurried through the crowds. The three men were only twenty yards in front, but there were at least a hundred other bodies between them. Higgs ducked through legs and pushed quickly past swinging arms, and Wilt had to reach out to slow him to avoid being left behind. He was too big to swim through a crowd like this.

'Wait for me, Higgs.'

They settled into a rhythm, slowly gaining on the three men.

'Well?' Higgs risked a quick turn to make eye contact with Wilt before focusing on the job at hand.

'Well what?'

'Are you going to tell me why we're following these men?'

'Lodan asked me to.'

'And?'

'And what?'

'And what else did Lodan ask you to do?'

'I'm not supposed to talk about it, Higgs, you know that. The Fingers—'

'Damn the Fingers!' Higgs stopped in the middle of the road and bodies all around them bumped and bustled into them. 'They would have got you back there if it wasn't for me. They were leading you into a trap. So who is he? And why had Lodan asked you to follow them? And what else has Lodan asked you to do? Tell me now or I'll scream thief and you'll never catch up with them.'

The crowd was thickening around them now, and angry mutterings could be heard.

'You wouldn't dare.'

'Thief!' Higgs shouted at the top of his lungs, and twenty pairs of eyes snapped toward them.

Wilt grabbed Higgs's hand and pulled him into another part of the crowd before anyone thought of following them. 'All right! Just don't let me lose them.'

They continued on, staying near the three men as the crowd moved ever onwards.

'They're ... well, one of them at least, is a Prefect.'

Higgs almost knocked an old woman over as he spun around to face Wilt. 'A Prefect! Of—'

'Yes, of Redmondis. They're here—'

'For a survey! They're going to survey the town to see if there are any students worthy of learning the skills!'

'Can I tell the story please?'

'Okay.'

'We don't know the reason they're here, but they're here for the festival. Maybe for a survey, but it doesn't matter. What matters is that Red Charley is also still here. Now, if a Prefect were to have something go missing ...'

'Even Red Charley knows better than to try and steal from a Prefect. No one knows what powers they have.'

'Yes but if someone were to steal something from the Prefect, and then that something was to find its way into Red Charley's hands ...'

'The guard would step in. They'd take control of his section, lock it down completely. They'd probably even ...'

'Yes, well what the guard would or wouldn't do to Red Charley once they got their hands on him isn't our problem. Our problem is getting our hands on something of the Prefect's.'

Higgs stopped abruptly and Wilt had to twist out of his way to avoid bumping into him.

'Now what?'

'They're doing it again.'

'What?'

'Listen.'

Wilt looked toward the three men but could no longer see them in the crowd.

'We're losing them!'

'Wilt. Stop and really listen. Can't you hear that? It's like an echo on the stones.'

Higgs's eyes had lost all focus and he was tilting his head slightly to the side like a dog. Wilt sighed in frustration and closed his eyes, willing himself to hear whatever it was Higgs was talking about. For a second he almost heard it, a whisper in the distance, a man's voice, but there was something wrong with it, something false. He could almost make out the words ...

'C'mon!' Higgs grabbed his hand and pulled him quickly to the side of the Way.

'Higgs, what—'

'They're doing it again. Leading someone else in. To the south.'

'But that's Red Charley's territory.'

'I don't think they care.'

They forced their way to the edge of the crowd and ducked through the nearest doorway into a tannery. Stretched hides hung from the roof beams, and groups of traders wandered around them, haggling over prices. Higgs started to run toward the back, but Wilt stopped him.

'No. This way.' He jerked Higgs around and pointed to the roof.

'But I can't—'

'I'll boost you up. Here.'

Wilt knelt on one knee and cupped his hands for Higgs to stand in. Once Higgs was balanced, he stood and threw his leg upward, propelling the small boy high into the roof beams. Higgs grabbed on and scrambled into a steady position. He looked down at Wilt and almost smiled.

'What about you?'

'Don't worry about me. Head to the hatch.'

Wilt pointed to the small hatch in the roof and Higgs started to edge slowly toward it, his arms outstretched for balance.

Wilt looked quickly around and sprinted toward the corner of the room. He ducked past two groups of men before they knew he was there, and ran full pelt directly at the wall. Just before he hit it he jumped, his right leg landing four feet up the right wall, then he pushed off again, toward the other wall, and his left leg hit another four feet higher. Then, as if it were nothing at all, he pushed off again, springing away from the walls now, and turned in mid-air to face the closest roof beam. His hand hit it dead on, and he allowed his body's momentum to swing him up to land feet first on the next beam across, coming to rest just under the roof hatch as Higgs arrived, wide eyed.

'Where did you learn that? You looked like a cat!'

Wilt winked at him and grinned. 'I've been practising. C'mon.' He pushed the small hatch open and they both crawled out onto the rooftop. 'Which way?'

Higgs raised a skinny arm and pointed. 'That way, three over.'

They sprinted across the roof, Wilt loping easily across the tiles and Higgs hurrying in his wake, trying not to make too much noise. The rooftops were joined here, packed in as they got closer to the centre of the town and the sprawling market that lay at its heart.

Higgs caught up with Wilt at the third building and stood panting behind him. The side of the next structure stuck out over the one they were on, offering a dark hiding place in its shadows. Wilt crouched at the edge of the roof, peering over.

'Wilt—'

'Shh! C'mere. Quietly.'

Higgs joined him at the edge. He peered over the gutter to see the dark alley below them. There was nothing there. 'Wilt?'

'The shadows on the east wall, below the window.'

Higgs fixed his eyes on the place and caught the slightest movement in the darkness, as though a body shifted impatiently.

'There are three of them. Must be Red Charley's. No discipline.'

Wilt and Higgs turned to the entrance of the alley as the three robed men strode in. The first two were chatting loudly to each other, the third walking quietly in their wake. As they approached the shadows where the attackers waited, they turned their backs to the wall as one. Two of the waiting thieves dropped from the wall and headed straight for them. The third held back, as if having second thoughts. Had to be Red Charley himself.

The attackers fell on the two large men quickly, then seemed to twist suddenly in mid-air as the men parried their thrusts and flipped them. The two young thieves landed heavily on the ground, their faces in the dirt. The men stepped forward and dropped heavy boots on their necks to hold them in place. The one on the right pulled something out of his cloak, and Higgs gasped as a glint of sunlight flashed off the long steel blade.

'Halt, Cantor!'

It was the third figure who spoke, but there was something different about the voice that rang out across the alley.

Deep silence descended on the area as the smaller man stepped forward into the sunlight and pulled back his hood. Her hood. Light gleamed off the long red hair that tumbled freely down the woman's back. That could only mean—

'A Sister.'

Higgs had only whispered the words, but they echoed in Wilt's ears. A Sister. One of the Nine. No one laid eyes on them outside Redmondis and lived. No one.

The woman—the Sister—paused as if listening, then continued on to the prone figures on the ground and the two large men standing over them. Every word she uttered rang out through the silence.

'That is not the way, Cantor Cortis. Not here. These two are not worthy of your blade.'

The Sister stopped her stride at the heads of the two thieves and peered down at them, scrutinising their faces with genuine curiosity, as though they were strange foreign specimens, pinned to a board for her study.

'Perhaps they have their uses after all. You! Come!'

Her voice seemed to coil through the air, writhing around its target. She pointed into the shadows as she called, and a third figure detached itself from the wall and strode slowly toward the group. As it entered the light, Wilt recognised Red Charley.

'You are not the one we sensed.' The Sister's tone was sorrowful, as if Red Charley had somehow disappointed her.

Red Charley halted directly in front of her and stood swaying. From the shadows, Wilt could see his features were slack, as if he was walking in a dream.

'Cantor Cortis. Hand this one your blade. We will test him here. He looks a quick study.'

The man handed the blade to Red Charley without a word, then stepped away from the two prone bodies.

The Sister spoke to Red Charley again, her voice softer now that she had complete control. 'These men have inconvenienced me. Remove their right hands.'

Red Charley didn't hesitate. He knelt quickly beside the first body as the Cantor pulled the poor man's hand out from under his body, and swept the blade down in a single chop. Blood spouted across the dirt and the man let out a choked cry, muffled by the dirt as the Cantor pressed down heavily on his neck again, his eyes blazing with an alien hunger.

The second man tried to scramble away then, choking out words to beg helplessly for mercy. Red Charley simply strode over and sliced quickly through the air, cutting into the man's out-stretched arm, removing his hand at the wrist. He turned away without a word, leaving the man to roll in agony in the dirt, then knelt quickly and offered the blood-soaked blade to the Sister.

'Good. But you have also inconvenienced me.'

Red Charley hesitated then, his sense of self-preservation pushing back against the Sister's will.

The Sister smiled at him. 'Not the whole hand, of course. We wouldn't want any true cripples to join the ranks of Redmondis. A finger will do.'

Red Charley looked down at his hand, then fell to the ground, splayed his fingers out in the dirt and cut the blade down quickly, chopping his little finger off with a single blow. He let out no cry, but his whole body shook as he raised himself to his feet and held out the blade again.

'Not to us. To your Master, Cantor Cortis.'

Red Charley spun on his heel and quickly walked the few steps to the man whose blade he held. He dropped to one knee and offered it up to the man, his head bowed. The man took the handle, wiped the blade on Red Charley's shoulder, and hid it within his cloak.

'It seems we have found one disciple already.' The Sister turned to the second Cantor, who was facing away from the bloody scene. 'Cantor Wrexley, you see, your doubt was misplaced.'

The second man spoke then, in a voice strong and clear, yet still deferential. 'Yes, Sister. Yet we were not sent here to recruit mere bodyguards.'

The man named Cortis seemed to stiffen then, and a smile spread across the Sister's face.

'You insult Cantor Cortis, Wrexley. You know he is quick to anger.'

'We each have our charms, Sister.'

'Yes. Come now. We still have work to do.'

The Sister raised her hood over her head and Wilt felt the pall of oppressive silence lift from him. His muscles suddenly screamed out for relief, and he realised he'd been clenched tight the entire time. Higgs had collapsed against his side, and Wilt knew he'd been under the same spell. They stayed in the shadows and watched as the three figures walked out of the alley.

Higgs finally rolled out of their hiding place and stood up. 'A Sister. We have to tell Lodan.'

'I know.'

Wilt struggled to his feet and walked slowly over the rooftops. Lodan would have to know, and the Hand himself. If Redmondis had sent a Sister to Greystone then everything was about to change, but that was not what worried him.

What worried him was the image of the Sister as she stood below him, her hair shining in the sunlight. What worried him was how beautiful she was.

Chapter 6

The news was passed up the chain and neither Wilt nor Higgs heard any more about the Prefects or the Sister until some days later, in the middle of the Greystone harvest festival. The festival was a two-week celebration of trade and plenty, a time when debts were put on hold and disputes forgotten. In the past the town had seen kings and queens make Greystone their home for the festival; nowadays the most prestigious visitors to share the duke's residence were members of the capital's merchant guild. But that didn't stop the town from celebrating, and it didn't diminish the festival's most important event: the battle for the flag.

To any visitor to Greystone over the festival period, the battle for the flag was just a day-long excuse for a party. To the locals, it was far more serious than that.

Two teams—guards versus guild. Win the game and you fly the flag for a year. Lose, and you face a year of taunts. At least, that was the official reward for victory. The unofficial ones were much more important. A guild victory would mean a year of guards turning a blind eye to the Greystone tax, stonewalling requests for investigations into missing goods, and generally letting things slide. There had even been stories of prisoners being set free; guild members who had pushed the guard's patience a little too far suddenly found their cell doors left unbarred. Of course, no one could confirm or deny these rumours; the guild hadn't actually won the flag for as long as Wilt could remember.

On top of this, there were a multitude of bets placed with unofficial bookmakers throughout the town. Guild members and guards couldn't help but back their team, and a victory either way always resulted in fortunes made and lost throughout the populace. The odds were always in the guards' favour, especially considering recent form, and bookmakers knew how to tempt even those who thought they knew better.

The game itself—named flagball in a typically Greystone show of practicality—was simple. Two teams of six: five outfielders and a goalie. Get the ball into their zone and take their flag. The zones were marked by two posts, five metres apart, and the flag hung between them, three metres in the air. There were no time limits. Full contact allowed on the player in possession—anything goes. Players weren't supposed to touch anyone without the ball, but the referee couldn't see everything. Games could last for two minutes or all day. Get the ball into the opponent's zone and take their flag. Simple.

Wilt knew better. He'd been playing flagball since he could run and catch, and watching the games since before that. He knew that what looked simple from the outside generally involved a lot of effort and skill, and usually a lot of pain. Still, when Lodan approached him about representing the guild, he couldn't help but be excited.

It seemed the guild was a man down due to unforeseen circumstances. At least, that's how Lodan had explained it. Wilt had a nagging feeling about that, but accepted his place with pride and tried to push any doubt from his mind. Later that night he mentioned it to Higgs, who giggled and reminded him of last year's game. The guard defenders had taken out the guild winger with a two-man assault that left their victim unconscious in the dirt with what later turned out to be two broken legs. All accidental, of course. Higgs laughed again and wished him a good night's sleep.

Lodan didn't give him any time to worry. A hundred little jobs seemed to appear, messages to be run from one end of town to the other, all apparently urgent, though Wilt suspected Lodan was just trying to keep him from dwelling too much on the game.

It was only a couple of days before the big game when Wilt finally managed to catch up with Lodan and ask him if they were ever going to work on any tactics or strategy. Lodan had smiled and clapped him on the shoulder. Apparently that simply wasn't how guild teams worked. The Hand was a believer in instinct above all else.

'Get the ball down their end and take their flag. Simple.'

'That's it?'

'That's it. And watch out for the guards. They like to play rough.'

Wilt couldn't be sure, but he thought maybe Lodan was making fun of him.

The day of the game arrived, and it seemed that the entire town had gathered in the centre of the marketplace. The stalls that usually cluttered the area had been cleared away, and a vast empty space of packed dirt was being roped off by town officials. Crowds lined the ropes, laughing and drinking despite the early hour. No man would begrudge you at harvest time. Wilt stood at one end of the field, staring blank-eyed across its length. He was trying to keep his mind clear of images of guards and blood and cheering crowds. His body felt distant and ready.

'Snap out of it!' Higgs's high voice brought him back to the present, and he turned to smile at him.

'What are you doing here?'

'Watching the game of course. Try not to mess up, will you? The guild's got a lot of money riding on you this year.'

'Oh?' Wilt hadn't thought of that. With their heavy loss last year the odds would be good. Maybe it was worth a flutter.

'Higgs, I know you know where I keep our stash. Behind the third brick up on the fireplace. Get half of it and—'

'I've already bet it. All of it.'

'All of it?' Wilt swallowed.

'All of it. Lodan's pretty confident.' Higgs smiled widely at Wilt's discomfort.

'Is he now?'

'Said the guards were looking old and slow. Said you should have no problems. Especially with the new gun recruit in the team.'

'He said that?'

'Of course not!'

Higgs burst into laughter and skipped away into the crowd. The Rats would be busy today, darting in and out of the crowd, siphoning up news and coin as they went. Harvest time brought a lot of visitors to Greystone, and that meant loose lips and even looser purse strings. Add to that the wave of drinking and betting that took over the town for the day, and opportunities for profit were widespread.

No time to think about that now though.

'Ho there!'

Wilt greeted the rest of the guild team as the crowd parted and they made their way toward him. Lodan, the team captain, was in the lead, his grey and blue guernsey stained and faded with use. The rest of the team were similarly attired, and Wilt panicked as he saw them approach. He didn't have the team colours. Was he supposed to organise that beforehand? Why hadn't anyone told him?

'Here.' Lodan flung something that hit Wilt squarely in the face.

'Nice reactions,' said Harry, the team goalie: a tall, solidly built man with an ever-present grin on his face.

Wilt pulled the cloth away from his face and looked at a shiny new grey and blue top.

'Now it's official. Our new winger,' Lodan said, loud enough for the crowd around them to hear, and a smattering of applause broke out.

Wilt looked at the rest of the team, not knowing what to say.

'Put it on, lad. Don't just stand there looking stupid.' Harry again, but he couched his words with a friendly clap on the shoulder.

The rest of the team stepped forward one at a time to greet him. Bolter and Bing, the two large defenders, were half muscle, half bulk, yet, as Wilt knew from watching them last year, they weren't half as slow as they looked. Griggs, the other winger, slowed now with age and injury yet still a match for most, covered one side of the pitch. Harry, the goalie, and Lodan, the centre, coordinated their team. That left him, the new guild winger.

He pulled the colours over his head and stood with the rest of the team, his head buzzing.

The sound of the crowd changed as the guard team stepped on to the other end of the field. Wilt swallowed and caught the panic in his throat before it could rise any further. Even from this distance, they were enormous. Twice the size of him, bigger even than Bolter and Bing.

Wilt finally found his voice. 'Big, aren't they?'

'Slow.' Lodan squeezed his shoulder briefly and smiled. 'Just get the ball down their end and take the flag. Simple.'

By the time the game was due to start, it seemed the entire population of Greystone was lining the sides of the pitch. Carpenters had been busy the night before constructing rudimentary bleachers, and the raised slope of the crowd seemed to amplify the noise. Wilt took his position on the left side of the pitch and the crowd there found an easy target for their attention. Calls and laughter reached him, encouraging and disparaging in equal measure, all determined by where the people had placed their money that day. Wilt knew well enough to ignore them. He'd done exactly the same thing only last year.

Wilt closed his eyes and relaxed his mind, letting the distractions of the day fade away. A cold wind blew through him, erasing all thought. When he opened his eyes again, the crowd was somewhere else; all that mattered was within the bounds of the pitch. He was ready.

A signal went up from the central dais where the town dignitaries sat to announce all was in readiness, and the game began.

Lodan took the ball from the centre of the pitch and passed it immediately toward their own goal, where Bolter took possession and waited for the guard forwards to approach him and make some room further up the pitch. Wilt stayed out on his wing and pushed up the field, trying to leave as much room between him and the rest of the guild team. He was aware of Griggs doing the same thing on the other wing. It was obvious that the more space the guild team had, the better. They couldn't compete with the guards for size, but they were quicker.

Bolter passed sideways to Bing as a guard forward reached him and stepped casually away from the late tackle that slid in toward his legs. He trotted forward and received the ball as Bing completed the quick one-two pass, and Wilt smiled at the effortlessness of the move. Wilt had his eyes on Bolter, ready for the pass, when he suddenly found himself on his back.

'Foul!'

A high voice from the crowd demanded attention, but the guard who had dropped Wilt simply smiled at him lying in the dirt, then ran toward the play. Wilt rolled to his feet in time to see Griggs skipping away from his man down the wing, the ball in his hands. Wilt's man had moved in toward Lodan in the centre of the pitch, seemingly assuming Wilt was no longer a threat. Wilt sprinted down his side of the pitch, raising his arm as he ran, signalling his openness to Griggs.

He didn't see the defender, but wouldn't be falling for the same trick twice. His sense told him of the approaching bulk of the man moments before impact, and he feinted toward the centre of the pitch before spinning away to his left again, leaving the charging guard defender to plough straight past him into the crowd.

Griggs already had the ball in the air, headed Wilt's way. The two guards on Lodan's shoulder watched the ball sail over their heads and turned to Wilt as he caught it and charged for the goal.

The world seemed to become still as Wilt took the ball. His mind cleared and mapped out his path as he went, the slow roar of his breath the only sound he now heard. He saw the massive guard goalie hurtle toward him, rolled the ball forward onto the ground, and watched the goalie's eyes widen and lock onto it. It was the easiest thing in the world to pull the ball under his boot and spin away from the charge, rolling the ball with his spin to leave the goalie clutching at thin air and himself with a clear path to goal.

The two guards that had left Lodan were rushing to cut Wilt off, and he held the ball almost too long before shaping to shoot. As he brought his boot down to the ball, he knocked it quickly forward with his standing leg and it rolled under the flying tackle of the nearest guard, straight to the centre of the pitch and the waiting Lodan. Wilt had just enough time to jump up and let the tackle hit him in mid-air, flipping him over the larger man.

He was already running as he landed, headed for the flag as Lodan calmly rolled the ball between the posts marking the guard's goal. The last guard futilely tackled Lodan to the ground, but the ball was already in. Wilt was too fast to stop now that he was closest to the flag. He sprinted toward it and leaped into the air, his hand grasping the cloth at the top of his arc.

The flag. He'd done it. They'd won. The sound of the world rushed back at him.

'Blade!' someone yelled out in a high voice.

The guard Wilt had allowed to charge past him into the crowd came stumbling back onto the field of play, a shining dagger in his hand, his eyes wild.

Wilt spun to face the man, the flag still clutched in his hand. Some defence that would be.

Time slowed. Details called out to him: the bright, unnatural silvery shine of the dagger; the red of the man's knuckles as he clutched it; the crazed, driven expression on his face; the dead eyes.

The guard stumbled in his charge as something hit him from behind.

'I got him!' Higgs sang out. He clung to the shoulders of the guard with one hand, and battered him about the head with a rock in his other. The guard bent over double to dislodge him, and Higgs rolled off, landing in the dirt at Wilt's feet.

'Catch!' Higgs tossed the palm-sized stone to Wilt, who snatched it from the air and wrapped the flag around it.

He set the makeshift sling spinning above his head and released it again in one motion, the rock flying straight and true directly into the guard's face. It dropped him facedown in his tracks, and blood poured over his face from the deep cut it had opened in the centre of his forehead.

A second later the rest of the players were there, both the guild team and the guards, holding down the maddened man.

'What mischief is this?' Lodan's clear voice cut across the confused babble of the crowd.

'Dawson! What are you doing, man?' It was the guard captain now, shocked at the actions of one of his players.

Wilt stared at the sprawled figure in the dirt. Bolter and Bing had him by the shoulders, and two guards held his legs. Blood covered his face now, but he managed to lift his head and look directly at Wilt.

'The blood within the stone!' His voice was deep and rasping, only half human.

He smiled then, an unnatural, twisted smile, before sending out a high cry and jerking his neck quickly around. Too far around. A deep crack echoed across the field, and the man's body fell limp.

'My oath!' Harry felt for the man's pulse. 'He's dead!'

The crowd seemed to swarm in on them as Wilt gazed at the broken body on the ground, at the man who just moments ago had tried to kill him. Some part of him still reacted, helping Higgs to his feet and brushing the dirt from his back, but the greater part of his mind reeled in silent shock. A high-pitched wail echoed through his mind, cloaking his thoughts.

Higgs grinned at him and mouthed something before pushing

through the press of bodies around them. Probably off to collect his bet, with no thought for the seriousness of what had occurred. Wilt wondered fleetingly when he had lost that innocence.

A clap on the shoulder jerked his attention back and he saw Lodan looking earnestly at him. He tried to smile in return but could tell Lodan saw through it. Lodan didn't say a word though; he twisted Wilt around and kept his hand on his shoulder as he pushed him through the crowd, away from the fallen guard.

The wail in his head faded as they stepped away from the scene, and Lodan's words began to leak into Wilt's awareness.

'—fastest game we've played since I've been in the team.'

Griggs was suddenly beside them. 'Never seen the like. Wouldn't have thought it possible if I hadn't just seen it with my own eyes. How can a man twist his own—'

'Griggs!' Lodan's warning voice was loud and clear, and Griggs changed the topic.

'That move of yours, Wilt, dropping the ball at your feet—where did you learn that?'

Wilt shrugged in reply.

'You'll have to teach me that one, and that spin with the ball. First one foot, then the other—that guard goalie didn't know which way to turn.'

'Fastest game I've been a part of,' Lodan agreed. 'I was just telling him.'

'Fastest game in thirty years, I'd say. Better watch yourself, Lodan. I reckon we've got a new star in our ranks. Won't be long before he's challenging you for the captaincy.'

'All challengers welcome, Griggs. I seem to remember a certain other winger trying to take that position from me not so many seasons ago.'

'Hey, any competition has to be good for—'

'Where are we going?' Wilt stopped in his tracks and the other two turned to face him.

'To the presentation, Wilt. We've won the flag.'

'Oh.' He resumed walking, seeing they were headed toward the official dais on the side of the pitch. They walked on in silence until Wilt found his voice again. 'Lodan? Have you ever seen anything like that? That guard?'

Lodan dropped his voice, his tone serious now. 'No, son. I don't think any of us has.'

On-duty guards finally moved the crowd from around their fallen comrade and cleared the scene, leaving all onlookers to gather in front of the official dais for the presentation. Word had spread that a Prefect of Redmondis was in town, and naturally he had been invited to join the duke and his entourage to witness the key sporting event of Greystone's calendar, but the sight of the three hooded figures standing beside the duke on the dais still sent mutterings throughout the crowd.

The duke—a squat, balding man ill-suited to public appearances—looked even shorter beside the figures in red. Even the smaller of the three—*the Sister*, Wilt reminded himself—towered over those around them. The crowd noise was beginning to grow as the mob found courage in its numbers.

Wilt looked around quickly. 'Where's Higgs?'

'Right here!' His small body seemed to melt through the crowd to appear in front of Lodan and Wilt. 'Thanks for waiting for me.'

'You did well, Higgs,' said Lodan, and Higgs smiled at him, keeping his tongue in check for once.

'People of Greystone!' The duke's normally weak voice blasted over the crowd, enhanced somehow and loud enough to drown out every other sound. The mutterings stopped as people looked at each other in confusion and awe at the magic.

The duke himself seemed surprised at the effectiveness of the small stone device he held up to his chin, a gift from the Prefect of Redmondis. It seemed to take his voice and throw it to the farthest point so the crowd could hear every word.

'Crafters,' Higgs whispered excitedly and locked his eyes on the contraption.

'People of Greystone,' the duke repeated in a more measured tone. 'We are honoured to welcome representatives of Redmondis into our midst on this fine occasion of the harvest festival.'

Mutterings among the crowd began again, and some of them must have reached the duke's ear, because he skipped the rest of his prepared speech and hurried his next words. The day of sun and drink was having its effect on the crowd, and they had no patience for long, official speeches.

'The Redmondis representatives have kindly offered to present our new flagball champions with their prize. Guild team, step forward!'

Wilt, Lodan and the rest of the team were pushed forward by the crowd until they stood directly in front of the two tall red-robed figures. The Sister had taken a step behind her two bodyguards but could still be seen, her dark hood floating at the level of their shoulders. Wilt found he was unable to keep his eyes from her shadowed visage.

'Captain.'

The voice was clear, with the hint of a smile edging its tone. Wilt recognised it from the encounter in the alley he and Higgs had witnessed: Cantor Wrexley.

Lodan stepped forward and bent his head as the Cantor hung a small silver medal around his neck. The Cantor whispered something and studied Lodan for a second, then seemed to be satisfied and moved on to the next member of the team. Griggs, Harry, Bolter and Bing all had the small ceremony repeated on them. Wilt was next.

'Wilt, that medal, it's not ...'

Wilt knew exactly what Higgs was talking about. He felt the power emanating from the small objects hanging around his teammates' necks. They weren't simple medals; there was craftier magic at work here.

'I know.'

There was nothing for it, no way to push through the crowd and get away. Wilt stepped forward and bowed, and heard the strange whispers from the Cantor as the medal was placed over his head.

A veil of darkness dropped over his vision, and he now stood in a large chamber, totally alone, a thousand eyes staring at him from the shadows, hungry for him.

Just as quickly the vision faded and he was back on the dais. He straightened, and felt a sudden heat where the medal rested against his chest. A sharp blue light shone from the small silver medallion, illuminating the shadows around them. Wilt locked his eyes onto the dark hood of the Sister, and thought he saw her eyes glowing grey, her deep red lips curl into a smile.

He bowed his head quickly, not losing eye contact. 'M'lady.'

There was a red swish of movement as the two Cantors fell on him, and all was darkness.

Chapter 7

There had been a blue light, then a smile, then a blow across the back of his head, harder than he ever imagined possible, hard enough to drive his mind past pain, directly into numbness. Claws. There had been claws, ripping into his scalp, a golden light burning through him, door after door opening inside his mind, the images gaining speed, rushing along until he could no longer make any sense of them, until they swirled into a whirlpool that sucked him into darkness.

Fever dreams, nothing more. They had faded into the stillness of sleep, and now that too was seeping away.

Wilt kept his eyes closed and his ears open. He was lying on his back, in a sling of some sort judging by the swaying movement that rocked him back and forth. Dark shadows flickered past him, guards he guessed, patrolling on either side of whatever he was riding in. Every now and then he caught a snatch of conversation, but the speakers may as well have been using a foreign tongue for all the sense they made. What little he could make out was all to do with patrols and how long each of them had been 'of the Nine'. None of it made any sense.

Finally he decided he'd learned all he could from lying still and opened his eyes.

His imagined situation hadn't been too far off. He was lying in a low hammock, strung up between the beams of a rickety old wagon. A thin sheet of cloth kept the high bright sun from burning directly onto him, but there were large rips in the cloth on either side through which he could see heavily armoured riders travelling alongside.

Wilt risked raising his head and regretted it immediately. A rush of pain burned up from his neck over the back of his head, bringing with it a wave of nausea. He slumped with a groan and closed his eyes again.

'You're awake!'

Higgs. Of course he was there.

'About time, too.'

Wilt heard a shuffle at his feet, then let out a deep sigh of relief as a cool wet cloth was placed on his forehead.

'We were wondering if you'd ever come round.'

The red lights on the inside of his eyelids danced and burned as the pain in his head faded. Finally he opened his eyes again and peered down at his feet. 'We?'

'Old Pete and I. Here.'

He opened his eyes and peered at the vague blur of colour at his feet approaching him and finally managed to focus on a small cup being held up to his face.

'Drink.'

Wilt reached out and took the cup with a shivering hand, holding it quickly to his lips to avoid spilling it completely. He almost gagged as the warm, brackish water hit his tongue, but he tilted his head back and forced it down.

'Nice huh? Pete says they save the oldest casks for us, the emergency stores. Says it helps weaken our will, make us more compliant, less trouble on the trip. Says that's why he never touches the stuff. It's clean water though—it won't make you sick.'

Wilt concentrated, and Higgs came into focus, crouched at his side. He was swimming inside a large rainbow-coloured cloak, far too big for him, and he sported a bright blue bruise across the left side of his face.

'Wha—' Wilt's throat screamed in protest as he tried to force out the words.

'Don't try to speak. Here. Drink some more.'

Higgs took the cup from his hand and held it up to his lips to drink. Wilt didn't notice the taste now, just the warm liquid coating his raw throat.

'You need to rest more. Pete said you'd fade in and out for a few days yet. The Cantor hit you a bit harder than he should have, Pete reckons. Says he heard some of the guards talking about it.'

'Wh—'

'The Cantor, the Prefect. Pete says they're called Cantors, that only folk outside Redmondis still call them Prefects.'

Wilt tried in vain to speak again but slumped back as a wave of pain smashed over him and left him to drown in the darkness.

The next time Wilt resurfaced and opened his eyes, the world around him was grey and still. He peered through a gap in the canvas and was rewarded with a view of a large camp rousing itself for the morning, breakfast fires being stirred into life, and heavily armoured figures stamping back and forth to get some warmth into their legs.

Wilt's headache was a dull thump behind his eyes now, and he risked raising himself onto his elbows. Pain flooded up from the back of his neck and over his skull again, but he gritted his teeth and clung onto consciousness. Stars danced before his eyes, then faded into nothingness. The wagon was empty apart from his hammock and a few bags of what looked like grain stacked roughly at his feet. Wilt thought about swinging his legs over the side and trying to sit up, but a second wave of dizziness and pain convinced him he'd pushed things as far as his body could handle right now, and perhaps he should just lie there and try to learn what he could from his view of the camp outside.

His wagon seemed to be one of many, arranged in a circle around the central camp. There were more still; he could make out the shadows of other wagons behind the first circle. A large caravan then. And judging by the number of guards, it was a well-equipped one.

The guards were well drilled, better organised than the Greystone guard Wilt was used to seeing. These men walked to their posts in step, they saluted each other with quick swings of their arms to their chest, and all looked like they knew exactly what they were expected to do. All wore long knives on their left hips—longer than daggers but not quite short swords—slightly curved steel blades that glinted in the sunlight. Wilt had seen one of these before; the Prefect—the Cantor—Cantor Cortis, he had wielded one against the thieves in Greystone. Wilt wondered briefly if the Cantor was here as well. He must be; wasn't he the one who had hit him? Probably based closer to wherever the Sister's wagon was.

Wilt pulled his thoughts back to study the guards outside. All carried the long knives, but the rest of their weaponry seemed to be a mix. Some rested their hands on the hilts of long swords, some had heavy axes swinging from their right side. Many held large double crossbows loaded with long, heavy quarrels. All wore steel plate armour, but seemed to move as if unencumbered. There wouldn't be any easy way out of here.

'So, you awaken at last!'

The canvas at the rear of the wagon flapped open and grey dawn light flooded over him. He looked past his feet at the old man pulling himself up into the wagon with a slight grunt.

'Feeling better?'

The man peered into Wilt's face. Wilt felt a small electric shock as their eyes locked, then mentally pushed back at the strange pull that seemed to call to him. The old man smiled then and patted Wilt's leg, and the feeling abruptly vanished.

'Aha, yes! You are feeling stronger. Good! Not long now before you're up on your feet again. The healing power of youth, you know. Nothing beats it!'

'Where's—'

'Your friend Higgs is sleeping. Been standing vigil over you for three days straight now, trying to keep awake. Finally had to slip him something in his evening meal to knock him out for his own good. Good lad, that one. Good friend. Hope you know that.'

'I know.'

'Friends are important. Especially where you're going.'

On closer inspection, the man seemed more weathered than old, as though the hard path he had trodden through life had worn him away. His face was lined with wrinkles, and his hands shook slightly as they moved through the air. Wilt could smell a thick cloud of alcohol surrounding him.

'Where are we—'

'No time for questions now. Pete will answer them all in time. For now, drink this.'

Wilt focused on the steaming cup being held in front of his face. It smelled vaguely spicy. 'What's—'

'No questions! Drink!' The old man didn't give Wilt any further chance to protest, holding the cup to his lips and pouring the warm liquid down his throat.

Wilt's mouth instantly numbed as he swallowed the drink.

'Now rest. All will be clear in time. Trust Old Pete here. Always comes clear in time.'

Wilt lay back and sank into unconsciousness. The last thing he saw as he faded into darkness was the hand patting his leg, its worn, weathered skin, and the small nub where a finger used to be.

Chapter 8

Time stretched and shrunk in upon itself as Wilt slept. Sun and starlight passed over his head, and the wagon train moved ever onwards, away from Greystone and everything he had ever known. His waking moments seemed to flash past in brief snatches, merging into his fevered dreams, and he swam between them, no longer knowing what was real and what was fantasy. Red Charley walked toward him, his hand still dripping blood, a grim smile on his face. He turned away to see the Cantors, long knives in their hands, reaching out for him, their flowing red cloaks leaving a trail of blood behind them. He turned again and saw Higgs run away from him, down a dark tunnel toward a fading blue light. He tried to call out but no sound came from his throat. A final turn and he saw the Sister standing in front of him, the blue light showing a smile curve her lips. She pulled back her hood …

'Wake up!'

A sharp pain in his side pulled him back into consciousness.

'Please, he is injured.'

'The Cantor wants him. Now. Wake up.'

Another kick and Wilt opened his eyes. A guard stood over his bed, one hand resting on the hilt of his sword, the other holding an old man back. Old Pete, that was his name.

'Please. Let me.'

'Get up! Now!'

The guard swung his leg back for another kick and Wilt sat up.

Stars flooded his eyes and the world around him lurched sideways.

Pete seemed to twist quickly away from the guard's outstretched arm and was suddenly beside Wilt, holding a cool cloth to his head. The world eased back into its rightful position, and he slowly focused on the guard.

'The Cantor. Now.'

Wilt swung his legs to the side of the hammock and tried to stand, only making headway once Pete lent his strength to the effort.

'Focus, Wilt. Centre yourself. Breathe.' Pete's whispered words snaked around his mind and wrapped him tight.

'Do I need to carry him?' The guard's voice seemed different now, not as harsh.

Wilt turned toward him. 'No. I'm all right.'

'Here.' The guard stepped forward and pushed Pete out of the way. He slipped Wilt's arm over his shoulder and took his weight. 'The Cantor will not wait.'

The tone was almost apologetic, and Wilt felt a small glow of satisfaction as they stumbled out of the wagon. Pete moved to take his other arm, but once Wilt's feet touched the dirt the guard barked at Pete to stay with the wagon.

Wilt seemed to float over the ground as they shuffled across the camp. Shapes lurched up in the darkness, and the orange glow of fires caused shadows to dance out of their way. For some reason Wilt found that funny. His body began to shake with laughter.

'What are you doing? Move your legs.'

The guard's voice was softer again, no longer a bark, almost a plea for help from his prisoner. That only caused Wilt to laugh more. There was something else too, something even funnier. A few more steps and Wilt recognised it.

'You smell nice.' He had to stop then, bent over double with exhausted laughter.

The guard let him go and stepped away from him, waiting for the fit to pass.

When Wilt raised his head again, he was clear-headed for the first time in days. He studied the guard in front of him, saw the way he stood with one cocked hip, and grinned again.

'You're a girl.'

The guard simply stepped toward him, swung her gloved fist into his face, and knocked him off his feet.

Wilt's nose was bleeding and his headache was back with a vengeance, but he felt better than he had in days. He stood swaying slightly outside the Cantor's tent, trying to catch his breath. He found that if he stared at his feet and really focused, he could almost stop the world around him from spinning.

The tent flap swung open and his escort from earlier stepped up to him. 'Feeling better?'

Wilt lifted his head and smiled at her. 'You sure know how to punch.'

'Watch your mouth or I'll use my right hand next time.' She led Wilt inside, and he was left mouthing silent words at her back.

The Cantor's tent was the biggest such construction Wilt had ever seen, and somehow seemed even larger inside. The first room was a guard post: two large, identically suited men barring the way with long pikes. Wilt's guard waved her hand and the pikes were swung up and out of the way.

The next room was the size of a small hall. The light from the fire in the centre of the room didn't reach the walls, and Wilt could only sense the figures moving in the shadows. A raised platform overlooked the fire, dominated by a single large throne occupied by the Cantor.

Wilt stopped in front of the fire and pulled himself up. May as well dive right in. 'Cantor Wrexley.'

The guard beside him swung a fist at the back of his head and Wilt found himself on his knees, only just stopping himself from falling face first into the red coals of the fire. He looked up and tried to focus on one of the three seated figures now dancing in front of him.

The Cantor chuckled lightly, and he slowly coalesced into a single image. 'Gentle now, Daemi. Our guest is simply unaware of our conventions. You see, Wilt, one must never speak to a Cantor unless spoken to. Think of that as lesson two. Lesson one, of course, was that one must never address a Sister at all.'

The guard stiffened and Wilt heard a sharp intake of breath.

'Of course, Daemi, you were unaware of our guest's earlier indiscretion. Perhaps that is for the best.'

A hand fell on Wilt's shoulder and pulled him roughly to his feet. 'Rest assured young Wilt here has his lesson. Cantor Cortis made sure of that. He was perhaps a little too eager to correct our young charge, but here we are.'

Wilt studied the Cantor in front of him. He was a tall, thin man, hair shaved close to his head, sharp, angular features jutting out from his heavy red cloak. His nose was beak-like, and his eyes glinted when he flashed his hard, steely smile.

'So we meet again. Wilt, that is your name, is it not?'

Wilt stood silently, and heard a quick swish of fabric as the guard next to him readied another swing.

The Cantor held up a single hand and the blow never fell.

'Now now, Daemi, once again, you are not giving our guest the benefit of his inexperience. Lesson three. One always responds quickly to a Cantor, no matter what the request. Again, your name is Wilt?'

'Yes.' Wilt heard his voice answer, though he hadn't intended to speak.

'Good. You saw the Sister at the medal ceremony for that quaint little game you played, but that was not the first time you had seen her, was it?'

The Cantor's voice seemed to be inside Wilt's head, swimming in the gap between his brain and his skull, poking at the soft parts of him, worming its way inside.

'No.' Again, Wilt's voice spoke without his control.

'You had seen her earlier, with me, and the Cantor Cortis. In the alley. She revealed herself.'

Part of Wilt heard the scrape of a blade being unsheathed, yet he couldn't even flinch.

'Daemi, I will not ask you again.' The Cantor's voice was calm and measured, yet there was no mistaking the threat. The guard sheathed her blade.

Wilt gazed at the flames dancing in a hypnotising swing. Then, as easy as breathing, he turned his eyes inwards and saw the Cantor's will wrapped around his brain, squeezing him, forcing him to do its bidding.

'You saw the Sister in the alley. Answer me.'

Wilt was too busy studying the thin black rope tied around him. The knot was a simple one, just a tug here and-

'Argh!'

Wilt watched the black snake slither away from him, toward the Cantor. The Cantor had let out a strangled cry and sagged back into his seat, holding his hand to his head as if in pain. Wilt's guard took hold of his shoulder and dark figures from the sides of the room slipped toward the throne, but the Cantor held his hand up again and they slunk into the shadows. He chucked ruefully and rubbed his hand back and forth over his shaved head.

'So. I should have known you would have some talent. Very well.'

The Cantor clicked his fingers twice, and the guard swung Wilt around and began to march him out of the tent.

'We shall talk again soon, Wilt. I shall pass word on to the Sister of your apparent recovery. She will be most pleased.'

Daemi pushed Wilt out into the clear night, and Wilt stumbled as a sudden wave of fatigue washed over him.

'So you are one of them.' Daemi's voice was laced with disgust. She gave him a shove and let him stumble on ahead of her. Once they reached Pete's wagon she stopped and spun him around to face her. Wilt could make out bright green eyes behind the scaled helm that covered her face. They flashed with anger and something else. Fear.

'Keep your worms out of my mind.'

She gave him another shove toward the wagon and stalked away, leaving Wilt to sink to the ground exhausted.

Chapter 9

'Rest now, let your mind relax, let the rhythm of your breath guide you.'

Wilt heard the voice through the heavy blanket of sleep, its soothing tone working at the pockets of tension in his mind.

'You are in total darkness, you see nothing.'

There was a point above his nose, between his eyebrows, a tight knot that still resisted.

'You are in total silence, you hear nothing but my voice.'

Wilt felt the lightest of touches directly on the knot, and it loosened and relaxed as he sank deeper.

'You are within and without. You are nothing.'

Wilt saw the blackness as a shape rising high above him, a writhing ball of oblivion, a tear in the substance of the world. He felt something close to fear, then put the feeling to one side and continued to stare into the abyss.

'Now, you know that which is and that which is not. Centre yourself.' The words were whispered as a command.

Wilt snapped back into his body and rushed into the light. A cold cloth was placed on his forehead.

'Open your eyes.'

Wilt obeyed and looked up at the slowly swaying canvas covering of the wagon directly above his head. A moment later he turned his head and saw Old Pete sitting beside him, studying him with his wild pale blue eyes.

'Feel better?'

Wilt sat up, and noticed a distinct lack of a headache. 'Yes.'

'About time!'

Wilt turned toward the voice and saw Higgs sitting impatiently by the foot of his bed.

'Pete says we're almost halfway there. Guess where there is?'

Wilt couldn't help but smile at the unconcealed enthusiasm in Higgs's voice. 'Redmondis.'

'Red— hey! Who told you?'

Swinging his legs around, Wilt sat up. He waited for a wave of dizziness or pain to slam into him, but only felt refreshed. 'What did you do to me?'

Pete chuckled and turned to the small pail of water by the side of the bed. He picked up the cloth that had fallen away from Wilt's head and began to wring it out. 'Me? I did nothing. I merely pointed the way.'

'He was brilliant, wasn't he? He was whispering all sorts of nonsense into your ear. I thought he was casting a spell on you, a spell of healing or something, but he said—'

Wilt tuned Higgs's voice out as he watched Pete drape the cloth carefully on the side of the bucket. His gaze was focused on Pete's hands, on the one knuckle where a finger used to be.

'You're one of them, aren't you?'

Pete chuckled again and held his hand up. 'This, you mean? The price of service? That was a long time ago.'

'I already asked him all about that, Wilt. Pete used to be one of them, one of the Nine, like the others here.'

Pete wiggled his fingers, his scarred knuckle dancing in the light. 'Of the Nine. A loyal servant of the Nine Sisters. A little joke of the Cantors.'

Higgs continued talking over them both. 'But that was years ago. He was one of the skilled ones, not a crafter, I already checked.'

'The skilled ones.' Wilt looked back up into Pete's eyes and held his gaze. 'But not—'

'Not a wielder either, not like you.' Pete held his stare, then suddenly smiled and turned away. 'I had some talent, a gift for bringing the best out of others, shall we say, but not enough for the Cantors to bother pushing me too far.'

'He still knows heaps though. He's been telling me all about Redmondis, about the three schools, about the Cantors and the Nine Sisters and—'

Pete silenced him with another deep chuckle. 'Enough, young man. Keep some of your tales for the campfire.'

Higgs couldn't resist one last flurry. 'And crafting! He knows some of the basics and he showed me. Look!' Higgs offered up a small glass pebble to Wilt, who studied it dutifully.

'Ah, that's great Higgs.'

'It's a sooth stone.' Higgs held it up in the sunlight and the glass turned a deep amber. 'Take it!' He tossed it quickly to Wilt, who caught it by reflex. As his hand touched it, the glass became clear again.

'Pete said he can show me all sorts of things, says he can see I've the talent for it.'

Wilt looked up from the sooth stone and resumed studying Pete. 'He does, does he?'

Pete held up his hands and shook his head with a smile. 'I only spoke the truth. Your young friend here does seem to have some talent for bringing out the power in objects. The life. The Cantors wouldn't have brought him along if he didn't.'

'Why did they bring him along? Why are we both here?'

'That you will have to clear up with the Cantors yourself, boy, but from my end the answer is obvious. You're a wielder, one who can read and, eventually, control minds. One who can access the deep wells of power that drives all life. The Cantors are always on the lookout for ones such as you. Probably travelled all the way to Greystone just to find you. While they were there they gathered whatever other skilled ones they could find. It's what they do.'

'But I'm not a— oww!'

The pebble in his hand had suddenly turned white hot. Wilt tossed it quickly in the air and Higgs snatched it with a laugh.

'Ha! I warned you it was a sooth stone. It warns when the holder isn't telling the truth.' Higgs looked at the stone in his hand and shook his head. 'It's only supposed to turn red though, not change temperature.'

'Something for you to work on then.' Pete ruffled Higgs's hair and turned to Wilt. 'You are a wielder, boy, a strong one. Even I could sense your presence. To the Cantors you must have sounded like a siren calling in the night with your uncloaked strength.'

'They can hear me?'

'If you like you can think of it that way. Anyone with the skill can hear you, some better than others. Some will be able to read you completely—read you and use you for their own ends. Open the way through you to the depths underneath, to the power that lies there waiting.'

Pete's words trailed off, as though they brought back memories he was not yet ready to share. He took a long, slow breath and continued.

'You must learn to control your strength, learn to conceal your skill if you wish to survive. Redmondis will teach you.'

Wilt studied the old man as he turned to leave the wagon. He was hunched with age, his body frail and sagging. Only his eyes spoke of a hidden strength. 'And you? What did Redmondis teach you?'

Pete chuckled and disappeared into the daylight.

The morning was bright and clear, the air crisp with the hint of winter. Pete had packed up their wagon and was huddled on the ground with Higgs, drawing strange symbols in the dirt with a stick and whispering to him. Higgs looked enthralled, and Wilt didn't want to interrupt. He wondered if Old Pete fully appreciated what he was getting into taking on a student of Higgs's enthusiasm.

Old Pete—surely not his real name.

Wilt had finally recovered from the blow the Cantor had struck him at the medal presentation all those days ago, and his mind was chugging back up to speed. Questions demanded his attention. Too many questions to address at once, so the thing to do was to start simple. Like finding out more about Old Pete, and maybe finding a way out of this camp and back to Greystone.

Wilt looked around the camp again. He'd given up the idea of simply walking out. Guards patrolled the boundary of the clearing, and even if he could make it past them, he had no idea in which direction or how far from Greystone they had travelled. Wilt knew all about surviving on the streets, but the wilderness was another matter. He'd been told stories of the Tangle and the dark dangers contained within it since he was a child, and although he knew most of them would be exaggerations and lies, he couldn't quite shake the nervous shiver at the sight of all those trees—as though they were watching him, waiting for him.

Wilt shrugged off the sudden gloom and continued his stroll. Apart from the problem of escape, there would be the issue of convincing Higgs. Seeing him with Old Pete, listening attentively, straining all his senses to soak in as much knowledge about crafting as possible, told him that Higgs wouldn't want to leave. Not now there was the possibility of learning to craft. Of course he'd still come if Wilt asked. He'd follow Wilt anywhere.

The thought was both comforting and suddenly troubling, and Wilt pushed it away, only to crash up against another uncomfortable possibility. Would they even miss him in Greystone, or would life have continued on as normal? He was only a lowly thief after all, not much more than a pickpocket. They were endlessly replaceable. Whereas here ... what had Old Pete called him? A wielder. Something special.

Wilt grinned and shook his head at the rush of excitement from the thought. He could almost feel the world opening up around him, the scales falling from his eyes.

Maybe that blow to the head had done more damage than he realised.

He left his jumbled thoughts behind and tried to focus on the immediate present. A guard stepped onto the path around the edge of the camp. Daemi. Wilt could tell by the way she moved.

Wilt trotted up and found himself waving awkwardly. 'Uh, hi there.'

She didn't acknowledge him, just kept marching away, eyes riveted straight ahead. Her face was still covered by the strangely shaped helm all the guards wore, but Wilt could make out the dark flash of her eyes beneath it.

'Daemi, isn't it?'

Daemi increased her pace, so Wilt hurried along beside her. He wasn't going to give up that easily.

'I was wondering if you could help me.'

'Do not speak to me.' Her voice was harsh and cold, her breath fogging out of the gap in her helm the only sign of humanity.

'Pete—the old man who healed me—he's a guard too, isn't he?'

Daemi swung around suddenly and shoved Wilt to the ground. She paused for a second to look down at him, and Wilt saw something new in her eyes. Fear perhaps, or regret. Daemi turned away quickly and resumed her march.

'I told you not to speak to me.'

Wilt lay in the dirt for a second, considering his predicament. She was faster than seemed possible in that armour. Maybe it wasn't as heavy as it looked.

He pushed himself to his feet and skipped after her. 'The reason I ask is, he's missing a finger.'

Daemi spun again but this time Wilt was ready. He ducked the blow and grabbed her wrist as it sailed over his head, then stepped in and twisted her arm behind her. Before she could react, he slid her glove from her hand. Sure enough, her little finger was missing, and a fresh bandage covered the wound where it had been.

'Just as you seem to be missing one.'

'You dare!'

Wilt heard the raw anger in her voice and let go, stepping well clear. She spun to face him, the long knife already clasped in her other hand, pointing directly at his heart.

Wilt held up his hands in surrender, her glove still clasped in one of them. 'Let's not do anything either of us will regret later.'

Daemi was beyond reasoning with. She let out a scream of incoherent rage and charged at him. Wilt barely had time to spin clear.

'There's no need for this. Here.' Wilt threw her glove back to her, making sure it sailed high enough to lift her eyes. Sure enough, he saw their green light follow the arc of the glove. As soon as they left him, he shot forward and kicked the knife from her hand.

The blade spun away and landed in the dirt. Wilt felt quite pleased with himself, for all of a second or so. Daemi's cry of rage turned into a grunt of effort as she dropped and spun, her back leg sweeping around to take Wilt's legs out from under him. He flopped back onto the ground and the air exploded from his lungs. Before he could roll away Daemi was on top of him, her hands clasped tight around his throat.

Wilt gaped up at her and felt himself fade as her image blurred. There was no air left in him, and no way to suck any more in. Bright stars burned through his vision.

No! He is reaching for me. I will not let him in, I must not let him in. I will kill him first.

Wilt saw himself lying prone, hands wrapped around his throat, his eyes grey and strange, all colour drained from them, yet still staring, peering into him, completely into him, taking him over. His hands loosened their grip.

Damn you! I will not let you take me!

But I do not want to take you. Just let go. Let me breathe. Like that.

Wilt saw his eyes begin to clear then slipped back into his own mind, the thick black rope that had linked their minds slithering away from her.

Wilt coughed and sat up, rubbing his throat. Her nails had drawn blood.

Daemi had rolled free and was on all fours, her body shaking. Something like a sob wrenched out of her.

'That will do I think.'

Wilt looked up and saw the long shadow of a Cantor standing over them, his red cloak blocking out the morning sun. Cantor Wrexley? No, it was the other one, the one who had hurt him. Cantor Cortis.

He was as tall as Wrexley, but his face was more weathered, as though he had spent long days facing the cold mountain wind, and a single scar dripped from his left eye, pulling his face into a hungry grimace, a hunger reflected in his strangely shining eyes.

'So, Wrexley speaks the truth. You do have some power.'

Wilt was suddenly very small and vulnerable, crouched on the ground at the Cantor's feet.

'I can see why the Sisters want you under their control. They scramble for anything now that the horizon darkens.'

The Cantor's eyes blazed as he glared at Wilt, and Wilt felt the world around him fade as he fell into their glow. There was something familiar about them, something from deep within his dreams. A golden light. His voice was strange too, as if he were calling to Wilt from a great distance.

'Still they do not understand, do not see the true path to harness such power. Perhaps we can find a way to better utilise it.'

A voice in his mind shouted a warning to him, but it sunk away as he stared into the Cantor's face, drowning in the heavy silence.

None can stand against the darkness. None can stand against the army that will come, that even now begins to grow. It would be best simply to let go. To surrender.

'Cantor Cortis.'

The world rushed back as Cortis dropped his gaze and turned to face the approaching figure of Cantor Wrexley. Wrexley frowned as he surveyed the scene.

'Daemi, gather yourself. You must learn to shield your mind.'

Wilt heard Daemi stand and move to pick up her blade, but couldn't shift his gaze from the tall figure standing over him.

'Though I doubt any shield would be able to withstand such strength. Such raw power. Dangerous when uncontrolled.'

Something tickled the back of his skull and he pushed at it. The touch flicked away, like a fly swatted clear, and suddenly the spell was broken.

'Cantor Cortis, I think I can handle this for now.'

Wrexley had appeared, and Cortis glared at him as if ready to argue the point, then turned on his heel and marched away.

'We all need to be more careful, I suppose.' Wrexley's tone deepened. 'Wilt. I had hoped to wait until we were safe within the gates of Redmondis, but as ever the impatience of youth trumps all. You are travelling with … Pete.' The name sounded strange coming from the Cantor, as if he had struggled to form the word. 'He knows the basics. I will instruct him to begin at once. Daemi.' The Cantor faced the guard, and she immediately snapped to attention. 'You will assist him. I am assigning you to special duty with our guest here. Perhaps it will help you in your own development.'

Wilt saw her stiffen, then salute and stalk away.

The Cantor chuckled softly. 'She is well trained, that one. Still, you should learn not to test her limits. Wielders do not need to risk physical engagement. The lighter the touch, the stronger the hold. But you will learn of this in time. Go.'

Wilt stood up immediately and quickly walked away. By the time he regained control of his body and turned around to face him, the Cantor was gone.

'Showing off again, were we?'

Wilt lay determinedly still.

'Get up, I know you're awake.'

Wilt sat up and opened his eyes to see Pete crouched in the

corner of the wagon, sifting through the various sacks that had accumulated there over time. His voice was slurred and angry.

'Seems we have been blessed with our own personal guard.'

'Daemi.' Wilt rubbed his throat and his fingertips grazed the small scabs where her nails had dug in. Except for a moment they had been his nails.

'Wrex—Cantor Wrexley also thinks it would be a good idea to start your training early. He always was a clever one.'

'Wrex?' Wilt smiled at Pete, but dropped the expression as soon as he saw his face.

'Forget it. Here.' Pete tossed something at him and Wilt caught it just before it hit him in the face. It was a carved wooden symbol held in a simple leather band.

'A necklace?'

'Put it on. Now.'

Wilt held the necklace up to the light to examine it. It was a smooth hollow circle of deep red wood wrapped around another smaller circle, this one of white wood. Whoever had carved it had made it seem like the smaller circle floated within the larger one, not touching it in any way. Wilt reached out to poke it with his other hand.

'Don't touch it. Just put it on.' Pete continued to stare at him until Wilt lifted the necklace over his head and settled the symbol on his chest. He tucked the symbol inside Wilt's tunic.

'There. The symbol should touch the flesh at all times.' Pete leaned back and studied him. 'Feel any different?'

Wilt thought for a moment, then shook his head. 'No.'

'Good.' Pete patted him on the shoulder. 'Good.'

Wilt rolled out of his cot and onto his feet. He threw back the canvas flap and bright daylight shone in. 'It's still morning?'

Pete chuckled as Higgs popped his head through the canvas opening.

'C'mon sleepy head. You've missed another day!' Higgs's head disappeared back outside.

Wilt turned to Pete. 'A whole day?'

'You wore yourself out wrestling with that guard, I expect. And the Cantor might have had something to do with it as well. He commanded you, didn't he? Made you move, overrode your own will? Not easy to do without wearing out both the driver and the passenger, that.'

'But I didn't feel tired.'

'No, you wouldn't. Your body was fine. You wouldn't feel sleepy or worn out, just turn off all of a sudden, like a candle being snuffed. The Cantor too. Knowing Wrex though, he knew what he was doing. Probably put a little something extra in to make sure you were forced to rest. Buy himself a little more time that way.'

'Time? Why would he need time?'

Pete's voice was suddenly angry. 'To use you boy! To wrap his tentacles around you, sink into your mind and twist you to his own ends. The more time he has with you in his control, the more access to your power he gains. You have the makings of a powerful wielder, boy. All the Cantors will try to have their taste.'

Pete spat the words at Wilt, overcome with an emotion Wilt knew came from somewhere, some time far removed from the present. Pete reined his emotions in, dropping his voice to a harsh, wounded whisper.

'They'll all want to take a piece. Best learn that now. Come.'

There was another edge in Pete's voice as he spoke, and the thought occurred to Wilt that the smell of alcohol was stronger this morning. Pete had been drinking more than usual. Trying to dull some hidden pain.

Pete threw a heavy leather jerkin into Wilt's lap and turned to go outside. 'Put that on. I don't think she's going to take it easy on you, not after what you did.'

Wilt looked at the worn leather in his lap and sighed. 'What did I do now?'

Chapter 10

Wilt felt himself flipping over in the air and slammed hard into the ground, the air rushing out of his lungs with a whoosh. He lay still and tried to breathe.

'That's four!'

Higgs's giggle snapped him back and he saw the boy grinning at him from the edge of the circle they had marked out for training.

'You don't have to enjoy this so much, you know.'

'I know.' Higgs's smile only widened before focusing on the small pile of stones arranged in front of him.

Wilt pulled himself to his feet and turned to Daemi, who stood with her back to him at the far edge of the circle. She wasn't even breathing hard. Wilt hadn't been able to get a word out of her all morning. She simply waved him on to attack, then each time managed somehow to sidestep him or duck under his charge, always with the same result: him flying through the air, usually with a hard punch or kick to the chest to help send him on his way. The heavy leather jerkin Pete had given him took the brunt of the blows, but didn't help his landings.

'Learn to roll, boy. You can at least do that much,' Pete said from the step of the wagon. He whittled away at a small piece of white wood in his hands and only bothered to look up when he heard Wilt slam into the ground again.

'Why am I learning to fight anyway? The Cantor said—'

Daemi spun and charged him. Wilt stepped quickly to the side but she'd somehow anticipated the move and was waiting for him, pivoting quickly and using his momentum to flip him onto his back.

He wheezed out the rest of his words: '—said there was no need for physical—'

Daemi dropped a heel into his gut as she walked past him and the last of the air in his lungs rushed out.

'Five!' Higgs giggled again and tossed one of the stones at his feet off to the side of the camp.

Wilt watched it disappear into the dirt. He was just like that stone. Being thrown from side to side.

'You're not learning to fight, you're learning focus and control.' Pete's voice echoed in the silence that had dropped over them. 'A true wielder knows how to shield his power from others, and knows how to call on it only when necessary. To preserve his strength for when it is truly needed. Then to be able to sink into it even when the world around him is in flux.'

The stone. Cold and clear. Wilt focused on the shape and feel of it and forgot everything else.

He stood up again and heard quick steps approaching from behind him. Feinting to the left, he then spun quickly to his right, meeting the flying kick Daemi was sending his way with a kick of his own. Wilt's muscles hardened momentarily with the memory of the stone's surface, and his boot slammed into Daemi's side, sending her sprawling in the dirt in front of Higgs.

'Uh, one,' Higgs muttered sheepishly and smiled at Daemi.

'Better.' Pete placed the small figure he had carved to one side and picked up another hunk of wood. 'We have ten days until we reach Redmondis, and for you that means ten days to gain some semblance of discipline. Again.'

Daemi was already moving.

The training, at least that's what Pete called it, continued each day as the wagon train made its way up the twisting mountain road toward Redmondis. The further north they travelled, the harder and colder the ground became, as Wilt discovered each time he landed on his back. Daemi never said a word to him; she simply charged in or waved him on, each time using his momentum against him and sending him sprawling into the dirt. Even Higgs had stopped keeping score, seemingly growing bored of watching Wilt get beaten up each day.

Pete sat witness for each session, carving away at his pieces of wood, only looking up when a particularly hard landing left Wilt wheezing in the dirt. Even then he simply shook his head and returned to his work.

Since that first session Wilt had managed to catch Daemi perhaps once every five attempts. He cleared his mind and felt which way she was going to move moments before she did, yet each time he caught her she seemed only to speed up again, moving quicker, hitting him until he managed to raise his awareness to that new level. Then again. And again.

Wilt tried reading her, sending out his sense like a rope to snare her, take control of her body before she attacked, but he couldn't seem to focus his will in that way. It was as if he was trying to push something very large through a very small hole, and only the smallest amount would leak through, too thin a rope for him to wield properly, too slow to react to her speed.

By the time it was dark, Wilt was battered and bruised and past thinking. He lay by the fire, gazing at the small wooden figures Pete had been carving, which were set out in a circle next to the flames. Each piece was the size of a finger, rounded in the middle and marked with a strange face. Arranged as they were, they each seemed to bear the same face, just twisted in a different expression. As the firelight flickered across them, Wilt saw flashes of someone he knew, or had known.

'Almost done.' Pete slumped beside the fire and placed another figure within the circle. It seemed complete now, no breaks left along its circumference.

'Almost?'

'We should arrive at the gates tomorrow evening, if this weather holds up.'

'So much for my training.'

'Oh, we've made some progress. You are much faster now than you were. Now you just have to learn how to fall.'

'Fall?' Wilt coughed out a harsh laugh. 'I've been doing nothing but fall.'

'But you still haven't learned how. Watch.'

Pete leaned forward and pushed the nearest figurine. It toppled backward, clipping the one behind it, then continued to tip completely over, spinning around to return upright. Meanwhile the piece behind had fallen as well, knocking the one behind that, and the one behind that, until a wave of motion pushed around the circle, the faces seeming to move as they passed before Wilt's eyes, one face grimacing in pain then smiling again. The pieces were so balanced that the wave continued around the circle, never ending, each piece falling and righting itself, falling and rolling back, using the momentum to always come around to standing.

'You see?'

The single face moved through its range of expressions, and Wilt suddenly recognised the features. They were his own. 'Clever trick.'

Pete reached out and held his finger on one piece, and as the wave moved around to it, it crashed to a stop. The piece showed a blank expression, exactly halfway between pain and a grin of triumph.

'Perhaps it is only a trick. Even so, it's not one you can afford to ignore.'

Pete lifted his finger and pushed the figurine again, restarting the wave of movement. Wilt stared at the circle until his eyes suddenly became heavy.

'Rest now. One final day of training, then the Cantors will have you. Let's hope you are ready.'

Wilt let his lids close and watched the circle now moving in his mind, smiling and falling, rolling and righting itself as he drifted away.

The final day was the longest yet. Daemi seemed determined to eke every last gasp of pain out of Wilt's body, to have him remember the feel of her boot sinking into his gut, her shoulder snapping into his solar plexus, her fist slamming into the side of his head.

Wilt had woken feeling strangely refreshed, as though his dreams had cleared away the dust and clutter in his mind. Even his body had felt good; for the first time in days he'd been able to stand and stretch without pain. Wilt grimaced at the memory now as he picked himself out of the dirt and tested the shoulder he'd just landed on. As always, just another bruise. Daemi seemed to know exactly how hard to hit him, as she never left any lasting damage.

She charged in again.

Wilt sprung to his left and rolled under the swinging arm, continuing his roll to end up behind her, but Daemi had anticipated his move and stepped back with the momentum of her swing, dropping low and letting her leg sweep his out from under him. He hit the dirt again with a groan and lay there for a moment, trying to suck breath into his lungs.

'Not doing so well today.' Higgs sat to the side of the fighting circle, playing with the small figurines Pete had carved. He'd arranged them in a figure eight and made them fall in order, his gaze following the wave of movement with a slight grin on his face. 'You know, this face looks a little bit like you.'

Wilt pushed himself up. 'Really? I hadn't noticed.'

Daemi moved in again and Wilt stepped sideways, edging around the circle as she stalked slowly toward him. He suddenly was aware of a brush on his mind, as if someone had tapped him on his shoulder, and he turned to face Pete sitting on the step of the wagon, eyes closed.

'Don't get distracted, boy.' Pete's mouth formed the words but Wilt seemed to hear them inside his mind.

Daemi's hand slapped hard into the side of his head and snapped his attention away. 'Don't get distracted, boy.'

Wilt saw the hint of a smile hidden under her helm.

A sudden suspicion led Wilt's gaze to Pete. They were working together. He looked toward Higgs, still transfixed by the figure eight in front of him, and saw the wave moving slowly around it. Falling and rising. Falling and rising.

Wilt took another breath and faced Daemi, his mind clear.

She ran toward him now, her left arm held straight out to the side, ready to swing at him. Wilt saw her approach in slow motion, and ducked under her arm as if it was the easiest thing in the world. He stepped out and around her, jumping backward as her leg swung out suddenly to try to catch him.

'Better.'

Daemi and Pete's mouths both moved and Wilt heard the words in his mind as well as his ears. He crept to the edge of the circle and let his mind sink deeper.

The world outside the circle seemed to blur into nonexistence. There was only his body, the circle, and the body of his enemy moving toward him again. And something else, a connection to the outside.

Wilt somersaulted backward as Daemi swung again, letting her fist swing harmlessly through the air in front of him. He kept his mind on the connection, the thread that drifted above them, the shimmering white connection that seemed so clear now. So easy to cut.

Daemi's heel slammed into the dirt beside him as he rolled away, springing to his feet and leaping backward to dodge another flying kick.

But cutting it would only sever the connection, would only leave him with two separate enemies. No, better to use it to snare them both. He reached out with his mind and pulled.

She stood very still between her parents, peering at the enormous armoured foot of the man in front of them, the man who towered even over her father, her father who was the second tallest man in the village behind Fern's, and Fern's father wasn't half as handsome.

Her father gripped her hand as he spoke to the strange man, quickly and urgently, squeezing her hand harder as he went, until she squirmed against the painful grip. He ignored her, lost in whatever it was he was trying to make the strange man understand.

Her mother stood silently, reaching out at one point and placing a hand on her hair, brushing it back from her face.

The strange man finally shook his head and reached out to take her hand from her father's. Her father resisted at first, then seemed to collapse into himself as he admitted defeat. Her hand was engulfed in the mailed gauntlet of the stranger, and he led her away.

She looked back and saw her father, tears running down his cheeks. He seemed so much smaller now, not tall at all.

Wilt pushed up from the depths and his vision returned to the physical plane. Daemi was swinging at him again, frozen in time, her right fist heading for the side of his head. Higgs was sitting outside the circle, his finger holding a single piece in place, gawking at the expression on it. Pete was still on the step, his hands clenched on the bench on either side of him, his face drawn, his eyes clouded and grey. Wilt saw a single breath fog out from Pete's lips before he sank back under.

He was standing in a large dark hall, lined up with the other acolytes, watching as the Cantor strode back and forth in front of them, gesturing to the large chart hanging on the wall. The chart described all the known welds, the different colours showing the different types and how to combat them. How to twist them and use them to control the weak. The Cantor held a long thin cane in his hand, and every now and then his arm shot out to whip a cut across the cheek of an acolyte. No one flinched. Those who were left were the strongest; each knew the consequence of showing any weakness.

He tried to focus on the lesson, on the chart, but his mind kept snapping back to the cane in the Cantor's hand, the pain that would come from it. His turn was coming, he could sense it. The Cantor strode up the line toward him and smiled as his hand shot out.

'Stop. Please.'

Wilt heard the voice in his mind and in his ears, strained and desperate. The air was deeply cold now, all warmth sucked out from the circle. The connection, what his vision had named a weld, still joined them, and he forced himself to let it go, let it float free of his control like a broken spider web in the wind.

Time sped up again as he pulled himself out of the depths, filled with an icy power he'd never known before. Daemi's fist resumed its arc toward his head, and he simply stepped into the punch, shooting out his hand to take her in the throat before she could connect. Wilt focused all his energy on the lunge, his hand smacking into the thin metal guard that hung from her helm to protect the vital area. It cracked under his hand, but he continued the movement, lifting her up and slamming her body back into the dirt.

'Stop.'

The voice was stronger now, calling out to him from beyond the circle.

'Wilt. Stop.'

It was Pete. Pete's voice. And Higgs.

'You're killing her.'

Wilt looked at his hand still locked around Daemi's throat, saw the grip that choked out her breath, the grey fingers that wrapped around her soft skin, and finally focused his attention on letting go. His hand seemed to hesitate before obeying, but finally surrendered and dropped away. Wilt sank back on his heels and felt the warmth of the morning sun seep slowly into his body.

Pete had run into the circle and was now crouched over Daemi, holding a cup to her lips and lifting her up into a sitting position. He turned to face Wilt, his eyes blazing with anger. Anger and fear.

'I told you never to remove that necklace.'

Wilt took a moment to figure out what he was talking about.

The symbol. The symbol Pete had given him, the symbol that still hung around his neck. He pulled it out from under the heavy leather jerkin and held it up. 'I didn't.'

'Whoa.'

Higgs's voice diverted Wilt's attention; he was still sitting by the side of the circle, his finger resting on a single piece of Pete's whittled characters. The piece was no longer white though; it had blackened and cracked, as though it had been left in a fire.

Pete stared intently at the symbol Wilt held up. The necklace too had changed. The red circle was still there, but the smaller white circle that had hung in the middle of it had been charred black.

Wilt reached out to poke it, then pulled his hand back sharply with a hiss.

'Is it hot?' Pete's voice was quiet.

'No.' Wilt watched the symbol swinging back and forth in the breeze. 'No, it's cold. It's ice cold.'

Chapter 11

Pete spent the rest of the afternoon caring for Daemi by his wagon. He fed her a strangely scented thin gruel and an even stronger smelling tea, and bit by bit she seemed to improve, eventually sitting up and allowing a weak smile to move across her face. Pete had removed her helm as soon as Wilt had let her go, and Wilt had seen her young face for the first time. She was around his age, pale of skin, and with a light scattering of freckles across her cheeks. She could almost be described as pretty. Yet when Pete lay her head down, her eyes remained closed and a bluish tinge coloured her lips. She looked half dead, and Wilt had slunk away as waves of guilt washed over him.

Wilt stalked around the edge of the camp, glancing over to check her progress every now and then and allowing the sight of her gradual recovery to lighten his conscience. Higgs had kept him company for a while, but his constant questions and blunt probing had yielded no answers from Wilt, and he'd eventually gotten bored and returned to studying the pieces Pete had carved.

Wilt was surprised to find he wasn't at all tired from the morning's exertions. If anything he felt stronger than ever, more energised, as if he'd woken from a long, refreshing slumber. Pete's necklace had been tucked safely inside his tunic, the intense cold of the inner circle having faded almost instantly. Wilt barely noticed it now, but its presence against his skin somehow reassured him. His mind was lighter too, as though a shroud had been shrugged off, a limit on his thoughts that had been burnt away. Frozen away.

For the first time in days he found himself thinking about escape, about returning to Greystone and the life he knew. Somehow those thoughts had dropped from his mind, pushed into the depths, and had only now returned to the surface. He played with the idea of Greystone, of Lodan and Griggs and the rest of the flagball team, of Master Turner, the Hand himself, of the busy streets and crowds ripe for the picking. Yet even as he had them, he knew such thoughts were only fantasy. That he could no longer simply walk away.

Guards patrolled around the edge of the camp, stamping their boots against the high mountain cold, their breaths steaming out from under their helms. Wilt idly watched them, wondering how old each of them was under their helms. Were they all as young as Daemi? As young as him? Most wore gloves, but some went without, proudly displaying the fresh scars where a finger used to be.

Wilt shook his head and kept walking. What kind of place was Redmondis, that it would demand such an offering from its subjects?

A light touch brushed across his mind and Wilt stopped in his tracks. He was on the far edge of the camp now, right at the boundary of the guard patrols and the open, wild forest beyond. The Tangle. He gazed into its depths and let his mind clear. The Tangle and the dark dangers it held had always been something unknown—something to fear. But standing at its edge now, Wilt recognised another feeling. A strange longing, as though the very trees called to him.

Suddenly he noticed how quiet the forest was, how the call of birds and chatter of hidden creatures seemed to have ceased. He scanned the trees, but saw nothing.

The touch brushed across him again, stronger now, as if clumsy fingers were trying to pry open his mind.

Wilt calmed his breathing and continued to walk deeper into the trees, readying himself to react to the next touch.

There.

Wilt felt the first scrambling claws across his mind and grabbed them, pulling the touch into him just as he had the weld between Daemi and Pete, suddenly seeing the thick black rope that snaked out toward him, trying to break through his defences. The weld slithered and flexed in his grip, no longer trying to break into him, now trying only to escape the vice of his mind. He fell back with it and dragged it into him, letting his vision follow the weld deep into the forest shadows, to the glowing golden eyes that was its source. He tightened his grip, and the animal squirmed under him, a silent yelp shrieking from its mind.

Then he saw Daemi's face again, her blue lips as the helm was lifted from her head, and he let the thing go. The black weld shot into nothingness as he released it, and a distant crashing in the trees told Wilt that its source had also fled in panic.

'You there!'

Wilt rushed back into the physical world and his body turned to face the voice.

'Stay within the camp boundaries.' The speaker was a guard, waving Wilt back from where he had wandered. 'Don't go wandering off. That's the Tangle out there. All sorts of creatures waiting for their next meal.'

Wilt trudged through the undergrowth and headed toward the campfires without another word.

'There you are.' Higgs trotted over to him as he entered their camp and grabbed his hand. 'Let me show you something.' Higgs pulled Wilt toward the far side of the wagon where he had been sitting all day, messing around with the carved figures Pete had given him.

Wilt allowed himself to be led, looking about but not seeing Daemi or Pete. 'Where's Daemi?'

'Huh?'

'The guard. The girl I hurt.'

'Oh, she's fine. Gone to report for duty or something. Look.' Higgs had arranged the pieces back in their figure eight pattern, the black piece standing alone in the centre. 'I thought it was just burnt, which was weird in itself, but now it's even better. Watch.'

'Higgs, I've seen this trick.'

'Not this one.'

Higgs bent down and touched his finger to the top of the black piece. He whispered a single word, and Wilt felt a sudden chill as the temperature dropped sharply. Then two separate ripples in the air spread out from the centre of the figure eight, moving as before, each piece flipping over to return upright, the two waves chasing around their separate circles to meet in the middle on the black piece and bouncing back around again.

Wilt focused on the pattern, allowing the display to sink into his mind, then let his eyes lose focus. He felt a surge each time the waves met in the middle, a heat in his belly that sent warmth up his spine and through his body, reinforcing something within him.

'The spiral shield. Good, Higgs.' Pete bent down and rested his finger on the black piece and whispered another word, and the movement suddenly stopped. 'You are making good progress. Don't overdo it though.' He picked up the black piece and held it in front of his face, studying the expression carved into the wood. 'Have you noticed the face?'

'Yeah. It changed just like you said.'

Pete held the piece out to Wilt. The face on it was still his, but seemed to have twisted into a dark smile, the blank eyes narrowed with an evil glint. Pete closed his fingers around the piece and tossed it to Higgs.

'Keep them safe. We enter Redmondis tomorrow. No need to show the Cantors anything but the basics. First rule of Redmondis: never let anyone know how strong you are. The strong are targets.'

Higgs sat the black piece down with the others, arranging them into a circle and muttering as he went, oblivious now to the rest of the world.

'Come, Wilt. There are some things we need to talk about.'

'Daemi is fine by the way. She was just a little shaken up. As was I.'

They were sitting in Pete's wagon, the canvas a dusty orange glow around them from the campfires outside.

'Higgs told me.' Wilt held the pendant Pete had given him out in front of his chest, letting the circle spin idly. The blackened wood seemed to soak in the light, not letting any escape from its shape, a black hole in the world.

'You shouldn't have been able to do that, you know.'

'Do what? What did I do?' Wilt dropped the pendant and looked up at Pete.

'You broke into our weld. We were joined, Daemi and I, sharing our strength to test you both physically and on another plane. You saw our connection.'

'It was white, not like the others.'

'The other welds you have so far encountered have been black, yes?'

Wilt nodded.

'That's because they were attack welds. Sent by the wielder to take control of their victim without their consent. Ours was mutual. A partnership. Stronger than any black weld, and proof against any outside interference.'

'There are other types of welds as well. I've seen them.'

'You saw what I saw, many years ago now. And you'll see them again. Even Redmondis still has to teach the basics.'

'And I saw other things. I saw Daemi.'

'You saw something of her past. Something important. A deep memory that served as the foundation for our weld. And yet you invaded it.'

'I didn't mean—'

'You could have simply severed the weld, broken our connection. But you did something else.'

Wilt picked up the pendant again and let it spin in front of his eyes.

'Something you should not have been able to do.'

'Why was it so cold?'

'You were draining us. Taking our strength to augment your own. If you hadn't stopped you would have killed us both.'

The black circle winked at him as the pendant spun.

'And lost yourself.'

'It was part of what you showed me. The pieces falling in order to stand again.'

'That's right. Using others' strength against them is the key to the strength of all wielders. But you can dive too deeply. You must be aware of the consequences of power. Strength alone will not suffice.'

The winking circle was making his eyelids heavy, and Pete's voice was fading into the background.

'Remember this, Wilt. The depths can be dangerous and the currents strong, and there are those who would tap into this strength if given the opportunity. The Sisters are already aware of your potential.'

Wilt's eyes closed and his body relaxed into sleep.

'Stay on guard. Tomorrow we arrive in Redmondis.'

Chapter 12

Wilt was shaken roughly awake and the canvas above him whipped away to reveal a clear dawn sky. He sat up and saw Pete scuttling around the wagon, untying ropes and flipping clasps. Pete worked quickly, collapsing the canopy and packing it away in a small wooden trunk. He seemed younger than ever this morning, no longer bleary eyed and broken. Wilt noted that he hadn't smelled the stench of alcohol on Pete's breath in days.

Pete pushed the trunk to the foot of Wilt's bed. 'Here. Put it with the others.'

Wilt stumbled out of the wagon and took hold of the trunk. 'Where—'

'Higgs will show you. Hurry now.' Pete and resumed his packing, leaving Wilt to search around the camp for Higgs.

'Good morning to you too,' he muttered.

Wilt finally spotted Higgs by the small campfire, blowing eagerly at the coals to try to spark some life into them. There was a pile of luggage beside the fire, and Wilt dumped the trunk with the rest of Pete's belongings.

'He's in a wonderful mood this morning.'

'Yeah. I think he's nervous.' Higgs finally got a coal hot enough to spark the dry leaves he had piled on top and a small flame flickered into life.

'What's he got to be nervous about? He's been to Redmondis before.'

'I don't think he likes it much. I don't think they like him much either—at least that's how it seems when the guards speak to him. I tried asking him about it, but he just growls at me.'

Higgs had a small pan on the fire and was now breaking eggs into it.

'Where did you get them from?'

The eggs spat and sizzled in the pan and as the smell wafted over him, Wilt suddenly realised how hungry he was.

'Some of the other wagons are surprisingly well stocked, especially the Cantor's. No meat, but eggs will do.'

'Been keeping your thieving skills in shape, have you?'

Higgs grinned up at him quickly before turning his attention back to the eggs.

'How do you know which one is the Cantor's?'

'Oh, he has more than one. You can tell by the number of guards patrolling them.'

That brought the image of Daemi into Wilt's mind and he caught himself just before he blurted out a question about her.

Higgs seemed to read his thoughts. 'Daemi left last night to join the other guards. Those of the Nine,' he said in a deep, joking voice, waving his fingers in the air.

Wilt shivered. He watched Higgs poking at the eggs for a few moments before speaking again. 'Have you thought about what you're going to do? Once we get to the gates?'

Higgs took the pan off the flames and drove a fork straight into the middle of the eggs. 'Didn't Pete tell you? I'm coming with you. I'm your ward.'

He took a hearty bite and grinned up at Wilt again, runny egg covering his chin.

'I asked you to help prepare the boy, not twist him to your ways!'

The Cantor's voice was raised as he paced in front of Pete.

Pete stood silently, a neutral expression on his face. 'They are not my ways, Wrex. They are the ways of the wielders. Your ways too.'

'The old ways. The weak ways!'

'They are not weak.'

'Don't think I don't remember, Petron! Wielders using wards as a crutch. The Sisters drove that heresy out of Redmondis, and the likes of you with it. Now you seek to weasel your way back in through this boy.'

Pete gazed at the Cantor, his eyes clear. 'You forget so quickly, don't you, Wrex?'

The Cantor dropped his head, apparently ashamed.

Pete continued, his voice calm. 'No one needs know of this. Their connection is well hidden. Deeper even than they themselves realise.'

'You think you can hide such a thing from the Sisters? From those who perfected the art of linking minds? Perhaps it is you who have forgotten.'

Pete let the words break against his blank face.

The Cantor paused in his pacing and studied the old man. Something passed silently between them as their eyes met, and the Cantor's voice took on a new tone. 'Still. I suppose you have shielded the boy effectively enough. I can no longer detect his power.'

'As you requested.'

'And Daemi? The guard I sent you? I hear she has returned to the company of the Nine.'

'Her assistance was most welcome and very effective. I recommend her.'

'Good.' The Cantor resumed his pacing, studying his feet as they trod the packed dirt. He seemed to be calculating possibilities, lost in his schemes. 'We will have to find some excuse to keep the ward near him.'

'I've already considered this. The lad shows real promise as a crafter—he can sense and shape the life within things. Surely he can earn his own place in their ranks.'

'A crafter? Yes. That might work.' The Cantor stopped suddenly as he seemed to reach a decision. 'Very well. We will arrive at the gates this afternoon. Send the boy and his ward to me at midday. I don't need to tell you to keep away from the gates do I, Petron?'

Pete's gaze didn't change, but his eyes hardened momentarily. 'No, Wrex.'

'Very well then.'

With that the Cantor strode away, and Pete relaxed from his position of attention. For a moment he looked a very old man, his shoulders slumped in weariness. It only lasted a moment, however, and he gathered himself together to continue readying his camp for the end of the journey.

Wilt sat with Higgs, watching him scrawl strange designs in the dirt at their feet. After each symbol was completed, Higgs would close his eyes for a moment, then shake his head and wipe the symbol clear before starting again.

Wilt could only hold his silence for so long. 'Pete's got you right into this stuff, huh?'

Higgs had finished drawing another symbol and was sitting with his eyes closed, contemplating. He opened one eye to peek at Wilt. 'It's what a ward is supposed to do for his wielder. I need to master these basics.'

'And what will they do for me, these drawings?'

'They're symbols of protection. Focus points for the power, the stuff the welds are made of.' Higgs rubbed out the symbol he had drawn with a stick and started another one, whispering while he worked.

'What are you whispering there? What language is that?'

Higgs ignored him and finished, then touched the stick in the centre of the symbol and whispered a final word. Wilt felt a sudden rush, as though a strong wind had suddenly whipped through the camp, and the symbol seemed to glow a faint red colour. A warmth spread over him, starting from the base of his spine and moving up his back and down his thighs. A slight smile crept across his lips.

'You see? They work.' Higgs wiped the symbol clear and the feeling abruptly left. Wilt was back in the real world, sitting on the cold ground.

'Enough of that, Higgs,' Pete said, walking over to them from the packed wagon. 'I think we have enough shielding to last for some time yet. Make sure you keep up your practice. Come now— it's time to join the others.'

Higgs bounced to his feet and wrapped Pete in a hug before he knew what was happening. 'Thanks. I know you can't come with us.'

Pete's face broke into a smile before he gathered himself and managed to push Higgs away. He tried to sound gruff. 'Spying on the Cantor and me, were you?'

'Just trying to keep in shape.'

Higgs flashed another grin at him before running off to gather his belongings. Pete had given him the set of wooden pieces he had carved, as well as a small, weathered book that looked even older than Pete. Higgs couldn't read the words, but he'd taken to studying the symbols each night before bed. He had wrapped everything in an old shirt Pete had found at the bottom of one of his chests, and looped this around the end of his favourite drawing stick, which he now slung over his shoulder.

'I take it Higgs told you about the Cantor and me?'

Wilt looked up at Pete and nodded. 'I already knew you were once in Redmondis. I saw it, remember?'

'Well. The less said about that the better. Just remember to keep your guard up, and try to keep that power of yours quiet. I've shielded you the best I can, and no one will take any extra interest in you unless you do something stupid. I can't make any promises when it comes to the Sisters, though.'

Wilt stood up slowly, brushing the dirt from his clothes. He reached out a hand and offered it to the old man. 'Thanks for your help, Petron.'

Pete seemed to stand taller as he reached out and shook Wilt's hand, his grip that of a younger, stronger man.

'And forget you ever heard that name. Some in Redmondis have long memories.'

Chapter 13

Higgs and Wilt waited outside the Cantor's tent, trying not to fidget under the disapproving glare of the two guards posted at the entrance. Higgs had tried greeting them, but had finally given up in the face of their stony silence. He contented himself now with pulling faces at them to try to provoke some sort of reaction.

'Stop that.' Wilt clipped him over the ears.

'I'm just testing their training. Good practice for them.'

'Why don't you practise your own training and try to keep still?'

Higgs relaxed his features out of a particularly gruesome expression and looked at Wilt. 'You know you've been no fun at all recently.'

'The Cantor will see you now.' A third guard had stepped out of the tent and ushered them inside.

Higgs was particularly impressed by the entrance room. 'I've never seen a tent with rooms before.'

Wilt was about to clip him again but the guard beat him to it, slapping a mailed fist over the top of Higgs's head and sending him stumbling forward.

'Silence unless spoken to.'

Higgs shot the guard an evil look, but the guard didn't seem to notice and led them on inside.

'I told you so,' Wilt whispered.

'He'll pay for that,' Higgs whispered back, his eyes suddenly hard.

The guard led them to stand by the large fire burning in the centre of the main room. Cantor Wrexley was seated on a raised platform, but had his head down studying an assortment of documents laid out in front of him.

They waited patiently for the Cantor, but he kept his head bowed, every now and then muttering to himself and scratching angry corrections into the parchments.

Higgs's patience gave out first.

'Excuse—'

He got no further as the guard slapped him hard on the back of the head. Higgs awkwardly stumbled sideways into the guard before catching himself and standing up straight again.

The movement seemed to break the Cantor's concentration and he finally noticed them. 'Ah, good. The final two. What took you so long?'

'We weren't the ones—' Higgs tried to splutter out an angry retort, but Wilt spoke over him.

'We apologise for keeping you waiting, sir.'

If the Cantor recognised Wilt's sarcastic tone, he chose to ignore it. 'Well, you're here now. Come, join the rest of our group.'

The Cantor stood and gestured to the darkness at the back of the tent. Their guard ushered them along behind the Cantor as he led them through the shadows and out a door neither of them had noticed. This led into another guardroom, then outside into a large open area where fifteen or so individuals stood about, trying not to look nervous. The Cantor waved Wilt and Higgs over to join them and proceeded to a large black horse waiting at the front of the column. He swung himself up easily into the saddle and spun the horse around to address them.

'We go now to the gates of Redmondis.' The Cantor's voice sung out across the small crowd.

Wilt saw the small gleaming gem he held at his throat.

'Crafters,' Higgs whispered. He looked from the Cantor to the guard standing next to his mount, the one who had escorted them here, and his eyes took on a mischievous glint.

'What are you planning?' Wilt whispered. He knew that look only too well.

'Me? I'm not planning anything. I'm not planning anything at all.'

The guard seemed to shift uncomfortably.

'My name is Simon. My father is a cobbler,' Higgs whispered to himself.

The guard's shifting took on significantly more urgency. The Cantor seemed not to notice him, and continued with his speech.

'You few have been selected to join us within Redmondis due to your potential. Potential that you may not yet be aware of.'

'I have three brothers and a younger sister. Her name is Alice.'

The guard had lost all composure now and was frantically clawing at his belt.

'Within Redmondis you will face many tests. Most of you will fail. But some will turn that latent potential into true power and join our ranks. Come! Today marks the beginning of your new life.'

The Cantor turned away from his audience and only then noticed the guard lying at his feet, now desperately tugging at his leggings.

'Werner? What is the meaning of this?'

The guard finally jerked his pants free and lay twisting in the dirt, his hands cupped around a bright red burn on his upper thigh.

Wilt saw Higgs now had a wide, satisfied smile on his face. 'Care to explain?' he whispered.

'Remember that soothstone I crafted? The one that got hot when the holder told a lie? I made some modifications.'

Wilt looked at the guard being helped up to his feet. The burn on his thigh was already beginning to blister.

'You have a terrible mean streak.'

'He'll recover soon enough.'

Higgs searched the ground at the feet of the horse, looking for where the soothstone had ended up. He had slipped it into the guard's belt when he'd stumbled into him, and it had been thrown free once the guard had wrenched his pants off.

'Daemi?'

The Cantor's voice snapped Wilt's thoughts back to the front of the crowd. A second guard had approached the Cantor and was standing at attention. Wilt would have known her without the Cantor speaking her name. After their days of duelling he would have been able to pick her out of any crowd simply by the way she held herself.

'Take Werner away. He seems to have done himself a mischief. You will lead our guard.'

Daemi saluted, then quickly moved to drag the suffering Werner out of harm's way.

The Cantor turned his horse to the trail and headed off without another word.

The small crowd around them began to follow. They were all around Wilt's age, teenagers and young men, looking tired and worn from the long journey. He didn't recognise any of the faces. They must have been picked up before the caravan passed through Greystone. For a moment he considered sending out a weld to get a reading of them, but he held himself back.

Don't do anything stupid. Petron's words rung in his ears. Besides, by the sound of things there would be plenty of time to get to know each other where they were going.

Wilt moved to follow the crowd and grabbed Higgs by the shoulder. 'C'mon, you can always craft another one.'

'But that was special, that was my first.' Higgs looked sad momentarily before giving Wilt a mischievous grin. 'Still. It was worth it, wasn't it?'

The high stone gates of Redmondis stood before them, rearing up out of the ground as though the earth itself had formed them. Sheer cliff face stretched out on either side of the gates, marked here and there by small windows carved into the rock. Wilt thought he saw movement in one or two of them, but didn't have time to study them further—there was too much else to look at.

The Cantor's column had joined with other caravans to form a single stream pouring in at the foot of the gates. The gates remained closed, and there was chaos where the caravans merged, with people and animals moving back and forth in confusion, jockeying for position and loudly asserting their right to stand their ground near the front.

Wilt and Higgs had stepped to the side of the confusion to better enjoy the show. There were at least four other columns of initiates, all doing their best not to look terrified. Cantor Wrexley had charged angrily to the foot of the gates and was haranguing the guards posted there, demanding to know what the delay was. Wilt saw Daemi and her small guard calmly organise space around the Cantor and begin pushing the rest of the crowd back: the initiates as well as various merchants and traders had come to dip their noses in the Redmondis trough.

'Is Pete in there somewhere, do you think?' Higgs gestured vaguely toward the milling crowd.

'No. He knows better than to get himself mixed up in this.'

'Do you think we'll ever see him again?'

Wilt thought about it for a moment. 'Yes. I'm sure we will.'

Higgs seemed to accept that. 'Good.' He smiled and resumed his study of the high stone walls. 'It'll be good to be back among stone again, don't you think? These wide open spaces make me nervous.'

Wilt turned a curious eye on his young companion. 'You're not worried about what might happen in there, are you?' Wilt stated it as a fact, amazed despite himself at Higgs's perspective.

'Oh, I expect most of those stories we were told of Redmondis are made up.'

Wilt was about to reply but was interrupted as a high-pitched horn blared out over the noise of the crowd.

Heads everywhere turned to see a huge horse charge toward the gates. The rider didn't slow as he approached the crowd, which split apart in sudden panic as men jumped out of the way to avoid being trampled. The rider pulled up at the gate and joined Cantor Wrexley in his angry diatribe at the guards. Wilt recognised the figure of Cantor Cortis, and a sharp pain stabbed at the back of his head as he remembered the last time he had seen that cruel face.

The Cantors seemed to make no headway with the Redmondis guards, and began arguing with each other. Wilt saw them both gesturing wildly at the crowd, who in turn took it upon themselves to raise the volume of their various disagreements.

'Not the most organised entry really.' Higgs had begun to pick his teeth with a long blade of grass.

'No. You'd think they would have had a bit more practice than this.'

Wilt kept his eyes on the two Cantors, and saw Cantor Cortis suddenly pull out a red cloth from his tunic and wave it wildly above his head. Cantor Wrexley seemed to know what this meant, and turned to his own guard, gesturing for Daemi to form them up around him.

A new note entered the symphony: a deep, driving bass of boots stomping heavily on stone. The crowd turned as one to face the column of guards bearing down on them, all other arguments dying in their mouths.

'Higgs, stay with me.'

Wilt headed for the foot of the cliffs, then slowly began to pick his way toward Cantor Wrexley at the gates, staying as far to the edge of the crowd as he could. He caught a glimpse of a red banner held high from a pike. Another horn rang out and the pike dropped suddenly out of view.

The crowd surged in sudden panic as the column of guards charged. Men and animals trampled each other in the rush to get clear of the pikes that were moving slowly, inexorably through the massed confusion of bodies. Those who were too slow to get out of their way fell and did not get up again, their broken bodies pounded into the ground by the guards' heavy boots. By the time the vanguard reached the gates their pikes were dripping with blood, and the guards' armour was splattered red from their grim advance.

Cantor Wrexley looked sickened by the display, but Cantor Cortis wore a triumphant smile. He turned and said something to Wrexley, who spun his horse and moved away from the gates without reply, his guard staying close.

Cortis's column stretched across the length of the area the crowd had filled. It was four guards wide, and as another horn rang out each guard took two strides to their side, opening a wide path through the middle of the column with two guards on either side. Through this gap drove a single covered wagon, with four red-cloaked figures standing at its corners, their heads hooded and eerily motionless.

Higgs jumped up and down beside Wilt, trying to get a better view. 'What's happening?'

'It's the Sister,' Wilt whispered.

As the wagon approached, the gates swung open, and Cantor Cortis bowed his head as it rolled past him and into Redmondis.

Wilt let out his breath as the wagon disappeared from view and the long column of guards filed in, leaving a bloody trail behind them. As they too disappeared inside the gates, the crowd flowed into the space as if nothing unusual had happened. He turned away from the scene and saw Cantor Wrexley wave to him from the front of the gates.

'C'mon Higgs. Looks like it's our turn.'

Higgs stared at the crowd, at the men who were picking over the remains of those unfortunate enough to have been caught by the guards' advance, their faces calm and their hands moving with business-like efficiency.

For once he had nothing to say.

Chapter 14

Wilt and Higgs joined the small group led by Wrexley as they walked through the gates of Redmondis. All chatter died, as though the weight of the heavy rock walls leaned in on them.

'You feel that?' Higgs whispered.

'It's just the walls. Changes in the air flow.'

'No, it's not. It's them. You can feel them.'

Wilt looked at Higgs's grim expression. 'You're just nervous.'

Higgs didn't reply, and Wilt thought better of pushing the point.

Their small column filed into a great open courtyard, lined on all sides by high white walls. From a walkway along the top of the walls, various figures watched them enter, chattering to themselves and pointing down at them.

Cantor Wrexley guided his horse to the side of the entrance of the courtyard and gestured his group in toward the centre. 'Don't let the other students bother you. Standard Redmondis greeting.'

Wilt examined some of the students standing near the walls. Most were dressed in simple black cloaks, though some wore common street clothes. The black-robed students seemed to stick to themselves, not mingling with the others. They scanned the newcomers below them as they entered, and Wilt shivered.

'You see?' Higgs whispered to him again.

Wilt felt the tingle along his spine again and let himself fall into it, his vision sinking to another plane. Suddenly the air danced with a thousand black snakes snapping at the crowd. Wilt saw the thin black ropes strike in and pull back, feeding on the thoughts and memories of the mob, squabbling for purchase. Some of the crowd seemed to be shielded, shimmering borders surrounding them and repelling each strike, and these shields attracted attention—more and more of the black welds moved toward them to try to break through.

'It's the students. The ones in the black robes.'

A group of welds suddenly broke through a shield and dived gleefully into an exposed man, who stumbled slightly but remained standing, his expression blank.

'The wielders,' Higgs whispered back.

'They're going after anyone they sense with the skill. Trying to remove any competition.'

Wilt saw another shield shatter under the onslaught of ten or more thin black welds. 'I can feel them fighting with each other.'

Higgs grabbed Wilt's hand urgently. 'Will they come after us?'

Wilt let himself sink deeper into the flow, before rushing back up to the surface. 'No. No, they can't see us. I think Pete shielded us.'

Higgs seemed to accept this and let go of Wilt's hand.

'Besides, I think the Cantors are about to put an end to it.'

The last of the initiates had filed into the courtyard and the great stone gates began to swing closed. The outside would be shut off for who knew how long. The sun had begun to break through the distant clouds, and the trees beyond the clearing swayed in a light wind. Wilt stared, drawn by something else now, the trees gesturing lazily, blocking out the sounds around him. One tree in particular stood out, a single bright shaft of light highlighting it. Halfway up its trunk a thick branch shot out to the side, and perched on this, gazing straight at him, was what looked like an eagle. Its bright golden eyes locked with his as the gates closed the scene off, and it seemed to nod its head to him. Then the vision was gone and the world rushed back in.

'Wilt!' Higgs was tugging on his hand again. 'They're calling your name.'

Wilt looked to the centre of the courtyard and saw Cantor Wrexley standing up in his stirrups, waving wildly toward him.

'The one called Wilt.'

The voice boomed across the courtyard, and a hundred heads turned to goggle at him.

Wilt stumbled forward to the front of the crowd and joined the small group that had formed in front of the mounted Cantors. As he walked up he saw Cortis lean over in his saddle toward Wrexley and whisper loudly enough for all to hear.

'Not the sharpest one there I see, Wrexley.'

The students lining the walls tittered, and Wilt felt his face turn a hot red. He glared at Cortis, who looked back at him with cold grey eyes. They weren't just grey though; there were flecks of gold in them, as if a second colour was hidden behind the first, trying to break through. Cortis broke the connection as the next name was called, leaving Wilt with a strange sense of déjà vu.

Wilt studied the group. There were ten of them, all of a similar age. He recognised some of them as the ones who had been shielded earlier. All welds had suddenly ceased as soon as the gates closed, as though a valve were shut off, but one or two of the initiates still looked dazed from the onslaught.

Wrexley sat on his horse at the head of the group, and on either side of him stood his guards. Wilt picked out Daemi immediately and smiled at her. Her face was covered by her helm, but Wilt could feel her angry grimace by the way her shoulders stiffened.

'The one they call Higgs.'

The voice continued its list, and Wilt turned to see Higgs trot over to join a large group of people on the far side of the courtyard. At the head of this group stood an old woman leaning on a carved wooden staff. This group was much larger than the one Wilt had joined, and they seemed a greater spread of ages. Higgs was perhaps the youngest, but there were men and women with him who looked old enough to have been his parents.

'The Lesser Skilled.' The young man next to Wilt sniffed.

'Crafters, healers, that sort of thing. Not a threat.' The boy was a tall, foppish fellow with blond hair down to his shoulders. His clothes hung loosely, and he looked like he needed more than a few good meals.

'Delco. At your service.' The young man placed his hands behind his back and bowed his head to Wilt in a formal greeting. Wilt stood there, not knowing the proper way to reply.

'Oh, you know one of them, do you?' Delco pointed his chin at the group and Wilt turned to see Higgs waving happily at him. He raised his hand slowly in reply.

A body bumped heavily into his shoulder, knocking him off balance and causing him to stumble slightly.

'Watch it, Meat.'

Red Charley strode past him and joined a third group forming in front of Cantor Cortis. He turned and smirked at Wilt, and one or two others leered back as well.

'Guards.' Delco sniffed again. 'Yet to learn their proper place. Always the last to be called out—we should be almost done now.'

'How do you—'

'How do I know so much about Redmondis?' Delco put his hands behind him. 'It's in the family. Both my brothers are full Black Robes now, and my father almost became a Cantor himself, though obviously he didn't.'

'Obviously?'

'Well, I wouldn't be here if he had, now would I? Cantors take a vow of celibacy, everyone knows that.'

'I didn't.'

An awkward silence descended before a wide smile broke across Delco's face, and he suddenly seemed much less formal.

'Well. I can see we're going to need to start from the beginning with you. Come.' Delco put his arm around Wilt's shoulders and led him along, following Cantor Wrexley as their small group filed out of the courtyard. 'I'll pull some strings, make sure we end up roommates. Won't take long to get you up to speed.'

Wilt allowed himself to be led, wondering briefly what sort of new world he had gotten himself into.

'I see you managed to survive the initiation well enough.' Delco smiled at him as they walked along. They seemed to be heading toward a high dome.

'Initiation?'

'Back there in the courtyard, when we came in.'

'Oh, you mean the welds.'

'The Black Robes do it every year, gang up and aim for whoever they can get their claws into. Drain what power they can. The stronger your shield, the more of a target you become. My brothers told me all about it. Said the best way was to not put up any shields at all, trust to luck. Besides, if they do get you they'll get bored soon enough if you don't put up a fight. Don't give them anything to feed from.'

'No shield?'

'Yes, though I expect you knew that. I didn't see you trying to shield yourself.'

Wilt smiled to himself at the knowledge that even another wielder couldn't detect the shielding Old Pete had given him. No, not Old Pete. Petron.

'My brothers got me anyway, gave me a bit of a waking nightmare just as I walked through the gate. Probably had me picked out from the get go. Didn't make it too bad though. I just feel a bit tired now.'

Wilt studied Delco's face. He had dark circles under his eyes, though Wilt had assumed that was how he always looked. He didn't seem the healthiest specimen.

'Still, we won't have to worry about any of that now,' Delco continued. 'Once the gates close, any wielding outside of class is forbidden.'

Wilt raised his eyebrows and Delco grinned at him.

'Yep, forbidden. Apparently they used to allow it, even encourage it if you listen to what my father says. Caused all sorts of problems. Wielders challenging each other over the silliest things. But the Sisters put an end to all of that.'

'The Sisters.'

Delco stopped and stared at Wilt, his grin slowly melting into a full-blown smile.

'You don't even know about that, do you? The Restoration. The Great Cleansing. Whatever they called it in your neck of the woods. My father calls it the return of the true faith. When the Nine Sisters rose, a single power linked between nine great minds. They stamped out any resistance and took control of Redmondis. Banished the weaker powers entirely, banned all wielding by any but those who wore the black robes. Even you must have heard about that.'

Wilt thought about Petron, about the argument with the Cantor, about wielders and wards. About the great bird he saw sitting outside the gates of Redmondis.

'I've heard a little.'

'Well, I can see the Masters will have their hands full with you. That's first grade history. Everyone's supposed to have a solid grounding in the basics before they get accepted here. How did you get in here anyway? I can't detect any power in you.'

Delco almost seemed angry for a moment, and Wilt smiled at him to try to break the tension.

'Oh, I don't know. Maybe they made a mistake.'

'Maybe.' Delco glanced a little uneasily at him before getting distracted by a new sight he could share his knowledge on. Wilt could tell Delco was the sort of young man who loved nothing more than showing off what he knew.

They had entered the large domed building, which turned out to be a single wide-open room. Wilt looked up at the ceiling and was shocked to see the sky instead, clouds moving across a deep blue expanse.

Delco grinned expectantly at him. 'It's an illusion. The ceiling is there, but they make it look as though you can see the sky outside.

Another crafter trick. At night it turns black and you can see stars moving across it. The Great Hall of Viewing. It's one of the oldest buildings in Redmondis. My father says—'

Whatever Delco's father had to say on the matter was lost as Cantor Wrexley's voice rang out, echoing off the high blue ceiling.

'Form a line. Present yourselves to the Sister.'

Wrexley himself stood to attention, facing the front of the hall, and the initiates all lined up behind him, murmuring nervously to each other.

'You do know about Sisters, don't you?' Delco whispered.

Wilt nodded quickly.

'Try to keep your mind clear. The Sentinels can sense your thoughts.'

Wilt felt a chill and a sudden oppressive pall in the air as five red-robed figures entered the room. Four were very tall, unnaturally so, and covered head to toe in red cloth. The Sentinels, Wilt guessed. Their faces were completely covered, red veils hiding their features. Their heads moved as if they were studying the students, then tilted back as though sniffing for any scent of danger.

In an instant the Sentinels were replaced by enormous, twisting pythons, heads bobbing from side to side as their tongues tasted the air. Wilt blinked and the vision was gone, the Sentinels back in human form, scanning the room. After a moment the four seemed satisfied and moved away from the fifth figure they had been shielding. The Sister.

She stepped forward and threw back her hood, and all air seemed to leave the room.

Wilt found himself floating in a deep stillness, his eyes locked onto her beautiful face, unable to even think. Her deep red hair curled down over her shoulders and was lost in the folds of her robes, and her alabaster skin seemed to glow in the sunlight shining down from the ceiling high above. But even more intense were her eyes: deep green pools lined in black, scanning the line of mere men in front of her with contempt.

Wilt watched her eyes move along the line and wondered how he would survive their glare.

'Initiates.'

Her voice seemed to echo inside his head, as though emanating from within his own thoughts. Finally her eyes came to rest on Wilt, and something caressed his mind as their eyes locked. A small smile curled her lips as she stared into him.

Wilt felt her wrap around his mind, holding him in the palm of her hand and weighing his power. He knew it would only take the slightest squeeze to shatter him into a thousand shards and leave him gibbering in madness.

'Welcome.' Her voice was a chorus, speaking in unison, a great linked swarm of welds, twisting around him, taking up the entire universe.

Finally her eyes moved on and Wilt's mind relaxed. Each initiate seemed to suffer the same judgment: their bodies stiffened and sagged in turn as she continued down the line. Eventually she reached the end and smiled at Cantor Wrexley.

'Good, Wrexley. Be sure to get them settled in.'

Wrexley seemed to relax at her words, and a wide smile of relief broke across his features. He bowed his head. 'Thank you M'lady.'

The Sister strode back to the safety of her four guards. She raised her hood over her head, and they formed around her protectively. Wilt felt the heavy air lift, though a slight chill remained. Relief rolled over him, but he kept perfectly still, all his senses tensed in warning.

Suddenly the closest of the four guards snapped his head to the side and looked directly at the nearest initiate. The young man's face had relaxed into a relieved grin and he didn't notice the sudden attention he was attracting. Wilt wanted to call out in warning, but he knew there was nothing he could do.

The Sentinel tilted his head, as though listening, then shot out an arm to take the young man by the throat. He lifted him effortlessly off his feet, a low screech now emanating from behind the

Sentinel's thick red veil. The initiate's face had drained of colour, and his legs kicked frantically in the air as he struggled for breath.

'Your thoughts betray you.' It was the Sister's voice, again echoing in each of their heads as though she was perched inside their minds. 'Let this boy serve as an example.'

Wilt saw another flash of vision, the great serpent's fangs striking into its victim.

A sudden spike of pain sank into each of them as the Sentinel closed his fist and the young initiate stopped moving. His body hung limply in the air before the Sentinel dropped him and turned away, escorting the Sister from the room. The young man's body lay crumpled on the ground, but no one moved toward it. All knew his spirit was no longer within.

'Come, gentlemen.' Cantor Wrexley's voice shook slightly as he turned away and led them from the Great Hall. Wilt risked a look over his shoulder as he walked, fixing the image of the broken body in his mind. He would remember this day.

The white faces of the other initiates told him they too would not soon forget their first day in Redmondis.

Chapter 15

Delco was as good as his word, somehow making sure he and Wilt ended up as roommates. Their chamber was high on the tenth floor of the large dormitory where all the skilled initiates lived. The more junior you were the higher your room, meaning the more cold stone stairs you had to trudge up and down each day. A single large window dominated the simple room, looking out across the dense forest below them. It was nailed shut, but Wilt surmised from the view that the window was cut into the cliff face—perhaps it was one of the windows he had seen before entering Redmondis. That already seemed so long ago, a pale and distant other life.

He didn't know how long he had been in Redmondis. Time seemed to have faded from importance. All he knew was the routine: up early each morning to trudge to the massive dining room on the ground floor of the dorm, forcing the tasteless porridge down his throat, and following his fellow first years out to begin their classes. Standing in bare stone rooms before various Cantors and lesser Masters as they droned on, all of them somehow merging into a single grey-faced figure in his memory. Always keeping a fixed, neutral expression on his face. Moving back through long enclosed corridors to the dining hall for another lukewarm meal of vegetable mush, then following the boy in front of him to attend afternoon classes. Never remembering exactly what was taught, simply soaking in the drone of words that washed over him. Back to the dorm before dark, to eat again and then trudge slowly back up the stairs, watching his feet to avoid stumbling on the irregular stone steps, worn down by centuries of feet just like his. Collapsing into a dark, dreamless sleep before starting it all over again as the sun rose.

The days were nothing more than a collection of fleeting images: heavy stone walls; flickering torches; high windows that revealed only snapshots of grey sky; empty shelves lining classroom walls, the wood bowed as though weighed down by invisible books; cramped, uncomfortable seats that stuck into the middle of his back; desktops rutted with carvings from another age, when students had the freedom to make their mark in such a way. It was as though the Redmondis they occupied was a shell of what it used to be: a tomb, a poorly remembered story, the details sketched out but the heart, the guts of it no longer there.

Part of him seemed to know something was wrong—something was missing that had previously been important to him—but the thin spike that had entered his mind on his first day within these walls throbbed briefly and that troublesome thought melted into the depths.

Delco seemed to be suffering the same fate; his constant educational chatter had dropped to a low mutter, not even addressing Wilt most of the time, instead talking to himself as he proceeded through the day. As for the other initiates, they were all blank faces. Wilt focused on the black-robed backs in front of him and followed where they led.

At night he slept within a cold, blank space of nothingness, floating without thought. Sleep became nothing more than a slice of death.

Then something changed. Though Wilt's days remained a strange grey blur, his nights bloomed into life. Dreams filled the void where reality used to be, until Wilt's entire world seemed turned upside down: his waking hours vague and still, his dreams vivid and full of life.

Each night began the same way. He closed his eyes and sank into the cold stillness that seemed so eager to welcome him, and the next moment he was floating beneath a thick layer of protective ice, watching strange figures above hunting him, yet oblivious to his presence. Red-robed guards and large, golden-eyed wolves padded past, eyes eager and hungry, but Wilt floated by them in the calm, cold waters beneath the surface.

And then he was elsewhere. In a warm room, sitting by a fire, paging through piles of books, soaking in their knowledge. Reaching over to pick up one of a pile of smooth stones, perfect for skimming, weighing one in his hand and muttering words he somehow knew. Feeling the stone heat in his hand and bend to his will. Placing it back with the others, its shape changed now, the beginnings of a face haunting its new curves.

A surge in the waters and he moved away, to another room, another set of eyes. Sweating as he bent and stretched his body, forcing every last gasp of effort out of his tired sinews, long knife flashing back and forth as he moved through the positions. Sweat dripped into his eyes, and he brushed it away to see himself standing in front of a tall mirror in the form of a familiar woman's tall figure, nightshirt clinging to the curves of her skin.

The rush of recognition brought on another wave that knocked the vision free, sending him on again, deeper now, the visions stranger. An impossibly beautiful woman, her red hair flowing down over her shoulders, surrounded by other red-robed figures, their hands joined, black chains looping out from within the folds of their cloaks, binding them together as they sunk away from his sight and into the depths.

A lone guard, his hands throbbing in the cold, a constant itch where his finger used to be. Standing and watching as other guards moved through the campsite, grabbing new recruits from their bedrolls and marching them to the high bonfire burning in the centre of the camp, where the Cantor stood surrounded by his wolves, his eyes bright and mad.

That same bright golden light reflected from another set of eyes, those of an eagle soaring high above the trees, banking in the wind that gusted from the high stone cliffs of Redmondis, curving toward a lone window cut in the stone.

Each night Wilt's dreams ended in the same way. He sank down, away from the ice that protected him, away from the light and movement of the visions, into the still dark of the depths. Sinking into the nothingness until it became his world. A blank slate, a cold finality that knew him and whispered his name.

One morning Wilt woke to a new sound, a scratching on the rough glass of the window at the head of his bed. At first he simply listened, allowing the sound into his mind and appreciating the way it ushered strange thoughts in through the thick soup. He watched one in particular rise up and strain against the black membrane encasing his mind. It kept expanding after the others had surrendered and finally popped as his eyes snapped open.

From the corner of his vision he saw a small shadow at the window leap away. Instinctively he rolled to his feet and reached the window in half a second, but the shadow had disappeared. All that was left was a single scratch running the length of the glass. Wilt ran his hand slowly across it, tracing the crack under his finger.

'What is it?' Delco's voice sounded strong and clear in his ears for the first time in days. Weeks perhaps.

'Nothing.' Wilt turned away from the glass. 'It's nothing.' His own voice felt strange in his throat, as though he hadn't used it in a long time.

Throughout the day Wilt's senses began to awaken. The still air in the corridor brushed against his cheeks as he moved through it, and he could smell the warm kitchen scents from the dining room before he entered. The sunlight bleeding through the thick glass windows of the classroom reminded him of other things, and his mind started to chug back up to speed.

The sounds of the world also returned. Whispered voices and clattering plates in the dining hall. Sandalled feet slapping against cold stone as the initiates marched to and fro across the halls. Even the voices of the Masters seemed to be coming alive; Wilt noticed a difference in their timbre from their usual dreary monotone.

'Eyes front!'

Wilt's attention snapped to the front of the class, where a particularly aged Master had been leading the class through a detailed history of the reasons behind the Restoration. He'd been caught staring out the high window at the spare grey sky outside. The Master seemed at a loss for what to do, as though such behaviour was hardly thinkable. In the end he shook himself and resumed droning.

At night Wilt's dreams returned—ripples and waves formed in the darkness. Somehow he knew it was only a matter of time before they rose over him again.

The scratching was there again as he woke the next morning. Wilt kept very still, his eyes closed and breathing regular to avoid spooking whatever it was outside his window. He let his sense float out of him as he lay there, allowing the image of the room to form in his mind. Delco was still asleep on the far side of the room.

The sound changed to a sharp tapping, and Wilt knew it was time to act. He rolled up and out of bed in one lightning-fast movement, snatching his hand through the window, where the pane of glass had been cut free just as the creature outside finished tapping. His fingers grasped at a leg, and he caught a confused glimpse of a large bird of some kind, one whose eyes stared straight into him with a familiar deep golden light. Then it was gone, leaping out into the great emptiness and flying out of his reach. Wilt leaned his whole body out the window to try to see where it flew to, but it had disappeared over the tops of the cliffs and out of his sight. He looked at the ground far below him, and felt the deep stillness of the air. It tasted indescribably sweet, as though he had been locked in a dank room for weeks away from the real world.

'What on earth are you doing?'

Wilt pulled back into the room and saw Delco sitting up in his bed.

'Oh. Uh, just getting some air?'

A wide smile broke out across Delco's face and they both melted into sudden laughter. It was as though a spell had been lifted.

Eventually the laughter subsided and Delco got out of bed to begin dressing. Wilt turned back to the open sky outside the window.

'Are you coming or not?' Delco asked, ready to leave the room to begin their day.

'Not, I think.'

Delco studied him for a moment, but seemed somehow to understand Wilt's reluctance to re-join the flow. 'You're staying here?'

'Yeah. Tell them I'm not well or something. If they ask, I mean.'

'Not well. Okay.'

Delco seemed to find that idea funny, but restricted himself to a wide grin. They both somehow knew Wilt's absence would not be noticed, could not be noticed in the grey flow of routine in which the world of Redmondis floated.

'I'll see you later then.' Delco closed the door behind him, leaving Wilt on his own with his thoughts, thoughts that began to speed up and present all sorts of new opportunities.

The glass pane had been cut clean against the frame of the window, and Wilt had knocked it completely out when he had snatched at whatever it was that had cut through the glass. It now lay somewhere far below on the forest floor, probably smashed into a thousand pieces. A light morning breeze had picked up and blew through the open window now, bringing with it the fresh smells of the world outside, the world Wilt realised now he had somehow begun to forget.

He sat on the ledge of the window, staring out across the tops of the trees far below him. The sunlight moved across the hundred different shades of green, and Wilt cleared his mind with slow, deep breaths. The stone window ledge was scratched as well, probably by the same creature that had cut through the glass. Three deep notches were carved into its surface, as though from the claws of a standing leg. Wilt rested his fingers in the grooves, closed his eyes and let his mind float free.

Wilt could smell the forest below him, the breaths of the trees filling the air. There was something else as well at this height, the scent of the far ocean perhaps, or the snow-tipped mountaintops—a clean, cold freshness emanating above the other smells. He felt his fingers slide back and forth in the scratches in the rock, felt his skin form around the shape of the grooves. Felt his nails dig in.

Another, much closer smell caught his attention. Sweet and smoky and completely irresistible. Wilt opened his eyes and sprang out off the ledge, not allowing his conscious mind to intrude upon the dream.

Wilt scrambled across the cliff face, his fingers finding the tiniest ledges in the rock, his toes digging into the hard surface. He scratched and clawed his way up to the roof of his building metres above his window. The possibility of falling, of slipping and losing the smell that overwhelmed his senses didn't even enter his mind until he pulled himself onto the cold slate rooftop and looked down at the yawning space below.

The rooftop was almost flat, and it was easy enough to trot over the slippery slate. The buildings of Redmondis had been built up around each other over the centuries, and left a path across the rooftops almost as complete as a night highway of Greystone.

The smell was much fainter now, though he knew he was on the right path. It was as though his senses had shrunk as he'd reached the roof and regained something of his conscious mind. Still, it was easy enough to follow. The air was still and clean at this altitude, and left little doubt as to the source.

Wilt leaped easily across a high gap in the rooftops, barely aware of the long drop that flashed below him. The scent led him on, in and around the centre of Redmondis. The high-domed roof of the Great Hall rose above the other buildings, helping him keep his bearings. He worked toward the far outer circle of Redmondis, where the lesser trades congregated, away from the stern silence of the Black Robes' areas. Other smells caught his attention as he padded along, as though the air was more alive there, full of activity and warmth.

The next building was a full storey higher than the one he was on, but a tight corner gave Wilt the purchase to jump up one wall and spring higher to the other, catching the lip of the roof and pulling himself up easily. A strange smile spread across his face as he rolled to his feet and continued on.

The scent was stronger again here; he was very close. The roof split into another higher tower, lined with windows. Another dormitory perhaps. The lesser trades probably needed more space; there were so many more of them. Still, they would be off on their own daily activities by now. The rooms would be empty.

Wilt ran up to the curved tower wall and examined the sandstone bricks. The tower had been built centuries ago, and wind and rain had had their way with the stone, cutting deep paths into its face. This would be almost too easy.

Again without conscious thought, he scrambled up the tower face, his fingers—no, his *claws*— finding easy purchase. For a moment the thought of claws panicked him and he felt his purchase on the wall slip, before the sweet, smoky scent wafted past him again, wiping his mind clear, pulling him along toward a single window cut into the face of the tower. Wilt climbed as he never had before, almost running up the tower wall. He reached the windowsill in seconds and perched there for a moment, scanning the empty room, before dropping onto the cold stone floor and hurrying over to the fire where a black iron skillet held the source of the smell.

Inside the pan, three fat sausages popped and jumped in hot

grease, and three long rashers of bacon bubbled alongside them. Wilt's mouth filled with saliva, and he was suddenly aware he was on all fours, crouched on the floor.

'Well there's something you don't see every day.'

Wilt spun around to face the voice coming from a shadow on the bed. Higgs sat forward, letting the light from the window shine across his grinning face.

'It took you long enough. I thought I was going to have to eat breakfast alone again.'

Chapter 16

Sausages, bacon, eggs, thick buttered toast and sweet, hot coffee now sat heavily in Wilt's stomach as he sat back on Higgs's bed and studied the room. It was smaller than his own, but the second bed here seemed to be unused, stacked high as it was with various books and strangely curved tools. He felt a flash of déjà vu as he scanned the room, as though he'd seen it somewhere before.

'I convinced my roommate it would be best for both of us if he found other accommodation,' Higgs said. 'I tend to have visitors you know.'

'Oh?'

'You didn't think I'd just forget about the world outside these walls, did you?' Higgs waved at the window and turned back to rummaging around the fire.

'No, I guess not.' Wilt's voice sounded small in his ears. He looked back out the open window, scratching idly at a tickle behind his ears, feeling vaguely guilty.

Somehow such thoughts, of Greystone and the Guild, of Lodan and Petron, of the entirety of his past life before Redmondis had dropped from his mind. How could he have forgotten?

'I've managed to organise some of the crafters already. Setup a network of supply. It's useful having this window facing the outside world. Makes receiving deliveries a whole lot easier.'

Wilt was only half listening. The tickle seemed to have moved south and he rubbed his sandals together, trying to scratch the itch on the arch of his feet.

'Petron is very helpful, of course.'

That got Wilt's attention. 'Pete? I mean, Petron? You've seen him?'

'Sure. He drops by every now and then. Tells me the news of the world, brings me various things. Can't carry too much of course.'

Wilt stood up and walked over to the open window. The wall he had climbed so easily seemed sheer and smooth from this angle.

'Petron climbs up here?' Another tickle fluttered behind his ears and he slapped quickly at the back of his head.

Higgs started to giggle. 'Of course not. He flies.'

Wilt turned around and Higgs broke into full laughter. He threw something in a high arc toward him, and Wilt's hands reached out automatically to catch it. It was a small, perfectly formed figure of a cat. As his hands wrapped around the stone figurine, a strange warmth spread over his body. He returned to Higgs's bed and stared blankly at the wall, trying to process this new feeling.

Higgs was still smiling, poking around in the high stack of papers on the other bed. 'Petron said it might come as something of a shock. Sometimes it takes years for the Black Robes to fully understand it. Something to do with the way they access the welds or something. Understanding gets in the way of opening access to all that power.'

'Petron. He's the one that broke through my window.'

'Yep. Said it would probably take him a few weeks to get through that glass. I put together a little cutting edge for him to help speed things along.'

'He's ... he's a bird?'

'An eagle. A golden eagle. He can take that shape.'

Wilt thought back to the jumbled image he had glimpsed out his window, and then back further still to the golden eagle outside the gates of Redmondis on that first day. He remembered the strange understanding that passed between them as their eyes locked.

'How?'

'That's not the right question at all. You know how—you did it yourself just this morning.' Higgs waved toward the figurine of the cat in Wilt's hands.

'But—'

'Course I helped a bit. Formed that for you, helped speed things along. Petron said I'd have the understanding to help decide on your other shape. A cat made sense to me. All that running around on rooftops you like so much.'

'But—'

'I'm not really supposed to show you that yet either, so don't tell Petron if you see him. You're supposed to come to an "inner understanding" or something. Sounds like typical Black Robe nonsense to me. I figure, if you can do it, that's all it takes for you to understand it. You fit your mind to reality, not the other way around. Besides, I wanted to show you what I can do. Watch!'

Higgs reached out to show Wilt another stone sitting in the palm of his hand. It was flat and curved, another of the perfect skimming stones he seemed to have such a talent for finding. Then Higgs closed his fist and the stone disappeared. He whispered something in a language Wilt didn't understand, then opened his palm again and the flat stone was gone. In its place was what looked like a lovingly carved cat's paw.

'I've been trying to work with other materials as well, but stone seems to respond best. All that time surrounded by rock in Grey-stone must have something to do with it.' Higgs tossed the paw into a small pile of similar shapes littering his desk and smiled at Wilt, waiting for a response.

'Uh, that's great, Higgs. You're a crafter.' The words sounded inadequate, but they were all he could come up with. Wilt's mind was reeling from the various shocks of the morning.

'Got a long way to go, of course. I figure we'll stay here long enough for me to get more of a handle on things.'

Wilt began to speak again but stopped himself. It all seemed so impossible, yet when he thought about how he had got here this morning, the feeling of the cliff face beneath his fingers (*claws*), his balance as he leaped from rooftop to rooftop, the way a simple smell had overwhelmed him ... it somehow all fit.

'What I'm really interested in is what happens to your clothes. I was half expecting you to appear here naked. I'd grabbed some bigger clothes just in case.'

Wilt glanced over to where Higgs was pointing, at a small pile of rumpled clothes in the corner.

'Thankfully that doesn't seem to be necessary. Petron had said it wouldn't, but I wasn't going to take any chances.'

'Petron.'

'You won't see him though, I suppose, at least for a while yet, so that's okay. He can't come within the Redmondis boundaries. He can stop by the window every now and then, but I suspect even that is hard work. He only does it once a week or so. I think it takes him some time to recover.'

'So how have you been speaking with him?'

'Notes. He writes me long notes and rolls them up. Carries them in a rather cute little pouch around his neck. It's a good thing eagles are the size they are too cause he's had quite a bit to say.'

Wilt tickled the small cat figurine on its belly and a warmth spread through his chest. He smiled and put the figure down.

'I'll take good care of it.' Higgs was grinning at him now, and Wilt had a terrible premonition of the sort of mischief Higgs could get up to.

'You won't—'

'Don't worry, it can't hurt you. It was just a way for me to get the idea into your unconscious mind. Look.' Higgs reached over, swiped the figurine from where Wilt had left it and tossed it casually into the fire.

'No!' Wilt sprang up to save the cat from the flames licking at its body, then froze. He felt nothing. No heat, no pain. Even the figure seemed immune to the fire, the stone not blackening from the heat of the coals.

Higgs giggled again and reached into the fire with a pair of tongs to retrieve the figurine. He tossed it toward Wilt, who once again caught it without thinking. It wasn't even warm.

'We're better than you think, us "lesser-skilled"'

Wilt smiled at the words, hearing Delco's disapproving tone. He suspected the Black Robes could learn quite a bit from those they considered beneath them, if they only chose to listen.

The thought of Delco snapped him back to the present. 'What time is it?'

'Almost lunch time, I expect. I was about to put the pot back on. I know you lot don't get fed properly. Figured you'd need some meat in you.'

'No. I have to get back.'

Wilt saw the disappointment in Higgs's eyes.

'Sorry. I'll be back tomorrow though, for breakfast?'

Higgs's face warmed up into a smile. 'Okay. Sausages, bacon and eggs all right for you? I'll make sure I'm stocked up.'

'And coffee. Thanks, Higgs, for everything.'

He placed the small cat back down by the side of the bed and walked over to the window. The sun was much higher in the sky now; it had to be past noon. At the window he hesitated.

'You know, it just occurred to me, this taking of other shapes. Perhaps that's why the Black Robes and the Cantors, the skilled, don't eat meat at all.'

Higgs laughed and nodded his head. 'You never know who you might be offending.'

Wilt smiled and turned to the window. 'So ... do I just change in and out of the shape whenever I want to?'

'Don't ask me—you're the one with all the strange powers.' Higgs sat on his chair by the fire and stared at him, waiting for something interesting to happen.

'Okay,' Wilt whispered, more to himself than anyone else. 'Here goes.'

Turning back to the open window, he emptied his mind of

everything except the image of the small cat figurine. He allowed himself to sink into it, everything else floating up and away from him, and the next moment he was running quickly down the outside wall of the tower, his four legs pumping furiously, his claws scratching for purchase in the rock, his mind free and clear.

Wilt's next conscious thought was that his room smelled different. He sat on the windowsill, his legs hanging inside the room, his finger idly rubbing along the sharp edge where the glass had been cut free.

If he had to describe how it felt to take on another form, Wilt would shake his head and shrug helplessly. It was a blur of image and surface, sharpened senses overloading any possibility of thought. The only reason he had made it back to his room at all was that his goal had been somehow implanted in his animal mind. He could only imagine how much worse such a terrible rush of freedom must feel were he to have the shape of an eagle, like Petron.

Delco was asleep on his bed, breathing easily in and out. Wilt jumped quietly on to the floor and Delco's eyes opened instantly.

'Oh. Hello. I didn't hear you come in.'

His voice had changed, the low mutter of the last few weeks replaced by the formal, nasal tone Wilt had first encountered when they entered Redmondis.

'Yes, well. Here I am. Sorry about ...' Wilt gestured over his shoulder at the open window. 'I'll have to look at getting some sort of cover for it.'

'No!' Delco sat up suddenly. 'No. I mean, it's quite nice really, the fresh air.'

'Might not be so nice on cold winter nights.'

Delco's shoulders slumped in disappointment. 'No. No, I suppose you're right.'

'I'll have a talk with my crafter friend. I'm sure he'll be able to knock something up for us so we can keep the window open when we want.'

That seemed to cheer Delco up instantly. 'Yes. Of course, your crafter friend. You know, I've been thinking about him this morning.'

'Didn't you go to class?'

Delco swung his legs over the side of the bed, and began to pace back and forth, a look of stern concentration on his face. 'I did, but it didn't seem right somehow. I got too distracted. Wilt, have you noticed that the Masters who teach us all seem impossibly old and, well, a little confused?'

Wilt watched Delco pace and kept his mouth shut.

'I've only realised myself, this morning I mean. It's the funniest thing, but you can't help but wonder what it is exactly they're trying to teach us here. I mean, if I'm honest, I don't think I've actually learned anything. What *is* that smell?'

Delco leaned in quickly toward Wilt and sniffed again.

'It's you. You smell like meat.' Delco's eyes were hungry. 'Where did you get meat from?'

'Oh, you know, the lesser skilled ones don't have the same restrictions we Black Robes do.'

Delco thought about that for a moment before nodding his head and continuing. 'And that's another thing. Why don't we ever see any of the other skilled ones, the crafters and healers and whatnot? Even the guards are separate from us. I'm not sure that's right.'

At the mention of the guards, Wilt saw Daemi's image flash across his mind, the image from his dream of her training in her room clear and sharp, as though it was more than a dream, as though it was a memory. He knew with a sudden certainty that he had to visit her the next chance he got.

'I mean, it's almost as if we're being kept in some sort of quarantine.' Delco stopped his pacing and faced Wilt, a troubled look on his face. 'I've been having the strangest thoughts all morning, Wilt. Heaven knows what my father would say.'

'I'm sure your father would be proud of that fact that his son had kept his questioning mind.'

'Yes, well, you haven't met my father. Still.' Delco strode back to his bed and lay down. 'I don't think I'm going to attend any classes this afternoon. I'm going to lie here and have a long think about things. Maybe I'm just feeling confused. Maybe you've passed whatever it was you had this morning on to me.'

Wilt smiled and turned to the open sky and the fresh breeze that caressed his mind clear.

Chapter 17

Wilt was woken by a cool mist on his cheeks. He opened his eyes to see the sky outside heavy with dark clouds. It took a moment for him to realise what he was looking at, his brain still slowly spinning up to speed.

It was raining. It hadn't rained in …

Now that he thought about it, he had no idea when he had last seen rain. As a Black Robe in Redmondis, he and his fellow initiates had trudged from room to room, staircase to staircase, always enclosed by one ceiling or another. Before the window was removed, the last time he had seen the sky at all, other than through blurred, rough glass, was the first day they had entered Redmondis, in the great courtyard where they had all assembled. Since then they had led very sheltered lives. Even Delco had begun to notice something lacking.

Wilt could see faint light struggling to push through the cloud cover and guessed it had to be late in the afternoon. Almost dinnertime. Some sort of tasteless, overcooked vegetable matter most likely. The same thing he had eaten for dinner every day since he arrived here. The thought made him grimace.

He remembered the sausages and bacon Higgs had served up for breakfast, and he smiled. The Black Robes were supposed to be the highest rank in the Redmondis hierarchy, yet they ate like beggars. He wondered what sort of feast Higgs had organised for himself.

And what of the others here? What of the Sisters? The Cantors? The guards?

Suddenly Wilt remembered the promise he had made himself that morning, to visit Daemi again. He didn't even have to talk to her; he just wanted to check in and ...

And what?

Wilt pushed that uncomfortable thought from his mind and stepped up to the window. It didn't matter why. They shared something now, a connection almost as strong as the one between he and Higgs. Maybe it had something to do with the training sessions, the constant dance they ran through day after day on the way to Redmondis. Or maybe it was deeper than that, due to the weld he had broken into, the way he had seen her deepest memories. The way he had drained her and almost killed her.

Wilt shook himself. He had to keep things simple now, couldn't afford to get distracted by too many thoughts. He fixed the image of Daemi in his mind and stepped outside.

The wall was slippery and cold and his claws scratched and struggled for purchase on the wet stone, but he somehow made it up to the rooftop and away.

Wilt's next conscious thought came as he lay hidden in a tree, overlooking a wide-open courtyard. He was on the far side of Redmondis, further from the Black Robes' buildings than he had thought possible while still within the high mountains that formed the Redmondis boundaries. It was colder here. A sharp breeze cut through the branches and sent thin fingers of ice down the back of his neck.

It hadn't taken long to get there. He'd scampered over the rooftops in the rain, dropping to street level as breaks in the buildings forced it. The Redmondis's night highway wasn't as complete as that of Greystone. He remembered smells and sounds, flashes of warning as he approached lights in windows and hidden guards, but his heightened senses had guided him past any danger. He wasn't sure how he knew where to find the guards. Perhaps his sense of smell picked up the sour scent of rusted metal and sharpened blades, or his ears had zeroed in on the creak and clank of armour. Perhaps it was something else entirely, something not at all human.

He swung down from the branch he was clinging to and crouched in the darkness. The courtyard in front of him was completely barren. Probably where they practised their marching back and forth. Beyond that was a small wall, only five feet high, and further still were the buildings that made up the guards' school.

It all looked easy. Too easy.

Sure enough, he made out a pair of guards patrolling the wall. Their shadows flickered back and forth along the length of the wall, meeting in the centre and turning to march away from each other as if they were taking part in some sort of duel. Wilt almost felt sorry for them. Probably part of their training, learning to stand guard. They'd be bored and miserable in this weather. They were nothing to worry about.

Wilt waited until they were marching apart, then kept his head down as he sprinted across the courtyard. He smiled as he ran, his blood singing in his ears. Finally a good use for the dark robe he wore—it would make him almost invisible this night.

He didn't slow as he reached the low wall, simply sprinting up it and leaping from the top to grab the ledge of the building in front of him, then pulling himself up into a roll and continuing on. The guards might have heard a light scuffle if the rain hadn't masked it, but in this weather they were oblivious.

Wilt scrambled over the heavy tiles to the apex of the roof to get a better look at his surroundings. The building he was on was one of a series of low single-storey buildings, all lining another open courtyard sprinkled with strange shadows from the various training structures that jutted up from the dirt. The back wall of the square was lined with taller buildings, lights dotting the walls. Must be the living quarters. That was his goal.

He resumed his low crouch and ran lightly over the top of the low buildings, his practiced feet finding sturdy footing on the slippery tiles, scampering along the spine of the roof, one foot in front of the other, as though on a high trapeze. If they were anything like the roofs in Greystone, every third tile on either sloping side would be loose, and all it would take was one wrong step to send a clattering alarm around the complex as a tile slid off and shattered on the ground below.

A gap appeared between buildings and, not slowing his run, Wilt jumped it easily. He was almost at the back wall now. Those guards should spend more time in places like Greystone, he thought, learning how to stop those used to the night highway. Perhaps he could make some suggestions to Daemi about improving their security.

Wilt stopped suddenly as the thought came to him. Stupid. How could he have been so stupid. Of course they knew about the night highway. Red Charley was here.

He dropped down and sent his senses out. It was hard to hear anything over the rain, and the darkness and unfamiliar surroundings made picking out any danger harder still. He reached out further, but found nothing. He couldn't smell anything with this nose anyway.

The next moment his much keener animal nose sniffed the air, sifting through the various strange smells it discovered. There were no images to go with the smells, just impressions of warmth and food and death. And something else, something that made his animal mind focus and tense itself. Men. Men coming.

Wilt sprang away from the peak of the roof, padding quickly down the sloping tiles to where the edge met the back wall of taller buildings, then scrambling up the vertical face to claw his way into the shadow of a window ledge. He lay low there, waiting for his night eyes to confirm what his nose had already told him.

Sure enough, a second later a shadowed head appeared on the far side of the roof, then dropped into the darkness. A few moments more and it was back, this time with another, and each pulled themselves up to the roof in a practiced roll. Wilt watched them run silently up to the place he had been standing, his eyes narrowing at the sight of the long thin blades glinting in their left hands.

'He was here.'

Red Charley. His whispered voice echoed in Wilt's ears as the wind whipped the sound straight toward him.

'There's nothing here.'

A strange voice, that one. Deeper. Uglier, somehow. Wilt studied the figure. Taller than Red Charley, more solidly built. He got the impression of authority and power, and something else. Something dangerous.

'He was here. I know it.' Red Charley was insistent, as if trying to justify himself.

'Well whatever you think was here isn't here now. Your trap didn't work.'

'Give it time, Funes.'

'We haven't got time. You haven't got time. You need to show Cortis you're capable of more than just marching in line if you want him to consider accepting you into the circle.'

'Give it time. I know these ones, these boys. They will come, and when they do, I'll show you and Cortis and whoever else needs to see. I'm ready.'

Red Charley was standing up to the other figure, but shrank back as the larger shadow faced him down.

'Well, I guess we'll see. Come. There's nothing here for us now.'

With that the two shadows dropped from the rooftop and disappeared into the darkness.

Wilt stayed frozen in place, breathing shallowly, not allowing himself to relax. His arrogance had almost cost him tonight; he would not allow it to endanger him again. The thought seemed strange in his mind, as though his brain was dealing with concepts foreign to it. It was used to simple things, pure things. Food, sleep, warmth, prey. Danger.

Wilt's eyes snapped open again as a new scent overpowered his senses. Without thinking, he sprang up and away from the window ledge, scrambling quickly up the wall to higher ground. He climbed quicker than he thought possible, a deep, angry panting breath on his heels. As he climbed he felt the danger drop away, unable to follow him up the wall. He reached another window ledge and stopped, turning back to see what had almost claimed him.

A large black wolf prowled the roof below him, glaring directly at him with bright golden eyes. As they looked into him, a new thought entered his mind, urging him to stop running, to come down, to forget his panic. Wilt's front paw edged out along the ledge as though to follow the command, before something in his mind slammed down on the weld trying to invade him, and the wolf cowered in pain and anger. It let out a low growl, leaving no doubt as to its intentions.

Wilt didn't wait for it to try again. He continued his escape, aiming for the one lit window he could see. The danger faded further as he climbed out of reach of the wolf's mind. As he pulled himself up to the window ledge he received his second piece of good luck. The window was open.

He dropped inside onto a thick rug and the heat of the fire wrapped around his body. A sudden wave of fatigue washed over him, and he trotted quickly into the safe shadows under the bed to rest and recover his strength. Now that he was free from danger, the adrenaline coursing through his veins drained slowly away, leaving him completely spent. He needed to rest, to close his eyes. Just for a little while.

Wilt opened his eyes and banged his head on the underside of the bed as he tried to sit up. Where was he?

A room. A strange room. Hiding. His fingers dug into the rug beneath him and memories came flooding back. The guardhouse. He had to get out of there before-

The door swung open and a bare pair of feet padded across the room to the fire. The feet merged with long legs, legs that disappeared up into a nightshirt. Female legs.

A hand reached down and poked at the fire with the short poker, then returned it to its resting place on the wall. The feet raised up onto their toes as the woman stretched lazily. Wilt swallowed and tried not to think about needing to breathe.

How long had he been asleep? It was still dark outside, no hint of dawn colouring the sky. Perhaps only an hour or so. Still, too long. Now he was trapped.

The feet moved further away then, toward the open window he had slipped through, and more of the body was revealed. Wilt's gaze lingered on the curves the thin material of the nightshirt clung to as they travelled up her body. Dark curls brushed against the milky white skin of her neck, and Wilt let out the faintest strangled gasp as his eyes confirmed who he was peeping at.

The feet paused in their step, and turned slowly to face the bed. Wilt closed his eyes and concentrated on trying to become invisible. If he could turn himself into a cat, surely this too wasn't beyond him.

The bed above him sagged with weight, and Wilt wondered if perhaps he was safe. Then the blade of a long knife cut through the mattress, stabbing the ground next to his head, and Daemi's face dropped over the edge of the bed to stare directly into his eyes.

'Well well well. Seems I'm the victim of an intruder.'

'Yes, well, um. You see—'

'Come out from under there.'

Daemi's face disappeared from view and the blade by his head pulled back with a low thrum. Wilt swallowed and crawled slowly out from under the bed.

'Don't get up. Stay there on the ground. It suits you.'

Wilt rolled onto his back and lifted his head. Daemi knelt on the bed, fingering the long thin blade, a disturbingly thoughtful expression on her face.

'You know, I'm not sure if there's been any precedent to this. A Black Robe invading a guard's room. I doubt they'd ask too many questions once they found your body though.'

'Yes, uh, listen. Sorry about this. It's just that …'

Wilt's explanation faltered as he realised he didn't really know what he wanted to say. Why had he come here anyway? It had seemed like a good idea at the time. Now though, seeing Daemi's face, her cold black eyes fixed on him, he wasn't so sure.

A thin smile crept across Daemi's mouth as she watched him flounder. 'Still, what can one expect of a Black Robe? A little boy.'

Wilt couldn't help himself; his gaze moved down from her face over her body, ending with the bare flesh of her legs stretching out from under her nightshirt. Daemi noticed and blushed slightly as she pulled the thin material over her knees.

'And that's quite enough of that.'

Wilt's eyes snapped back to hers. 'Sorry. Look, I didn't mean to barge in like this. It's a little hard to explain. I was—' Something by the side of Daemi's bed caught his attention. Something familiar. He held out his arm and pointed. 'What is that doing here?'

Daemi turned to see what was pointing at, and now it was her turn to stutter. 'Er, just something Higgs gave me.'

Wilt rolled to his feet and strode quickly over to the bed, snatching the small cat figurine from its resting place. It wasn't exactly the same as the one in Higgs's room, but the same hand had carved it. As his fingers wrapped around it, a familiar warmth spread through his body.

'Higgs.'

'Yes, he said it was a gift. It's pretty, don't you think?'

He wasn't sure he liked her tone. 'Pretty?'

'Yes.' She smiled at him then, and he felt himself faltering again.

He looked at the figurine in his hand. It was him. Higgs had given her another figure of him. Perhaps that explained the calling, the pull that had guided him here in his other form. He thought for a moment, then placed the small statue back where it had been.

'He comes by to visit at least once a week. Brings all sorts of news.'

'Oh yes?'

'He told me I should be expecting you. He knows you very well, doesn't he?'

'He sure does.' Wilt kept his eyes focused on her face, but couldn't help noticing other things as well. Like the way her long fingers spun the knife in her hands. The way her tight black curls were pulled back around her ears. He was beginning to feel very strange.

'So. Where have you been hiding then? Higgs said even Petron couldn't get in touch with you.'

Wilt's attention snapped to her words. 'Petron? You know his name?'

'Of course. Old Pete has been part of Cantor Wrexley's entourage since, well, since forever.'

Wilt saw the flash of stolen memory again, the image of her mother's hand brushing back her hair. The tall man taking her hand and leading her away. 'Well, he got to me eventually.'

'Can't have been easy for him. He's banished from Redmondis, you know. Something about what happened during the Restoration. Many Black Robes were banished that day.'

'Black Robes?'

'Oh come on, surely you knew that much. Petron was a Black Robe, just like you. He and Cantor Wrexley, they ... were roommates. But when the Nine Sisters rose to power, Wrexley was savvy enough to keep his head down.'

'Savvy. So that's what it was.'

Daemi's eyes flashed in anger. 'I won't have you speaking ill of Cantor Wrexley in my presence!'

The blade was held out in front of her now, and Wilt raised his hands in surrender.

'Okay, okay. No need to get all stabby now.'

A grin broke out on Daemi's face as she studied him silently.

Wilt blushed. 'Look, the reason I snuck in like this ... I didn't mean to ... it's just there was this wolf—'

Daemi shot to her feet and grabbed him by the shoulders. 'A wolf? What kind of wolf?'

'Uh, a big wolf. Black, with golden eyes.'

Daemi jerked the window further open and held her head out in the rain, scanning the rooftop below. 'Cortis. He's getting more confident to take that form here.'

'You mean, Cantor Cortis? He's the wolf?'

Daemi faced him again, her hair streaming with rain. 'The wolf is his other form, just as Petron's is the eagle, and I imagine yours is …' She nodded toward the cat figurine by the side of her bed. 'But that power, the power to take on another form, that was one of the magics forbidden by the Sisters. Apparently they aren't able to do it themselves—at least, that's what Wrex told me.'

'Wrex?'

'Cantor Wrexley, of course. Don't be dumb.' Daemi stamped over to the other side of the room and grabbed a towel to dry her hair. 'If it was Cortis, and he's confident enough to flaunt his power so close to the heart of Redmondis, then things are further advanced than we thought.' She threw down the towel and began to pace across the room. 'Petron needs to hear about this. Perhaps now he'll be convinced to let me approach Cantor Wrexley as well.'

'Wrex.'

Daemi stopped pacing and glared at him. 'Wrex. Yes. Is there some sort of problem?'

'No, no problem. Sounds a little familiar, that's all.'

There was a pause as Daemi considered what Wilt had meant by 'familiar'.

'Why, you dare—' Daemi didn't bother to finish her sentence; instead she swung a high kick at Wilt's head that he was only just quick enough to duck.

'Look, I can see that you're very busy—' Another kick shot out toward Wilt's stomach, but he spun away and rolled to the other side of the room. 'So if it's all the same to you, I should probably be going.' Daemi continued her spin into a low foot sweep with her trailing leg, but Wilt jumped over it and landed on the windowsill. 'Give my best to Higgs, and Petron. And Wrex.'

With a final grin he dropped out into the rain just as Daemi's fist shot toward him. The next moment he was on four legs, scampering away over the rooftops, Daemi's angry yell chasing him into the darkness.

Chapter 18

Wilt remembered nothing else from that night. He'd clearly made it safely back to his room, for that was where he found himself when he woke, but there was no trail left in his mind to prove he had made the journey. Instead, broken images had haunted his dreams, slices of another life. His small hands crafted a figurine, shaped its flowing lines and whispered words of power into it. Words he did not understand, did not even know. Still he spoke them.

He felt a pull from the dream, as though it wanted to suck him into it, join with it completely and let its views become his own. For a moment he was tempted, then his gaze returned to the surface and the vision burnt away.

The early morning sun was streaming in through the still open window, and Wilt allowed himself to stare out at the open sky.

'Good morning.' Delco was sitting on his bed, already dressed. 'I was beginning to wonder if you'd ever wake up.'

Wilt sat up and rubbed sleep from the corners of his eyes. 'Am I that late?'

'Late? No, not for today at least.'

'Today?'

'You slept through all of yesterday. I tried to wake you when I got back here after lunch, but you were dead to the world. I would have called someone for help if you didn't have such a pleasant smile on your face. You must have been having good dreams.'

Wilt swung his legs out of bed and his stomach lurched. 'I slept all of yesterday?'

'Yep. I didn't see you come in, but it must have been late.'

Wilt's stomach twisted again in protest at its emptiness as he hurriedly dressed. 'I guess it was. I'm starving.'

'I'm not surprised. C'mon then, I'm sure there'll be plenty of porridge left for us.'

They didn't talk again until they were in the dining hall, steaming bowls of porridge on the table in front of them. Delco nibbled at the edge of his with his spoon, but Wilt dived right in, shovelling thick globs down his throat, ignoring the distinct lack of flavour. He finished one bowl and Delco swapped their plates, setting his spoon on the table and watching Wilt dive into the food.

'Guess your appetite has returned.'

'Hmph?' Wilt swallowed and wiped his mouth. 'Yeah, I guess so.'

'You'd have to be hungry to enjoy this stuff.'

Wilt continued eating. He didn't look up again until his spoon scraped the bottom of this second bowl.

'Better?' Delco smiled at him, a genuine fondness in his eyes.

'Much.'

Wilt looked around the room, taking in his surroundings for the first time. Other Black Robes sat along the long benches, heads bowed over their food, not talking. Those who did venture to talk did so in hushed whispers, as though they were passing on dark secrets to each other and didn't want to be overheard. The light was different as well: a pale grey glow that seemed to drain all colour from the room.

He felt a familiar heavy pall settle down over his shoulders. He looked at Delco, who was still staring at him, as if waiting for something.

'You see it too.'

'The light. There's something wrong with it.'

Delco nodded. 'The light, the air. The way sound travels. It's not natural. I only began to notice it myself yesterday.'

Wilt watched a group of Black Robes walk past them, their step completely in time. 'It's like they're walking in a dream.'

'Exactly. A dream we have only just woken from.'

Wilt randomly chose one of the Black Robes sitting around them. He focused, then reached out for him. There was nothing. Nothing there at all. It was as though his mind was a blank slate, a cold yawning space scrubbed clean and ready to be occupied.

'Have you tried reading them?'

'What?' Delco's voice rang out far too loudly across the room, but no one looked up. His voice dropped to a whisper. 'Of course not. You can't wield inside Redmondis like that.'

'Have you tried?'

'No! And you're not to try either. Even if you could, they'd find you.'

'They?'

'The Sisters of course. Who else do you think put such controls in place. You saw what happened that first day.'

Wilt remembered the crumpled form of the boy on the ground of the Great Hall, the whisper of the Sentinels as they turned away and left the body there, empty and broken.

He pushed away what remained of the porridge, no longer hungry. 'C'mon. We're late for class.'

Delco stood and Wilt followed, waiting for him to lead the way.

'You can't remember, can you? Which way to go. I noticed that yesterday too. We never had to decide before. Here, just follow along.'

Another group of Black Robes marched past, and Delco quickly matched their step, joining the back of the column. Wilt dropped into step behind Delco and bowed his head. He focused his eyes on Delco's back and didn't look up again.

After a few minutes the air around them changed, and he realised they had entered another, much smaller room. Each boy dropped into a seat in line, and Delco and Wilt followed, keeping their heads down. Wilt fixed his eyes on the cold stone beneath his sandalled feet, and drew his toes around the edge of the two deep indentations worn into it. For how many centuries had men sat where he did now?

'Welcome, class.'

Wilt looked up automatically, and every other head lifted as well to face the Master who had just shuffled into the room. He looked impossibly old: a short, weathered body worn away by time, wild white hair springing up above an eroded, lined face. Even his eyes seemed old, white and cloudy, as though he were half blind. The Master moved slowly to the front of the room and dropped into the chair behind his desk with a deep sigh.

'So. We begin. The third mandate.'

The Master's voice slipped into a low drone, barely audible, but the eyes of every Black Robe were riveted on him, heads cocked as if listening intently, soaking up the wisdom being bestowed upon them. Wilt looked around, confused. Was he missing something? He caught Delco's eyes, but he just shook his head sharply and looked at the Master, feigning interest in the lesson.

The Master's head had begun to droop, as if his own droning tone was putting him to sleep. The only movement was the slow drum of the Master's fingers on the desk, one after another. Something about the movement held Wilt's attention. A wave. A circle of small wooden figures, each falling in line, each wearing his face.

Wilt looked into the Master's face and let his mind fall, sinking into the depths. His eyes lost focus in a silver haze of swirling fog.

'Ah, so at last you hear me.'

The voice was clear and filled his mind. It was the Master's voice, yet changed. Younger. Much stronger. The silver haze shifted and began to spin in a shining whirlpool.

'Come, join with me.'

The whirlpool began to form a tunnel, a long silver weld that Wilt began falling toward. The command urged him on, ever deeper, drowning him in the glimmering light.

'Open yourself to me.'

As Wilt fell, something in his mind separated, as if it had split into two, one half eagerly sinking into the depths, the other side-stepping the weld and holding itself back, hovering just over the edge of the vortex, balanced on the edge of oblivion.

The fog in front of his eyes faded, and he was back in the class-room, empty now except for himself and the Master. The Master sat at the front of the room as before, and his hair was still white and wild, but that was where the similarities ended. The years seemed to have melted away from him, his eyes were bright and probing, his face clear and shining with power and energy.

'Just the one? I thought I … yes. One moment.'

The voice echoed and fuzzed in Wilt's ears, as though he were listening to voices in another room. A moment later Delco appeared in the classroom, looking dazed and slightly nauseous.

'Yes, two of you. A good start.'

The Master seemed pleased with himself and sprang to his feet, striding back and forth across the front of the room.

'Now, where to begin. It has taken much longer this year than in the past. We only have so much time. Never enough time.'

Wilt looked over at Delco and tried to smile at him. His face seemed unwilling to cooperate, but eventually the muscles woke up and responded. His voice came easier. 'Delco?'

At that, the Master's head shot up and a bright smile lit up his face.

'Of course! Yes, names! How silly of me.' He pointed at Delco. 'You, Delco, is it? You look familiar. Brothers here?'

Delco seemed to stir from his daze and nodded slowly.

'Well, answer me, boy, no need to stay silent, they can't listen in here.'

'Y-yes, Master. My father and two brothers are all Black Robes.'

'Names?'

'Er, Sensi and Plaxo, sir. My father's name is—'

'Hurley. Yes, a good enough man. Not too strong, but a clear mind. Not one who came under their spell.'

'Er, yes sir.'

'Your brothers, on the other hand, are both completely useless. You won't turn out like them I hope, Delco.'

'Er, no sir.'

'Good!' That seemed to satisfy the Master, and he turned his attention on to Wilt. 'You then, name?'

'Wilt.'

The Master studied his face as he replied, and cocked his head sideways, as if listening for something. 'Repeat that please, boy.'

'Wilt, sir.'

Again the Master seemed to be straining to hear something, and a slightly pained expression came over his face. 'You sound distant, boy. Muffled.' The Master strode forward and leaned down over Wilt's desk. 'Once again.'

'Wilt, sir.'

'Ah! Yes, I see now.' He reached forward quickly and grabbed Wilt's collar, pulling it open to expose the carved wooden figure hanging around his neck. For an instant he seemed ready to rip it from him, but his long fingers pulled away at the last moment, as though scared to touch it.

'Now this work I recognise.'

The Master looked into Wilt's eyes again and regarded him with a strange respect.

'You know, I shouldn't be able to hear you at all while you're wearing this. You shouldn't even be able to make the most basic welds. Unless Petron's losing his touch. Is he losing his touch, boy?'

'No. No, I don't think he is.'

The Master jerked Wilt's collar back over the carved figure and stood up straight. 'Don't ever remove that within these grounds. Petron told you that, didn't he?'

'Yes sir.'

'Good.' The Master turned on his heel and strode back to the front of the classroom. 'Now then. I don't suppose either of you can tell me how likely it is that others will be joining us here? Others from your class? Any discernable talent among them, or are they all weak-willed like most of them these days?'

Wilt and Delco gaped at him, not knowing how to respond.

'Well. All we can do is wait, I suppose. Some of them might wake up one day.' His voice dropped lower, as though he was muttering to himself, though his voice still rang out clear in Wilt and Delco's minds. 'Never easy getting started.'

After a moment he seemed to come to a decision and lifted his head, re-energised.

'Now then. I don't suppose either of you know what is happening right now? Here, I mean, in this room.'

Wilt kept still, his mind still churning over the thought that this Master and Petron knew each other. Of course they could. Petron had been a student here, and this Master had to have been at least a student then, if not already teaching.

'Sir? It's a silver weld. A group sharing of minds,' said Delco, even going so far as to raise his hand.

A bright smile broke out on the Master's face. 'Good! That's right, boy, a silver weld. We're not completely lost then. And how many other types of welds are there?'

Delco's hand dropped down a little, then reached up again tentatively. 'Er, there's black welds, attack welds, and for reading others' thoughts.'

Wilt thought back to his days with Petron, to the final day he duelled with Daemi, to the thick white rope joining them that he had broken into. He finally found his voice.

'White welds.'

Delco looked across at him, as if he had said something wrong, but the Master nodded eagerly.

'Yes, white welds. Strong, a full body joining with another. Useful for when the one you wish to join with isn't skilled. Good. Others?'

Delco's hand returned to his lap, and they both sat still. After a moment the Master turned away again.

'Well, a good start at least. There are many other forms of welds, and many other types of connections between minds. Shared thoughts, shared points of view. Shared lives in some extreme cases. None of this is taught here in Redmondis anymore, of course. Too dangerous, so they say. But here, in our little private classroom, here we may be able to change that.'

'Sir?' Delco raised his hand again.

'Yes?' The Master looked up at him. 'Oh drop your hand, boy, you look ridiculous.'

Delco's hand dropped into his lap with a loud clap.

'Well?'

'You sir? You know our names, but who are you?'

'Ah, of course, how silly of me. Master Biore.' He took a quick bow. 'At your service.'

'That's impossible,' Delco spluttered. The Master raised a single eyebrow and Delco rushed to explain. 'Master Biore was an old man when my father was a student here. There's no way—'

'No way an old man could last so long here, under the very nose of the Sisters? No way he could hobble along, unnoticed?' The Master seemed amused at the thought.

Delco persisted. 'No way he could still be alive.'

At that the Master's smile twisted and a bright gleam sparked in his eyes.

'Come, boys. There is much to teach you.'

Part 2

The wind is rarely still now, as though it too senses the growing stain blackening the land. The visions come more frequently, figures raised from their victim's nightmares, stalking the earth, leaving only dust in their footsteps. Even the trees sense the danger, though the threat has yet to reach their edge. They bend away from the taste of death in the wind, they groan and mutter to themselves, their dreams troubled. Still, the threat remains too distant for those without deep roots to sense.

The spark, the one we have watched so closely, is now cornered within the high stone walls of Redmondis: a place once so welcoming, now blank and cold to all but those the Sisters feel they can control. The wild ones, the others like me, the ones they cannot bend to their will, are broken within its depths. Discarded.

The memories of the stone, of the still, numb air troubles me. The Nine Sisters sought recognition, then control, then power. Now they wallow in the depths they have plumbed, unaware of the dangers. Unaware or past caring. Those they consider their servants twist themselves around their minds, numbing them to their peril.

Redmondis no longer stands guard against such powers, against those who threaten the human world. Its eyes are turned inwards, its ears deafened.

The trees whisper patience. Time is nothing to them, and a spark can blaze into a flame in moments. All it takes is a breath of wind to blow the embers into life.

Already progress is being made. The first cracks of awareness have appeared, the first mergings of perception. If only there was more time. And yet there are still those within the Redmondis walls who can help fan the flames, even if they do so unaware of the true nature of their task.

Our enemy also has agents within the walls, instruments that cannot help but try to sound their own tune. The chaos and cacophony they create may be just what is needed to finally bring the ages-old prophecy to life.

Chapter 19

Higgs sat at his window and peered out across the open sky, his fingers drumming idly on the hot mug of coffee clasped in his hands. The morning was bright and clear, and the new sun was burning off the mist that clung to the tops of the trees far below him, just as the steam from his coffee tickled his nose as he sipped it.

He waited as he always did in the morning, keeping an eye out for birds in the sky. Petron hadn't come for days now, although that wasn't unusual. The last time he'd visited, in bird form of course, Higgs had tied a long list of items to his leg, and Petron the man was probably busy out there trying to fill his requests before he next passed this way. The next trade day, when the gates of Redmondis would open to the outside world for a day to restock and resupply, might still be days away. Higgs doubted he'd see Petron before then.

As for Wilt, he hadn't seen him for over a week either. Petron had warned him about that too, his scrawled note telling Higgs to maintain his patience, to give Wilt time to make his way back. Wilt had been awakened now—at least that was the term Petron used—and it might take him some time to get used to his new world. Higgs sipped his coffee and suppressed a sigh. He knew Petron was right, but he still missed his friend. His brother.

Still, there were lots of things to keep him busy. The information link he'd established with the outside world through Petron had made him popular with the other crafters. They weren't sure exactly how he did it, but mention to Higgs you were after some item in particular, and sure enough by the next trade day that item would be available for purchase, usually at a fair price. In the past the crafters and other lesser skilled had had to rely on passing messages out through the guards, and even when they managed not to mess up the order completely, the prices asked were extortionate. Yes, Higgs had proved very useful since his arrival.

Not everyone appreciated this shift in power. The guards, who in the past had managed to live off the money they'd skimmed from every trade, had found their profits dwindling of late and were beginning to take notice. Daemi had warned Higgs about this, but things were only now beginning to come to a head. Some of the other crafters had mentioned that the latest guard patrols had refused to take any orders at all, their logic being to starve the crafters back to paying their high fees. They clearly didn't yet understand Higgs's connection to the outside world if they thought that was going to work. It had only driven more customers Higgs's way, and Petron was more than capable of filling orders on his end. When he couldn't fill the orders himself, he passed on the information to one of the other traders on the outside, and the item would arrive in Redmondis on the next traders' day. If anything, such deals only helped disguise Petron's role.

Higgs tipped the dregs of his coffee out the window. Yes, things were going very well right now. It was going to be another good day.

He turned to the little table pushed up against one wall of his room and sat down. The table was bare except for a small leather pouch that he untied and upturned on the table, and small wooden figures tumbled out across the surface—far too many of them to actually fit in the container. Higgs smiled to himself as he always did when he encountered clever craftsmanship, and patted the pouch absently.

After a few moments he sighed and started to pick up some of the figures and set them upright. He hadn't been able to read anything in them, and knew he shouldn't expect to be able to yet. Pattern prediction was an advanced craft, one only a few had been able to master. He'd only been studying for a few weeks, but every other aspect of crafting had come so easily to him that Higgs had begun to expect instant success, and couldn't help but feel frustrated when things didn't go his way.

It probably had something to do with their makeup. Higgs still couldn't quite unlock the potential of wood; it never responded as clearly to his wishes as stone, and though he continued to work at it, he was beginning to accept that his particular skills didn't lie in that direction.

Petron had told him to expect such hurdles, told him that each craft comes to the crafter in its own time, and he understood that. But that didn't mean he had to like it.

Higgs placed a group of the wooden pieces in a figure eight, took a breath to focus himself, then touched the top of the centre piece. Immediately, they began to fall in order, a wave moving around the shape, blurring as it sped up. Higgs felt the power of his craft warming the air above the table. The spiral shield. One of the first wards Higgs had been taught, and one he still practised every day, layering the protection, strengthening the connection between him and Wilt.

He was snapped out of his contemplation by the sound of running feet, and had already begun pushing the pieces back into their bag when his door swung open and a short, flustered young girl came rushing in, panting with excitement.

'Higgs! The caravans have been sighted. The traders, they've come early!' The girl seemed to run out of words at that point, and stood bouncing up and down on her toes, waving her hands frantically as if she had just burned her fingers on a stove.

Higgs smiled easily at the sight. 'Okay, Heather. I'm coming.'

It wasn't unusual for the traders to arrive ahead of schedule. The twisting mountain paths through the Tangle were tricky at the best of times, and no one could ever be sure how long it would take to get from A to B, especially if they were leading a caravan loaded with goods. Sometimes they came early, sometimes late; the Redmondis trading days occurred whenever the next caravan arrived.

He packed the last of the pieces away and pulled the thin strap tight to close the leather pouch. Heather stopped shaking her hands as she watched, a new expression on her face.

'Higgsy, when are you going to make me one of those bottomless pouches?'

Higgs grimaced at the pet name. 'I told you I'll show you how to make your own. And don't call me that.'

Heather smiled at him until his face melted into his normal easy grin. 'I'd prefer you to make me one. It'd be a nice gift.'

Higgs didn't miss the cunning glint in her eyes and held up his hands as he walked past her out of the room. 'You don't need any gifts from me. You get more than your fair share from the others.'

Heather stamped her foot before trotting after him. 'Oh, those boys couldn't even think up a bottomless pouch, let alone craft one.'

Higgs ignored her and continued down the corridor, smiling to himself. After him, Heather was the most talented young crafter in Redmondis. When he first arrived, she'd spent weeks trying to best him, then undermine him, then finally turn him to work for her somehow. Higgs was unlike any of the other crafters here though; he'd been raised among beggars and thieves, and knew all the tricks. Eventually Heather seemed to have settled for a kind of grudging respect. Troublingly, this was beginning to morph into something deeper. Perhaps it was just her new tactic. Higgs preferred not to think about it too much.

Other crafters had heard the news, and a small crowd was milling around the courtyard as Higgs stepped out into the sunlight. Word had passed around the other trades as well. Healers, stone and wood shapers, potion brewers—all the skilled trades that Redmondis housed in its twisted halls seemed to be represented. He would need to be quick to make sure he got his hands on what he needed first, to avoid any bidding wars. Higgs fixed a confident, calm smile to his face and stepped into the crowd. He chatted pleasantly with everyone who greeted him as they made their way toward the gates, trying not to let any of his nervous excitement show.

The trade caravans had made their way to the gates of Redmondis early that morning, and were setting up their stalls in the large open area outside the gates. Surrounding them was a ring of guards, first years mostly, there for show more than to offer any real security, to remind the outside world of the strength nurtured inside the high walls. At least, that was their official purpose. Higgs had found early on that certain tradesmen knew certain guards very well, and certain items never seemed to be for sale to any until a quick nod was received by a guard posted conveniently in the trader's line of sight. When Higgs had mentioned this to the other crafters, he'd been told such practices were common.

On the short trip up to the gates, Higgs had managed to manoeuvre himself near the centre of the growing crowd, aware that his popularity was turning him into a target. His short stature served him well here, though he found it hard to resist testing his cut-purse skills with the sound of coins clinking in pouches on every belt surrounding him. He jammed his hands in his pockets and kept his head down as the gates swung slowly open and the crowd spilled out into the courtyard.

Higgs felt the eyes of the guards at the gate pass over him like a beam of heat. He fixed his eyes on the man in front and kept walking. Time seemed to slow as the crowd reached the bottleneck of the gate and bodies bumped up against each other. Then a hand grabbed his and he snapped his head around to see Heather smiling at him.

'Thought you'd gotten away, didn't you? C'mon. I want you to introduce me to your trader friend.'

Heather pulled him through the crowd, weaving their way out of the crush into the open air. A wave of relief passed over him as they left the gates behind them, as though a tension was lifted from his shoulders simply being outside Redmondis.

Once they were free of the worst of the crowd, he pulled Heather to a stop. 'You know Pete won't be here. He came last time.'

A glint flashed in Heather's eyes that made Higgs feel decidedly strange. 'I know.' She pulled him into motion again and they wandered over to the nearest circle of stalls.

The traders had their own unofficial hierarchy and arranged their wagons and stalls in various rings according to their rank, the most favoured closest to the gates, the less so further away. Usefully, these ranks also mostly equated to the sort of items the trader specialised in. When Higgs first arrived in Redmondis, those traders specialising in fine clothing and materials had been toward the front, but with the recent rumours of strife in the south, the traders most focused on weapons and armour had begun to move up the ranks. The circle Higgs and Heather moved into was one of these, with dozens of shining blades hanging from the sides of the stalls, and shining platemail stacked in the back of the wagons close by.

Naturally the guards favoured these items, and a small group of them were standing about, haggling lazily with one of the traders. Higgs hesitated, but Heather pulled him on and he pushed away his misgivings. The guards seemed preoccupied, and it wasn't like they were doing anything wrong anyway.

He turned his attention to the goods on display. The first few stalls seemed to specialise in swords, daggers, and well-made but unremarkable heavy iron blades. Higgs had been thinking recently about trying his hand at crafting a special blade of some sort, but not like these. He walked on as Heather examined some of the smaller daggers more closely.

Higgs stopped as he passed the third wagon, an interesting glint catching his eye.

'Ah, a discerning customer.'

The trader was unfamiliar to Higgs, but seemed to practise the same fawning act as all the others. Higgs ignored him and headed directly for the glinting object.

Hanging high at the back of the stall was a large curved silver dagger, almost the size of a short sword or scimitar. Its metal was strangely blue, as though a secret power glowed within it. Higgs reached toward it and the glow brightened.

'Yes, yes. A very special blade. Moonsteel. Crafted in the Eastern Dales.'

Higgs lifted the blade from its place and felt its weight in his hands. It seemed impossibly light.

'It is said that moonsteel is nothing more than the light of the full moon captured in a certain shape, lighter than the very air, yet able to cut through even the strongest steel.'

Higgs had never heard of moonsteel, and doubted the trader's story was anything more than an interesting fiction designed to close the sale, but the blade was lighter than he could ever have imagined, and its blue glow seemed to shift and dance in the light in a way that suggested hidden power. He knew he had found what he wanted.

'How much?'

'Alas, it is not for sale.'

Higgs smiled, familiar with the first steps of the dance. 'Everything has its price.'

'Three hundred silvers.' The trader almost spat out the words in challenge.

Higgs's smile widened at the extortionate price and tore his eyes from the blade to focus on the trader's face. 'I'll give you fifty.'

The trader seemed pained, as though a tight cramp wracked his insides. 'It is not possible, this price. For you, two hundred silvers. The lowest I can go. As I said, I should not even be considering—'

'Seventy-five.' Higgs would pay whatever it took, but he still had his principles. Two hundred silvers was enough to buy a wagon filled with blades and four horses to pull it.

'A hundred-fifty.' The trader's accent seemed to be getting stronger as they haggled, and Higgs saw the greed tugging at the corners of his lips.

He took out his pouch and poured a pile of heavy silver coins onto the table beside them. 'One hundred silvers. Here. Take them.'

The trader hesitated only a moment before reaching out and grabbing the pile of silvers with both hands. 'Very well. You rob me this day. The one this blade was meant for will not be pleased.'

Higgs smiled and hid the blade inside his coat. 'I'm sure you'll be able to do more than replace it at that price. Enjoy your new wealth while it lasts.'

One hundred silvers was a massively inflated price, but something about the blade called to Higgs, called to that part of him that sparked whenever he encountered true crafter work. Besides, with his recent successes, he could afford it.

He walked out of the stall into the sunlight, and stumbled straight into the back of a large armoured man standing in front of the stall.

'Well well well, what do we have here?'

The guard peered down at Higgs as though examining something he'd stepped in. Over his shoulder Higgs saw Heather being held by two other rough looking guards.

'What's the meaning of this?'

'The meaning?' The guard seemed to chew over those words as if examining their taste.

'It's okay, Funes, leave this to me.'

Another guard pushed past the large man and grabbed Higgs roughly by the shoulder. 'I know this one.'

Higgs found himself staring up into Red Charley's leering grin. 'What do you want?'

'Ah, well now, that is a very large question to answer.'

Red Charley marched Higgs away from the traders' wagons and stalls toward the cover of the trees that ringed the clearing. Behind them, Higgs could hear Heather being dragged along as well by the two other guards. The larger one—Funes, Red Charley had called him—led the way. Traders and crafters all moved quickly out of his way as he marched toward the edge of the clearing.

They moved a few metres into the shade of the trees and Funes stopped them. 'This'll do. Guards know better than to bother us anyway.'

Red Charley kicked Higgs in the back of the legs and sent him sprawling on the ground. 'Have a seat, Higgs.'

Higgs rolled into a sitting position and began to brush himself off. The blade he'd just bought was still inside his coat. They hadn't even bothered to frisk him. 'Again. What do you want?'

Funes bent down lazily and clapped him across the mouth with the back of his hand. The blow sent him sprawling again, and stars burst across his vision.

'Smart mouths get smacked.'

'Now now, Funes, that's no way to treat our little guest here. Come, Higgs, sit up.' Red Charley pulled Higgs into a sitting position and patted him softly on the head. 'Funes is impatient, you see. Probably best not to anger him.'

Higgs's mouth twisted, ready for another reply, but he saw Funes had stepped toward Heather and the sight stilled his tongue.

'Now, what we want, Higgs, is information. Apparently someone has been passing messages out to the traders, skipping the middleman. Skipping us. Wouldn't know anything about that, would you?'

Higgs shook his head and glared into Red Charley's eyes; they had a yellow glint to them, as though the whites of his eyes were sick.

'Wasting time.' It was Funes again. 'Hit him again.'

'No.' Red Charley met Higgs's look with his own, as though they were locked in their own private battle of wills. 'No, there's no point. Higgs grew up in Greystone, like me.' He stood up, but kept his eyes locked on the young crafter. A slow grin made its way across Red Charley's face as he finally broke eye contact and pointed at Heather. 'Hit her instead.'

Funes didn't need to be asked twice. He stepped forward and slapped Heather across the face with the back of his hand, knocking her head sideways. The two guards holding her staggered with the force of the blow but kept her upright.

'No!' Higgs tried to struggle to his feet, but Red Charley kicked him back down.

Funes swung again, this time into Heather's body, doubling her over. She let out a strangled cough and vomited the contents of her stomach onto the guards' feet.

'It's me. I send messages out to the traders, requests for goods. I send them via bird. To ... Old Pete. The trader who brought us here.'

Red Charley had been enjoying the sight of Heather suffering, but now faced Higgs. 'We thought as much. Thank you for confirming our suspicions.' He nodded and Funes stepped forward again, smacking Heather across the face with an open palm, knocking her completely out of the grasp of the guards and sending her sprawling onto the ground, unconscious.

'Stop!'

'Oh dear, it seems Funes doesn't know his own strength. Pity. She looked such a pretty young thing. Won't be pretty much longer.'

Higgs found he had tears in his eyes, and hot anger rushed through his body. He controlled it, stored the anger up, and let his hand creep slowly inside his jacket to grasp the hilt of the dagger hidden there.

Red Charley had moved toward Heather to better drink in her pain. His eyes had a sick hunger, as though the sight of Heather fed some twisted inner desire. Funes too was breathing hard, a wide grin plastered over his face. The two guards who had been holding her looked sheepish, as though they weren't quite prepared for what they'd gotten themselves into.

Higgs's anger didn't let him worry about such fine lines. The two guards were closest to him, and he scrambled toward them, pulling the moonsteel dagger out of his jacket as he rolled to his feet. He swung it in a wide arc at the back of their legs, and the blade cut quickly across them without any resistance.

The two guards collapsed with a strangled cry, clutching their severed hamstrings. The noise got Red Charley and Funes's attention, and they turned to see Higgs waving the blade back and forth in front of him.

'Well now, it seems this pup has teeth.' Funes leered as he said the words, and stepped toward Higgs.

Higgs swung at him, but Funes was too fast and stepped outside the swing, then forward again, wrapping his arms around Higgs's much smaller body. Higgs had expected as much, and continued his swing down and through his own legs, sinking the blade into Funes's thigh.

Funes let out a yelp and dropped his arms away quickly, as though the blade had caused much more pain than it should have. He skittered backward, out of Higgs's reach, his eyes pained and wary now, locked on the strange silver blade Higgs wielded.

Red Charley looked at him as though he had gone mad. 'What's the matter with you? It's just a dagger. You get worse cuts in training every morning.'

Funes breathed heavily, his gums drawn back over his teeth in pain. 'Not just any blade. Moonsteel. The essence of pain. You'll pay for this, pup.'

Red Charley looked bewildered, but Funes didn't bother to explain any further. He dropped into a crouch and began to circle Higgs, a low growl emanating from the back of his throat.

Higgs watched him carefully, trying to keep the blade between them, wondering briefly how long he would last in this fight, whether he would get the chance to hurt Funes again before he was killed. That was all he wanted: the chance to inflict some pain on the man who had hurt Heather.

'Hold, soldier.' The command came from the edge of the trees, and a body of warriors pushed into the small clearing. They were led by a helmed guard, obviously of higher rank. 'What is the meaning of this?'

Red Charley snapped to attention and saluted quickly. 'Nothing, Captain. Just some trouble with thieves.'

'Thieves you say.' The captain turned toward Higgs and cocked his head, studying him. 'You don't look like a thief to me.' The captain's voice was slightly muffled by the helm, which bore a strikingly realistic picture of a tiger across its full-face plate. The tiger's head moved from Higgs back to Funes, then to the two guards rolling in pain, then saw Heather sprawled unconscious in the dirt.

'It took four of you to detain these two "thieves"? Cantor Cortis will be most displeased.'

Funes glared back at the captain, fury coursing through his eyes. Red Charley began to stammer an explanation, but was cut off with a wave of the captain's hand.

'Leave us. We will question these thieves ourselves.'

'But Captain, I—'

'I order you to return to the barracks.' The tiger face stared at Red Charley, who dropped his head and moved to obey. 'Guards. Ensure they don't get distracted on their way back.' The captain then motioned toward the two guards rolling in the dirt. 'Take these two dogs with you.'

Red Charley and Funes marched back toward Redmondis, the two hamstrung guards propped between them, and the captain's escort marching behind. When they were gone, the captain turned to Higgs, who still held the small blade in front of him, as though he had forgotten it was there.

'You don't need that anymore, Higgs.' The captain lifted his helmet clear and Higgs almost collapsed with relief to see Daemi standing in front of him. She smiled at him and he let the blade drop to his side. 'Come. Let's see if we can't get your friend here to a healer.'

Chapter 20

The man sat shivering with fear in the middle of the room, his eyes roaming wildly around him, as though unsure from which direction the next blow would come. Grime streaked his face, and his thinning hair was plastered across his scalp, dripping with sweat. His shoulders shook, the muscles jumping and twitching against the bonds that held his hands firmly behind him.

Wilt stared silently at the man from his seat in the front row, trying to keep his mind clear of even the slightest pity, clear of any thought at all, while Delco attempted to break into this victim's mind.

Delco stepped in front of the man, who flinched as if expecting a slap across his face. Delco leaned in closer, locking eyes, and brought his will onto him.

Wilt felt the crackle of energy as Delco forced himself into the man's mind. The man's face twisted in sudden agony, then slackened and went blank, his whole body slumping into surrender.

'Good. Good, Delco. Don't let him go now. Bring him back.' Master Biore stood to the side of the scene, his eyes bright.

Delco's mouth twisted in effort as he focused, and the man's head lifted up. His eyes were wide and white, and rolled completely back in their sockets. Delco let out a gasp of effort and the man slumped into unconsciousness.

Wilt held his hand over his nose as the stench of opened bowels wafted across the room.

Delco shook his head. 'I'm sorry, Master. I couldn't hold him.'

Master Biore stepped forward and put his arm around Delco's shoulders, turning him away from the sight of the broken man and walking him toward the seats. 'Don't let it worry you, young man. It was an excellent try.'

Behind them, Wilt saw quick shadows move to clean up the mess they'd left behind. The man in the chair was lifted out of the room, and the offensive smell left with him.

'Well, young man, ready for your turn?' Master Biore asked Wilt.

Wilt sprung to his feet and moved to the front of the room. Waiting for him was another man. No, the same man. The same grimy face, the same sweat-streaked greasy hair. But this man was conscious and seemingly undamaged. Wilt shot a confused look at Master Biore, who gestured for him to continue. Wilt turned to face his task and pushed all doubt from his mind.

The world around him froze into silence, leaving just him and his victim. He took a deep breath and sent out a single weld into his mind.

Nothing. No thoughts at all, just an endless, terrifying void. Wilt plummeted into it, falling away from the world, from himself.

'That's good, my boy. Now bring him back to the surface.'

Master Biore's voice sounded at him from all sides, cradling him in the emptiness. Breath moved in and out of his lungs, then a rush pushed him upward out of the depths and his eyes opened again.

He stared out across a small classroom, a young Black Robe standing silently before him, his eyes endless pools of grey. Another, older one standing behind him.

The older one spoke. 'That's it! You see through his eyes now. You have taken control.'

Wilt looked at the younger man in front of him. Both his and the younger man's lips moved as one. 'But there is nothing here, just emptiness, just a shell. He isn't real.'

The older man clapped his hands happily. 'Oh, very good, my boy. You are right, of course. This victim was cleansed long ago, used now for training exercises like this one. It wouldn't do to have a constant stream of broken victims resulting from our classes here, far better to use and re-use this one.'

The young man frowned at this, as though troubled by some thought the older man hadn't voiced, but kept his mouth shut.

'Of course, once we do succeed in gaining control, there is nothing much to see. This man's mind was scrubbed clean long ago.'

No. A single flicker of pain, a flash of endless misery and anguish sparked way down in the depths, and the young man's frown deepened, but the older man seemed not to notice.

'Now, young Wilt, return, and we will both help Delco to catch up.'

The young man was with him still, and he felt the small flame within lick against the walls that held him. He felt the young man drawing away, the endless void return, the familiar torment of waking death overwhelm him again.

Wilt swam up and away from the mind of the victim and found himself looking through his own eyes back at the man again. For a second there had been something, some spark of consciousness hidden in the depths. A deep pity washed over him as he wondered how many times the man had been brought back to this shell of a life only to die again.

He turned to Master Biore. 'It isn't right, to use a man in this way.'

Master Biore gazed at him, his smile frozen in place and a dangerous glint in his eye. 'And what would you have us do, young Wilt?'

'Release him. Let him die completely. Don't hold him on the edge like this.'

Master Biore paused, as if considering his words carefully. 'And how would you have us do that? Slit his throat where he sits?'

'There must be a way.'

'There is certainly a way. But it is dangerous, and only for the advanced. Isn't that right, Delco?'

Delco sat quietly in the front row, hands wrapped together in his lap, his eyes wide with fear. The answer seemed to fight its way out of him.

'Yes, Master Biore. But—'

'But it is very dangerous, young Wilt. Ask Delco about it some other time. I'm sure he'll give you a full explanation.'

Wilt studied Delco, but he seemed unwilling to meet his eyes.

'Come now. We have been at this long enough for today. It is time to return to that curious grey world we call reality.'

Wilt walked to his seat and sat down, and immediately a dim silver haze began to whirl slowly around them. The whirlpool sped up to become a bright wall of light, wiping the world away, before slowing again to reveal a classroom full of Black Robes and a frail, mumbling old Master bent over his desk at the front of the room. Seconds later the mumbling stopped, and the students stood up as one.

Wilt risked a glance at the old Master sunken into his seat. The Master didn't raise his head, and Wilt headed silently out of the room, biting back the long list of questions he needed answers for.

Any questions he wanted to ask Delco would have to wait. The students filed into the dining room that evening to find the long wooden tables removed, leaving a wide open space. In the centre of the room stood Cantor Cortis, flanked by four heavily armed and fully masked guards. A cruel grin stretched across the Cantor's face as he watched the Black Robes mill about in confusion before him.

Finally his smile dropped and he barked out an order. 'Form a line!'

Wilt bustled his way into place before the Cantor, his eyes scanning the guards standing either side of him. Despite their masked helms, he recognised two of them immediately. One was massive, too big to be any other than the one called Funes. The other he recognised by the arrogant set of his shoulders. Red Charley. Wilt lowered his eyes and focused on the floor. They would find some excuse to single him out. He had to be ready for anything.

Once the Black Robes had formed into something resembling a line across the room, the Cantor shook his head and shouted down their muttering. 'That will have to do. Silence!'

His voice echoed across the high ceilings, shocking the room into complete silence. Cortis enjoyed the effect his words had for a long moment, then began to prowl back and forth in front of them, like a great caged beast.

'It has been brought to my attention that Redmondis is no longer as secure as it might be. These great walls surrounding you are manned by my guards, but we also rely on your particular … talents … to help ensure no threat can enter from the outside world. In this task, it seems, you have failed.'

Cortis stopped pacing and reached out to lay his hand on the shoulder of the nearest Black Robe.

'You. Your name.'

'Er … Bertrand, sir.'

The young man looked frozen in place, his eyes locked onto the Cantor's, his shoulders stiff and attentive. There was a whisper in the air, and the young Black Robe's body suddenly slackened. He was lost, Cortis was in control now.

'Bertrand. You would like to help us secure our walls, would you not?'

'Of course, sir.' His voice was more confident now. Not his own.

'Good. Because there have been reports of merchants trying to smuggle in certain items, certain dangerous items. Items that have no place within these walls. Do you know of what I speak, Bertrand?'

'No, sir.'

'I would hope not. But Bertrand, you and your fellow students here possess skills that might help in our investigation of this security breach. Will you use them to help us, Bertrand?'

The young man stiffened to attention again and almost saluted as he blurted out his agreement. 'Yes, sir!'

'Very good. Bring in the witness.'

Cantor Cortis dropped his arm from Bertrand's shoulder and spun away to watch two more guards enter the room, dragging a slumped body between them.

'Funes, get our witness a chair.'

Funes spun his massive frame surprisingly quickly and marched to the side of the room to return with a single chair, which he placed in front of Bertrand. The two guards dropped the body into it, kicking his feet under the chair. They pushed the man into a sitting position and looped a rope around his chest to hold him in place. Wilt caught a glimpse of bruised skin and hastily patched cuts all across the man's face.

'As you can see, Bertrand, some of my men have been overly eager in questioning our witness already.'

Funes and Red Charley stiffened at the words, but Cortis ignored them.

'Unfortunately, this has left our witness somewhat unconscious. What I need you to do, Bertrand, is get inside there and wake him up for me.'

Wilt raised his head to get a better view of the scene, but quickly dropped his eyes to his feet. It was a trap. Focus on being silent and still. Hidden. A calm pool. Untroubled and shallow.

Sure enough, as soon as Bertrand nodded his head and focused on the victim, Wilt felt clumsy fingers brush over his mind. They weren't here to question the witness. Cortis could have done that himself, far more effectively than any others here. No, the witness was merely an excuse to scan them, the Black Robes.

Cortis saw them as a threat.

The witness stirred then, a low groan escaping his lips. Even Bertrand seemed surprised that he had succeeded in making some sort of contact, and he lost his concentration. The pawing touch on Wilt's mind faded away.

Cantor Cortis's voice seemed to slither across the room now, worming its way into their minds. 'Very good, Bertrand. Now go deeper. Find out what he knows about the contraband.'

Bertrand took a deep breath and refocused on the victim. His eyes clouded grey and small beads of sweat sprung out on his forehead as he strained, clumsily pushing into the victim's mind. Wilt winced at the thought of the damage being done to the poor man by Bertrand's heavy touch, but dropped the thought as soon as it appeared. There was nothing he could do. This whole scene was merely theatre. He had to stay silent and still. Hidden.

Wilt felt the light touch on his mind again, as though soft fingers trailed across the surface, seeking out any irregularity.

The victim stirred again, and a low murmur escaped his lips. 'Boy. Sold to boy.'

Cortis seemed unsurprised by the information, but leaned in closer and placed his hand on Bertrand's shoulder, as though to give him support. 'Very good, Bertrand. What did he sell to the boy?'

Bertrand's face was drenched in sweat now, and he swayed slightly on his feet as he pushed deeper into the man's mind.

'Blade. Moonsteel.' The last word was squeezed out of him in a gasp, and the victim slumped forward in his chair.

'Moonsteel.' Wilt risked another glance up and saw Cortis savour the word, a distant look in his eyes. The pawing at his mind returned, but he was confident he could resist it now.

'Anything else, Bertrand? Go deeper for me.'

Cortis was almost holding Bertrand up by now, but he didn't break the connection, and bore down further on the shrinking figure tied to the chair.

The man groaned again, a final death rattle as he pushed the words out of his cold blue lips. 'Higgs. She called him Higgs.'

Wilt's head shot up and at the same time the soft pawing at his mind became a set of sharp claws digging under his skin, pulling at him, trying to get inside his shell. A great roar rushed through his ears and he dropped down, away from the world, away from the threat that sought his scent. He was a fish in a deep still pool, swimming under solid ice. Far above, a great grey wolf paced on the ice, but he stayed always out of its sight.

As he dived, another part of him sent out a weld to join the connection between Bertrand and the victim. Mallow. Mallow the merchant. Trader in fine and mysterious goods from all ends of the land. That was his name.

Mallow's mind was collapsing, its foundations smashed by Bertrand's fumbling. He was lost and dying, though Wilt was coldly satisfied to see he would take his killer down with him. Bertrand was floundering as the walls around him caved in. Cortis had left him down there, sending all his power away to try to break into Wilt's mind. No, there was no return for Bertrand from this. A spark of pity tickled his mind, but he quickly snuffed it out.

Wilt's weld rushed through Mallow's shattered mind, flashing through thoughts and scenes from his life, rifling through his being to find what he was looking for. Higgs. He had said his name.

Finally, deep inside the core of Mallow's mind, Wilt found what he was looking for. Hastily he built supports around the small chamber to hold it steady as he dived into the scene.

He was standing at the entrance to his tent. Coin was heavy in his hand, and he felt the slightest twinge of regret as the young boy walked outside into the waiting guards. It had been a good trade. Rare to enjoy such trading skill here, where the crafters and Black Robes were often so desperate for goods. He preferred it this way. Yes, he had liked trading with the boy. Now though, now it looked as though the boy had made some powerful enemies. He stepped behind the tent flap of his stall to view the scene, making sure to stay out of the guards' sight. One never knew what those dogs could do. Best to stay out of their way.

He watched the guards question the boy, saw them strike the young girl standing with him, the boy lash back, reaching into his tunic to pull out the glowing moonsteel blade. Recognised the sharp pain flash across the large guard's face as the blade cut across him. The moonsteel had hurt him badly. That meant he was one of them. At least, he was on his way.

Wilt pulled Mallow's thoughts back to the scene in front of him, though he knew something important was there. He had no time.

The thoughts suddenly stopped and Wilt found himself being squeezed as the walls in Mallow's mind crumbled inwards. He pulled himself out quickly, a part of him still under the ice looking up, seeing no predator above him now, but feeling wary nonetheless. Then a great crack appeared in the ice and a bright light burst into him, searching him out and burning him away.

Wilt opened his eyes and stumbled forward before catching himself and returning to the line. The scene in front of him had changed. Bertrand was collapsed on the floor, his eyes white and lifeless. Mallow was slumped forward in his chair, the stench of sudden death wafting from him. Cortis and his guards were standing at attention, eyes locked on the far side of the room. Wilt turned his head to join the others and was almost lost.

The Sister stood at the far side of the room, her hood thrown back and the full terrible glory of her gaze locked onto his. Wilt caught a glimpse of her red-robed guards standing on either side of her, heads back, tasting the thoughts in the room, but couldn't do anything more than stare into the Sister's wondrous green eyes and sink into their depths. The thick ice protecting his mind warped and cracked as nine coiled minds burned into him, and the medallion around his neck became impossibly hot. They had found him. They had found him and now he was theirs.

With a gasp he dived deep into himself, reaching out for Higgs as he did so, reaching out for his fellow Black Robes as well, dragging them all down with him, trying to draw any support he could. He felt their struggle as his mind locked onto theirs, their frantic kicking as he pulled them deeper than they had ever been before, away from the terrible burning light of the Sisters. For an eternal moment he held each of them within his mind, weighing their strength. A secret voice whispered to take them. Squeeze them and drain them and make their power his. To fight back. Instead he turned away, dropping all the welds he held except one, the strongest one, the true connection to his ward. He dived into it, leaving everything else behind.

He stood in a small candlelit room, at the foot of a bed. The old healer leaned over Heather and dabbed at her forehead with a cloth. It was his room. Daemi stood at the door, impatiently tapping her foot, and he turned to shush her. Something in the movement twinged his neck, and he grabbed at it as he looked at her.

'Higgs? What's wrong?'

Suddenly there was too much, too much inside him. Not enough room for them both. He smiled helplessly at her and collapsed.

Wilt opened his eyes to find himself prostrate on the ground. He was still in the hall, and a quick glance around showed him he wasn't alone on the stone floor. Bodies lay crumpled on either side of him, and a soft whimpering could be heard across the room, as though a dog was crying in pain and fear.

He considered sitting up, then thought better of it, closing his eyes again to let his ears tell him the story.

'We pushed too hard.' It was the Sister's voice. No longer a pleasant song though—now a harsh, cold female choir. Not in keeping with his vision of her at all.

'We taste thoughts here.' A lisping, slithering voice, not wholly human, answered her. The Red Robes. 'Sweet thoughts. Dangerous thoughts.'

'I did sense something. There is old craft here.' The Sister's heels clicked on the stone floor as she strode across the room. The whimpering got louder, then was abruptly silenced.

'You have disappointed me, Cortis. How long have you known about this violation?'

'Only since this morning, Sister.' His voice was a high whine, desperate to please. 'My guards, they found evidence.'

'Your dogs picked up a scent and you thought to sniff it out yourself rather than come to us. Foolish Cortis.'

Wilt felt power grow in the room, and Cortis let out a strangled cry before collapsing onto the floor in silence.

'You are fortunate we sent Wrexley away. He would not let such an intrusion pass.'

'The thoughts, Sister. We taste them still.' The Sentinel again, its sucking whisper pushed out through lips no longer suited to the purpose.

'Enough.' The Sister's voice was final. 'We will find nothing here. Not today. The old craft has returned to Redmondis. We Sisters must consult and decide our next steps. Come.'

The sound of the Sister's steps receded quickly down the hall, and the ghostly brush of the Sentinels' floating strides followed her. A weight lifted from the room, and the bodies either side of Wilt began to stir.

He could smell burnt skin, and a separate channel of his mind told him it was his own, from where the medallion around his neck had melted into his chest.

'Come.' Cortis's voice was an angry bark. 'You have disappointed the Sisters. You will discover the consequences of this.'

Cortis strode out of the hall, his guards limping along silently behind him. Wilt smiled to himself as he listened to them leave. He imagined Cortis's punishment would be most imaginative.

A body to his side sat up and he heard Delco's familiar voice.

'What happened?'

Wilt sat up, his mind feeling free and clear and wild for the first time since before coming to Redmondis. The freedom was terrifying, as though he were perched on a ledge above a yawning abyss, the open sky stretched out in front of him, inviting him on.

'I ... I'm not sure.'

He stood up slowly and watched as the rest of the Black Robes began to stir into consciousness. Their eyes were confused and clear, as though waking from a dream. They too no longer had the cold spike of control throbbing within their minds. It had all melted away.

Wilt pulled Delco to his feet. 'But I think things are about to get a whole lot more interesting around here. Come on, I have to check on someone.'

Chapter 21

Once inside their room, Wilt sat Delco on his bed and bent over to study his face. 'How are you feeling?'

'I'm okay. Different. Tired.'

Wilt smiled at Delco's slightly stunned face and patted him on the shoulder. 'Rest. Whatever it was the Sister did, she did it to all of us. I don't think she meant to either. We can talk about it in the morning.' He looked out the window, the grey dusk sky just beginning to darken into black.

'What are you going to do?' Delco's voice was faint, as though he were already drifting off to sleep.

Wilt pulled the blanket up over Delco's shoulders. 'Don't worry about me. Sleep.'

As soon as he said the words, Delco's eyes closed and his breathing dropped into a slow, steady rhythm.

Wilt turned to the open window and pulled himself up onto the sill. He fixed the picture of Higgs's room in his mind, blocking out all other thought, and the next moment was springing lightly down the wall.

Night had closed in as he approached Higgs's window, and the light from inside threw strangely twisted shadows against the glass. He hesitated as he studied the window, his nose twitching. Then he was on the window's ledge, balanced on two human feet, tapping lightly on the glass with his knuckle.

Daemi threw open the window and grabbed him by the collar,

pulling him quickly inside and tossing him roughly onto the rug. Wilt rolled easily to his feet.

'Nice to see you too.'

She didn't reply, and turned to face the bed. Wilt saw two bodies lying there. One, a small girl, her face bruised and split, the girl he had seen through Higgs's eyes—Heather. The other, larger figure's eyes were shut and his face twisted in silent pain. Higgs.

Wilt stepped toward the bed, but was shooed back by the healer standing over the two prone figures. 'Leave them be, young man. They will survive.'

'No thanks to you,' Daemi muttered angrily under her breath, barely loud enough for the words to carry.

'What happened?' Wilt addressed Daemi, but it was the healer who replied.

'The girl has been cruelly beaten, but nothing is broken and the bruises will heal. The boy has a deeper problem.'

Wilt examined the healer: a hunched, hooded figure whose voice was suddenly familiar. 'Petron?'

Petron pulled back the hood of his cloak and allowed Wilt a smile. 'Well, it's good to see I'm not completely forgotten.'

'But—how are you here? I thought—'

'You thought I was incapable of returning to Redmondis? That I had to remain outside its walls? I hadn't entered in case the Sisters detected my presence. Now, however, it seems that no longer matters.'

'Now that you've announced yourself to the world.' It was Daemi again, angry sarcasm dripping from her tongue.

'Me?' Wilt looked between them, stepping back and shaking his head in denial. 'I didn't do anything. It was the Sister.'

'The Sister and her minions followed your scent.'

'Now, now, Daemi.' Petron lifted his hand in a calming gesture. 'It is not Wilt's fault that he has been discovered. We all knew it would happen eventually. I was hoping for a little more time. Still,' he smiled again, a tired tension in his eyes, 'here we are.'

'And where was Wrexley? Cortis should never have been allowed—'

Daemi interrupted Wilt, her voice low and dangerous. 'Cantor Wrexley was sent on an important task. He asked me to stand watch until he returned.'

'So you just wave Cortis inside the tower to line up the Black Robes one by one to seek out any threat?'

Daemi dropped her head and Wilt flushed with both victory and shame.

'Quiet, both of you.' Petron's voice was calm and steady, but somehow wrapped itself around them and melted the tension away. 'Daemi could do nothing to stop a Cantor from going where he pleased. Especially not one as single-minded as Cortis. There is no blame there.' He sat down in the chair next to Higgs. 'No blame anywhere. Or rather, blame for each of us in our way. Even this young man.'

Petron dipped a cloth into a bowl of strangely scented water by the side of the bed and patted it gently across Higgs's forehead. 'The curiosity of youth.' As he wiped his patient's face, Higgs's troubled frown relaxed slightly, the tension knotting his brow melting as he fell into more peaceful dreams.

Wilt found he could almost feel the flow of thought and desire wash across the impossible landscape of Higgs's mind, feel the coolness of the cloth as it wiped across his brow.

'And you, young man. How do you feel?'

Wilt jerked away from his thoughts and looked at Petron, who was studying him curiously. 'Me? I'm ... fine.'

'Your chest?'

'My chest?' For a second Wilt didn't know what Petron was talking about, then raised his hand inside his tunic and traced the fresh scar burned into his skin. 'My chest is fine.'

'Show me.'

Wilt hesitated for a second, a voice inside him screaming for him to run, to leave them, to save his power for-

'Wilt.' Petron's voice was louder now, though still gentle, as though he too could hear the secret voice. 'Open your shirt.'

Wilt pulled open his tunic to reveal the deep red scar where the medallion had melted away. The edges of the scar had blackened, and it seemed to glint cruelly in the flickering light of the fire.

Daemi let out a small gasp, but Petron stepped forward and traced his fingers lightly over the rough, ridged flesh.

'Interesting.'

Petron's fingers left a tingling warmth as they traced the design, and Wilt's mind cleared, as though he were dropping into a weld. He caught himself before he plunged into the depths, breathing slowly, holding himself back from the edge.

'Good, Wilt. You have made progress.' Petron's eyes glittered in the firelight, yellow and strange, as though another creature peered out from behind them. 'Let me try something.'

The voice inside Wilt tried to protest again, but it was quieter now, weak and distant. It faded into silence as Petron began to whisper and trace his fingers along the scar.

The room faded, and Wilt found himself at the top of a high cliff, the sky grey and clear. A slight breeze ruffled his hair, carrying the strange words Petron whispered along with it. Soon a second voice joined it, and after a few moments Wilt realised it was his own. The words he spoke were meaningless, but his lips formed the strange, slippery syllables without difficulty.

The wind grew in strength, but Wilt stood firm, his robes whipping around his legs.

A third voice joined the chant. A familiar, boyish voice. Weak, but growing stronger with each word. Higgs. Wilt heard his friend's voice come from the yawning darkness in front of him and from the bed in the room far away where his physical form still stood.

The wind grew again, and Wilt stumbled as he held himself back from brink. The darkness beyond seemed to suck him toward it now, beckoning him on. He heard the voices grow impossibly loud, forcing him ever closer to the edge.

The three voices became one inside his mind, then a hand reached out and pushed him, away from the noise and frenzy, away from the light and the world, and everything but the darkness.

He fell forever, through conscious thought and black stillness. The secret, hidden part of him, the voice that spoke only to him, watched in silent interest as the three voices followed him down, wrapping around him and sucking something free. Then they left him to the emptiness and he hit the floor.

Wilt opened his eyes to see Daemi standing over him, her concerned face twisting into annoyance as she saw his eyes clear.

'What are you doing?' she whispered angrily at him, as if he had somehow embarrassed her. 'Get up.' She pulled him roughly to his feet and caught him as stars broke across his eyes and his legs buckled. Daemi pushed him upright. 'Behave yourself.'

The stars clouding Wilt's vision faded as the room returned into focus.

Petron was there, leaning over Higgs again, a slight smile on his lips. 'Good. Very good.'

Higgs's breathing seemed normal now, and his face relaxed and clear. He seemed to be simply sleeping.

'Let the boy rest now. He will be fine in the morning. Maybe with a little headache.' Petron turned toward them and ushered them over to the far side of the room. 'Here.' He pulled a chair toward Wilt and pushed him into it. 'You too. Rest.'

'What happened?' Wilt was surprised by the faltering weakness in his own voice.

Petron sat down heavily in a chair and sighed deeply. He too seemed exhausted.

'What is wrong with you two?' Daemi pulled her own chair over and sat down angrily, glancing between the two and trying not to look concerned.

'I haven't delved so deeply in many years. Not since—' Petron's voice faded into silence and a distant smile twitched his lips. 'Since the last time I was within these walls.'

'With Master Biore, you mean.' Wilt wasn't sure where the sudden flash of intuition came from, but as soon as he said the words he knew them to be true.

'Yes. Biore.' Petron's smile twisted and died on his face as he said the name. 'I should have known he'd seek you out.'

'He's been teaching us. Me and Delco, I mean. Though I think we'll have more students in the class next time, now that—'

'Now that they've woken up. Yes. I think any wielder with the slightest trace of the skill felt what has happened this night. The Sisters overreached.'

'There was only one of them. I've only ever seen one. A redheaded woman, very beautiful.'

'Really.' Daemi seemed unimpressed with Wilt's description, but Petron continued on, ignoring her.

'The Sisters are not like us, Wilt. When you face one you face all nine of them. They are forever linked. That is part of their power.'

'Biore says they are skilled, but not like us.'

'No, not like us at all.' Petron seemed to pull himself out of his reverie and snap back to the present. 'Still, what Biore says is of no importance right now. Just promise me one thing, Wilt.' Petron leaned forward to clasp Wilt's knee, his eyes bright and clear. 'Promise me you'll be careful of him. Biore has a habit of using people up.'

Wilt didn't know what to make of that, but nodded helplessly in return, and Petron seemed to be satisfied.

'Good. You will have to be careful of many things now, Wilt. You are no longer shielded from them.' Petron waved his fingers toward Wilt's chest, and a dull throb of heat pulsed from his skin.

'Whatever the Sisters did trying to break through to you, they made sure of that at least. You only survived by instinct, using your ward, hiding inside Higgs's mind while the whirlwind passed above you. That is also how we managed to save him. When you came back out, some part of him came with you. You are both strongly linked, now more than ever.' Petron's voice was getting weaker as he spoke, and his head began to nod forward. 'I must rest now, and you must return to your room before the guards discover you. Cortis's dogs will have free rein now, and will be hunting you.'

Wilt looked at Daemi for some explanation, but she seemed just as confused as he was.

'Go. I must rest.' Petron sat forward suddenly, his eyes wide. 'Wilt! Remember your strength. You are stronger than any wielder I have known, stronger than any there has been, I suspect. You are a danger to them. Be always on your guard.'

Chapter 22

Cortis sat alone in his tent, his eyes closed, listening to the sounds of activity in the camp. Soldiers marched back and forth, breaking down the tents, moving quickly, not wasting any effort. Only the best of the guard were still here. His personal selections. Those who would not question any order.

He opened his eyes and looked at his right hand, cupped in his left, his long fingers curled into claws. He turned his hand over, and for a moment in the flickering light of the fire his nails were long and yellow and no longer human.

'Cantor Cortis.' The guard snapped into a salute.

Cortis nodded a reply. Rokley. That was his name. An eager young pup. He had definite potential.

'The patrol has returned to Redmondis. We shadowed them the entire way and they were none the wiser.'

'Good, Rokley. And the form?'

'All held it without difficulty, Cantor.' The guard didn't try to hide his obvious pride.

'Very well. Continue with the preparations. We must be ready to move by dawn.'

'Yes, sir!' Another salute and the guard backed out of the tent to resume breaking camp.

Cortis watched him leave, his mind elsewhere, his thoughts buoyed by the sounds of activity filtering through the heavy canvas.

Redmondis was blind, its patrols careless. The time to strike was now. They needed to shake off the leash the Nine Sisters had flung around their necks. Show them the true meaning of power, the real darkness that—A sharp bolt of pain drove into his mind suddenly, driving all thought away. He immediately clutched his brow, forcing his mind elsewhere, away from the pain.

The dream faded and Wilt's contact was lost. He found himself floating toward the surface, Petron's words echoing in his mind: *be always on your guard.*

Wilt woke to find the sun high in the sky. It was long past time for the first lesson of the day.

Delco sat beside his bed, a steaming mug of coffee in his hands. 'Here. I don't know how you managed to find coffee in this place.'

Wilt sat up and took the mug Delco offered gratefully. 'Lets just say I have friends in useful places.'

'Oh yes, your crafter friend. I'd almost forgotten about him. But never mind about that now. I was beginning to wonder whether I was going to have to wake you.'

'It's late.'

'Lessons have been cancelled for the day. For the foreseeable future, I expect. No Masters are around. No one seems to know quite what's going on. Some of us have things to do, however. Get dressed.'

Wilt heard something in his tone and looked at him, confused.

'The Sisters want to see you.'

The Nine Sisters dwelt in a separate area of Redmondis, cut deep into the mountains that formed its walls. Wilt had noticed guards and Black Robes wandering aimlessly as he left the tower, but they had gradually disappeared from the streets as he approached the Sisters' compound. As he stood before the high stone gates, the streets were completely deserted. There weren't even any guards by the gate; nothing but a great stone ring set in the wall, far too large for any human to lift. Wilt hesitated for a second, then reached out to touch it. A spark of heat zapped his fingers as they met the stone, and the doors swung open.

Beyond the doors, a wide staircase led down into darkness. Wilt felt as though he were walking down the throat of an enormous beast, a feeling only compounded when the stone gates swung shut behind him with a low thud.

It wasn't completely dark inside. The walls seemed to emit a low green glow, as though from some mineral in the rock. Wilt traced his fingers over the stone as he walked down the stairs. Whatever caused the glow was beyond his power to sense. He thought how fascinated Higgs would be by the sight and smiled to himself, suddenly no longer afraid.

Wilt lost count of the number of steps, but the closeness of the air around him told him he was far below the surface by the time he reached the bottom and was faced with another door. This one was wood, and swung open on his approach. He sensed a pulse of power, quite deliberate, as though someone wanted to make sure he understood what he was walking into.

Beyond the door was a small waiting room cut into the smooth stone, two Sentinels standing on either side of a single door on its far side. Both lifted their heads to sniff the air as he entered.

His earlier vision of serpents tasting the air returned, flashing across his consciousness. For an instant he panicked, then his chest throbbed and a wave of heat rolled through his mind, calming him. Wilt stared at the Sentinels, unafraid. Their probing thoughts slithered over the surface of his mind, but he was deeper now, beyond their touch. Some part of him whispered that they no longer posed him any threat.

He understood suddenly that, if he wished, he could shield himself completely from them, move himself absolutely out of their reach, and that simple understanding gave him control. For a second he considered reading one of them, diving in to see how it reacted, to see what was inside its twisted mind. He held himself back, however; aware that now was not the time for pointless displays of power.

Wilt didn't need to read them to see they had lost their humanity long ago. He almost felt sorry for them as he walked past them, their animal snufflings following his step. Then he remembered the sight of the young Black Robe lying on the floor on his first day at Redmondis—the broken shape of his body, the emptiness in his eyes—and forgot any notion of pity. Wilt tore his thoughts back to the present and walked through the final door.

Inside was a large, curved stone room, shaped like a theatre with rows of seats cut into the stone. Wilt walked directly onto the stage at the front of the room, and stopped abruptly, his body following a whispered command that his mind had not heard. In the rows of seats in front of him, nine red-robed figures sat silently. Their heads were hooded, their faces shadowed, but Wilt could feel their eyes and minds focused on him. He stood perfectly still and let their senses scan him, feeling the light touch tickle over the surface of his mind.

After a moment a decision seemed to be reached and one of the figures in the centre of the room pulled back her hood to reveal the long flowing red hair of a Sister, the same Sister Wilt had met before. The sparkling green eyes held his, and her full red lips curved in a knowing smile. A thick blanket of silence and stilled power covered him—the same sensation he had felt back in Greystone, and again on his first day in Redmondis. It was no longer magical, however, and Wilt knew that if he so chose he could push against it. He was master of his own mind now, no longer subject to these simple tricks.

The Sister's smile seemed to widen as she watched him, as though she read his thoughts. 'You have made progress.'

Her voice was low and husky, half whispered, but the words were clear in Wilt's mind. Something in the voice was off though, as if the words themselves didn't completely match the movement of her lips. They seemed to echo in the high silence of the room.

'Master Biore seems to think that you may be of great use to us.'

Suddenly Wilt was aware of a second figure standing on the small stage, the shadows pulling away to reveal Master Biore, a strangely simpering grin plastered over his face. The aged disguise he wore had dropped away to reveal his true self, but he still stood hunched and frail.

'Wilt, my boy. I've been telling the Sisters about—'

'Master Biore has been most informative.'

Wilt realised what it was about her voice now. It was as though many voices had been merged into one, a crowd of people speaking through one set of lips. His eyes moved over the nine hooded figures before him, and he remembered Petron's words. Forever linked.

'He has told us of your power. And of your protection.'

Suddenly a great invisible hand wrapped around Wilt and held him in place as his jerkin was ripped open to reveal the scar on his chest where Petron's medallion had been. A whisper of wind moved over it, tracing the scarred edges of his flesh.

'Yes. This work is familiar to us.'

The power holding Wilt vanished, and he pulled his shirt closed, suddenly shy. The Sister facing him smiled wider.

'That protection has gone now—burned away by our power, the power of the blood and the stone. But that protection also limited you, held you back behind its walls. It seems we have unleashed you.'

Something about their words stopped Wilt's thoughts. The power of the blood and the stone. The blood within the stone. There was something …

'Now you stand before us and we must decide what we will do with you. Biore,' the Sister's words changed into a single stern voice, 'you may leave us now.'

Biore seemed to sag in relief, but a desperate glint remained in his eyes. 'Yes, Sister. And the … er … compensation?'

'The Sentinels will ensure all is in order. Leave us.'

The Sister turned to Wilt, but his mind was lost in the past. He was standing on the flagball field in Greystone, staring down at the broken body of the guard who had just tried to kill him. The blood within the stone.

Wilt blinked and was back in the present. 'The blood within the stone. I've heard those words before.'

As soon as he spoke, a veil seemed to lift from his mind. For the briefest moment he saw the Sisters before him as they truly were, a twisting nest of nine great serpents weaving their magic upon him, holding him down and dancing around him, just waiting for the right moment to strike. He reined his thoughts back immediately, his face blank.

'Oh yes, the words of the prophecy. You are the one from Greystone. The one that assassin was sent for.'

The voice was soothing and warm, and despite himself Wilt's doubts and fears began to fade.

No. They no longer had power over him. They could not.

'He was not sent by us, you know. We would not be so clumsy.' Again the Sister smiled, and Wilt had to push back against the surge of trust and hope that her expression brought welling up inside him.

'There are … others who would have such power as yours removed from the game, rather than risk it falling into the wrong hands. We hope this will not be necessary.'

The pure threat behind her words poured into his ears like warm honey. Wilt clenched his entire body, holding himself still as the charms washed over him. He could feel himself weakening, sinking under their spell.

'Cantor Cortis has also shown an interest in you. He sees you as a threat, though whether this is to Redmondis or to his own position is not yet clear. We would put his mind at rest were the times not as they are.'

Put his mind at rest. Such simple words.

'But the times are what they are. You have been sheltered inside these walls, inside our protection. You do not know the world as it is. There is a storm building in the south, a storm that is only now beginning to be glimpsed on the horizon. Such power as yours is not easily discarded when threats appear.'

The Sister smiled at him again, her green eyes boring into his mind. Wilt felt the hot want inside him, to surrender to her, to rip his mind open and expose himself totally to her. He did the only thing he could instead.

Wilt read her. It wasn't easy. It was as though the room itself held some power over welds, as though the curve of the walls or the nature of the stone rebuffed their use. Wilt had to concentrate his entire mind, forgetting the Sister's charm, forgetting the power that tried to work its way inside him. He forgot all about welds, about black welds and white welds and the various ways Redmondis had taught him to use his power. He simply focused on the Sister and forced himself to read her. Thoughts broke over him like a wave.

Kill him!

No, he could yet prove useful.

Feed him to the worms!

They hunger as we hunger.

Food today or food tomorrow—what does it matter to us?

The blood and the stone have spoken. It is not our place to respond.

The prophecy. It is written—without his power we may be lost. The storm builds.

Let Biore have him. Let him sate the hunger.

He is only a man. A simple man. He is no threat to us.

Wilt wrenched his mind away from the tangled thoughts he had found himself in. He felt unclean. No wonder he had only ever seen one Sister. By the taint of their minds, the other Sisters would no longer be recognisable. Whatever faces they wore, the owners of those thoughts were not human. Not anymore.

The Sister sat before him, unaware anything had changed,

confident in her power to charm. 'Cantor Wrexley is due to return this evening. We will inform him of all that has occurred. You will want to stay close to him, under his wing.' The Sister smiled then, as if at some private joke. 'Your fellow Black Robes have also had their eyes opened. It seems we pushed harder than we intended. This is perhaps for the best. If nothing else they will help muddy the waters.' The Sister tilted her head to the side. 'Be ever on your guard. These walls no longer protect you as they once did. Those who attempted to remove you in Greystone may yet try again. And of course there are more immediate threats—Ah, Cantor Cortis.'

She spoke the final words to the figure who had just entered the room, and Wilt turned to see Cantor Cortis glaring at him, his lips curled back in a snarl.

'Leave us now, Wilt. We will be watching you.'

A grip Wilt had been unaware of suddenly loosened, and he stumbled where he stood. Cantor Cortis continued to stare, and Wilt thought he could hear a low growl emanating from the back of his throat. He walked off the stage quickly, toward the gap Biore had disappeared through earlier.

'Cortis. What news …'

The words faded into silence as Wilt hurried down the curving stone corridor. He had to concentrate to stop himself breaking into a run. Eventually, after numerous blind curves and a maddeningly slow incline, the tunnel spat him out into the open air. He found himself in a small walled courtyard, and was surprised to see the sky was grey with the first touches of the evening. How long had he been down there?

'How do you feel, boy?'

The voice came from a shadow on a nearby bench, and Wilt could just make out the face of Master Biore, though his voice sounded weaker than normal.

'Okay, I guess. Strange.'

'Yes. Strange.' A low chuckle emanated from the shadows. 'The Sisters tend to have that effect on people.' Biore reached out and offered something to him. 'Here. Drink this. It will help ground you again.'

Wilt took the cup automatically and sipped it. It was warm and thick, with a slight metallic twist that sent a rich glow firing throughout his body.

'Not too much now.'

Biore held his hand out for the cup, and Wilt was surprised to feel a sudden reluctance to give it back. He pushed the thought away and passed the cup to Biore.

'To the blood and the stone.' Biore raised the cup quickly, a twisted grimace on his face, and drained it. 'Come. You probably have a few questions. I'd rather not try to answer them here.'

Biore stood up and put his arm around Wilt's shoulders, leading him out of the courtyard and into the shadowed night.

As the night set in around them, Wilt's clouded thoughts began to clear, as though the darkening air strengthened him somehow. His vision sharpened, and he found it easy to make his way along the twisted lanes that led out of the Sisters' quarters and back toward the high towers. Biore, too, seemed to have no trouble seeing in the dark, though he leaned heavily on Wilt's shoulders as they walked in silence.

Finally Biore spoke. 'The Sentinels. You saw something of their true nature in there, didn't you?'

The vision of serpents Wilt had experienced twice now came back to him. 'Serpents. They were great snakes of some kind. No longer human.'

'Never human to begin with. The Sisters have delved very deeply, and not all that they have returned with belongs in this world. Be always on your guard around them.'

'Did they tell you of the prophecy?' Biore continued.

Wilt nodded. 'The blood within the stone.'

'Ah yes. *"Within you and without you. The blood within the stone. Writ for you and about you. Together and yet alone.'* Do those words mean anything to you?'

'No, nothing. Though I've heard some of them before.'

'Yes, many of us have.' His voice dropped into a whisper. 'For a long time I believed they were written for me.'

Biore seemed to want to say more, but held his tongue, and Wilt continued on in silence, not knowing what to make of it.

Soon they approached the first lights of the short walls surrounding their towers, but Biore guided Wilt away from the light, toward the outer walls of Redmondis.

When his voice came it was weak and distant. 'The crafters, those some still foolishly label the lesser skilled, they have always known the truth. That within all objects is a pulse of life. Of blood. And those who can access this power, who can truly harness it … A wielder with such reserves, such access to the black depths themselves. Why, one who could control that …' Biore shook his head suddenly as if to free himself of some troubling dream. 'But duty calls, young Wilt. No time for rest yet. We need to make sure the Sisters' messenger has returned unharmed.'

Wilt didn't question the order, the habit of obedience still clinging to him. He was surprised to feel a moment of hesitation, however, as if his mind considered rebelling, then thought better of it. He smiled to himself as he realised he had almost forgotten what if felt like to break the rules.

Biore steered them toward the stables lining the eastern side of Redmondis. The various guards and lesser skilled workers all ignored them as they walked in and inhaled the strongly scented air. Wilt's sense of smell was reawakening after weeks of wasting away.

'The smell. It's—'

'Yes. Strong, isn't it? You forget how raw the real world can be sometimes.'

'No, it's … wondrous.'

Biore chuckled at this, then led him through the stalls and

toward the back of the stables. Eventually they found themselves alone in the shadows again, the silence of the night broken only by the infrequent whinnies and snorts from the various beasts sleeping in the stalls behind them.

Biore pulled them to a halt and stood up on his own, rolling his shoulders as he looked around. 'Here. This will do.'

He cupped his hands in front of his face and blew into them, a low owl's call hooting out. Then he fanned his fingers, and the hoot trilled into a series of notes, moving up and down the scale as his fingers rolled back and forth.

Biore dropped his hands and listened to the empty night. Wilt watched him survey the empty sky, and was about to send out a weld to scan the area when he heard the sound of beating wings approaching. He took a step back as a large bird dived out of the darkness and landed in front of them. Petron. What was Petron doing with Biore?

The bird blurred into human form and Wrexley stood before them.

'Biore.' Wrexley nodded his head quickly toward the other Master, then looked hard at Wilt.

'What is the boy doing here?'

'The boy is no longer a secret, Wrexley. The time to scurry about in the shadows has passed.'

Wrexley continued to stare at Wilt for a few moments, then seemed to resign himself to the idea, and a tired smile broke out on his face. 'I suppose we need all the help we can get these days.'

Wilt couldn't hold himself back any longer. 'Cantor Wrexley. Your other form. It's the same—'

'The same as Petron's,' Biore interrupted him. 'Of course it is, boy. Didn't you know?'

Wrexley's smile twisted into a grimace before melting away. 'Yes, Wilt. Petron was my ward. We still share many things. Now, however, is not the time to reminisce.' He turned to Biore, his face serious. 'I need to make my report to the Sisters. I take it from the fact that I was able to land here that they are beginning to recognise the seriousness of things. Our enemies are beginning to move.'

'From all sides. Much has happened since you were sent on your little errand.'

Wrexley's voice hardened. 'It was not an "errand", Biore. Forces are being mobilised. We need to know how much time we have.'

'Of course. I forget you still hold to the belief that the Sisters will save Redmondis.'

'The Sisters *are* Redmondis.'

'Your other form may have something to say about that.'

'We cannot all hide in the shadows.' Wrexley's jaw clenched as if holding back further insult. 'I don't have time for this. What did you call me for?'

'The Sisters have unleashed their dogs. The barriers to Redmondis have fallen. It is time to call on old friends. We need all the help we can get—you said as much yourself.'

Wrexley grimaced again, as if the possibility Biore raised caused him actual pain. 'Those days are gone.'

'Those days are now, Wrexley. Petron is here, inside Redmondis. Can you not feel him yourself? Have your senses become so dulled?'

Wrexley stood shaking in front of them, holding himself clenched and still. 'I … I know. I will see him once I have made my report.'

'Good.' Biore smiled quickly, his teeth shining red in the moonlight. 'Be on your guard. Cortis will no longer hesitate to remove you should you get in his way.'

'Cortis knows better than to get in my way.'

Biore grinned again. 'Ah, it is good to see this side of you again, Wrexley. Something tells me we will need it soon enough.' He bowed quickly then, and Wrexley stalked past them and into the shadows.

Wilt had a thousand questions for Biore running through his head, but he settled on one. 'Wrexley and Petron are wards? Does that mean something important?'

'Only that they share the same shape, the same thoughts. At times the same mind. It is as close as two people can be. They were once a very strong force within these walls. Then the Nine Sisters took control, and such pooling of power was named anathema.'

'Why? Why should the Sisters care?'

'For the same reason anyone cares about what others do. Ignorance and fear. The Sisters are linked so deeply they have lost all individuality. They have no mind of their own, and are therefore unable to share themselves fully with anyone. Their bodies are not their own, merely vehicles for a part of the greater mind. They cannot take other forms, so ban such expressions of power in others.'

'They cannot change shape? But Cortis—'

'Cortis is useful, nothing more. He knows that well enough himself. A dog at the beck and call of its mistress. The Sisters would do without him if they could.' Biore looked up at the night sky and took a deep breath, closing his eyes as if drinking the cool darkness in.

'And you, Master? What do the Sisters use you for?'

Biore sighed and looked at Wilt, his face still and calm and suddenly sad. 'That, Wilt, is best left for another time. Come. It is late, and it looks like tomorrow will be an interesting day.'

He turned and walked toward the light of the stables. Wilt stood alone in the dark, listening to the night sounds until a wolf's howl sung out from the darkness and he hurried to catch up.

Chapter 23

Wilt had intended to head straight to Higgs's room once he returned to his own, but when he closed the door and saw Delco fast asleep in the darkness, a wave of exhaustion crashed over him. He climbed into his own bed and collapsed into sleep.

His dreams were vivid and confused, peopled with eagles, wolves and serpents, and red, sharpened teeth glinting in the moonlight. His body faded into an ethereal mist as a great cold sunk into his bones.

Wilt woke to find his bedding thrown back and his body shivering in the cool of the early morning. He sat up, hugging his chest to push away the deep chill that had wrapped around him. Delco stood by the window, gazing out at the dawn, totally oblivious to Wilt. Wilt wrapped a blanket over his shoulders and swung his legs over the side of the bed.

'Morning.'

'Hmm,' Delco grunted in reply and continued staring.

Suddenly aware he was intruding, Wilt stood up and began fussing with the small stove squatting in the corner of the room.

Delco's voice suddenly cut across the silence. 'I never noticed the trees before. Isn't that strange? The way they move, like the whole forest is alive.'

Wilt looked up, but his intuition told him not to reply, not to talk at all.

'My brother—Rawick—he used to tell me that the trees had a

consciousness too, a language, and that if you could find the right weld, you would be able to understand them. Of course, those trees were nothing like these. Imagine the stories they could tell.'

Delco turned to face Wilt. 'I never told you about Rawick, did I?'

'Your brother? I think you mentioned him. There were two who were Black Robes.'

'Plaxo and Sensi. I had a third brother, Rawick. He was always the strongest. And the kindest. Here, let me.'

Delco nudged Wilt away from the stove and began to organise the coffee pot. Wilt surrendered it easily and sat on his bed, pulling the blanket tighter around his shoulders.

'Rawick was the eldest. When my father was away, which was most of the time, he was placed in charge of me. Of all of us really. Sensi and Plaxo were only a year apart, and old enough to look after themselves, so they spent most of their time away too. I was much younger. Most of the time it was just Rawick and me. I preferred that anyway. Plaxo and Sensi were … they were not kind.'

Delco poured the coffee grains into the pot and set it on the stove, his hands practiced and calm.

'Rawick was the first one to teach me about welds, about what it can mean to be a wielder. A real wielder, he used to say, not just a Black Robe. He didn't think much of Black Robes. I think he saw how Father suffered. He used to call it the "Redmondis yoke". He was never really cut out for all of this.'

He set two cups on the table as the smell of the coffee brewing filled the room.

'Rawick didn't think much of Redmondis. When the time came to enter its walls, he refused. Said he'd rather stay and complete his studies on his own. His research, he called it. Father knew better than to argue when Rawick put his foot down. I think Rawick reminded him too much of my mother.'

Delco poured the thick, rich liquid into the cups and handed one to Wilt. He took it gratefully, his hands wrapped around the hot cup as the steam tickled his nose.

'He used to take me out with him, into the forest. We'd swim in the river until dark, then make camp. Not have to see any of the others for days.' Delco took a quick sip of his coffee. 'They were the best days. After Plaxo and Sensi had left one day, Rawick took me out again. Showed me what he was studying.' He walked back to the window and leaned out, staring blankly out at the sea of trees far below them. 'He used a white weld on me. Took control of me completely. It was as though we shared the same mind. But more than that, the same thoughts, the same desires. It was as though suddenly there was no such separate thing as Delco and Rawick. There was only the one. For a moment it was wonderful.'

Delco sipped his coffee and placed it carefully on the sill, watching the steam rise and disappear into the sunlight.

'He wasn't trained, you understand. He didn't mean it to happen. But my mind, my child's mind, it couldn't maintain the weld. It collapsed.'

Silence stretched out between them for a moment.

'I don't remember much more than flashes now. Rawick screaming at me, inside me, to try and hold it back. Hold what back? My mind wasn't fully formed, I couldn't grasp what he wanted me to do. It was like I was drowning. I remember panic, as though a heavy blanket had been pulled tight over me, then a great sadness, then cold, the cold of death and nothingness.'

Delco picked up his cup and held it to his lips. Wilt could see the cup trembling in his hand.

'When I woke up, Rawick was gone. It must have been hours later—it was dark and cold. I was on the floor of our basement, and I could hear Plaxo and Sensi stomping around the kitchen above us—above me. There was only me.'

The coffee seemed to strengthen him, and he turned around to face Wilt.

'I was changed. From that moment on I could wield as well as my brothers. Better, even. There were other differences. I had thoughts I'd never had before. I liked coffee. I'd always hated the stuff before.'

'You'd picked up something of Rawick's?'

'Exactly. He'd left some part of himself inside me, some imprint. It was all we had left. When Father finally returned, I told him what had happened, tried to describe it as best I could. He was never very good with us, with his children. I think he knew that. He was no help. I used to catch him staring at me, sometimes, studying me as if I was an interesting specimen. As if he was trying to catch me out at something.'

'What happened to Rawick?'

Delco put his cup on the table and sat down on his bed with a sigh. 'I don't know. He was … absorbed. Not by me, but by the weld itself. Something in the power. Something Biore knows.'

'You don't trust him, do you?'

'I'm afraid of him. He's dangerous.'

Wilt could see the pain and loss behind Delco's eyes. And something else. Guilt.

'I know.'

Wilt walked down the worn, curving staircase toward the dining room, lost in his thoughts. As he descended, he became aware of a change in the air, something unusual that brought him out of his musings. Noise. The sound of people talking—arguing and laughing over their meals.

It was just as the Sisters had said. The block had been lifted. The Black Robes were free.

The normally orderly room was in chaos. Tables and chairs were pushed together in haphazard patterns across the room, and black-robed figures were leaning forward, talking excitedly, greeting each other as if they'd each woken from a long sleep.

Wilt hovered at the base of the staircase, suddenly proud. This was what he'd first imagined Redmondis to be. Like minds revelling in discovery.

There was something else, too. Power. He let himself drop into the well within himself, and suddenly he saw the welds dancing across the room. Welds of all colours and sizes, wrestling with each other, snapping back and forth like playful animals with minds of their own. The students were testing themselves, finding their strength, no longer afraid to experiment.

Wilt's chest itched where Petron's amulet had rested, and he reached absentmindedly under his shirt and traced the scarred skin. His fingers could still make out the shape, carved forever now into his chest. A heat flared within himself as he pictured the shape in his mind, a warm rush of power that surged up and settled over him.

He finally entered the dining room. Welds bounced off him as he walked, sliding harmlessly away from his mind, unable to find any purchase. Those who wielded them frowned in frustration momentarily before heading off to find other, easier targets. There was no malice in it, but Wilt preferred to keep his mind to himself. It was trifling to keep these welds away.

Wilt contented himself to sit and eat and watch the eager madness surrounding him. The faces of the young men positively glowed. They were vaguely familiar, yet so changed, so lit up with life that he abandoned trying to remember who was who. A tall boy next to him sent out a bright red weld toward a smaller boy sitting two rows over. The weld flew across the room, burning a path through two other welds that got in its way, before shooting down onto the boy's head and bursting in a shower of sparks. The victim yelped in quick pain and snorted his mouthful of food all over himself. He looked around, trying to identify his attacker. The boy next to Wilt doubled over with laughter, and it didn't take long for his victim to notice.

'No fair! No sparking at the dinner table!'

That brought even more laughter, and the smaller boy went bright red.

'Right. Two can play at that game.'

A thin green weld slithered out from him, bending and sliding its way across the room, dodging other welds before striking at the tall boy. The boy's face immediately went green, and he swayed slightly in his seat as a deep nausea took hold.

'No—' he started to protest, but had to stop as his stomach flipped and his cheeks suddenly bulged.

The others on the smaller boy's table crowed with laughter and patted him on the back. Wilt grinned as the tall boy struggled to hold his breakfast down. The nausea passed in seconds, and his face returned to its normal colour.

He smiled at the boy who'd attacked him so effectively. 'Nice one. I'll have to remember that.'

'Hey!' A voice called out from the front of the room, demanding everyone's attention. 'The seniors have challenged the guards to flagball! In the courtyard!'

The owner of the voice ducked out of the room, eager to spread the news. The Black Robes in the dining room looked at each other and grinned. Flagball. Why not? It seemed to make sense in the mood of giddy celebration that had engulfed Redmondis.

Wilt leaned over to the boy next to him and tapped him on the shoulder. 'Flagball? I thought only Greystone played that game.'

The boy pulled a face and shook his head. 'Oh no, it's been played here in Redmondis for years. At least, it used to be. The central courtyard was built specifically for it. My father would never shut up about his games. Used to boast about not having lost to the guard team in over a decade. Made his fortune always betting on black.'

The boy grinned and sprang from the bench to rush out with the others, and Wilt was left on his own. He finally pushed himself up and followed the crowd out into the sunlight toward the courtyard.

The streets were teeming with life, crowds of crafters wandering to and fro, discussing their various trades and chatting loudly with the Black Robes as they passed, offering their services. They too looked as though they had woken from a long dream. Wilt had never before considered the hold the Sisters must have had on all levels of Redmondis.

A single voice called out through the gabble of the crowd, grabbing his attention. 'Interested in a mind mirror, boy?'

Wilt turned toward the voice. It belonged to a strange old man, a crafter by the look of him, and a not very reputable one at that. The man was short, with a few thin strands of grey hair sticking out from his weathered scalp, his hands deep in the pockets of his long overcoat. He took Wilt's momentary interest as a sign to continue his spiel, and swung one arm out to reveal a collection of strangely shaped baubles hanging inside his coat.

'Best of their kind in Redmondis. Never get caught out again. Guaranteed to deflect any and all welds coming your way. Favourite of all the players.'

Wilt stopped to examine the objects. They were small spheres of polished glass, but as he looked harder, he realised they showed no reflection.

'Players?' he asked, trying to keep the man talking to give him time to study the mind mirrors.

'The flagball players. Can't do without them playing here. Too many wielders trying to influence the game. You take a step out onto the field without a mind mirror and you're lost before you start. Had some of these stored away for years, since before the Restoration.' The old man leaned sideways and spat on the ground, as though the word itself left a bad taste in his mouth. 'Go ahead, boy. Take a closer look.'

Wilt reached out for one of the mind mirrors. The surface of the sphere seemed to be liquid glass, silver waves washing back and forth under the glass. Higgs would like these.

'How much?'

'Twenty. But for you, you being a Black Robe and all, I'll take fifteen.'

Wilt smiled as he reached into his tunic for a coin. 'You'll take five.'

He flipped the coin in the air and grabbed the mind mirror he had been examining, then walked away as the crafter grabbed the coin out of the air and began to protest. Wilt stepped quickly into the road and lost himself in the growing crowd, the crafter's angry calls fading into the general chatter. As he slipped the mind mirror into his pocket, he smiled to himself. Higgs would never have forgiven him if he'd paid full price.

The thought of Higgs brought a twist of melancholy into Wilt's thoughts, but he pushed the feeling down and tried to enjoy himself. Higgs was probably still sleeping anyway. He'd go visit him this afternoon, after the game.

The walkway lining the courtyard was teeming with people by the time Wilt arrived, three and four deep in places, but he knew how to move through crowds quickly, and he slid his way to a place at the front and surveyed the scene.

Sure enough, a flagball court had been marked out in the packed dirt. Two groups were loosely gathered together, one at either end; obviously the two teams who were about to compete. One seemed mostly made up of guards, though they weren't wearing their helms. The other seemed a rough mix of Black Robes and older crafters, thick set and heavy shouldered, as though the Black Robes had found the largest bodies they could to try to offset whatever physical advantage the guards would have. Wilt turned to the guard team and stopped as he spotted the tall slender figure who strode confidently toward the opposing team.

The world around him was suddenly silent as Daemi moved, her curled black hair dancing in the wind. She looked toward him and a smile broke out across her face, and the world rushed back in.

Wilt realised he was grinning and waving like a fool and quickly dropped his hands as Daemi continued on to talk to the opposing captain.

'Know her, do ye?'

Wilt looked to his left to see a heavily bearded old crafter peering up at him.

'Excuse me?'

'The guard, the captain. You know her?'

'Er—yeah.'

'She any good?'

'I've no idea.' Wilt thought suddenly of Daemi dancing through the air as she came in to strike him, and her quick, cat-like movements and impossibly fast feet as they'd duelled daily on the road to Redmondis. 'But yes, I imagine she's very good.'

That seemed enough for the old man, who nodded quickly and moved away. 'I'll wager ten gold on the guards!'

His voice was lost in the crowd as he pushed through, and Wilt turned back to the field to watch the game.

The players had arranged themselves across the court, and a weathered ball had appeared from somewhere to sit expectantly in the centre circle. The crowd noise rose into a dull roar as Daemi stood alone in the centre of the field, resting the ball in her hands, and Wilt felt a thrill run through him.

He looked around the courtyard again and suddenly saw how it had been designed as a flagball court originally. The dimensions of it, the way the walls sloped up to provide the crowd with a view of the action. How long had it been since it had actually held a game?

The air seemed to vibrate with excitement, as though the stone of Redmondis itself was taking a deep, cleansing breath.

The noise of the crowd changed as Daemi started, and Wilt lost all thought of anything but the game.

It was obvious both teams had played before, though they appeared a little rusty at first. Passes went wayward, tackles flew in late, but after just a few minutes the pace of the game lifted. Daemi was just as fast and skilled as Wilt had imagined she would be, and always seemed to have time whenever the ball came her way, as if everyone around her suddenly slowed down. Her direct opponent, an older Black Robe that Wilt hadn't seen before, was almost as fast, however, and his teammates seemed to know each other better. They would step into position for the pass a moment before their opposition, and eventually worked their way through the guard's defence to score a clever goal, though the guard's flag stayed safe for the time being.

Wilt cheered the goal just as heartily as those around him, happy to be witness to such a skilled game.

'What're you cheering about? We're losing!'

Wilt looked down to see Daemi glaring angrily up at him, her fists balanced on the points of her hips.

'Um, just happy to see everyone enjoying themselves.' His voice faded into a mutter.

The game restarted, and this time the guard team began to make better progress, switching the ball out to the wing and using the pace of the young guard on the left who had at least a couple of yards on his direct opponent, a heavily built crafter who looked like he had been enjoying himself a little too much this morning.

The young guard feinted past his opponent, bumping him to the side and leaving him sprawled awkwardly in the dirt, and sent the ball into the middle, where Daemi rose above the small pack that had formed to crash her fists against the ball and send it flying toward the Black Robes' goal. Only a fantastic diving save from the last defender kept the ball out, and Wilt could see the spirits of the guard team lift as they chased after the ball again. Eventually the Black Robes cleared it high over the crowd and the players moved back to their positions as someone went to fetch the ball.

The wing crafter trotted over toward the sidelines, gesturing for someone. Wilt's gaze was drawn to him by instinct. There had been something about that last tackle attempt, the way the crafter had stumbled too easily into the young guard. He'd seen that kind of move before. Sure enough, the crafter reached out to a Black Robe in the crowd, and Wilt caught a glimpse of shining silver in his hand before the Black Robe grasped it and nodded.

The crafter jogged back to his position, a new spring in his step. Wilt then saw the Black Robe huddling with some others. They were planning something.

A high whistle brought Wilt's attention back to the game as it resumed, and the guards quickly moved the ball out to their winger again. The crafter backed off him this time, seemingly happy to give ground rather than be caught diving in again. The winger grinned broadly, jogging upfield with the ball. Daemi and the other guards pushed forward, waiting for the cross to come in.

Then Wilt felt it. A rush of cold, as though a breeze blew directly from the snowy mountain tops high above them.

The guard stopped where he was, then turned and began to run back the way he had come. The wrong way.

The guards and half the crowd shouted at him, but the young guard seemed completely oblivious. The crafter jogged happily behind him, as though he had been waiting for just such an occurrence.

Wilt looked toward the Black Robes in the crowd, but there was only an empty space where they had been. He felt the cold wind again, from farther down the court now, and turned to follow it. He saw the small group of Black Robes scurrying behind the crowd, their heads huddled together as though deep in discussion, the young winger on the court following directly parallel to them, as though they were attached in some way.

Wilt concentrated and reached out for the cold.

A thick black weld filled the air above the court, joining the young winger and the group of Black Robes in the crowd. But the Black Robes weren't just reading him; they were taking control of his body. For a full second, Wilt admired the power and skill it took to craft such a powerful weld. Then he dived in.

The weld swarmed around him as he joined with it, a deep cold sinking into his bones and stopping his breath. Wilt almost gave in to the panic, then regained control.

The weld was actually a rope, a twisted braid of five individual black welds. Wilt pulled at them experimentally, but they slipped out of his grasp. These Black Robes were well trained.

Some other part of him was aware of the winger reaching the

far end of the court and heading toward the guards' goal, the crowd screaming now, the other guards charging toward him, waving their hands in the air.

Suddenly Wilt remembered Master Biore grinning at him, his teeth glinting red in the moonlight. The weld couldn't be unpicked, but perhaps it could be drained.

Wilt grasped the nearest cord and pulled it into him, dropping through the cold into the deep silence beneath.

Three things happened. On one plane, the young winger stumbled to a halt and looked around, as if waking from a strange dream. On another, deeper plane, the black weld suddenly frayed as one part of it was sucked away. And deeper still, Wilt felt a surge of cold so deep and satisfying that it awoke a deep hunger in him. He reached out again, desperate for more.

The weld bucked and twisted away from him, stung by the sudden drain on its power. The group of Black Robes on the sidelines milled in confusion as one of their number collapsed to the ground, completely comatose.

Wilt wasn't finished. He clawed toward the weld, sucking it into himself, revelling in its icy touch. The winger had been released, now free of the weld's control, but Wilt's hunger didn't care. It wanted more. It wanted everything. The empty stillness wrapped around him, held him in a deep, silent embrace.

Another of the Black Robes fell, and the weld continued to shrink in size. The remaining Black Robes tried to rally then, gathering their strength and pushing desperately at Wilt's draining touch. The weld surged at the young winger, sending a pulse of power that knocked him completely off his feet, leaving him stunned in the dirt. Wilt felt the surge as a brief splash of warmth, a spark that flickered and died as it drowned in his depths.

The three Black Robes who were still conscious buckled to their knees as their weld turned on them, sucking them dry. They were beaten; the weld had snapped back from the young guard on the field, but Wilt held it and continued to drain. There could be no thought of releasing them, no thought at all except that of his hunger.

'Enough.'

A hand was on his shoulder, a warmth surging into him, into his conscious mind.

'Release them, Wilt.'

Master Biore. It was his voice, something beyond his words telling him he understood the hunger, he understood it and controlled it, and that Wilt could too. Wilt stared at the weld in front of him, a thin, sickly umbilical, and let it go.

The Black Robes on the sidelines had collapsed to the ground, and a small crowd had formed around them. A healer was bent over one of them, patting him on the cheek, whispering secret words. Wilt saw the Black Robe stir, then looked away.

'How do you feel?'

Biore was standing beside him, his hand still resting on his shoulder. Wilt brushed it off as he faced him. How did he feel? Power surged through him, ready to strike.

'The hunger must be controlled, Wilt. You must not lose yourself in its depths.'

Biore peered into him, as though watching an inner struggle Wilt was only partly conscious of. Some part of him wanted to reach out to Biore, take hold of him and revel in the cold satisfaction of power.

A call from the field distracted them both. 'Wilt!'

Daemi's voice. Wilt saw her image in his mind and suddenly felt a great release as he let the hunger go and his mind cleared.

'Wilt! Come down here. We need a winger!'

'I'm okay,' he whispered, as much to himself as to Biore, who simply nodded in return. 'Okay!' Wilt leaped onto the field.

Daemi watched him jog over, her gaze cool and steady. 'You don't look like much, but Higgs told me you're not half bad at this game.'

Wilt grinned at her and began cinching his Black Robe up around his legs. 'I've had my moments.'

'Well, just keep yourself out on that wing. And watch that crafter. He's faster with his hands than he looks.'

'I know. I saw him lift the mind mirror from your man.'

'Joyce should have known better, but he's young. Of course, we shouldn't need the damn things anyway. Still, that's what you get for playing with Black Robes. Can't trust any of you to play fair.'

Wilt just smiled in reply and jogged to his position on the field.

Daemi's idea of fair play began as soon as the whistle blew to restart the match. The two largest guards charged straight at the Black Robe with the ball, who saw what was coming and passed it quickly toward his own goal. The two guards ignored the ball completely and ploughed straight into the man, crunching their shoulders into his chest to leave him wheezing in the dirt.

Daemi jogged past and threw a lazy foot into his ribs. 'One all.' She looked up then to see Wilt gawking at her and waved angrily at him. 'What are you staring at? Keep your eye on the ball!'

The ball had been thrown toward his wing, and Wilt started toward it, easily catching the ball and outpacing the crafter still manning his position.

The two were in yards of space, Daemi's guards having continued their earlier charge to take out another of the Black Robes' defenders.

The crafter slowed his heavy sprint as he got closer to Wilt, who was waiting patiently for him, his foot resting lightly on the top of the ball.

'Here.'

A silver glint flashed in the air and caught the crafter's eye as Wilt tossed the mind mirror toward him. He looked up to follow its path through the air, and Wilt suddenly cannoned the ball into his face with a quick, powerful kick, sending him sprawling in the dirt, his eyes dancing with stars.

The ball had bounced high off the man's face and Wilt gathered it in as he skipped past the barely conscious crafter.

'Eyes on the ball.'

Wilt sprinted toward the goal, the ball rolling easily at his feet. The Black Robes must have had other friends in the crowd, because light touches passed over his mind as he went, as though other welds were striking at him but slipping off, unable to find any purchase. Wilt recognised the part of him that wanted to reach out to each one, feel its power within him and drain it, suck it dry. He could do it now, he knew how. He wouldn't even have to break stride.

Wilt pushed the thought away and reached out instead to Daemi. It wasn't a weld as such, at least not any kind he recognised, but he felt a true connection with her mind, telling her where to be and knowing she would understand. Then he curled a sharp, whipping cross into the box directly into her waiting hands. It was easy.

But Daemi wasn't there. Wilt stumbled to catch himself after kicking the ball, and felt a rush of wind as the noise of the world returned. The sound of the crowd had changed; they were no longer cheering, they were crying out in panic.

A wolf's howl cut across the courtyard from the direction of the main gates. No words were needed. The howl spoke directly into each man's heart. Death was coming.

The crowd lining the pitch pushed and trampled each other in their rush away from the gates. Wilt caught a glimpse of Daemi running to organise her guard, but the crowd had spilled out onto the pitch and he lost her in the panic. Another howl sounded, much closer now, and following it was the steady cadence of marching feet.

High above, a lone eagle cried out in answer, circling slowly above the chaos. A flurry of arrows arced toward it and it banked easily away from the gates.

Petron. No, not Petron. Wrexley. Trying to warn them. Cortis was taking control. Wilt knew the thought to be true as soon as it came to him.

'Wilt!' Daemi pushed through the crowd, her ten-man guard fighting against the bodies that rushed past them, trying to maintain formation. 'Cortis. The wolves. Get to Higgs.' She pulled her sword free as the first of the wolves entered the courtyard.

Wilt didn't wait to watch. Suddenly he was running, his four legs pumping, dancing through the clumsy bodies above him, darting up a wall to the empty freedom of the rooftops, the slate cool and sure under his padded feet.

Higgs.

The idea throbbed in his animal mind. A high window. The scent of food and warmth. He ran on, faster than thought, leaving the human chaos behind.

Chapter 24

Wilt's dreams were of whispers and smoke, slithering welds and the heat and suck of promised power. He was a wolf, racing along in the hunt, its maw bloody from a fresh kill. The pack behind him followed eagerly, taking back what should always have been theirs.

No. It wasn't his dream. It was another's, someone else's mind. Cortis.

The darkness began to spin and a wave of nausea forced him into consciousness.

'Here. He's waking up.' Old Pete's voice. There was something comforting about that.

'About time! I'm supposed to be the one in recovery.' And Higgs.

Wilt began to sit up, and immediately regretted it.

'Whoa. Slow down there, Wilt. One thing at a time.' A hand pushed him down on the bed and Petron's face leaned into view. 'Not feeling too good, I expect?'

'You look terrible.' Higgs pushed in beside Petron and frowned at him. 'Your skin looks green.'

A fresh roll of nausea rumbled in Wilt's belly and he took a deep breath to keep the contents of his stomach down.

Petron nudged Higgs out of the way. 'That's enough of that. Get some coffee going. Make yourself useful.'

Higgs's mumble faded to the far side of the room. 'Comes in and kicks me out of bed …'

'Do you know where you are?' Petron stared into Wilt's eyes, studying them.

'He's in my bed is where he is.'

'Silence!' Petron threw an angry look across at Higgs, who sank into a low grumble as he pottered about the fire.

'Higgs. I'm in Higgs's room.'

'So, not completely lost then.' Petron patted a cool damp cloth across Wilt's forehead.

Wilt thought about trying to sit up again, but decided against it.

'You've been draining people.'

'I ... Yes.' He felt guilty, though he wasn't sure why.

'Not the most worthy use of your power.'

'Why do I feel like this?'

'Because you deserve to.' Petron's face broke into a smile. 'At least, that's what my father would have said to you. And many of my teachers. Yours too, if you had any who knew what they were talking about.'

'Here.' Higgs handed a steaming cup of coffee to Petron, who held it out for Wilt to sip.

'Take it slowly. You took in a lot of power from others, then used it all up at once. Your body wants more. It hungers for it.'

'Sounds like a hangover to me.'

Petron chuckled and nodded his head. 'Yes, yes, I suppose that is an apt analogy. A hangover.' He frowned suddenly at Higgs. 'What do you know about hangovers?'

'I know enough to not want to have another one. I know the best cure too!' Higgs ducked away and resumed his pottering.

'Sometimes I wonder about that boy. Far too worldly for his years.'

Wilt smiled and felt better immediately.

'There. That helps, doesn't it? There is a reason draining the welds of others is dangerous, Wilt. You lose something of yourself each time. And each time the hunger grows.'

Wilt closed his eyes and saw a cold white face gazing back at him. 'Like Biore.'

'Yes.' Petron's voice was suddenly sad. 'Like Master Biore. He was one of our best, once.'

'And now?'

'Now? Now he suffers for certain choices he has made.'

'Nothing like a fry up to cure a hangover!' Higgs popped back into view, bringing with him a plate stacked with bacon, sausages and greasy eggs.

Wilt groaned as his stomach protested.

'Get that out of here, rascal.' Petron pushed Higgs toward the fire and out of Wilt's sight, mercifully taking the plate with him. Petron glared at him, making sure he stayed on the other side of the room, but continued talking to Wilt. 'Biore is a man stuck in between worlds. No longer quite human.'

'In between? So what else is he?' Wilt sat up slowly, relieved to feel his stomach stay where it was supposed to.

Petron looked like he was considering how to answer him, but Wilt's attention was suddenly taken by something else in the room.

In the far corner, leaning against the wall, was what had to be the moonsteel blade Higgs had purchased, the one Cortis and his dogs had been so keen to find out about. It was glowing.

Wilt held out a slightly shaking finger and pointed at it.

Petron glanced across the room and frowned. 'Yes. Moonsteel. I never thought I'd see one within these walls. We have all heard stories, of course. It is dangerous, especially for wielders. It shares something of the same power.'

'Something from within the welds?'

'Perhaps. It is said the craftsmen of the Eastern Dales have very different ideas about power and what price we should be willing to pay for access to it. There is a reason such tools were named anathema. As for the glow ... it senses the presence of those it was forged to destroy.'

Higgs skipped over to grab the blade. 'Great, isn't it? Something in the metal reacts to the presence of the wolves. I've been trying to work out exactly how they did it but—'

The wolves. Cortis.

'Daemi!' Wilt tried to swing to his feet, but was pushed down by Petron as another wave of dizziness struck.

'It's okay, Wilt. Daemi is safe. We know all about Cortis's latest gambit.'

'How?'

'Young Higgs here does have his uses, it seems.'

Higgs leaned back into view, holding a new object: what looked like a small stone chess piece. Wilt could see it was a soldier, its helm pushed back to reveal Daemi's face. The figurine seemed to come to life, moving its mouth as though whispering something.

'Just a little something I picked up from Heather—er, one of the other crafters. They're made in pairs. Daemi has the other one—looks like me—and they can talk to each other.'

Wilt looked at Petron, wondering whether he should believe what Higgs was telling him.

'Oh yes, they seem to work well enough. This one told us about the invasion of the courtyard. Daemi rallied the troops still loyal to Wrexley and managed to push them back. Saved a lot of innocent people, I expect. Cortis must have decided he's had his fill of waiting in the shadows. Daemi and the others have barricaded themselves in the armoury at the guard barracks. Cortis and his dogs are ignoring them for now—they're too busy rounding up all the Black Robes.'

'What do we do?' Wilt's voice was weaker now, and the room began to blur at the edges.

'We? For now we rest. You especially. We'll need all your strength soon.'

Petron patted Wilt's forehead with the cloth again, and Wilt sank deeper with each touch. Some part of him was aware that he was being drugged, but another, stronger part knew he could trust Old Pete and he let himself go.

Wilt sank gratefully into the void, a dead weight floating in the still, dark air. Below him a black vortex writhed and twisted, aware of his presence, calling to him. Waiting for him. He floated above it, out of its reach, cradled in a web of thick welds, each of them disappearing into the light, into separate minds he shared a connection with. Every now and then a shiver vibrated down one of them and his dreams changed, visions communicated from the world above. From other eyes.

In his sleep, Wilt's lips moved in response and whispered her name.

The first Daemi knew of any trouble was on the pitch, just after watching Wilt blast his way past the fat crafter with a not entirely legal move. Still, it was the least they deserved. Daemi shouldered her way past another of the Black Robes, sending a quick elbow into his ribs for good measure, leaving him crouched over and gagging in the dust. If they wanted to play dirty, she was happy to oblige.

She was manoeuvring herself into position to receive Wilt's cross when she heard the first howl. No one else seemed to have heard it, but Daemi knew to trust her instincts, and turned to the crowd just as the first of the wolves broke over the top of them.

It was massive, easily three times as large as a natural wolf, and its eyes were red and gleaming with an all too human hunger. It landed on the shoulders of a Black Robe at the front of the crowd, pushing him face first into the ground and knocking him unconscious. Then it leaped toward the next nearest Black Robe, eager to engage.

Daemi dropped into a crouch and pushed her way through the players, trying to keep pace.

The wolf reached its next target, swatting the Black Robe across the back of his head with a heavy paw, knocking him senseless. For a wicked moment it stood over the prone man, long teeth glistening, mouth eager. Daemi thought it was about to bite down on the man's neck, but it sprang away instead, heading toward another small group of wielders. She lost sight of it in the crowd.

They were making sure there would be no resistance. Where were the guards?

'To me!' Daemi stood up straight and pulled her long knife from its sheath, its honed metal shining in the sunlight.

'Captain!' Two of her guards responded immediately and drew their blades, standing either side of her.

'Come. We have to try and protect them.'

The guards froze, only nodding as howls sang through the air. More were coming.

The crowd was in chaos now, bodies rushing past in panic. Daemi darted through the waves of people to where she had last seen the wolf.

She stumbled into a sudden gap in the crowd to find the wolf standing over another victim, this one bleeding from a long gash across the back of his neck, whimpering slightly as he lay there.

'You!' Daemi lowered her blade and held it straight out at the wolf. Its mouth twisted into something like a grin. 'Come play with someone your own size.'

The wolf sprang at her with lightning grace, and Daemi only just had time to roll underneath the heavy body. It turned in mid-air and snapped at where her head had been, its body crashing lengthwise into the other two guards, sending them sprawling.

Daemi rolled to her feet and charged after it, keen to get in a strike before it found its feet again, but the wolf was too agile, springing straight at her. She fell backward, her knees bending as she skidded through the dirt, her shoulders almost touching the ground behind her. She held her blade tightly above her, and the wolf landed directly onto it.

Hot blood sprayed onto Daemi as she slid out from under the wolf, leaving only a corpse behind her.

Standing, she reached down and pulled the closest guard to his feet. 'Go! Gather whoever you can find. Head to the armoury. They won't hurt the Black Robes unless they have to, but any guards they'll happily kill. I'll circle about the other way and do the same.'

She turned toward the latest howls, pausing only to wipe her blade clean on the pelt of the dead wolf at her feet.

The vision faded and again there was only darkness, cold and still as death.

No, there was something else. Something inside the darkness. Within it. A self, a mind. Wilt's own mind.

Wilt slowly became aware of the boundaries between his mind and the nothingness that was everything outside himself.

Then a sound. A voice. Petron.

'You should never have led him down your path.' He was angry at someone, though controlled.

'I led him nowhere. His own power brought him here.' Biore. Unflinching in reply. Calm, as though stepping past old arguments.

'Now is not the time to place blame, Petron. We must decide on the best action to take.' Wrexley now. Weariness in his voice. The world he knew was gone, replaced by one he always suspected lurked beneath.

'Cortis has taken control of the streets. His dogs guard every corner. The Black Robes have been confined to their tower.' Biore again. Waiting for something.

'The guards?' Petron, back on track, trying to find a way forward.

'Those who resisted are mostly dead. Daemi has organised a few—twenty or thirty of them at most. They've barricaded themselves in the armoury. She awaits my order.' Wrexley, pride in his voice. A father's pride, nothing more.

A warmth moved through him at the thought, but let it sink away into the darkness. He was conscious of his body now, lying still on the bed, the heat of a fire on one side of him, his eyelids closed.

'Something else. They have captured one—one of Cortis's dogs. Penned it in. She wants to know what to do with it.'

'Put the thing out of its misery.' Petron, always mercy first.

'No! Let me try to break into its mind. We must know more about Cortis's plans,' Biore said, unable to disguise the hunger in his voice.

'Isn't it obvious? The Sisters lost control. They have moved quickly to regain it.' Wrexley again. So that is what his disappointment stemmed from. He had lost his faith.

'There must be more to it than that. Petron, you must be able to see.'

A pause. Wilt's mind saw them each glare at the other. Old friends, grown apart.

'He's right, Wrexley. We need to make the most of any advantage we can find.'

'But what good can it do? What can we learn from such a thing? Can you even get through to its mind?'

'Perhaps.' Biore, still calm, still waiting.

Suddenly Wilt realised what he was waiting for and opened his eyes. 'No.' He sat up as they turned toward him. 'He can't. But I can.'

As soon as he was satisfied Wilt was in good hands, Higgs had left to check on Heather. He told himself he was duty bound to do so. Higgs didn't stop to analyse his feelings about it; he simply gathered his things and headed into the tunnels that joined all the crafters halls, over to her room in the neighbouring tower where most of the female crafters lived.

There was no official segregation of the sexes; crafters tended to gravitate toward those who shared their particular interests. Healers lived together, as did the weapon smiths and potion makers, as did those who had yet to decide on their particular specialty, such as Higgs. Heather had decided long ago to focus on crafting jewellery, charms such as mind mirrors that gave the wearer protection from uninvited welds. Her tower was full of other crafters with similar interests, and Higgs had to stop himself from getting too distracted by the rows of sparkling goodies lining the walls as he proceeded through the narrow hallway toward her room. His fingers itched as his eyes scanned the treasures, noting the location of certain items of interest in his mind. Perhaps he would drop by here again when he had more time. Keep his skills up.

When he'd last seen her, Heather had been unconscious, her face swollen with painful bruises where the big guard—Funes, Higgs spat the name in his mind—had knocked her down. The healer had promised the damage looked worse than it really was, that she would be fine after some rest, but Higgs still felt some trepidation as he knocked lightly and pushed open the door to her room.

His worries disappeared in a second as a high squeal greeted him.

'Higgsy!' A body flew into him and pushed him against the door as light, quick kisses rained over his face. 'My hero ... You stood up to the guards for me ... I've never ...'

Higgs wasn't sure how she managed to get the words out between kisses, and he was surprised to find he didn't mind the attention, but he pushed her away and looked at her face. She seemed completely healed; the purple bruises had faded and the swelling was completely gone. The only sign he could see of the recent travails was a small red scar at the side of her nose. It was almost cute.

'Oh! You've noticed it already, haven't you?' Heather stepped back and held her hand over her nose to hide the scar.

'Don't be silly. It's nothing. And don't call me Higgsy.'

Heather smiled again and dropped her hand. She looked like she was about to resume the kissing and hugging, so Higgs side-stepped her quickly and walked past her into the room.

The healer's potions and herbs had been packed away, and Heather's charms and works in progress were spread throughout most of the room. The sight made him feel better still. She was obviously working again already.

'Here. I've got something for you.' Heather began rummaging in a small chest next to her bed, tossing half forged trinkets aside as she delved in. Finally she found what she was looking for and held it up triumphantly. 'A present for my hero.'

Higgs looked at the necklace hanging from her hand, spinning slowly in the air, and swallowed. 'Uh, thanks.'

He slowly reached for it, but Heather stepped past him and threw it around his neck, standing behind him to fasten it securely in place.

'There's no need to—'

'Oh yes there is. I know you, Higgsy. You'll shove it into your pocket and forget about it. Probably already have three other gifts from me already in there. This one is made to be worn, and I'm going to make sure of it.'

She whispered a strange word then, and a sharp heat pierced the back of his neck.

'Hey!'

'Oh, stop fussing.' Heather slapped him lightly on the shoulder and spun him around to face her. 'There. Looks very smart.'

Higgs held the charm up to inspect it. It was a small red stone, the size of his thumb, oval shaped and cut in a way that seemed to hold the light inside it rather than reflect it. It was actually quite modest compared to some of Heather's other efforts.

'What is it?'

'A heartstone.'

'A what?' Higgs dropped the stone as if burnt and pulled on the chain holding it around his neck.

'A heartstone. It will help me keep track of you, my love.'

'Love? What are you talking about, woman?' Higgs desperately pulled at the chain, but it seemed unnaturally strong.

'Wherever you are, I'll be able to find you, just by following the heartstone's song. And stop playing about with the chain—you can't remove it.'

'This isn't a gift, it's a trap!'

'Oh, stop being silly.' Heather patted him lightly on the cheek and turned to her bed. 'Now, let me just get these things packed away and we can have a proper talk.'

Higgs watched in growing horror as she began sweeping things off the bed. Whatever it was she meant by 'talk', he was sure he didn't want any part of it. It was bad enough she'd put this leash on him. He stepped out the door quickly, calling back as he jogged away.

'I … uh … have to go. Speak to you later!'

'Higgsy!' Heather rushed to the door, but he was already gone.

Chapter 25

By the time Higgs returned to his room, Wilt was up and about, looking like there'd never been anything wrong with him.

'You're all better then?'

'Yep. The "hangover" has passed.'

'Good. Guess I can reclaim this then?' Higgs slumped onto his bed and lay back, his hands behind his head.

Wilt smiled at him silently.

'What?'

'Nice necklace.'

Higgs sat up quickly and stuffed the heartstone inside his shirt. 'It's nothing. A gift.'

Petron stepped into the room, carrying a steaming pot of tea. 'A heartstone, if I'm not mistaken. Seems young Higgs here may have met his match.'

Petron poured the tea into three cups and offered them around, then he and Wilt sat down and stared at Higgs, grinning like idiots.

'Now what?'

'Aren't you going to tell us all about it?' Wilt could barely disguise the laughter in his voice.

'Shut your face.'

'Forming a heartstone is one of the most basic crafts, though difficult to perfect,' Petron explained to Wilt. 'You pair the stones, then give one to your—' He took one look at Higgs's face and thought better of it. 'To the one you have chosen. When the stones part, the connection between them remains. You can use one to find the other, usually through following basic signals, like vibration. Some go further still. I've seen heartstones be placed in special sounding bowls, so the vibrations become music. The heartstone's song. It can be quite beautiful.'

Wilt hid his face behind his tea. 'Sounds delightful.'

'She trapped me.' Higgs pulled forlornly at the chain around his neck, his gaze flicking back and forth between Wilt and Petron, pleading to be believed.

'Oh, to be young again.' Petron smiled again and placed his cup on the table. 'But we have no more time for such things.' He stood and moved to the window, looking out onto the streets below to see a troupe of guards march past.

Wilt joined him. 'I'll leave tonight, as soon as it's dark.'

Higgs shot up out of bed. 'What's this? Where are we going?'

'I'm going to see Daemi. You're staying here.'

'I bloody well am not. I can move through the streets better than you.'

'Maybe. In human form. But that's not how I'll be going.'

Higgs turned to Petron for support. 'But that's not fair. They need my help.'

Wilt interrupted. 'Unless you can think of a way of turning yourself into a cat …'

'You only managed to do it yourself with my help. I carved your form.'

'That is true,' Petron muttered, lost in thought. 'Perhaps it is time.'

Wilt and Higgs answered together, their voices in perfect unison. 'Time for what?'

Petron looked back and forth between them. 'Yes, perhaps it is time at that.'

In the hours remaining before sunset, Petron explained to Wilt and Higgs some of the possibilities in the wielder and ward relationship. When the two were close, so close as to be almost one person, their powers could be shared. Take him and Wrexley. At one time they had been as close as two individuals could get, sharing everything. That closeness was what allowed Petron, not a natural wielder himself, to display some of Wrexley's power. He learned to form basic welds. Most importantly, he learned how to take on Wrexley's other form.

'Haven't you ever wondered how I did that?'

'I just thought you were a wielder,' Wilt answered.

'But you know better than that. You know how weak I am compared to the others,' Petron said, without any sense of self-pity.

'I guess I never really thought about it.'

Higgs paced with excitement. 'So I can do it then? I can become a cat too! How? Let's get on with it!'

Petron smiled and waved him back into his seat. 'The first thing you have to do is calm yourself.'

Higgs stopped pacing and made a valiant effort to keep still. 'Next?' he gritted out through his teeth.

'I said calm, not merely still, and definitely not clenched. Sit down.'

Higgs obeyed immediately.

Petron reached into his pocket and removed eight small stones, two-inch figurines with vaguely human faces on them. He arranged them in a circle and touched one, beginning the wave of falling and rolling upright again.

'Close your eyes and try to empty your mind. Think about the spiral shield, about the stones falling in order. Around and around. Never ending.'

Higgs's breathing became deeper, a regular pulse in and out as he sat there, perfectly still.

'Good.' Petron turned to Wilt. 'Now, the hard part. Sit down on the bed, facing Higgs.'

'Are you sure about this, Petron? Maybe I should just go now while you've got him ... hypnotised, or whatever.'

'Sit down.' Petron's voice was deep and stern now, and Wilt obeyed him automatically. 'You need to concentrate now, Wilt. We need a white weld, strong and firm, a complete sharing of your minds. But you have you remember not to sink too far, not to lose Higgs's mind within yours. You have to hold the power back. Resist it.'

'I can do that.'

'Just beware of the hunger. It will be stronger than ever now. The stones, think of the stones.'

Wilt closed his eyes and saw the stones in front of him, their faces forming into recognisable features as the wave of movement circled around them. Wrexley fell into Daemi, fell into Biore, fell into Petron, fell into the Sister. And onward.

Wilt floated within the flow of his power. He was aware of the hunger to dive into it, send it striking out, but he held back and formed a single white weld. He opened his eyes and sent it sliding into Higgs's mind.

There was a rush of heat and noise as Higgs tried to grab hold of him, tried to squeeze the weld within himself, desperate to hang on, desperate for this to work. Wilt gently pushed him back and wrapped the weld around him.

'Now. Take your form.'

The voice came from somewhere outside, somewhere other than the two minds that were the universe, but Wilt recognised the command and followed it. He changed, then forced the weld around Higgs's mind to change as well, ignoring the protests that squeaked from within it as it was bent into a foreign shape. The next moment they were two again, two separate forms in separate bodies.

'Now, go. Wilt, you need to keep control of Higgs. He doesn't know how to contain himself in this vessel.'

Wilt sprang to the open window and turned to wait for his companion. Higgs, that was his name. Ridiculous name for a cat, but it fit nonetheless. Not even a cat. A kitten. Need to keep an eye on this one.

The smaller cat leaped up quickly to join him and almost toppled out the window before catching himself, using his tail to find balance.

Wilt sniffed disgustedly and turned to lead him away.

'Remember your goal. Find Daemi, and keep an eye on Higgs.'

The human voice followed him out the window as he padded down the wall to the flat rooftop below. He landed softly and turned to watch the kitten scuttle awkwardly down the wall and land beside him. The young cat rolled onto his back, waving his four paws in the air like this was the greatest game ever.

Wilt swatted him quickly to knock some sense into him and trotted away.

Kittens. There was no teaching them anything.

Daemi.

The command pulsed in his mind, bringing with it images of warmth and safety, a fireplace, an open window above a low rooftop. That was the way.

Wilt scurried over the rooftops, dodging chimneys and leaping easily across gaps. Every now and then his nose led him away from his target, skirting around the scent of a guard standing forlornly in position, eyes half open. If he didn't have the kitten in tow, he could probably have snuck right past the guard, but he couldn't trust the young one. He was having a hard enough time keeping up as he was.

He heard the kitten pad up behind him and let out a low purr. Higgs was hungry and curious and wanted to know why they were rushing along, ignoring the scents of food they passed.

Wilt swatted him on the head again before prowling away.

Higgs tried to catch hold of his thoughts, but couldn't seem to grasp any of them. Impressions raced through his mind, pulling him this way and that. The world was a series of bright snapshots flickering before his eyes. His nose told him to go this way and that, but something deeper kept him following the larger cat in front of him.

It was as though his mind had taken on a foreign shape, packed him inside a box that was too small. If he let them, his thoughts could turn to panic and push back against the form that contained him, but then he heard another command and saw a strange sight—a series of stones falling one into another, and the panic faded.

He sprung easily across the gaps in the rooftops, losing himself in the joy of his agility and speed.

Two large dogs paced the rooftop in front of them, more alert than the human guards they had passed so easily. The two cats sat perfectly still and watched them.

They moved together, the larger one—a massive beast, almost a wolf in size—led the other along. The smaller one—still a large dog, at least five times the size of Wilt—seemed less sure of itself. It paced along haltingly, as if not used to the feel of the rooftop beneath its feet.

No, it was something more. It was not used to walking on four legs.

The thought passed through Wilt's mind and faded again without troubling him. Such thoughts were for other times. Other forms. Right now he needed to get past the dogs to the tower behind them, to the scent he could barely make out past their heavy stench.

The kitten nuzzled up against him, wanting to purr but knowing now not to make a sound.

The dogs sniffed the still air. There was no breeze to carry the cats' scent, and the dogs' noses must have been poor indeed if they hadn't picked up anything yet. Wilt waited for them to move to the furthest point in their patrol before sprinting toward the gap.

He was across in a flash, springing up the next wall to a high window ledge, where he stopped to make sure they weren't following. Wilt would have made it easily were he alone, but the kitten wasn't as fast or sure-footed as he.

Higgs missed his footing as he tried to follow Wilt up the wall to the safety of the perch. He scratched helplessly at the wall before falling onto the roof below, the soft thump of his landing the only break in the silence.

The two dogs turned as one and leaped toward the sound. The larger one got there in two great strides, growling and snuffling furiously around the base of the tower. The other stumbled, getting its legs confused and almost toppling off the wall.

The next moment, Red Charley lay in its place, out of breath and panting in pain. 'I can't … can't hold the form.'

The larger dog growled loudly at him and resumed its hunt. It circled around the spot where the kitten had landed. The scent wasn't what it had been expecting, but it was something. Something to find, to chase down, to sink its teeth into.

Wilt crouched on all fours and watched helplessly from the windowsill. He'd heard Higgs scramble for purchase, saw him fall, then lost him in the darkness. The kitten had rolled out of immediate danger, but had to be down there somewhere.

Red Charley was on his feet, bent over in pain, limping around next to the dog, trying to help. 'Do you smell anything? I couldn't make sense of all the different smells up here. So much information … it was overpowering.'

The dog let out a low growl and continued on its search.

Red Charley seemed to take it as a personal rebuke. 'I'll be okay next time, Funes, I promise. It just felt wrong, I couldn't get my mind around it. Next time I'll do better.'

Wilt smiled smugly: Red Charley whined like a beaten dog.

Something nudged his thigh and a soft purr rumbled. He turned to see the kitten nuzzling against his back leg, pleased with himself. Wilt considered swatting him again, just to teach him a lesson in overconfidence, but thought better of it and bounded up the wall of the tower, away from the hunters below.

They made the rest of the trip without incident. Guards were posted on the rooftops, but they snuck past easily enough and were soon peering through a thick glass window into a small, bare room. Someone was sitting in a chair—no, tied to the chair—his head lolling senselessly, and a woman paced back and forth in front of him, her head bowed in thought.

Daemi.

The thought came immediately into Wilt's mind, bringing with it a wave of strange emotions that his current form couldn't grasp. He let them sink down into the darkness and patted a paw on the window.

Daemi looked up to see a pair of cat's eyes watching her. Two pairs.

She slid the window open and the two cats tumbled into the room. The larger one sprang easily onto the floor, while the kitten jumped straight into her arms and started nuzzling her chest. She held its warmth against her, stroking its back.

'I wouldn't let him get too familiar.'

Daemi turned to see Wilt standing behind her, a strange smile on his face.

She raised an eyebrow, the kitten eagerly licking her neck now. 'This?'

'Is Higgs. And he's enjoying himself a little too much, wouldn't you say?'

Wilt's meaning suddenly clear, Daemi almost threw the kitten across the room. The next moment, Higgs was lying on the floor, giggling helplessly.

'Aw, c'mon Daemi! We were having such a nice time.'

Daemi's face flushed, and she strode over to haul Higgs to his feet. 'How?'

'It's great, isn't it? Petron showed us. Something about a ward being able to take on some of his wielder's powers. It was like Wilt took my mind and forced it into a new shape. I didn't really understand it, but it worked! Oh, Daemi, you should have seen me. It was awesome!'

Daemi couldn't hold her anger in the face of Higgs's enthusiasm and so turned it on Wilt instead. 'Why didn't you tell me?'

Wilt didn't seem to know what to say. He held his arms out to his sides. 'I just did.'

Daemi huffed and dropped Higgs to the floor. 'Boys,' she spat, as if that was all that needed to be said to sum up the matter.

Wilt and Higgs looked at each other sheepishly, then almost broke out in a giggle again, before both thought better of it.

'How did you get past the guards?' Daemi began striding back and forth across the room.

Wilt answered, happy for the change of topic. 'It was easy enough to sneak past most of them, though there were a couple of dogs patrolling the rooftops that caused Higgs a little problem.'

'No problem at all,' Higgs protested. 'Bet I did better than your first time on four legs.'

'How did you get past those two anyway? I lost you when you fell.'

'I didn't *fall*. Just had a minor hiccup with my footing. Luckily us cats always land on our feet. Amazing feeling that, by the way, turning in mid-air, just knowing which way is up. When do you think we'll be able to do it again?'

'The dogs, Higgs. How did you get past them?'

'Oh, I heard the big one as soon as I landed, and knew I didn't have much time, so I just went where I knew they wouldn't be.'

'Which was?'

'Where they were. When I landed, I mean. I sprinted back to where they had been. The big dog jumped straight over me, and Red Charley was too busy turning back into a human to notice. Daemi! Red Charley was there, in dog form!'

'What's this?'

'He's right. Red Charley was one of the dogs, and the other one was Funes. It was big enough.'

'You mean they were wolves, like Cortis?'

Wilt shook his head. 'Not wolves. Dogs, but not those either. It was as though they were poor copies. Not truly sharing the form.'

'And Red Charley couldn't hold it! He turned back and I ran straight between his legs. Stupid lump. After that it was easy enough to circle them. Funes was too busy trying to sniff me out and Red Charley was too busy whining at him.'

Daemi had stopped listening and stood in front of the guard tied to the chair. 'I was wondering what to make of this.' She leaned down and pulled his head roughly by the hair. The man groaned and his lips pulled back in a half conscious snarl.

Wilt could see immediately what she was talking about. The man's teeth were long and yellow, as if they were halfway to being a dog's.

Daemi pushed his head down in disgust. 'Cortis must have found some way to turn his guards. Get them to take on his form. Some of those who invaded were full wolves though. When this one wakes up again, I'll be sure to ask him all about it.'

Wilt grabbed a chair from the side of the room and slid it in front of the seated man. 'I don't think we need to wait that long. Higgs, go and make yourself useful somehow.' He sat down and faced the prisoner, a strange glow in his eyes. 'Daemi, it might be best if you leave the room for a bit. Just make sure I'm not disturbed.'

Daemi was about to protest, but something in Wilt's expression stopped her. She ushered Higgs out of the room.

'What's he going to do?' Higgs whispered.

Daemi shut the door, her face cold. 'I don't think either of us want to know.'

Once he was alone with the guard, Wilt wasn't actually sure what he planned to do. He studied the man, allowing the silence to wash over them.

The prisoner was a young man, only five or so years older than

Wilt, probably only a couple of years out of training. His skin was drawn and weathered from hours spent standing at his post, facing the wind and the cold. There was something more though, as if he had aged from what he had seen, what he had experienced. Wilt stored the thought away in his mind and continued his study.

The man's hands were rough and calloused, the nails too long and pointed, again as if the other form he had taken was trying to push its way out of him. Whatever Cortis was doing, it didn't look like it was good for the long-term health of his guards.

Wilt sat back and gathered himself. Enough delay. Time to find out what he could. He sent out a weld and hit a strange resistance immediately, as though the man was shielded. His weld slid over the top of the shield, unable to find a way through. There was no time to waste with this. Wilt pulled the weld back quickly and struck down hard, shattering the shield and driving into the man's mind.

The man let out a low groan that Wilt barely noticed. The room faded into insignificance.

He was standing in a field, throwing a ball back and forth with his brothers. Berni, the youngest, kept dropping it, and he had to keep the others from teasing him too badly. He tried to lob easy ones up for him, but Berni kept misjudging the distance, his hands clapping together just after the ball had passed between them. The others kept laughing and Berni looked on the edge of tears, which he knew would only make the teasing worse. The others were just the same at Berni's age; he just had to practise. He lobbed up another one, silently urging Berni to keep his eyes on it, to reach out at just the right time.

'Maron!'

The ball landed in the dirt as the brothers all turned toward their father's voice.

'Maron! Now, boy!'

Their father was standing at the door to their house, his hands on his hips, chest out as he always held himself when they had company. A man dressed all in black stood silently beside him, watching them.

It was time.

He turned back to Berni, wanting to kneel and hug him one last time. He wouldn't be seeing them again for years, his father had told him. Proud to have a son chosen for the guard. To have a son following in his footsteps. To have at least one son worth the cost of raising.

Berni stared at him silently, knowing he wasn't to cry. Knowing he wouldn't have Maron's protection anymore.

'Maron!'

He smiled at Berni, trying to make it all right, wanting to reach out and wrap his arms around him. But he just turned away, leaving it all behind.

The door to the room opened for a moment and Wilt was aware of his hand waving the interruption away. The door closed again and he was back inside his victim's mind.

Maron was older now, still a teenager but more confident in himself. His training had taught him that. Taught him to be cold and proud, to act without thought. To follow orders.

'Hand out.'

He thrust out his left hand, moving his fingers in turn for one last time.

'On the block. Keep still, boy.'

The captain spoke and he followed. He was the best of them, the first to be chosen. The first to be one of the Nine.

He thought suddenly of Berni, and saw him standing alone in the field outside his father's house, watching the sunset, staring at the lone tree, at the thick high branch that was low enough to sling the rope over and strong enough not to break. Ignoring the cries from the house, from the man who was supposed to care for him. Waiting for the darkness.

When the axe fell he felt no pain, just a sudden cold fire as he moved his hand, leaving his finger behind on the block. A cheer went up from the troop, but he ignored them. The captain clapped him once on the shoulder and he turned away.

A rush of images then as more years passed. Nothing to note but a growing coldness.

He was fighting beside Cantor Cortis, the best of the Masters, the one who shared his fire with the guards and stood beside them as they fought. The one they all followed without question. The village was burning, the heathens streaming away from the flames straight into their blades. It wasn't even a battle now, just slaughter.

Each child wore Berni's face, though he had heard news long before of Berni's suicide. Each child wore Berni's face and each man his father's. The women and children streamed toward him and he cut them down, just as the Cantor ordered. He felt nothing at all.

Deeper. Wilt pushed through the layers of his victim's mind, diving into the rush of hunger and power to find what he was looking for.

He stood in the circle of firelight, watching as Cortis reached out to each of them in turn, his hand a wolf's paw, a golden light shining in his eyes. As the paw touched his forehead, his mind became a whirlwind of animal urgency. He was aware of pain, of his body screaming as his limbs bent and bones twisted into foreign shapes. The pain was a vehicle of change, a new presence rushing in with it, a new form taking over his consciousness. He left any thought behind and became one of the circle, one of the pack.

Wilt opened his eyes and coldly considered the man slumped in front of him. The world around was still and incorporeal. There was nothing here for him, nothing to hold him back.

He was aware of the door opening again, of voices calling his name, and he was troubled. Why did they have to bother him now? He had his victim. He had the power.

Cortis. The voices kept saying that name.

Wilt sighed and pulled from the dark warmth inside his victim. The warmth that spoke only to him.

Cortis. He had to find out more. Pain was the key.

The paw touched his forehead and pain wiped his mind away. Something else rode in on the pain: another consciousness, another drive.

Wilt held the memory still and dived into it, past his victim's consciousness, into what lay beneath.

He rode up the clawed hand, the arm, into Cortis's mind. Animal, twisted and cruel, yet still human. Still driven by human feelings, human desires. Eager to please his master, eager for his promised reward.

Master? Not mistress?

A nest of snakes writhed beneath him, twisting about Cortis's mind like a tangled weed, wrapping themselves into him. The Sisters had a firm hold on him. On part of him.

A deep cold sank over Wilt's body. Deeper. Beyond. A low groan of dread escaped him.

He dived past the writhing forms, into something beneath. Something altogether blacker. It knew he was there. It held him and whispered into his ear, then flung him away.

Wilt was on the floor, Higgs leaning over him, patting his cheeks. 'Wilt!'

Daemi pushed him aside and peered down worriedly at him. 'Is he all right? Are you all right? What's wrong with your eyes? What happened, Wilt?'

'Look at the guard,' Higgs said, awed. 'He looks drained, like something sucked all the life out of him. I—I think you killed him, Wilt.'

Wilt pushed himself into a sitting position and peered at the slumped figure in the chair, its cheeks hollow, its skin grey. His vision was clouded, as though a film covered his eyes, but he saw what he had made of his victim. A husk where a man used to be.

He heard the darkness whisper to him, the words spilling out over his lips.

'The blood within the stone.'

The darkness smiled and took him into its arms.

Chapter 26

'What's wrong with his eyes?' Daemi said, panicked.

'They go grey sometimes when he's reading others, but I've never seen them like this. I'm sure it's nothing.' Higgs swallowed, not believing his own words, remembering the times Wilt had told him the same thing. 'Nothing to worry about.'

'What do you mean nothing to worry about? Look at him!' Daemi exclaimed, her cheeks flushed and her eyes wild.

'It's okay, Daemi. I'm sure he's okay. I'd know if he wasn't.'

Daemi stared at him as if struggling to recognise who he was, then seemed to gather herself together, aware that she was exposing something secret.

Higgs looked away, giving her time to pull herself together. She really did care for Wilt. How about that?

Wilt stirred and whispered something he didn't catch, his eyes still flooded with black.

'How long does it last?'

'I don't know. Not this long.' Higgs chewed his lip. 'I think we should get him into bed.'

Daemi seemed pleased to have an order to follow. 'The living quarters are just down the hall. Plenty of beds free.'

'Good. Do that then.'

Daemi bent down and pulled Wilt's arm over her shoulder. She lifted his dead weight easily to his feet.

Higgs reached over and placed his hand gently on Wilt's

forehead, pulling his eyelids closed. The next moment they popped open again, and he found himself staring into two deep black pools. An involuntary shiver danced up his spine.

Daemi moved toward the door, Wilt's boots dragging on the timber floor. She paused as she reached it, as if she'd forgotten something. 'What are you going to do?'

'Get some help.' Higgs noticed her worried glance and tried to make his words sound confident. 'Don't worry about me, Daemi. Look after Wilt.'

Daemi nodded quickly and moved away, leaving Higgs alone in the room.

He turned to the open window and the cold night outside, thinking about the feeling of four paws leaping across the rooftops, of speed and balance and heightened animal senses. A slow grin crept across his face.

No one said getting help couldn't be fun.

It was much easier the second time. It was as though the change with Wilt had carved a door in his mind; now all he had to do was open it again, and there he was. Rushing across the rooftops in the cold morning air, his senses alive.

The guard patrols seemed to have lessened in the daylight. He only had to sneak past two or three tired looking men, slumped at their posts, their breaths steaming out in long regular draughts. Eyes closed. At least half asleep.

Humans. So numb and closed off.

The kitten tumbled down from a wall and rolled as he fell, still unsure on his feet. There was an image in his mind, a room with a fire and a silver blade, a warm bed. A voice, calling him.

He tried to hold the image as he ran, but it was difficult. There were so many interesting smells to investigate, small creatures to chase. To hunt. That brought the thought of the large dogs into his mind and he forced himself to concentrate on his goal. There was danger here. He had to stay focused. Get to the room. Get to the voice.

Finally he arrived on a familiar roof, looking up at a high window in a tower. The voice called again and he didn't hesitate, bounding up from one fragile foothold to the next, scampering to the window ledge and in. On to the lap of the one who had called him.

'Higgs.'

He opened his eyes to see a fire in front of him. He lay on the ground, curled in the foetal position. Some part of him tried to hold on to his dream, but it drifted away.

'Higgs.' The voice that called him here. Petron.

'Getting in some practice, were we?'

'You. I heard you.'

'Yes. It's a good thing Daemi has a head on her shoulders, unlike some others I could name. She let me know you were coming.' Petron gestured over toward the small, carved stone figure of Daemi standing beside Higgs's bed. 'She told me what had happened, what you were planning. I thought I'd better try to help out.'

'How?'

'We're linked, you and I. Perhaps not as strong a link as that between you and Wilt, or me and Wrexley, but linked nonetheless. We all are, somehow. The skilled simply know how to access these links, take advantage of them. Those like you and me who have limited access to the skill can access them too, though to a much lesser degree.'

Higgs let Petron's words sink in. 'We're all linked? But that means—'

'That means even our enemies can lead us astray should they be strong enough. You took a risk coming here in that form. It is still new to you. You are still young, still weak.'

Higgs thought about his other form. He couldn't quite hold the memory in his mind. All he caught were glimpses and a feeling of lightning excitement.

'Still, you are here and we are wasting time. Daemi sounded worried. Tell me what happened to Wilt.'

Higgs sat up and quickly explained what had happened—how they'd left Wilt with the guard, how they'd heard a strange scream and returned to the room to find the guard dead and Wilt unconscious—or something. His eyes black and senseless.

Petron looked troubled. 'So. He has taken his first victim.'

'Victim? You mean the guard?'

Petron lowered his eyes and shook his head, then stood up. 'Come. Now is not the time for regret. I must find Biore.'

Higgs tried to jump to his feet and stars swamped his vision. Petron saw him falter and laid a hand on his shoulder.

'You stay here. Rest. The change takes more out of you than you realise. Besides, the other crafters will need your help. I think you'll find yourself busy enough to stay out of trouble for a while.'

They both turned around as the door swung open and Heather burst into the room. She was holding a small bowl out in front of her, a strange song emanating from its hollow.

'I knew it!' She pushed past Petron and threw her arms around Higgs's neck, knocking him to the floor.

Petron stepped quickly out of the room. 'I told you you'd be busy.'

Wilt's dreams were of shadows bouncing into each other, growing larger with each turn.

'Wake up.'

Wilt opened his eyes to see Petron sitting beside his bed, holding a steaming cup of what smelled like coffee.

'Here. Drink.'

He felt fuzzy from tiredness, but nothing more. Not damaged in any way. As he sipped his coffee, the dread that had haunted his dreams dripped away and was forgotten.

'I warned you about going too deep.'

Wilt finally noticed Petron's tone. 'What are you angry about?'

His bluntness seemed to break Petron's mood, and he turned away, shamefaced.

'I'm not angry, boy, just—'

'Disappointed,' Biore finished.

'No! Not disappointed either.'

'They're always disappointed in us, I've found, though happy enough to use our particular skills when they need them.'

'He's not like you, Biore.'

'No? He seemed to do an awfully good job of pretending.'

'What are you two talking about?' Wilt swung his legs off the bed and sat up. Each sip of the coffee seemed to bring him closer to reality, pushing the numbness away.

'You drained that guard, Wilt. He's dead,' Petron said softly.

Wilt watched him pace the room and realised what it was he heard in Petron's voice. He was ashamed.

'He did what he had to do. Didn't you, Wilt?' Biore leaned forward, peering at him, the hunger that always danced beneath his eyes blazing up. 'You went deep into his mind, to find what we asked you to. You had to use something up in order to get back.'

Wilt recognised what he saw in Biore's eyes. But Biore didn't see all of it. The darkness lay too deep for his sense.

'I found something.'

'The Sisters?' Biore spat, already knowing the answer.

'Yes, but—'

'I knew it! Wrexley has gone on a fool's errand, Petron, right into the snake's nest. And you let him.'

'I couldn't stop him. I never could.' Petron's voice was quiet and final, and even Biore recognised the pain within it.

'The Sisters were there, in Cortis's mind, but there was something else.'

'Cortis's mind? You mean the guard's.'

'No, the guard—Maron—was just a shell. A vessel. He had lost himself long ago, gave up his mind as he joined Cortis's circle. His pack of wolves. Cortis changed him, took him over, twisted him around, and I could take that part and go back, into Cortis. At least into what he had been.'

Petron and Biore both gaped at him.

'Pain. Pain was the key. It took over Maron's mind, rode in on it as it twisted him into another shape. I could see it, grasp it like a weld, dive into it. The Sisters were there, but underneath there was something else.' Wilt looked up at them, his eyes clear. 'It recognised me.'

Petron shot a look at Biore. 'Have you ever heard of this, been able to do this?'

'No.' Biore seemed awestruck. 'I don't think anyone has.'

'The darkness within him, it's using him. It spoke to me. The prophecy. The Sisters' prophecy. It's part of that.'

Neither Petron nor Biore knew what to make of that. Both stared back at him, strange expressions in their eyes. As if they were afraid of him.

Wilt looked around, studying the strange room. 'Where are we?'

Petron was pleased to be able to answer. 'Still in the armoury. It's been a day since you ... interrogated the guard. Since daylight, Cortis's guard have lessened their patrols, though the streets are still closed. We think they're holding most of the Black Robes in their tower—at least Wrexley and I saw none when we took a look around.'

'A bird's-eye view.' Biore smiled. 'I saw nothing either, from a much lower vantage point.'

'How did you get past—'

'Oh, I have my ways. Old ways. Silent ways.'

Petron seemed to find Biore's words distasteful and twisted his mouth sourly. 'Daemi and her guard have started to retake sections as they can. Most are empty. The crafters halls were ransacked, but most of them were left unharmed.'

'Higgs?'

'He's been busy with the crafters. His number one fan tracked him down easily enough—she won't let him out of her sight. They're reorganising things in the crafters halls, though I'm not sure how long Higgs is going to last. He looks like a trapped rat.'

'And Wrexley? He's gone to the Sisters?'

Petron nodded and looked away.

'Then that's where we start.' Wilt stood up. His eyes danced with stars for a moment, but they burnt out and his vision cleared. 'I think they need to know what I saw.'

'The Sisters?' Biore's reluctance was clear. 'Are you sure about that?'

'I am. The darkness, the thing I saw inside Cortis. It's their enemy too. We need to convince them of that.'

Petron was already hurrying about the room, readying things, eager to be on his way.

'You can lead us to Wrexley?'

Petron looked up and nodded. 'It won't be easy, I'm afraid. Cortis's dogs patrol in packs around the Black Robes tower and the path to the Nine Sisters. Even one as talented as you won't be able to slip by unnoticed.'

Biore smiled coldly back at him. 'Perhaps not in his form. But there are other ways, Petron.'

Wilt faced Biore knowingly. 'Old ways. Silent ways.'

The eagle soared high above the rooftops, well out of bow range, circling slowly in the warm currents of air. Wilt and Biore stood far below, huddled in the shadow of a doorway, peering out at the empty street in front of them. At least, it looked empty. The afternoon sun was sinking behind the mountaintops and long shadows lurched over the streetscape.

'Good. The shadows will help.' Biore's eyes glowed in the dim light.

Wilt could feel the hunger emanating from him.

'Now, prepare yourself.'

'What are we going to do?'

'It will be quicker for me to show you.' Biore noticed Wilt's hesitation and smiled. 'Don't worry. A man of your talents shouldn't find it any problem.'

The next moment, a weld pushed at Wilt. He held it back easily, feeling it slide over the glassy surface of his mind.

'Relax, Wilt. Let me in.'

With a conscious effort, Wilt dropped his defences and the weld sank eagerly into him. He felt the rush of Biore's presence in his mind, then another rush of knowledge as doors opened in his awareness. The weld led him along new pathways, showing him how it was done.

In an instant Wilt understood. 'Okay. I'm ready.'

Biore seemed taken aback by the speed of Wilt's comprehension. 'Are you sure?'

'Yes. Enough Biore.' Wilt could feel the hesitation within the weld, the hunger eager to delve deeper. To feed.

In an instant he realised the truth: Biore's power was more than just a part of him. It was almost a separate being, growing each time Biore loosed it. Taking over his mind. Soon he would be helpless to resist it.

Wilt began to push the weld away just as Biore withdrew. A moment later they were both back fully in the world.

Biore's gaze dropped away. 'Come then. Let's see how quickly you learn.'

Then he was gone, his physical body fading into a dark grey mist that blew through the doorway and away. As it left, Wilt made the change too.

Like all such skills, it was simple once you knew the trick. Taking his other form required him to shrink his mind into another physical shape, that of a large cat. This new change, however, required he forget his physical existence entirely. He created a weld in his mind, then forgot everything else.

His body faded into the cold, replaced by something less, yet more. The world around him sunk into black and white, light and shade. He saw the thing that had been Biore move through the doorway and wondered briefly why he bothered. A doorway meant nothing in this form. A wall was merely another idea. With a thought he melted straight through it, into the open space beyond, feeling nothing more than the brief cold breath of the living world whispering in his mind.

An eagle's cry resounded and Wilt looked up to see it arc out of a spin and turn away, heading deeper into the centre of Redmondis. Wilt saw the eagle as a bright light. Energy. The hunger within him sparked rapidly, urging him toward it. The hunger was much stronger in this form. It was something he had to consciously resist.

Biore ignored it. Wilt saw his form drift toward an unsuspecting guard standing alone in a doorway. Saw the man's breath mist in the sudden cold that enveloped him. Saw his cry freeze in his throat as Biore took him and he collapsed into death.

Wilt felt nothing. No horror, no regret. Merely an angry rumbling of his own hunger.

The eagle's cry echoed again, snapping him back to his task.

He drifted into the long shadows of the street, willing his insubstantial form to move silently through the air. Biore was still ahead of him, the husk of the guard he had drained left lying where it fell. Wilt studied it as he passed, trying to feel something at the grim sight, but he felt nothing.

Wilt saw another guard's form glowing at him, the warmth of his life force calling like a siren's song. *Take me. Drain me. Become death.*

He drifted through another wall, coursing toward the unsuspecting victim.

Again the eagle's cry brought him back, and he was forced to change tack. Back onto the street, drifting past the guard, who shivered in the sudden cold that passed him by. The guard flexed his stiff fingers in his gloves and rested his hand on his hilt. Wilt moved away, taking the cold with him, then was aware of a deeper chill as Biore drifted from a nearby doorway and cut toward the waiting guard. The guard had time to draw his sword and make a single thrust, which disappeared harmlessly into the black mist that surrounded him. Wilt watched his eyes glaze over into death, then turned away.

Wilt had no concept of how long they travelled this way. Biore drifted in and out of his awareness, eagerly removing what he saw as obstacles from their path. Petron curved above them, a constant reminder of the real world he drifted through, the one he would return to. The one of light and warmth and colour and life.

A great sadness sank over him as they moved through the streets. A foreboding. As though each of them walked a path already foretold.

The patrols and guards they passed grew in number as they went. Cortis had strengthened his hold on these areas, as though he expected an attack.

In this form, the guards were nothing but a temptation. Wilt drifted past them, the dogs whining quietly and sniffing the air, the guards huddling in their cloaks and telling grim jokes to each other about someone walking over their grave.

Eventually Petron curved away from the street and down a series of dark alleys. Wilt moved through the walls as easily as he did the shadows. Finally he saw the eagle dive onto a nearby rooftop and disappear, to be replaced by the bright glow of a human form.

For a second he felt the hunger again. The possibility of death.

'Come, Wilt.' Petron stood before him.

Wilt returned to his natural form and stood shivering in front of Petron, who held out an arm and patted him softly on the shoulder.

'They are dark paths you walk. Be sure you can return from them.'

Wilt returned Petron's stare, nodding in understanding.

'Come. Biore will follow in his own time. He has spent too long in that form to discard it so easily.'

Petron led him through a doorway to the back of a disused storehouse, thick dust stirring in their footsteps. Petron pushed a heavy looking barrel to one side to reveal a trapdoor beneath.

'Even Cortis can't know all of Redmondis's secrets.'

Chapter 27

The small bowl sat alone on the table top, the heartstone resting within it, the song emanating from its shape quieter now yet still present, tingeing the air with its notes.

'Does that thing ever shut up?'

Higgs threw his bag into an empty corner of the room and slumped wearily on the bed. He'd been working all day, helping the other crafters restore their rooms and goods to their previous state, and hunting down tools and ingredients for those who found important items missing. He'd also found himself playing peace broker between crafters who squabbled over a much smaller pool of resources now that Cortis and his dogs had locked down the streets. Higgs was heartily sick of it all.

'That "thing" is a sounding bowl. Our sounding bowl, as a matter of fact. It tells me when the heartstone is near. When you are near. I think its song is lovely.'

Heather faced Higgs's scowl with a smile and he forgot his anger despite himself. Still, he tried his best to stay grumpy.

'Ball and chain is what it is.'

'Don't be ridiculous. Now tell me, how are the healers getting along? Did you tell them about the three barrels of forest dew we found in the basement?'

As simple as that, Heather steered the conversation back to practical matters, and Higgs's mind began to wander. It hadn't taken them long to get the other crafters organised, and now that the chaos was abating he found himself straining to be back out there, on the streets, taking a more direct hand in things. He glanced at the moonsteel blade resting against the far wall of his room.

'I'm going tonight.'

Heather's stream of chatter stopped. 'Okay.'

'There's nothing left here that others can't handle, and Petron said—'

'Higgs, I said okay.'

Higgs spluttered to a stop, a strange warmth rushing over his face. 'I promise I'll be careful.'

'I know you will.' Heather stood up and stepped over to him, planting a quick kiss on his cheek before he could protest. She turned away and swiped the bowl off the table as she went. She waved her hand quickly over the bowl and its song died away.

'I'm going to try and contact Wilt's roommate, Delco. Maybe some of the other Black Robes are still free.'

'Good. I'll be waiting here for you.'

Her voice sounded different, and Higgs stared at his feet to avoid seeing the tears he imagined on her face.

'Maybe when I get back you can show me how that thing works. The sounding bowl, I mean.'

Heather stopped at the doorway and smiled. 'Okay.' She walked out, leaving Higgs alone with his sudden guilt.

Higgs was still alone hours later, sitting on his floor, the moonsteel blade resting on his lap. The sky outside was sinking into dusk and it was almost dark enough for him to sneak past whatever prowled the streets at night. He was confident he would have more control this time, and not get distracted from his goal. Not need Petron to call him home.

His fingers traced over the blade in his lap, sensing the strange power forged into the metal, and the tingle of electricity and warmth. His last trip had given him another idea. He'd half hoped he'd return wearing only his clothes, the heartstone that hung around his neck forgotten as he became human again. But all was as it had been. And if that was the case, what was to stop him including some other handy tools next time he took the other shape?

The shadows outside the window stretched across the rooftops, and the low moon washed a blue-grey light over the buildings below. It was time.

Higgs held the moonsteel blade up to the light and its surface turned to liquid silver. He closed his eyes and returned to the door inside his mind, where the other form waited for him.

The next moment he was standing on four legs on the windowsill, his tail flicking back and forth slowly. The kitten stretched languidly, his bright silver claws shining.

Good. Not so defenceless anymore. If any dogs discovered him they were in for a nasty surprise.

He sprung out the window and ran down the wall to the rooftop below. There was a target in his mind, another tower, another high window. But he would have to be careful. Humans and worse patrolled the night. Their scents tainted the air already. Guards in their stinking armour, and their dogs, which smelled even worse—unnatural. There was something else too, something worse on the edge of the air, souring its taste.

Higgs pushed such thoughts from his mind and dived into the world, leaping across rooftops, dancing through shadows, skipping past the few guards posted in the streets. His new claws helped, grabbing easily into the hard stone walls like they were soft timber, allowing him to scamper up even the sheerest walls in his path.

The scent of wrongness became stronger as he approached the tower. For a second he hesitated in the shadows, unwilling to expose himself to whatever was causing such a stench. A strange thought pulsed through his mind and he pushed on, ignoring the warning screams of his instincts.

Something in a high window in the tower called to him, beckoning him with the warmth of reflected firelight. He began to climb the wall toward it, claws cutting into the stone.

A sharp cry rang out from somewhere beneath him. A horrible, strangled, guttural moan of pain and terror. He froze in place and waited for the cry to die out in the wind. A guard to the side of the tower looked around nervously, then bowed his head, as though he were used to hearing such things and knew best to ignore them. The man's fingers shook as he pulled his cloak tighter.

Higgs's goal was an easy climb, no more than a few leaps away, but he felt drawn to investigate the cry.

The guard took no notice of the small shadow ghosting past it. On the street below, one of the dogs raised its nose and sniffed as a new scent wafted into range, but it was gone as soon as it appeared, and the human tugged on the dog's chain to pull it back into step, and the scent was forgotten.

A loud bang rang out as a wooden door slammed open and another pair of guards stumbled out. One leaned heavily on the other, a thin stream of drool hanging from his mouth. The second guard struggled to hold his weight, and almost fell himself as he dropped his friend and stood over him, panting.

'C'mon solider. On your feet.'

The guard on the ground let out a whimper of protest and shook his head.

'You can't stay here. They'll take you next.'

The soldier responded in a burst of panic and energy, rolling to his feet and stumbling toward the cat hiding in the shadows, before bending over and loudly losing the contents of his stomach.

The second guard held him upright and patted him weakly on the back. 'That's it. Get it out. No shame in being sickened by it.' He murmured the words quietly, then pulled his friend away into the darkness.

The cat turned his attention to the door. It was only metres away, unguarded, but too many eyes watched it, glancing up nervously whenever a new cry sang out in the night. No. The door was not the way.

The cat's gaze travelled to the boarded up window near the door. It was high in the wall, half shadowed by the low roof hanging over it. The boards covering it looked old and rotten and were no match for the cat's new claws.

He waited for another guard to walk past the alley entrance, then sprang into action, nothing more than a blur of movement as he sliced easily through one of the wooden boards covering the window. He squeezed through the gap and dropped into the room beyond, ready for anything.

Empty.

The room was small, a dusty storeroom of some kind, with a door leading into the tower beyond. The strange scent of wrongness that pervaded the courtyard outside was stronger here, more focused, and the cat's hackles stood on end.

He slipped through the ajar door into what turned out to be a large kitchen, sneaking past the single nervous guard posted by the main door, the man whispering to himself and shaking his head like a madman.

Another cry ripped across the air, much closer now. The cat stopped in his tracks, legs shaking as the agony evident in the scream echoed through the air. It left only silence, filled quickly by the lone guard's whispered prayers.

The cat slinked on through the shadows, over benches and past pots and pans, careful not to knock any of the teetering piles of dishes stacked haphazardly in its way. The kitchen looked and smelled like it had fallen into recent disuse.

Three large shuttered openings led through to the dining hall, one propped open by a small stack of metal pans. Flickering orange light bled into the kitchen from the gap, and the cat squirmed through it, dashing quickly for the shadows again.

A great open bonfire glowed in the middle of the hall, fed by what looked like broken benches and tables. The thick smoke from the ages-old wood pooled in the gaping archways high in the ceiling, flattening into a strange grey cloud. Guards stood close to the bonfire, clearly afraid of what waited for them away from its light.

The sense of wrongness was almost overpowering. The cat's body shook as his senses screamed to flee. Something deeper, something foreign yet understood held it in place.

A man stood amongst the guard. *Cortis.* His eyes were alive with power and madness, scanning the room in triumph. He was flanked by two enormous wolves, glaring coldly out at the men. Waiting.

Human guards stood nervously around them, trying to stay stone-faced and passive, yet giving themselves away with small shifts of weight. To one side stood a row of Black Robes, beaten and broken in spirit, heads drooping and some swaying on their feet as if ready to collapse at any second. From this group one was chosen, dragged in front of Cortis, who seemed to take an age to notice his presence.

Cortis stared through his victim at something only he could see, before reaching out his hand, grasping the young man by the chin, and whispering to him. The young man instantly stiffened, his head thrown back as if trying to break free from the rest of his body. A cry of anguish broke from his throat, and his body began to sink into itself, bones twisting and snapping with sickening wet thunks. A moment later the young man was replaced by a large dog, whimpering slightly and shaking on four strange legs.

'Thank the gods,' muttered a nearby guard, standing as close to the shadows as he dared, unaware that he could be heard.

The cat followed the guard's glance to the far side of the bonfire, where the light broke over a pile of strange, shifting forms—those who hadn't been able to accept the full transformation thrust upon them, half formed bodies writhing in agony, screaming through mouths and throats that no longer worked—and was glad of the emotional disconnection of his own current form. He could watch and remember. Feelings would come later.

The cat moved along the edge of the room, away from the guard and the light of the bonfire. He circled the room easily, the thick shadows hiding his sleek form. At the far side of the hall, a large stone staircase curled up into the darkness, and he trotted quickly up it, away from the horrors on the floor below. Even in his current form the sight of such abject suffering and pain filled his mind, distracting him from his surroundings. He almost stumbled into the back of a large dog guarding the top of the stairs, only catching himself at the last moment and leaping quickly to the side, but not before giving his presence away.

The dog sprang around with an angry growl and snapped at empty air, the cat racing past it into the darkness and up another flight of stairs beyond, but a bark from behind him was answered by more ahead. They knew he was there.

The stairs curved up into thick darkness, but the cat jumped up onto the wall, his claws digging easily into the cold stone, leaving the heavy pants and padded feet below as the dogs raced in from both directions. They milled about in confusion where the two packs met, trying to isolate the cat's scent amid the chaos. Human guards waded in, trying to organise the ranks, but the dogs were mad with hunger and snapped at them. More than one guard sank beneath the pile.

This way.

The call came from above the cat, two or three floors, a whispered request, not a command, as though not wanting to scare him away.

Come. This way.

The dogs on the level below had gathered into some sort of order, and one or two were sniffing at the wall where the cat had scaled to safety.

He didn't have time to question. He leaped across the stairway to the other wall, trying to break up his path.

Good. Come. This way.

He ran along an empty corridor, past rows of closed doors,

toward one that was half open. Pale firelight called to him, promising warmth and safety. He slunk into the room, right into the waiting arms of the one who had called it.

A heavy cloak shut out the world and thin, strong arms wrapped around him.

'There you are.'

Chapter 28

'What is it?' Petron peered at Wilt, trying to make out his face in the dim light of the tunnel.

'Nothing. It's—' Wilt stuttered to a stop. For a sharp moment he had felt the world collapse over him, shutting out everything else. Suffocating him.

Then it was gone.

'It's nothing.' He waved Petron on down the tunnel.

'How much farther?'

It had to be soon. They seemed to have been travelling along this same tunnel for hours now, the air getting closer and staler as they went, as though the whole universe was narrowing its focus on them.

'You can feel them, can't you?' Petron asked.

Wilt thought about his words, about the feeling of a hundred pairs of eyes turning toward him, suddenly aware of his presence.

'Yes.'

'Take it as read they can feel you too. The Sisters are more powerful than any of us. Always assume they know more than you do.'

Wilt almost muttered a reply, but held his tongue and continued on. Petron couldn't understand. It wasn't that the Sisters were more powerful. It was something else, something deeper. Something they were more open to.

They would have been in complete darkness were it not for the small torchstone Petron had uncovered from inside his cloak. As it was they walked as if through a thick grey fog, seeing just enough to make out the single set of footsteps pressed into the thick dust at their feet.

'Did Wrexley come this way?'

Petron didn't answer at first, and Wilt almost repeated his question before he heard him let out a tired sigh.

'No. No, these footsteps are older. Wrexley found his own path. I can feel his presence.'

'Is he okay?' Wilt regretted the words as soon as they were out of his mouth; even in the dim light he could see Petron hunch his shoulders against some hidden pain.

'I think so. It's … difficult to tell.'

The air seemed to shift as he spoke, as though the strange force watching them found some grim humour in Petron's words. They had come close enough now for Wilt to sense more of the Sisters' power. They were waiting for them.

Petron led them around a final corner, and light from a room ahead spilled against the walls. Petron pocketed his torchstone and quickened his pace, eager to get whatever was coming over with.

Silence slammed over them as they stumbled into a large, well-lit room. Petron let out a pained whimper and hurried over to the figure lying crumpled on the far side of the room. It was Wrexley, lying still, not even seeming to breathe.

'Cantor Wrexley disappointed us.'

Wilt stopped and faced the far wall, where a chorus of voices called out to him. Sitting on a bare bench was a hooded Sister, her hands clasped before her. Wilt felt power spilling from her, as though she were the gate in a dam, holding back the full force of the collected might of the Nine Sisters. Focusing them to a single deadly point.

'Wrexley. What have they done to you?' Petron whispered as he rolled Wrexley face up and gazed into his blank eyes.

'Cantor Wrexley forgot our instructions. He lacks the required discipline.'

The voice was only vaguely human, a chant of voices not completely in time, some slithering in and out as though struggling to wrap foreign tongues around long forgotten syllables.

On the wall behind the Sister, Wilt saw a twisting nest of serpents. Then the image was gone, leaving only stone.

Petron stood up slowly and glared at the Sister. 'Why have you done this? He only ever wanted to serve you.'

The Sister turned toward him, her face cold. 'You. We know you.'

Petron's shoulders shook as he stood before the Sister, his eyes flashing with barely contained rage. 'No. You don't know me. Not yet.' He spun toward Wilt and grabbed his hand. 'Come boy, it is time we showed these vipers what you're capable of.'

A sudden warmth spread up Wilt's arm from Petron's grasp. With the warmth came a whisper in his mind, unfurling itself as it rushed through him.

Come. Let me direct your power. Open yourself.

A great weld formed in his mind, gathering strength as it spun like a hurricane inside him. Suddenly a voice broke from him.

'Sisters. You do nothing but take.'

Wilt spoke clearly, though the words were not his own. Petron was guiding him, moving his tongue, forcing the words out. As he did so, the silent command continued to race through Wilt's mind, opening pathways, pushing back boundaries as it went. A whole universe was blossoming inside him.

He pointed at Wrexley, broken on the floor. 'All he ever did was serve you. Despite what it cost him. What it cost me.'

A thick silence dropped over him as the Sister slowly raised her hands and pulled back her hood. 'You. We have seen you before.' The silence became a vacuum as the Sister's deep red hair spilled free and her bright green eyes shone at Wilt. 'We know you.'

The twisting snakes burrowed into Wilt's mind, eagerly chewing through his soul as though desperate to sate their hunger.

No.

With a surge of effort he slammed the walls down around him, banishing the Sister's weld as he did so. Petron let out a cry of triumph inside his mind as he stared at the woman. Beautiful. Evil. No longer a threat.

'You have lost your focus.' Wilt spoke clearly again, stepping toward the Sister. 'You have let your welds weaken. You have failed to see the threat within your walls.'

The vortex of power within him, spinning faster now than he could comprehend, reared to strike.

Petron's voice continued to speak through him. 'You discarded so many, only to replace them with these serpents, these slaves of the dark. Blinded by the power they offered, you did not notice as they burrowed under your skin.'

With that the weld was unleashed, darting straight into the Sister, piercing her mind and going beyond, into the serpent's nest.

The Sister collapsed into the stone wall, and it shattered to reveal eight hooded figures. Unable to stop him.

Wilt wasn't sure what was real and what was illusion. The power of the weld had overwhelmed his senses. There was nothing else. The darkness wrapped its arms around him and welcomed him into its depths.

Before his eyes the nest of serpents twisted and writhed in pain as he dived through their minds, their perpetual link opening a single path for him to follow.

No! It is not possible!

He sees us!

The worms. There is no other way. Give yourselves to them!

Some of the minds wrenched away from him, losing themselves in the process to become pure animal, turning onto the other Sisters, feeding on them.

No! We must not give in to them!

It is too late. We have already begun.

'Stop this,' choked out the crumpled Sister, and some part of Wilt was aware of the pleading tone in her voice.

No. They must pay. All of them.

Petron's voice inside his mind was a triumphant shout of power. Wilt had broken into their shared link, their hive mind, and in response the Sisters were destroying themselves.

'Please.'

Wilt looked at the Sister at his feet, her eyes glistening with pain as her shared connections tore away from her. But it was more than her tears that called to him. She looked different. Human.

Wilt clenched down on the weld pouring out of him, trying to redirect it against the serpents that gnawed into the Sister's minds.

No.

Petron pushed back, sending his power toward the Sisters. Wilt felt a strange warp in his mind as they pulled in different directions.

'Petron. Let him go.'

The words came from somewhere else, somewhere outside the power that consumed them.

No.

Wilt felt the resistance as he began to tear in two.

'Petron. Do not become like them. Let him go. Wrexley needs you.' Biore. He must have caught up to them.

The separate urge inside Wilt's mind weakened, then faded away as Petron surrendered his hold. Wilt found himself in total control of the weld, and he directed it on the serpents that still fed on the Sisters' minds. It wrapped around their slavering maws, muzzling them and pushing them into the depths. Where they belonged.

The waves of power battered the serpents down, and slowly they began to loosen their hold on the minds of their victims. They took most of the Sisters' minds with them; the serpents—the Sentinels the Sisters had considered their servants—were too deeply ingrained in their very being to be discarded without cost.

The Sister at Wilt's feet stood slowly, taking his hand. The power within him strengthened, and with a final surge of power that knocked him off his feet, the weld blasted closed, leaving Wilt with stars dancing in his eyes.

'I know you.' The Sister's voice had changed. She was just one woman now, no longer connected to the power that their shared weld had given them.

'Greystone. You are the one we—I—sensed. Why have you done this?'

Wilt looked coldly at her, recognising the hurt and anger in her eyes. He couldn't speak, but heard Petron answer for him.

'You did this to yourselves. You should never have allowed them in. Any of them.'

'What has happened?' Wrexley's weak voice echoed across the silent room. 'I was, somewhere, being held there. Awaiting punishment. The Sentinels—the serpents. They were going to give me to them, then the Sisters holding me simply … left.'

Petron hurried over to him, cradling his head in his hands. 'Be silent, Wrex. They are gone now. They are—'

'They were consumed.' The Sister pushed her shoulders back, her voice gaining authority.

'They were their own victims,' said Biore, no longer wringing his hands in supplication before the Sister. 'Such things should never have been allowed out of the depths.'

'Their power was ours to control.'

'And yet it controlled you,' Biore responded fearlessly. 'You lost your focus. All of you. The Sentinels. Cortis. Your slaves have turned on you.'

The Sister's eyes flashed. 'It is not possible.'

'And yet it is so.' Biore shrugged off her angry glare and turned to where Petron was supporting Wrexley. 'The blood within the stone. You think yourselves the only ones to have tasted of its power?'

'My Sisters.' For the first time she sounded less sure of herself.

'How many survived?'

The Sister hesitated, as if searching herself for something that was no longer there. 'I … I do not know. I can no longer feel them.'

Biore looked at her, unsure whether he should believe her words. But Wilt somehow knew she spoke the truth.

'Forever linked,' he whispered.

The Sister turned to face Wilt. 'Please. Help me. Help me find them again.'

'No.' Petron stood, lifting Wrexley and supporting him on one shoulder. 'Your dog Cortis has taken over Redmondis while you and your—' he caught himself before he spat out further insults, 'your Sisters hid down here in your nest. First you will help us.'

The Sister moved her lips as if trying to find the right words, and finally spoke. 'How? What can I do? I am alone.'

'You are a Sister, still more powerful on your own than any of us.' Petron then glanced at Wilt standing off to the side. 'Than most of us anyway. I'm sure we will find a use for you.'

Chapter 29

Higgs woke to find himself curled on the floor in front of a low fire. In his dreams darkness was enveloping him, holding him down, trapping him in its depths.

He stretched slowly and stared dully at the licking flames, then instinctively shot his hand to his hip. The moonsteel sword was gone.

'Looking for this?'

Higgs turned to see a thin pale figure sitting on the bed across from him, the blade twirling slowly in his fingertips.

'It is very fine work. Moonsteel, is it not? I've never seen its like.'

He tossed the blade to Higgs, who caught it easily in mid-air and slid it quickly into the sheath on his hip.

'You are Higgs? You've nothing to fear here, at least, not from me. I am Delco. A friend of Wilt's, just as you are, I think.'

'Where is Wilt?'

'Ah.' Delco smiled sadly. 'I was hoping you would be able to tell me that.'

Higgs sat up and began patting himself down, making sure everything was still in place. He felt stiff and a little strange, as though his clothes no longer fit him as well as they used to.

'You are close to him, aren't you?'

'He's ... he's my friend.'

'And you are his ward. I have read about such things, though the Sisters banned the practice long ago. I suppose that doesn't matter now. Many things have changed.'

'While I was a cat, you called to me. You called me here.'

'What? Oh, yes. I heard the ruckus out there. Figured anyone who could cause the guards that much trouble would be worth talking to. Sorry about grabbing you like that.'

Higgs felt the black cloak drop over him again, holding him still. He shivered and banished the thought from his mind. 'It's okay. You saved me, I think.'

'The dogs aren't too smart but there are many of them now. Too many.'

That thought seemed to trigger a wave of sadness. Higgs had a sudden vision of the hall downstairs, the line of waiting victims. The strange, writhing pile of half formed bodies.

'Cortis. What is he doing down there?'

'Cantor Cortis is growing his army. And searching for something. Something he will not find with any of them.'

Higgs stood up and sat on the bed opposite Delco. Wilt's bed, he supposed. 'I saw them. What he's doing. It's … evil.'

'Evil.' Delco grimaced. 'Yes, it is that.'

'Why are you letting it happen?'

Delco reared back, a sudden fire sparking life into his eyes. 'You've seen the others. Those they've captured. You've seen what becomes of them. I—I tried at first. Me and some of the others. Tried to fight back. But Cortis and his wolves were too strong, too many. We don't … our skill isn't yet fully formed. We can't …'

He paused, finally continuing in a much lower voice.

'The others were captured. I was lucky. I got away, managed to climb back up here. Where those of us who are left hide. They haven't bothered to clean us out yet. But they will, when they run out of victims.'

Delco's eyes radiated deep fear and shame. 'I'm scared. Too scared to move.'

Higgs nodded. 'Good. Scared is a good place to start.' He bounced to his feet and began to pace the room. 'You said there were others up here.'

Delco nodded, something else coming into his eyes now. Something like hope.

'Show me.'

Delco led Higgs along the deserted hallway, away from the staircase, toward the far end of the floor. They moved silently, though there was no sign of any other guards.

'How do you keep the guards away from here?' Higgs asked, keeping his voice low.

'We—me and some of the other skilled ones—we put up a barrier. A weld wall, I suppose you could call it. It only works on the weaker minded ones. When they get too close they suddenly feel like turning around, patrolling somewhere else. Whatever suggestion works for them.'

Higgs mulled that over, thinking of the possibilities.

'It won't work for long though,' Delco continued. 'It's only held this long because they haven't bothered to send anyone with any strength. Cortis or his wolves would see right through it.'

'His wolves.' Higgs saw an image of the two great wolves sitting silently on either side of Cortis downstairs, hungrily glaring at each victim before them. 'Who are they?'

'His personal guard. I don't know how many there are. They were the ones who swept through Redmondis, removing any true threats. The rest of them, his dogs, they're just humans twisted into another form. The wolves are something more. Something worse.'

Delco's voice had found strength as he talked, and Higgs noted he no longer crept along the hallway.

'Here.' Delco stopped in front of a door and knocked quickly in a strangely syncopated rhythm.

After a moment a small voice answered through the wood. 'Who is it?'

'It's Delco. Open up, Frankle.'

Higgs's practiced ears picked up at least four separate locks sliding open before the door eventually swung open, allowing them through.

Delco led him in. 'You know, the point of a secret knock is that you don't need to ask who it is.'

The young boy who had answered the door was about to reply when he noticed Higgs and gave a small yelp, hurrying away to the far side of the room.

'What are you doing, Delco? You can't bring strangers here,' an older voice called out.

Higgs scanned the room as Delco held up his hands to calm the growing murmur of angry voices. There were at least ten young men sitting against the wall, as far from the door as possible; sick, scared looking boys, their black robes hanging from their frames. Little boys whose world had caved in around them.

'It's okay. This is Higgs. He's a friend.'

'How do you know? He could be a spy,' the older boy said, then dropped his eyes, as though scared Higgs was going to fly into a rage.

'He's not a spy. He's a friend of Wilt's.'

Wilt. They knew that name; they'd all seen his power.

Eventually the same boy spoke up again, above the eager murmur of the others. 'And where is Wilt now? Gone. Along with everyone else.'

'Wilt is doing what the rest of you should be, instead of hiding here in the dark,' Higgs said. 'He's fighting back.'

The older boy found some courage at those words. 'Fighting back? Have you seen what they're doing down there? What happens to those who fight back?'

He had tears of helpless rage in his eyes, and Higgs felt a momentary pang of pity. He forced it down; he had to break this one in order to lift the others.

'I've seen them. Up close, unlike you. I've seen the wolves sitting proudly in front of their master, hunger in their eyes. Seen the line of those you once called friends, like cattle for the slaughter. Seen the guards sickened by the sight of what awaits them. And I say to you again, why aren't you fighting back?'

The boy stared silently at Higgs, his tears flowing freely now down his cheeks.

Delco laid a hand on Higgs's shoulder. 'Because we're scared, Higgs. We're terrified.'

'We're all scared, Delco. Wilt is scared too. We have very little idea of what we're up against, but that doesn't mean we shouldn't try.'

The other boys stared at him, each trying to find within themselves the courage to answer his call.

Finally, the older boy wiped the tears hurriedly from his cheek and sniffed. 'And where would you start?'

Higgs drew the moonsteel blade with a flourish and held it out before them, letting the light dance off the bright liquid silver blade.

'I've got a couple of ideas.'

Delco waited in the doorway, chewing his lip as he watched the others alter the weld wall they had built. Higgs's suggestion had certainly been an interesting one. Now they just had to trust it would work.

He examined the surface of the wall as each boy drew his hands back from the barrier—some quickly, as if eager to be away from it; others, a pleasing number of others, much more slowly. Studying the wall as they backed away. Eager to see the plan in motion. Each wielder added to the weave of welds forming the wall, opening them where needed, altering their form to better accept the new power Higgs had offered.

Finally it was his turn, and he stepped forward, Higgs's moonsteel blade in his hand.

'Are you sure about this?' he had asked Higgs earlier that afternoon, once he'd heard Higgs's plan.

'No. But it's as good a plan as any.' Higgs had smiled, and Delco couldn't help but return it.

'You think we can just merge the moonsteel into the wall? Force it into the weld?'

'Why not? I don't understand welds as well as you do, but I know crafting. We forge materials and powers all the time. From what I understand, those powers are just reflections of welds—or to put it another way, welds are just focused concentrations of those powers. Think of it like this—when I take on Wilt's other form, I merge into his power, in a way. And last time I did it, I also brought the moonsteel with me. There's something about it that allows for this sharing of forms. I think that's what it's meant for.'

Delco had simply looked at Higgs and finally taken the moonsteel blade from his hands. 'And where will you be during all of this?'

'I'll be downstairs. Bringing the party to you.'

'Oh.'

Delco banished the memory as he stepped toward the wall and focused his concentration. Merging into the weld. Sounded simple enough. He took a deep breath and tried to forget the fact he had no idea how he was going to do this.

For an age he stood silently in front of the wall, watching the slight ripple of light move along its surface. The moonsteel blade tugged at him, pulling itself toward the weld wall. Delco's surprise dissolved quickly, however, with a sudden rush of pure power.

Delco flailed helplessly in it, drowning in the tumult that almost knocked him senseless. He staggered back from the wall, but the blade seemed to grip him tighter, hauling him to his feet and slapping him into lucidity. Something yanked him up and out of the madness, and for a second Delco saw himself above it all, the rush of power beneath him, the blade cutting through and melting into the wall, coating its surface as it went. Guiding him where it needed to go.

You see? Like this.

Delco heard the familiar voice, somewhere far away, and a smile formed on his face.

He was sitting huddled by the side of a river, a thin blanket around his shoulders, trying to catch the heat from the fire to warm himself. His dripping clothes were staked close to the fire to dry, and he watched sparks float up from the flames and float over them, out into the darkness beyond.

Rawick strode suddenly into the light, his skin still dripping from the water. He smiled as he reached out and grabbed Delco's hands, pulled them out so the blanket billowed out behind him like a great sail. Instantly Delco could feel more heat become trapped in it, and his shivering began to subside.

You see? Like this.

Now go, little brother.

He was dropped into the depths, his memories wiped away, through the rush and out, back into his own body. He staggered away from the wall and landed on his backside.

'Delco!'

Frankle hurried over to him, but Delco waved him away, a stunned look on his face.

'I'm okay, Frankle. Back to your post.'

Delco turned back to the weld wall, noticing the silver shimmer to its surface now. He felt dazed but curiously warm, as though something inside him had been sparked into life.

Well, Higgs. Our part is done. The rest is up to you.

Chapter 30

Wilt followed the others up the gently sloping corridor to the surface. At regular intervals they passed heavy red cloaks piled carelessly on the ground. It was as if they had been purposely discarded, left as markers of how the Sisters' guards—the Sentinels—had cast aside their physical selves and returned to their true serpent forms.

The Sister walked a few steps ahead of him, and Wilt noticed her shoulders tighten as they passed the abandoned cloaks.

'You still feel them?'

'No. Not anymore.'

The Sisters had discovered the serpents in the depths and brought them up to the human world. They'd harnessed the serpents' power, keeping them as weapons and trophies, yet the Sisters had remained unaware of how the serpents has woven themselves into their hive mind. Gradually taking control.

Wilt was broken from his thoughts by bright sunlight as they turned the last corner and walked through a doorway into the open air. The street was completely deserted.

Petron and Biore supported Wrexley between them, but the sunlight and fresh air seemed to help revive him. After a few moments he pushed Biore away and took his own weight, one arm still slung around Petron.

'Where is everyone?' Wilt whispered, afraid of breaking the spell.

Petron patted Wrexley on the shoulder, then pushed him gently away to stand on his own. 'Come. That's what we're going to find out.'

They waited for Wrexley to take one or two halting steps, slowly regaining control of his limbs.

The Sister stood off to the side, her eyes wide. 'Redmondis.'

Wilt wondered what was going through her mind.

She noticed him staring and answered his unspoken question. 'I—I've never seen it like this … Never …'

'Never paid too much attention. Never thought it necessary.' Biore finished her sentence for her and moved off down the empty street.

The Sister tossed her head back proudly before following after him.

Wilt watched her move gracefully down the street, the aura of power and authority gathering around her with every step.

'Daemi!'

Petron's voice rang out from further up the road, and Wilt hurried to catch up. From a side street, a tired looking party of guards shuffled toward them, still scanning the rooftops and doorways suspiciously. They were led by Daemi, striding confidently in front, ready to take on any threat.

Wilt smiled as she approached, then wondered what was wrong as she stiffened to attention, her face cold.

Petron waved his hand as if to dismiss a spell. 'Oh, don't worry about all that, Daemi. This Sister is no longer your commander.'

The Sister threw an angry glance at him and was about to speak when Wrexley interrupted her weakly.

'Many things have changed, Daemi. Too many to explain now. Tell me, where are the others?'

Daemi looked back and forth between the Sister and the Cantor, unsure if she was being tested. 'Gone, Wrexley. We are all that remain—at least, all that I know of. We've lost contact with the rest of the guards from the barracks. Cortis's wolves swept through, scattering us like leaves. I only hope some of the others had the sense to retreat. We're trying to work our way back to the barracks now.'

She stopped to catch her breath, panting silently.

'We ran into a small group of them, humans and dogs, led by a couple of wolves. We were outnumbered. Something happened though—the wolves fled, as though following some silent call. The pack fell apart. The dogs … it was as though they wanted to die. They threw themselves on our swords.'

'Cortis felt the rupture,' the Sister said proudly, as if defying any of the others to comment further on the matter.

Petron studied the sorry group of guards standing behind Daemi. They were out on their feet with exhaustion.

'We're going to pay Cortis a little visit. We can pass by the armoury on the way—make sure your men get back safely. Stay behind us.'

Daemi stiffened to attention, her eyes flashing. 'Cantor Wrexley. It is my sworn duty to protect you at all times. I will take my rightful position in the vanguard.'

Wilt smiled as she glared at Petron, daring him to say another word.

Wrexley chuckled and waved his hand to calm her. 'Of course you will, Daemi. But your men have extended themselves beyond what can be expected of them. Let them guard the rear to ensure we aren't taken by surprise.'

Daemi seemed ready to respond, but looked over the troop and noticed for the first time their obvious exhaustion. 'Very well,' she squeezed through gritted teeth, and turned back to organise her men.

'If it's all the same to the rest of you,' said Biore, 'I might just scout ahead. Ensure there aren't any nasty surprises waiting for us. Wilt, care to join me?'

Wilt saw the hungry glint in Biore's eyes and felt the answering pull in his gut. He was about to accept when the Sister spoke up.

'No. This one should stay. We … I … can better use his power.'

Biore chewed his lip for a moment, then nodded and moved away. Within moments Wilt felt the change, and a dark shadow moved off ahead of them, seeking out its first victim.

Wrexley shuddered suddenly and Petron hurried to his side. 'I'm all right,' Wrexley protested, but let Petron throw his arm around his shoulder. 'Just a little weak.'

Petron glared briefly back at the Sister, then slowly hobbled off. Daemi trotted past to catch up with them and resume her march, her cloak thrown back and her hand flexing eagerly above the long knife at her hip.

'What did you do to Wrexley?' Wilt asked the Sister, surprised that he was able to speak freely now, as if the stunning power of her aura had faded in the daylight.

'We ... we emptied him.' The Sister halted over her words, as if trying to form foreign concepts into a language that wasn't designed for them. 'The Sentinels ... they convinced us to question him, to seek out the truth. We were quite thorough.' She paused. 'He should not have lived.'

'And yet he does.'

'Yes. He does. Because of you, and the other ... Petron. He held some part of the Cantor inside of him, some part that called him back. Back from the depths.'

'They share a strong connection. Petron is his ward.'

'His ward, yes. That is what you men call it. It was forbidden.'

'By the Sisters? Or by your so-called servants?'

The Sister ignored him and glided silently away to follow the others.

Wilt sighed, pondering what she had meant earlier when she said she could better use him. He was beginning to tire of being used.

They had no trouble on the way to the armoury. The streets were still deserted, and though Wilt felt the hot rush of hunger and joy once or twice as Biore claimed a victim, they saw no more guards on the street.

Daemi's exhausted troop tried to protest being left behind, but a few choice words from their captain silenced them soon enough. Petron attempted to order Daemi to stay with them, but all it took was one glare in reply for her to make it clear she would be going with them.

As they travelled through the streets, Wilt could feel power drawing into the Sister with each step, as though from the stone of the streets itself. She walked in silence, her eyes eagerly scanning the buildings, drinking in every image.

Finally he trotted up beside her. 'What did Biore mean before? About you never seeing Redmondis like this—never finding it necessary?'

The Sister studied him, as if searching for an insult in his words. Eventually she answered. 'When we—the Sisters—when we first gained power, many years ago now, we recognised the strength within these stones. We delved into the depths, both physically and in other ways.' She glanced at him. 'You know the depths I speak of.'

Wilt saw a flash of a rushing river, the flowing power that called to him, inviting him into the darkness below. 'Yes. I know.' His voice suddenly sounded very small.

'You are unusual in that respect. Most of your kind, most wielders, they keep their power on the surface. Like Wrexley.' She nodded toward the front, where Wrexley still hobbled along on Petron's shoulder. 'This allows them certain talents, like the form shifting they take such pride in. But it misses so much more.'

They continued on in silence for a few seconds.

'Biore was hinting at a truth, I believe.' The Sister's jaw was clenched, as though she was fighting not to spit out the words. 'We spent too long within the depths. Too long blinkered by those we thought our servants. We forgot about all of this.' She gestured around them and dropped her head. 'We were made to forget, perhaps.'

For the first time Wilt saw something like sadness in her eyes, her cold beauty dropping away to reveal something human. 'What is your name?' he blurted.

The Sister glared up at him in surprise, then her expression melted into a weak smile. 'We—I—have no name. Not anymore.' She picked up her pace and strode away from Wilt, ending the conversation.

'Having a nice chat are we?'

Wilt spun around to see Daemi behind him, a twisted grin on her face. Her eyes weren't smiling, however.

'I—I thought you were up the front.'

'I was. I wanted to drop back and see what all the fuss is about. I've never actually met a Sister before, you know. She's very beautiful, isn't she?'

Wilt knew immediately he couldn't answer with any honesty and expect to keep his nose unbloodied. 'Um … I suppose so. I hadn't thought about it.'

'Really?'

'I mean, if you like that sort of thing. Not my type at all, of course.'

'Of course.' Daemi scowled, and Wilt rushed to change the subject.

'What about you—I mean, how are the other guards?'

Daemi hesitated, scanning the rooftops, though Wilt knew Biore had already thoroughly scoured the areas ahead.

'They're tired, but they will survive. This will provide them with good experience at least. They will all find their swords bloodied.'

'Was the fighting that bad?'

'At first. The wolves are the worst. They are cunning: they know each move before you make it, and their reflexes are better than ours. But they don't improvise well.'

Daemi suddenly shot out a foot and pushed Wilt over it, tripping him and sending him flying through the air. He rolled as he landed and came to his feet, grinning.

'Not bad. Shouldn't have let me catch you at all though. What are you grinning at?'

Wilt moved his arm out from behind him to reveal Daemi's long knife, still in its sheath, Daemi's belt still trailing from it. His hands had been quicker than ever. Higgs would hardly believe it.

Daemi stormed toward him and Wilt backed away, dropping the knife.

'Careful now, without your belt you're liable to lose your trousers. Wouldn't want to create a scene.'

Daemi's face went a shade of red Wilt had never seen before as she snatched up her belt and buckled it back on. He took another few paces away just to be on the safe side.

She took a deep breath and her face slowly returned to its normal shade. Eventually she held up her hand. 'I might have deserved that. Truce.'

Wilt wasn't sure he could trust her, but knew better than to openly doubt a soldier's word. 'Truce.'

They resumed their march behind the others, trotting along to catch up.

'Yes, the wolves are the worst. They were his best soldiers. Are, I suppose.'

Wilt remembered the guard, Maron, the one Daemi had captured. He remembered the feel of his mind, the twisted thoughts and cold distance. 'Cortis changed more than just their form.'

Daemi waited to see if Wilt would say any more on the subject, then continued. 'But there are only so many wolves. The others, the humans, are not as well trained. You can tell when you fight them—they don't have their hearts in it. They fight from fear of the consequences of not fighting. They outnumber us, but we will overrun them given time. As for the dogs—' She seemed to find the thought unpleasant, and twisted her mouth at the words. 'I'm not sure what they are. They seem … unnatural.'

Wilt thought about asking more, but saw pain in Daemi's eyes. It wrenched something inside his chest, and for a moment he thought about putting his arm around her.

Another good way to end up with a bloodied nose.

'Daemi!' Wrexley called from up ahead, and Daemi immediately trotted to the front of the group to answer the call.

Wilt watched her go, then broke into a run to catch up with the others. He felt a change in the atmosphere, as though they had just passed through an invisible wall, and it suddenly seemed crucial to make sure Daemi was safe.

Biore stepped out from a laneway to the side and waved as he approached. 'Up ahead. Cortis's dogs are rounding up the last few hideaways.'

Wilt couldn't help notice the bright glow of energy in Biore's face and knew he had been feeding well. Biore met his gaze levelly before gesturing down the road.

In the distance, figures ran to and fro across the road, and smoke poured out of a couple of the larger buildings.

The Sister stood tall, glaring at the chaos as though judging it. 'Come. We can remove these vermin easily enough.'

'Wait.' Petron held up his hand and took a step away from Wrexley. 'No point simply charging in there.' He knelt down and brought a small polished stone out of his cloak, then began tracing strange designs in the dirt with it.

The Sister watched him work, her face twisting in disgust as the design became clearer. 'Such skills were declared anathema.'

Petron didn't look up from his work, but Wrexley answered for him.

'A lot of mistakes were made in the Great Cleansing. Perhaps we can start fixing some of them.'

Petron clapped his hands above the design and sat back on his heels. The intricate pattern glowed with a bright light, then disappeared immediately, leaving no mark in the road where it had been.

'There,' Petron whispered. 'Let's see what our little trap can summon.'

Daemi drew her sword as a large dog lumbered down the road toward them.

Wrexley held up his hand and waved Daemi back. 'It's okay, child. Move back. It cannot see us. It cannot see anything but the design that summoned it.'

The dog moved awkwardly, as though it wasn't sure how exactly its back legs should work. At times they bounded forward together; at others they trotted one at a time like a horse.

'Gods,' Petron groaned as the creature approached.

Its skin was stretched strangely over its bones, bald patches appearing in its dark coat. It was as though it were wearing a much smaller dog's skin. Its breath wheezed, and great streams of drool dripped from its jaws. As it reached the summons, it raised its head and sniffed the air. Then Wilt saw the worst of it.

Its eyes were human, great wide panicked eyes filled with pain and despair, as though it were living a waking nightmare, watching from somewhere deep inside its head.

'Cortis, you monster. What have you done?' Wrexley whispered, swaying slightly on his feet as though the very sight of the thing weakened him.

'I will end this.' The Sister stepped forward and raised her hand. Power surged around her, then shot out from her fingers in five thin welds, wrapping around the dog and weaving a net around it.

The dog let out a single whimper of pain before collapsing into death.

'This creature should not be,' the Sister said coldly, her hand still outstretched. Wilt saw the net around the dog glow as more power poured into it, stripping away what had been to reveal its true form.

'Enough,' Biore whispered, and the Sister dropped her hand, her weld vanishing instantly.

On the ground in front of them lay a young man, a Black Robe judging by what was left of his clothing. His limbs were twisted unnaturally, his face warped and wrenched with pain, his eyes open and staring out from the other side of life.

Daemi sheathed her sword and moved away, then one by one the others followed, until Wilt was left alone, staring into the young man's eyes, unable to grasp true extent of the suffering that had ended here before him.

Cold rage churned inside his mind, whispering of the possibilities should he allow the power and darkness within him to flow free. For a moment he allowed it to rush over him, the dizzying swell of it wiping the world around him away. Then he clamped down on it, pulling himself back from the darkness to join the others.

Each member of the group made a vow silently, in their own words, but for each the vow was the same.

Cortis would pay for what he had done.

Chapter 31

Higgs found it easier each time he changed form. It was as though he knew every aspect of it now, and could slip in and out at will.

The cat trotted smoothly out of the shadows and down the stairs, his senses on guard. It smelled like the dogs and their guards had returned to the ground floor after their earlier chase. The cat proceeded cautiously, his human side still not trusting his nose.

Two flights down and he still hadn't encountered any guards. He couldn't be certain, but he recalled running up the wall from this spot to avoid the guards. Sure enough, the wall next to the staircase was scarred with claw marks from his earlier ascent.

But something had changed. The guards had gone.

He sniffed the air again, sorting through the troubling scents that rose from below, then continued silently down the stairs.

'I told you why.'

'You gave me excuses. Complained about the pain. Always complaining.'

'I just don't understand why it's necessary. I'm good with a sword, why not use it?'

The cat slipped his head through a gap in the banister to peer down on the two men. Something told him to wait. Wait and listen.

'Good with a sword, yet always waiting for someone else to strike first. Never quite at the front of the queue.'

'Funes, I proved my use to you, didn't I? When I showed you the trail on the rooftops?'

'Stop whining. If you can't bring yourself to follow orders, at least keep your mouth shut.'

Funes. The big man was Funes. Smelled of dog, and wolf, and sweat and blood. So the other, much smaller one, the one who smelled of fear and nervous excitement, that one was-

'Red Charley. Seems to me we should look at changing it. Maybe Pink Charley is more your style. Or Yellow Charley.'

The smaller man just grinned weakly back.

'Something is up. Cortis and his wolves moved out in a big hurry to go take care of it. That means I'm in charge. And I say, we get everyone together and sweep out what's left of the stragglers in here. Show Cortis we're good for more than just guard duty and chasing phantom trails on rooftops in the night. C'mon.'

Funes grabbed Red Charley by the shoulder and pulled him away. Angry voices called back and forth as they formed their patrol.

The cat sat back on his haunches and began idly licking his paw. Perhaps this would be easier than he thought.

After a few minutes the voices returned, followed by the sound of many pairs of heavy boots.

'Right. Those of you who can, change. We can use your noses to ferret out the last of the rats.'

The cat felt a change in the air, though there was no sound. Dogs. He readied himself.

'Red Charley?'

'No Funes, I can't. I'll—'

'You'll stay as weak as you are. Very well. I'll be sure Cortis hears all about this when he asks me to join the circle.'

The cat saw Funes change and the patrol of guards and dogs begin to march up the stairs. Now he just needed to add a sense of urgency.

The cat dropped onto the floor, rubbing across the cold stone. A little scent to help things along the way.

Once the steps were thoroughly marked, he danced back

upstairs onto the banister, where he would have a good view of the action to come.

Seconds later the first of the dogs came panting up the stairs, diving straight for the spot where the cat had left his scent. The dogs snorted eagerly at the floor, consuming the scent, as if it fed some hunger in them. More and more of them gathered around it, nudging each other out of the way in their eagerness.

Human guards pushed through, shoving the dogs aside, examining the floor to see what all the fuss was about.

'What is it? Move back, you fools. You can't all stand in the one spot,' Red Charley called out, trying to maintain some sort of order.

The largest dog, Funes, shoved its way in and begin snorting at the ground.

Now was as good a time as any.

The cat leaped off the banister, claws out and ready. He landed right on Funes's back, his claws ripping into the hair on the dog's haunches. He had time for one extra touch, an angry nip at the dog's ear, drawing blood as he tore the exposed flesh. Then he sprang away and the chase began.

The great dog bucked, spinning and snapping at where the cat had been, then pounced after the cat as he darted through the crowd of humans and dogs.

Most of the others hadn't even seen the cat, just felt him rush past, and were immediately bounced off their feet as Funes charged after him.

Red Charley was the first to find his voice. 'After it!'

Those still on their feet charged up the stairs after Funes, and the others pulled themselves up and hurried after them.

Red Charley waved them past, making sure he took up a position toward the rear.

On the floor above, the cat raced from step to step, jumping sideways to dodge the snapping jaws of the large dog on his tail. The dog was quicker than it looked.

Not long now. Just a few more steps.

He reached the landing and raced across the floor. He heard the hungry joy in the dog's heavy breath. It had him now. There was nowhere to hide.

The cat raced toward the strange, shimmering silver wall, then at the last moment jumped into the air. His mouth closed around the thin, almost invisible rope they had left hanging from the ceiling for just this purpose, all four legs hugging himself as the rope swung with sudden momentum toward the silver wall, tail coming within a hair of the surface before swinging back to safety.

The dog had no chance at all. It raced straight through the barrier, and the cat heard a yelp of terror before the sound was suddenly cut off, as though a door was slammed shut. Several dogs skidded through after it, but the stragglers managed to stop before they hit the wall, sniffing and whining at strange silver barrier, confused that their pack had completely disappeared.

The cat had pulled himself up onto the ceiling beams and settled down to watch the scene below.

Human guards began to push through the mess of dogs, angrily slapping them around the ears and ordering them forward, but never getting too close to the silver wall.

'What is it?' one of the guards yelled to another nearer the front of the bottleneck.

'Some sort of Black Robe trap. Go through it, Scriver.' The dog at the guard's feet whined and shrunk away from the wall.

'Lead it through, why don't you?'

The guard at the wall looked back at the other and shook his head. 'Oh no. After you.'

At that moment the silver wall vanished and the corridor beyond was revealed. Funes and the other dogs who had crashed through the barrier lay on the ground in their human form, their eyes empty. Beyond them, stepping out of the doorways, were Delco and the other Black Robes.

Delco waved his arm forward, a grim smile on his lips. 'Attack!'

Instantly a weave of welds shot out from the Black Robes into the guards and dogs that stood before them, welds of all colours that struck their victims like snakes. Guards fell to their knees and dogs dropped on their bellies to whine for mercy as the welds burrowed in.

As each body dropped into unconsciousness, the welds jumped to the next. Lightning bolts of power arced between the bodies, searching for the next victim. Soon those who could began to flee, pushing and trampling each other in their rush to escape. Within moments, all that was left were unconscious bodies, and the Black Robes let out a cheer of victory.

Higgs dropped to the floor, landing on his two feet. He brushed himself off and smiled at Delco and the others. 'Victory!'

'Your plan worked,' Delco said, though didn't join the others in their cheer. At his feet lay the piled bodies of those who had crashed through the weld wall.

Higgs stepped through the bodies toward where Delco stood, above Funes's giant form stretched out on the floor. He kicked it quickly with the toe of his boot. 'Dead?'

Delco nodded, then looked away to study the others. 'The moonsteel stripped their form from them, and didn't allow their minds to change back. It left them to drown in pain and madness. Still, at least it was quick.'

Higgs kicked Funes's body again, not so lightly this time. 'I suppose we can't have everything. And the others? The ones who didn't go through the wall?'

'Most will probably survive. I didn't aim to kill anyone, just knock them senseless for a good day or two. Some of the others might not have been so forgiving. Or so precise.'

Higgs watched the Black Robes smiling and congratulating each other, then scanned the bodies around them, noticing more than one pair of dead eyes staring back at him. 'It had to be done.'

'Did it?'

Higgs simply turned away, unable to give him the answer he required.

'Now what?' Delco asked, his quiet voice bringing silence to the corridor as the other Black Robes noticed his sombre mood.

'Now we take the fight to Cortis.' Higgs began poking through the bodies at his feet. 'Has anyone seen my sword?'

Frankle stepped forward. 'Uh, I saw it fall. When the weld wall came down, I saw it fall to the ground. But—'

Higgs turned to him expectantly.

'But one of the guards. One that got away. He grabbed it.'

'One of the guards took it? Did you see where?'

'He ran down the stairs. He had red hair, I saw that much. I wanted to stop him but—'

'It's okay, Frankle,' Delco said. 'At least you saw something.'

Higgs swore silently under his breath. 'Red Charley.'

Delco looked over at him, a questioning look on his face.

'An old friend. C'mon, he'll be heading back to Cortis. At least he can show us the way.'

Chapter 32

The garrison was one of the few buildings in Redmondis designed with no thought for aesthetics. The Black Robes' tower reached high into the sky, each spire seeming to urge the others on in their pursuit of architectural glory. The crafters' towers, on the other hand, twisted around each other like vines, curving and dipping in unexpected ways. Even the guards' living quarters, where Wilt had stumbled into Daemi's room days earlier, were built to enhance light and fresh air, if not as intricately designed as the others.

The Redmondis garrison, however, was built purely for defence. It squatted alone between sheer cliffs, only accessible from one side, a single open road where any advancing threat could be seen early and dealt with efficiently. It was the most easily defendable area in Redmondis, and it was where Cortis had made his base.

Wilt and the others surveyed the wide open road to the compound ahead, noting the trenches dug at intervals down the road's length, and the tall thin guard towers dotted alongside, no doubt manned with archers. Even at this distance they could see the brunt of Cortis's guard moving between the trenches and mulling about the towers that stood between them and their goal.

'Well I suppose the element of surprise was too much to expect,' Petron grumbled.

Wrexley sagged against Petron's shoulder and patted him weakly. 'You forget our secret weapon.'

The Sister strode forward and raised her chin toward the road in front of them. 'Come. This should not be a problem. You.' She waved dismissively at Wilt. 'Stay by me. I may need you.'

Daemi grunted something under her breath as Wilt sidled up beside the Sister.

'The rest of you stay behind us.' With that the Sister began striding down the middle of the road, her head high, as if she was leading a parade. Wilt walked behind her, trying not to look too out of place.

The first guards were still a longbow shot away when Wilt felt it. A warm wave of power washed out from the Sister, straight down the middle of the road, crashing over him and leaving him wallowing in its shallows.

The guards didn't know what hit them. One minute they were readying their arrows, the next they were thrown fifty feet into the air by a great invisible force, crashing down to the packed earth once gravity regained its hold. The lucky ones lost consciousness, or were left writhing in pain with broken bones. The less fortunate lay still, never having known what power had ended them.

Wilt stared at the back of the Sister's head, trying to work out what she had done. It was unlike any use of the skill he had encountered. There was no surge, no rush or release. It was something else, something alien to him.

They continued down the road, the wave of power having moved beyond them now, slowly weakening as it pulled away. Guards in the distance lost their footing, then pulled themselves to their feet. Another wave rushed out, even larger than the last, blowing the bodies before them into the air.

On the Sister continued, never breaking her stride.

Wilt couldn't help himself. He sent a weld toward her, reaching into her mind.

Ah. I wondered when you'd get here.

Wilt almost jerked to a stop as he felt the Sister's mind close around his weld, dragging him inside her.

Come. Do not fear. This is the way.

He doubted he could resist anyway. A wild vortex sucked him through the weld into her mind, into the great pool of power that raged inside her.

You see? This is the way.

Wilt recognised the panic that rushed into him as he fell, yet it felt somehow distant, as though he were watching a copy of himself drowning in the surging tide. He knew he should feel something, but he was beyond that. Only one part of the power. There was no he. There was only—

We. We are one.

His consciousness of himself was wiped clean, leaving just the ebb and flow of the power, tides surging through his mind. Thoughts became clear, but weren't limited to any one mind to make or share them. Time became meaningless.

Now you see. We see. The true way. The true meaning of the skill. Within you and without you.

Some part of them moved an arm and another wash of power pulsed out, wiping their feeble enemies away.

We were not sure your kind could share this. Other men have been too wrapped up in their self, their power fixed to their image of themselves. They take on other shapes but always return to their base selves.

The power swirled and twisted around what used to be Wilt. Spiralling and gathering speed, sucking further into the darkness.

But this—this aspect of power. This focus. The prophecy told of this. This is what we have been missing. Ah, my Sisters. How could we have known?

The waters tore around his mind. Not, not waters. Blood. Blood that throbbed with a heat and life that coated the stone walls of their heart. Obliterating awareness.

We have found the key.

The darkness became complete. The thoughts were now just a whisper.

Too late. Too late. The blood within the stone.

An explosion of movement and light knocked Wilt back into himself and threw him out of the now still waters. For an instant he was aware of a slithering body twining around him, a gaping maw ready to swallow him whole, then the serpent's head was knocked aside and it twisted away from him. He reached for its tail and held on, letting it pull him back up to the light and movement. To the real world.

Wilt was on one knee, his eyes clearing to focus on the toe of his shoe in the dirt. He flexed his foot and was mildly amazed to see his thought become action in front of his eyes.

'Wilt!' Daemi's voice cut through the numb silence, and he turned to see her running toward him, waving her arms. She was so far away.

The sound of the world popped back into existence, and everything sped back up. Wilt pushed himself to his feet and turned to face what he knew would be there.

Just in front of him the Sister lay crumpled in the dirt, her eyes open and aware, her body straining against invisible bonds. Surrounding them lay the stunned and broken bodies of Cortis's guard, and in the doorway in front of them stood two red-robed Sentinels.

Wilt could feel their contemptuous judgment as he stood to face them. Their mocking dismissal of his threat.

The Sister let out a low groan. They were killing her. Removing the last of their constraints.

Wilt gathered himself and sent out a weld. He knew he couldn't hope to penetrate their minds, so he entered that of their victim instead. The weld slipped into the Sister, and into pain.

We are lost.

The waters foamed as the serpents thrashed inside it, hunting down every last scrap of awareness that still muddied its depths. Wilt tumbled and struggled as the surf knocked him back and forth, pushing into his nose and throat, choking him. Instead of fighting against it, he let the panic wash through him, refusing to react to it, watching himself drown.

They come, desperate to feed. They are beyond our control. We are lost.

He was aware of the other Sisters' minds now. Those who had survived the earlier assault, those who were in hiding but still linked as one. The source of the Sisters' power now served as the means to discover and hunt them down. The serpents consumed them, burrowing through the connections of their hive mind to end them forever, using this final act of betrayal as the means to generate the power they needed to separate from the sucking depths completely

I am lost.

Wilt saw the Sister at his feet, the life fading out of her as the serpent closed its jaws around her, saw her meet death suddenly alone.

No.

Wilt pushed into the weld, through the waters, into the depths where the serpents lay. In a cold rage he sliced through the strangely twisting link that served as the weld between their mind and that of the Sisters, ignoring the jumble and panic of the alien minds of the serpents, then moved into the darkness beyond.

He was aware of an overriding sense of size, of the still enormity of the world around him. A world that suddenly became aware of his existence.

You.

The voice was both within and without him, wiping away his ability to think. He was an ant. Less than that. A single being. He was nothing. Nothing at all.

The blackness swallowed him whole, absorbing and erasing him.

Not yet.

A single voice sung out through the darkness, a single white light floated by. Another. There was another.

Not yet. Too soon. Go back.

Wilt was in himself again, in his own mind and body. The darkness was separate.

Go back. Too soon.

The light trailed away from him, and he pushed himself after it, swimming through the blackness.

This way. This is the way.

Wilt pulled away from the sucking darkness, felt it lose its hold on him. He was too small. Too difficult to grasp.

You see. Like this.

The light hovered in place, speaking in a voice so familiar, someone he knew.

Delco's lost brother. He was here, inside the depths of the welds.

Wilt approached the surface, saw the movement and life beyond it, and pushed through, a single name on his lips.

Rawick.

Wilt broke through into the rush and disarray of the serpents' dance. They instantly twisted around him, darting in at their prey, bustling each other in their rush to strike. A serpent knocked its rival aside and bore down, its mouth gaping as it closed over him. With the lightest rush of power, as though a delicate wind brushed against Wilt's hair, the serpent was gone, absorbed, sucked into the great well of nothingness that lay inside him. The well he now controlled.

The other serpents didn't seem to notice the fate of the first and rushed at Wilt, hungrily snapping their jaws. He waited for them to come, let them take him, let them dive through him into the nothingness beyond, let them die in the darkness, in the place that had born them, the place they had so desperately tried to escape.

One by one the serpents broke on him, wiping themselves away. Eventually the waters quieted, the waves rolled out and the foam melted into clear stillness. Wilt looked around at the empty waters of power, the nothingness that remained of the Sisters and their linked minds.

It could be his, all of this. If he wanted it. If he remained.

'Wilt!' Daemi's voice called him, and his human mind took hold.

Not yet.

He heard the words again as he pushed back up to the surface, away from the darkness, away from the power. Power that would be his.

Wilt opened his eyes to see Daemi peering into his face, her hair tumbling around her head, her mouth twisted in worry. He allowed himself a smile then sat up, pushing his mouth against hers.

The world disappeared as the heat of her lips against his blocked out all else. Then she shoved him to the ground and pushed away, wiping her mouth.

'That's quite enough of that!' She stood up quickly and hurried away, leaving Wilt grinning stupidly at her back.

'Well, well, it seems there's life in him yet!' Petron chuckled and patted Wrexley on the shoulder.

Wilt scrambled to his feet, and saw Biore in the middle of the road, crouched over the Sister's body.

'She's dead.' Biore stood up. 'Not drained though, something else. Something *they* did.'

'The serpents,' Wilt whispered, then turned quickly as he remembered the red-robed figures standing in the doorway.

Daemi was stamping on the robes, as if checking for mice hiding in them. 'There's nothing here. They're gone.'

Biore continued to stare at Wilt, who returned his look calmly.

'They're all gone now.'

Chapter 33

Higgs jogged down the middle of the deserted street, hardly noticing the bodies strewn here and there by the side of the road. Victims of earlier battles, guards and crafters and Black Robes, humans and dogs. No longer any threat.

'C'mon!' He waved impatiently to where Delco and the other Black Robes were crowded together, nervously scanning the road, waiting to be set upon by some hidden enemy. 'They're all gone. Or dead. Either way, hurry up!'

They didn't raise their step above a walk, exhausted and terrified, still in shock from what they had seen and done in the tower, and especially from the shuddering movement of the failed transformations they had found on the ground floor—evidence of what Cortis had planned for them.

Higgs could see they were at their limit, but he urged them on nonetheless. 'We have to get that blade back. Hurry up!'

'What's so important about the damn sword anyway?' Frankle muttered, his eyes darting back and forth across the road, jumping from victim to victim, each sight worse than the last.

'I'm not sure. But it is important. Moonsteel. And something more, something to do with the welds,' Delco answered calmly, trying to distract his young friend from the scene around them. 'Cortis wants it for some reason, which means we have to stop him from getting his hands on it. Or at least try. Try our best for the others, the ones who weren't as lucky as us.' He patted Frankle gently on the shoulder, and the boy looked up sadly and nodded in reply. 'C'mon then. Let's put Higgs out of his misery. Speed up.'

The group took their lead from Delco, and they quickened their pace.

Higgs grunted in frustration, but knew they were trying their best and kept his mouth shut. At least it was clear which way to go.

The road ahead led through the centre of Redmondis, and straight toward the high cliffs where the garrison squatted. It made sense that this was where Cortis had made his camp and, from the increasing number of bodies on the road as they approached, they knew they were on the right track.

Red Charley had come this way. Fled from the fight, like he always did. Higgs was determined to have a few words with Red Charley when they caught up with him. More than just a few words.

At first the group had been slow to creep out of their tower, afraid the guards below would rally and they'd face another attack. But the guards seemed to have lost all fight, as though their leaders had fled the field, deserted them and left them to their own devices. Those guards they did encounter were quick to surrender at the sight of a group of Black Robes approaching them. Higgs had tried questioning the first couple they found, but hadn't been able to get more than a few grunted replies. Each had seemed damaged in some way, as though they'd surrendered some part of their will to another, and now it had gone they'd lost all sense of direction or focus.

He almost pitied them. Almost.

Eventually Higgs's angry questioning had led to them being waved down the road, toward the garrison beyond. They were on the right track, but they'd lost valuable time, and Red Charley was well ahead of them now. Red Charley and the sword.

As they continued, Higgs noticed something change in the air. The bodies strewn along the road changed too. There was no longer any bloody evidence of fights or gruesome victims of pack attacks from Cortis's dogs. The bodies they found now lay still and calm, knocked senseless by some great force.

Higgs slowed to peer at each face he passed, unable to completely convince himself they weren't about to jump up and attack.

'Great power has been used here. Can you feel it?' Delco spoke softly, as if unwilling to disturb the silence.

'A tingling,' Frankle answered.

'Yes. Someone took care of these guards quickly, with a minimum of fuss or care. And didn't mind what sort of trail they'd leave.'

'Cortis?' Higgs asked. The tingling became a strange tickle down his spine, an itch he couldn't quite scratch.

'No. Not Cortis. This power was not … male.'

Higgs stared at Delco, who let the silence stretch. 'Wilt was going to the Sisters. Perhaps they are helping.'

Delco didn't seem to like that thought at all, and his mouth twisted in reply. 'Perhaps.'

They strode on toward the garrison, through the broken rubble and bodies that fanned out from the road in front of them.

The tickling gained intensity as they approached, and Higgs could tell by the silence of the others that each sensed the power around them. His crafter sense often picked up force and power in objects, able to feel its presence like an electric field around the object he was studying. This was more like that, but still different. Something familiar, as if some lost part of him was calling out, leading him on.

A lost part—that was it. The blade. The moonsteel blade.

Higgs's fingers itched where his claws had been, as if they wanted to break through his skin. He looked over at Delco, who was frowning at some private thought.

'It's not just that, is it?' Higgs asked him. 'It's the blade. I can feel it.'

Delco shook his head slightly and continued on, unwilling to pursue the conversation.

If Higgs felt the pull in his fingertips, where would Delco feel it?

Delco, who had merged the blade in with the weld wall, and who had given over something of himself in the process.

They walked past a deep trench scarred into the ground, and the crumpled remains of a high guard tower collapsed over half of it. Suddenly Higgs felt the pull change, away from the road.

'Wait.'

The others stopped, eager for any excuse not to continue into the growing sense of dread and power settling over them like a blanket.

'This way.' Higgs pointed to the trench, into the shadows below the broken crossbeam of the tower. 'The blade—Red Charley went this way.'

He jumped into the trench, not waiting for the others. Ducking under the heavy wooden beam, he could see the markings of a trail in the dirt. A single set of footprints. He followed them quickly, hearing the others drop behind him. The trail twisted around broken parts of tower, sinking deeper into the ground, and ended at a small wooden door cut into what looked like rock.

'It must be a hidden entrance, some sort of shortcut. The guards probably had them everywhere to move between positions without being seen.'

Higgs pulled at the door, and it swung open easily to reveal dark, curved tunnel. 'We're close. I can feel it.'

'Can't you do something about the dark?' Higgs whispered, and winced at the sound of his voice slithering down the tunnel. They had been walking for at least an hour, and even his practiced night vision was ineffective in the complete darkness. He walked with one hand on the wall, fingers tracing along the dirt and rock; his other stuck out in front of him, hoping to prevent any collision. Higgs knew that time had a way of stretching out when one had no sense or data to rely on—he'd spent many hours running through underground tunnels in Greystone, secret passages between warehouses for those who didn't trust the night highway or the streets themselves. Still, even he was beginning to feel the air close in around him. He could only imagine how Delco and the other Black Robes were suffering.

Delco didn't need any further prompting. A torchstone was produced from the folds of his robes and passed up to Higgs, who tried to avoid looking at it directly but waved its light in front of him. Nothing but blank passageway stretching for as far as he could see. He passed the torchstone back to Delco.

'Keep it close so the light shines past me.'

Higgs saw the drawn, traumatised faces of the young men as the torchstone was passed back. 'Everyone all right?'

'We're fine, Higgs,' Delco answered firmly, hoping his confidence would catch on with the others. 'Go on.'

The tunnel was no more than an arm-span wide and high enough for Higgs to walk through, though Delco had to hunch his shoulders and some of the taller guards would have to bend over almost completely to move through it. Every twenty paces or so they'd cross the entrance to a similar tunnel, leading off no doubt to another trench cut into the road above them. At first Higgs had paused at each branch, unsure as to which way to continue, but the pull of the blade became stronger as they went on, and now he didn't even hesitate. He felt the pull in his fingertips and his chest, urging him onwards.

Higgs.

Delco whispered directly into his mind, as though he had held his lips right up to his ear. Higgs jumped at the sensation and almost stopped in place.

Sorry. Don't panic. It's me, Delco.

He was about to reply when the voice in his head cut him off.

Don't try to answer. I don't want to panic the others, but have you thought about what exactly we're going to do once we catch up with Cortis?

Higgs hadn't really considered that. He was hoping to catch Red

Charley before he got back to Cortis, though he had to admit that now they were here, that possibility looked less and less likely. Red Charley had the blade and they had to get it back, it was as simple as that. Worrying about Cortis wouldn't help anyone.

Just then the light over his shoulder revealed the tunnel walls ending and opening into a larger space. Higgs waved his arm behind him quickly, and Delco was sharp enough to cover the torchstone before too much light leaked out, giving away their position to anyone waiting in the chamber beyond.

Higgs stood completely still, waiting for his eyes to adjust to the empty darkness again, hoping to pick up some hint of movement.

Nothing.

He slipped back toward Delco and held his lips to his ear. 'I'm going to try and see if my other eyes have any more luck. Stay here and keep quiet.'

Delco nodded slowly and stepped back a few paces, touching each of the other Black Robes on the shoulders, ensuring they were all still together.

Higgs pushed to the front and took a deep breath.

The next moment the small cat peered through the tunnel into the great chamber beyond, his eyes wide, scanning the darkness. Even his night vision struggled here, but there were shapes in the centre of the room. And scents. Men and wolves. Waiting for them.

The cat slipped silently out of the tunnel and crept low along the edge of the wall.

The pull of the blade was stronger now, in this form, an urgency calling to the cat, luring him in to the centre of the room where his prize waited. The cat started to creep toward it, then stopped and shook himself, as if shedding the heavy air that threatened to overwhelm his other senses.

A muffled clatter of metal shot out through the silence from the far side of the chamber, and the cat jumped away from the shadows just as a heavy, panting body landed where he had been, and an angry voice shouted: 'There they are. Get them!'

The shadows poured toward the entrance of the tunnel where Delco and the others hid. The cat saw a flash of light as someone tried to fight back, then his attention was taken by the large wolf that suddenly dropped out of the darkness, the cat's senses only warning him at the last moment. He ducked out of the way of the snapping jaws and sprinted away, sharp claws slicing through the air and just catching the end of his tail, leaving a burning slash.

Chaos broke out everywhere, and a light flared from the centre of the room, a single guard standing on a rock, waving a torch to try to make some sense of the action. The struggling from the tunnel entrance had already died down, and another guard called to the one holding the torch.

'We have them. Stand down.'

'No!' Red Charley's voice called out, and the cat saw him standing at the edge of the light, wide-eyed. 'The cat. Get the cat. He's the one we want.'

Another shadow loomed, and he ducked and rolled away moments before the wolf landed. There were too many of them, and the room was too small to hide in. He was trapped.

But perhaps he could take one or two down with him.

He sprang away from another wolf and danced through the scuffling legs and chaos of the guards. Red Charley was only a few feet away now, peering out into the shadows, trying to make sense of the scene. He couldn't see the small cat slipping through the bodies around him, eyes locked on his face, ready to spring.

The cat leaped and landed on Red Charley's shoulders, reaching around to drag both sets of claws across his unprotected face, feeling them dig into his skin, searching out his eyes. The next moment he felt hot breath behind him and a monster set of jaws clamped down, pulling him free and shaking, threatening to break his back.

'Don't kill it,' another voice called out. 'Cortis's orders.'

The pressure of the jaws lessened slightly and the cat caught a glimpse of Red Charley on his knees, hands locked to his eyes, blood streaming through his fingers. Then he sank into unconsciousness.

Chapter 34

'Wilt!'

Wilt opened his eyes to see Daemi standing next to him, shaking him by the shoulder.

'Are you okay? You look—strange.'

Wilt smiled weakly at her, part of him craving the attention but another, deeper part whispering warnings. 'I'm okay. Just had a … spell.'

Daemi glared at him, studying his face for a moment before striding back to the front of the party. Wilt sagged against the wall, grateful for the darkness. Another vision had overwhelmed his senses. He'd felt hot breath on his neck, then a trap clamping down on him, shaking him like a rag doll. And blood. There had been blood, too.

He breathed in slowly and his mind cleared. Higgs. It had to have been Higgs.

'Wilt?' Petron was standing with him now, his eyes kind. 'Another one?'

'Yes. What?' Wilt looked up, confused.

'Shared visions. They are common among wielders and their wards. They become more so as each share each other's form. I know.'

Wilt relaxed again and nodded to Petron.

'Try not to let them trouble you too much. They are often simply dreams, not grounded in reality.'

Wilt gazed into Petron's sad eyes and forced himself to smile. It hadn't just been a dream.

'Come. Cortis can't be much further. Then we can end this.'

They were inside the garrison, deep underground now, somewhere in the maze of tunnels that twisted and snaked toward the heart of the structure. Daemi had warned them about it, told them of the way the tunnels had been constructed to confuse and exhaust the enemy. Each tunnel took unexpected turns in order to disorientate, and sloped gently up and down at irregular times to tire the mind and body. She had seemed confident she knew the way though, and the others trudged obediently behind her, trying to conserve their strength.

Wilt in particular was tiring badly. His battle with the serpents had taken more out of him than he first realised. The world around him seemed dim and indistinct, as though he'd left something important behind in the depths, something that still called to him, urging him to return. It was draining simply to resist.

Wrexley and Petron leaned on each other for support, and marched with a determined gleam in their eyes, as though both knew they were facing their last battle. Knew and embraced the fact, ready for what would come next.

Biore walked along quietly, keeping his eyes on his feet, a strange expression on his face, listening to faint music only he could hear.

Eventually Daemi stopped and held up her hand. 'Here. The central chamber is up ahead. Cortis will have guards waiting for us.'

Biore placed his hand gently on her shoulder and moved her aside. 'Please. Allow me.'

A shudder of longing passed through Wilt as the shadow form slipped away down the tunnel toward its waiting victims. He closed his eyes and saw still, calm waters—cold dark depths that waited for him.

He felt Biore latch on to his first victim and heard a clatter as the armoured guard, hidden in an alcove ahead, collapsed onto the stone floor.

'Come. While they are distracted.' Petron strode ahead as the sound of heavy marching boots rang out in the silence.

Wilt saw a flash as Daemi drew her long knife and pushed past Petron, an eager expression on her face. She let out a high cry of challenge as she dived toward the guards headed their way.

Wilt moved to help her, but Wrexley grabbed his collar and pulled him to the side, away from the mass of bodies and clashing steel.

'She can look after herself. Come. We must find Cortis.'

They stepped over the first of Biore's victims, his eyes blank.

Petron moved quickly to the centre of the room and bent down to scratch a strange design in the dust. Wilt sensed Biore move in front of him, picking off individual guards who dropped away from the edges of the group circling Daemi. Suddenly Daemi let out another high cry of triumph and four bodies fell away from her.

Wrexley pulled Wilt with him, hobbling awkwardly toward the far door where the reinforcements had appeared.

Petron struggled to his feet just as another group of guards saw him and charged. He hurried toward Wrexley and Wilt, waving frantically at them as he went. As soon as the first guard's feet crossed the markings on the floor, a bright flash filled the room and a great bang shook the air. It was as though lightning had struck inside the chamber, and the group of guards closest to the circle fell senseless to the floor.

Daemi took advantage of the stunning effect of Petron's work to finish off the guards around her, and suddenly the group was alone.

'This way!' Wrexley called out as he pushed Wilt through the door and up the staircase behind it.

Wilt stumbled up the stairs but caught himself and followed Wrexley, who seemed to have completely recovered from his wounds now that the battle was joined.

The stairs led up a level and opened out into a much larger chamber. Wrexley strode to the middle, his arms held high, a challenge on his lips. 'Cortis! Time to answer for your crimes!'

He brought his hands together over his head with a great clap, and another shock of thunder and lightning cracked across the room, knocking over the troop of guards closing in.

Wilt held onto the wall behind him, stunned and weakened, as though all power was being drained from his body. He watched helplessly as the guards and wolves closed around the group in the centre of the room.

Petron hurried past him to stand beside Wrexley, and each threw their hands out, sending out shockwaves of force to knock back any who came too close. Daemi, her eyes gleaming with battle hunger, darted back and forth, each time her blade finding its target. On the far edge of the room, Biore's shadow enveloped victim after victim, his cold touch leaving only death behind.

'Enough!' Cortis barked across the room as the last of the guards fell to Daemi's blade. He stood alone in a high alcove cut into the rock. 'Enough foolishness.'

Wrexley and Petron turned together and raised their voices in unison. 'Cortis!'

Cortis smiled in return. 'Gentlemen, please. Haven't you drained your friend enough?'

His words seemed to shock Petron and Wrexley, who both looked over at Wilt slumped against the wall.

'He has given so much for you. Must you take more?'

Wilt saw the image in front of him double as his vision blurred, and he sunk to his knees.

'Your young friend has opened the door, and you have each fed from the darkness, just as I have. Just as our Master intended.'

Petron continued to stare at Wilt, who was unable to do more than smile weakly. Wrexley looked at his hands, at the power that crackled between his fingers, the power he had wielded so easily just moments before.

'Don't tell me you didn't realise what you were doing?' Cortis chuckled coldly as he saw the effect his words were having.

Suddenly a shadow reared up behind him, and Biore's cold fingers wrapped around his throat. For any other man, that would have been the end, but Cortis simply grimaced in pain and spun quickly, the moonsteel blade in his hand glittering as it plunged into the heart of the shadow.

The shadow seemed to warp around the blade, spinning in a whirlpool of darkness before disappearing completely, leaving Biore standing there, the blade buried in his belly, a look of incomprehension on his face.

'Oh yes. I almost forgot about you. Poor Biore. Tell me, how does this side of death feel?'

Biore tried to choke out a reply, but all that came was a low, gurgling rattle. He stared into Cortis's eyes, who observed him like one would a particularly interesting experiment.

Wilt and Biore both collapsed to the ground together.

Cortis turned from Biore's dead figure at his feet to smile coldly at Wilt. 'I should thank you, I suppose. You returned my prize to me.' He yanked the sword free of Biore's body and held it high in the air. 'Moonsteel. Known in the east as a weld blade. I was wondering if I'd ever see it again. Beautiful, isn't it?'

The silver blade darkened as a black ink flowed from Cortis's hand to cover the blade.

'So powerful, so wonderful.' Cortis seemed hypnotised by the sight.

Wrexley suddenly shot his hand out, sending a glowing ball of energy hurtling toward Cortis. As the crackling ball approached him, Cortis swiped the flat of the weld blade against it and it disappeared, seemingly absorbed into the blackness.

Wrexley's effort surged in the base of Wilt's gut.

Cortis chuckled again. 'Wrexley, you were always so slow on the uptake.' He twisted the blade slowly in the air, then swiped it quickly downward and the ball of energy shot out from it. The ball was dark now, a black spot of emptiness aimed straight for

Wrexley. It impacted with a low crack, and Wrexley was thrown senseless against the far wall.

'Wrexley!' Daemi rushed to where he lay, shielding his broken body from Cortis and any further attacks.

'As I was saying,' Cortis continued. 'A weld blade. The very thing I was looking for. Of course, it seems your young friend discovered it before my guards could secure the delivery. Quite fortunate, in the end. Gave me the excuse I needed to finally act.'

'You,' Wilt whispered, unsure of his voice.

'Yes. I was the one the blade had been ordered for. I should have known better than to trust a Daleishman like Mallow to keep his word. Still, he paid for his treachery.'

Cortis moved the blade again, swaying it in a figure eight pattern through the air in front of him, and to Wilt's eyes a long trail of shadow was left in its wake, as though the blade had cut through the surface of the world to reveal the darkness beyond.

'Of course it wouldn't do to have such a weapon lying about where any old fool could get their hands on it. Isn't that right, old fool?'

He sliced the blade quickly downward, and another ball of shadow arced out and headed for Petron. Petron tried to shield himself, but the shadow enveloped him, covering him with a thick black film that then ignited with a heavy whisper. Black flames danced around his body, and Petron fell to his knees.

The next moment the darkness was gone, and Petron was left kneeling, his hands over his head, his face twisted in panic.

Cortis chuckled again, an evil island of sound in the silence. 'Forged from the very power that forms the welds themselves. A tool for merging with, and severing, every connection possible. You could have held this power, Petron. But you were too scared. Too scared and too foolish. As always.'

Wilt tried to lift himself to a sitting position, but his body wouldn't cooperate. He felt numb and distant, as though he were watching the world through a long dark tunnel.

Empty.

No.

A spark of light danced across his vision, taking his attention from the darkness around him. Leading him away. Leading him back. A warmth of life.

Cortis continued his rant, his eyes crazed. 'I had spent years preparing my guard. We would take control of Redmondis. Cast down the Sisters from their seats of power. Turn their very weapons against them.'

That thought seemed to give him pause, and he glared at Wilt.

'Yes. The serpents. You. You stopped them, somehow.' He lowered the blade slowly to point at Wilt and shook his head. 'No. You didn't stop them. You only delayed the inevitable. They still haunt the darkness, the depths. You know.' Cortis shook with barely controlled rage. 'You know. And you will help me rouse them again. Guards!'

Wilt heard the heavy stomp of boots on stone as more of Cortis's guard marched into the room.

'Take them. We have much to do.'

The sudden hopelessness was too much for Wilt. He collapsed to the ground and let his eyes close, watching the single spark of light that danced in the darkness.

Chapter 35

Wilt floated in darkness, until the face appeared. A familiar face. Higgs's face. Etched on a stone figurine.

The face tilted backward and the figure fell, knocking into another behind it, and another, stones falling and rising in a circle of never-ending movement. The shadows seemed to shy away from the sight, and Wilt became aware of another world.

He lay on a cold stone floor, rough paving pressed against his cheek. He was in a cell.

The world was black and white, as though all colour had been drained from it. A body on the far side of the cell moved toward him in slow motion, and he was aware of a strange sound in his ears, a voice that spoke too slowly for his ears to comprehend. A stretched, moaning voice.

His voice.

He tried to make out what he was saying.

The face leaned down toward him, and the world tilted as he was pulled into a sitting position. Delco, that was the face's name.

Delco peered into his eyes and said something, shaking him by the shoulders as he called to him, but Wilt couldn't make out the words. He was far below, under the waters, and the sounds couldn't penetrate.

Nevertheless, he seemed to answer.

Something in his reply shocked Delco, and a desperate hope bloomed in his eyes. The next moment, Delco sprang to his feet and moved out of Wilt's vision. Wilt's world leaned to the side again as his body crumpled to the floor.

The cold stone kissed his cheek, and he was surprised when it stopped him, when he didn't sink down any further. His eyes closed, and the strange spark of light faded into the darkness within him.

The door clanged shut, and Higgs opened his eyes.

He was in a cell, underground, beneath the heart of the building. He'd regained consciousness as they carried him along the tunnels, and he'd tried to keep the map of their route in his head, but the twists and turns had been too much even for his practiced senses, and he hadn't dared open his eyes.

Heavy boots marched away from the cell door. Higgs sat up, straining his eyes wide to try to make some sense of his surroundings.

It was a small cell, cut into the rock. The cold stone bench on which he sat was hollowed out of one wall. Other than that, there was just the door: a thick wooden gate with an ages-old lock, judging by the noise it had made.

Higgs jumped to his feet. Shouldn't be too much trouble.

They'd searched him thoroughly when he'd been out, after he returned to human form. He'd felt heavy hands press into him and large, wet noses burrow around his clothes, seeking out any hidden weapons. They'd taken everything, but he was a crafter and needed nothing more than his skills.

Higgs's fingers explored the edge of the door, feeling its coarse wood beneath his fingertips. It wouldn't respond to him. The lock itself was simple, but heavy. He needed something to turn it, something strong. Even the most basic key would do.

He sunk down to the floor and held his hand over the stone, his head raised as if listening.

There. A whisper of life within the stone. The cell had been cut directly into the mountain, into living rock. Rock that he could speak to. Rock that would follow his commands.

Higgs settled on the ground, his legs crossed, and began moving his hands back and forth over the spot of rock directly in front of him. He pictured the shape he wanted. The shape that was within the rock. The shape that was waiting for him to reach in and take it.

He closed his eyes, seeing the shape clearly in his mind, seeing nothing but the shape. Slowly, he reached his hand directly into the stone floor, closing his fist around something and pulling it back. When he opened his eyes, he saw a small stone key lying in his palm. It was warm to touch.

With a grin, he sprang to his feet, slotting the key into the waiting lock. He turned it quickly, and the bolt shot back with a heavy, satisfying clunk. For a moment he stood there, congratulating himself on his work, then he pulled the key out of the lock and bent down to the ground, whispered a word of thanks, and pushed the stone key back into the floor. Seconds later there was no sign of any disturbance.

Higgs smiled to himself again as he thought of the confusion and trouble his little crafter's trick would cause.

The next moment he was moving silently along the dark corridor outside his cell, his eyes wide in the dim light, his fingers tracing along the wall beside him. Every few steps they ran along another cell door, each one empty. He had to be in dungeons beneath the garrison. Somewhere dark and silent where he could be put out of the way and forgotten.

Well, he would see about that.

Higgs moved along in silence, toward where he thought the door to the dungeons should be. The air seemed less stale as he went. Sure enough, after a minute or so the light seemed to improve slightly, as if a half moon had broken through thick clouds, and sounds of movement began to leak from the rooms up ahead.

Sound travelled strangely in the hallways, and he almost stumbled into the guard before he saw him—a large, well-armoured man standing outside another door, kicking his feet in the dust. Higgs shrank into the shadows and waited.

The door swung open, revealing bright firelight behind it, and another guard walked out and spat on the ground. From behind him a low groan of suffering filled the hall. 'Won't shut up, that one.'

The second guard snorted and resumed kicking his feet. 'Always was weak. Could tell by looking at him. Not cut out for anything but sneaking around. Serves him right, he'll spend his life in darkness now.'

'Could be a short life, if he keeps up that noise.'

Both guards looked into the room, and Higgs took the opportunity to duck along the hallway past them. As he went, he caught a glimpse into the cell. Red Charley sat by the side of a small fire, with dirty looking bandages wrapped around his face.

So, Red Charley had finally gotten what he deserved. Higgs allowed himself a grim smile as he crept down the hall. Things were looking up.

As he continued, the air became fresher and lighter, until he reached a point where he no longer needed to feel the wall for direction. A passage and what looked like the entrance lay ahead—a thin stone staircase leading up into the shadows, with a small table and two chairs placed beside it. A single torch burned on the wall where the staircase began. The passage seemed deserted.

Higgs stood for a moment, silently studying the scene. There was something …

A cough barked from behind one of the doors, and Higgs recognised what his senses had picked up. A smell, a good smell. A female smell. Daemi was here.

He moved quickly to the door and slid back the metal peephole cover. Daemi sat cross-legged on the floor.

'Daemi!' Higgs's whisper seemed impossibly loud in the silence, and he cringed as he heard it echo down the hall.

Daemi shot to her feet and moved to the door. She held her mouth to the peephole and barely whispered her reply.

'Want to make any more noise? Get me out of here.'

'How?' Higgs had immediately reverted to taking orders in her presence, waiting for her to take the lead.

'I don't know, you're the damn thief. Figure something out. There must be keys around here somewhere.'

Higgs sank away from the peephole, a sheepish expression on his face. A key. Of course there were keys. Perhaps he should just make his own again, show Daemi what he was capable of. A part of him wanted to show her, prove his worth.

He got as far as bending down to feel the stone at the foot of the door before heavy footsteps echoed through the hall. Voices joined the chorus as the two guards he'd passed earlier came trudging out from the darkness.

Higgs looked around desperately. His eyes were used to the darkness now, but the grey light revealed no obvious hiding place. The only possibility was by the staircase where the torch burned against the wall, throwing deeper shadows across the walls around it.

Daemi had moved back to the floor at the first sound, and Higgs only had time to wave urgently at her before moving toward the staircase, the voices chasing his every step. He ducked past the torch, hoping the guards weren't looking this way as he passed it, and moved up the stairs into the safety of the shadows.

A desperate wave of dread swallowed him. What if the guards didn't stop there? What if they were heading up the stairs, straight toward him? He'd run himself into a trap. Higgs cursed his stupidity under his breath as the two guards approach.

'Never understood why Cortis kept him around. Funes I could understand, but these other rats?'

'All one and the same. Not made for real work. Sneaking around in the dark. Look what comes of it.'

The guards paused by the door to Daemi's cell, and one of them peeked through the metal slot. After a moment he grunted and moved away.

'Still out of it. I'm thinking we might have to wake her majesty up soon enough.'

'Wrexley's little pet captain. We'll show her what good her rank does her down here. Give her a nice little wake-up surprise.'

The first guard chuckled and slapped the other across the shoulders. 'Little? Speak for yourself!'

With that they both broke into rough laughter and moved away from the door.

Higgs clenched his fists, waiting for them. Part of him suddenly wanted them to start up the stairs, just so he'd have to fight them. His fingertips tingled where silver claws had once been. Maybe he could take them even without the sword.

The guards were still both laughing as they slumped into the chairs around the table at the foot of the stairs. Higgs's eyes were drawn immediately to the large, heavy key ring hanging from the closer man's hip.

Higgs stood and chewed his lip, trying to formulate a plan of attack. He rested his hand against the cut stone wall beside him, and the low warmth of the stone responded to his touch. Yes. That was a way.

'Guards!'

Daemi's muffled voice brought both the guards to their feet.

'Wakey wakey.' One of them chuckled. 'Me first. You had the last one.'

'That doesn't count, we haven't had a woman down here in months.'

'A turn's a turn. Don't worry, I'll just warm her up for you.'

The first guard hitched his pants up around his waist and moved off into the darkness toward Daemi's cell door, keys clanking by his side. The other stood with his back to the staircase, hands on hips, oblivious to the world.

It was now or never.

Higgs put all his force into the fist-sized rock he brought down on the back of the guard's head, and the man dropped to the floor with a grunt. He hurriedly stepped over the prone body and moved out of the torchlight.

Another grunt echoed out from the shadows, and the next moment Daemi strode out to meet him.

'Amateurs.' She spat into the darkness and moved past Higgs, who was holding his rock up stupidly. 'You take care of the other one? Good. C'mon, we have to find the others.'

'I hit him with a rock.'

Daemi stopped and looked at Higgs, then allowed herself a smile and reached out to tousle his hair. 'Well done. Now let's go, Killer.'

Higgs's face burned and he was thankful of the darkness as he trotted along behind Daemi, up the stairs and out of the dungeons.

'You always were too cautious. Too careful. Too smart for your own good. Now look at you.' Cortis spat the words at Wrexley, who lay strapped to a rack, his hands stretched high above him, his face a mask of grim pain. 'You served and smiled and made your clever remarks. And I waited.'

Cortis strode around the rack, his hand trailing lightly across the wood, his fingers caressing the thick wooden handle by the side of Wrexley's head. 'You could have shared in this.' His fingers tapped the handle, then paused above it.

'Shared?' Petron said from the corner of the room where he sat slumped and shackled against the wall. 'It is not yours to share.'

'Silence!' Cortis screamed and spun to face Petron, his eyes blazing with madness. 'Do not speak to me, filth. Abomination. You have no place here.'

Petron let out a low chuckle in reply. 'Still you cling to the Sisters' rules, even as you overthrow them. Do you not hear yourself?'

'Silence!' Cortis's hand dropped to the handle and spun it quickly, stretching the rack and wringing a scream of pain from Wrexley.

'Stop. Please stop,' Petron whimpered. 'You're killing him.'

Cortis looked at Wrexley, at his hand on the handle, seemingly noticing it for the first time. His fingers shot back as if burnt.

'You could have shared in this,' he whispered.

Wrexley's scream died into a low babble, and Petron spoke up again, his voice stronger now. 'Me. Use me, Cortis. I'm the one you hate.'

'Yes. You.' Cortis seemed to be considering the idea, before shaking his head. 'No. I have other plans for you. He wants you.'

'He?'

'Our Master. Our true Master. The one who waits in the dark.' Cortis nodded to himself. 'He has touched you, but you have not seen. Not yet. You have no idea what power he wields.'

Petron sat up straighter and raised his voice again, hoping to distract Cortis from his grim task.

'Where is Wilt, Cortis? Where are the others?'

'Oh yes. The young one. The key. The one you so easily tapped. Without even realising it. He showed you the truth.'

'What is the truth, Cortis? What did he show me?'

'That all of this,' Cortis spread his arms, encompassing the world around him, 'all of this, this surface, is nothing. Nothing to the depths. Nothing to the darkness below. No. You have not seen. But you will.'

Cortis looked at Wrexley on the rack and reached out to stroke his sweat-soaked face. 'You could have shared this with me, so I offer you one last mercy.' His fingers moved back to the handle. 'I offer you death. The darkness will not have you.'

'Cortis, no!'

Petron strained against his bonds, but Cortis didn't even look at him. He spun the handle wildly and stood back, his body shaking, as Wrexley's body broke on the rack and a final agonised scream ripped from his throat.

Finally the scream was choked off, and Cortis glowered at the shattered body before him, his eyes glazed and wild and forever lost to sanity. His mouth moved as if he were struggling to find words, then he strode quickly out of the room.

Petron dropped his head and sobbed.

Chapter 36

In the darkness a cell door clanged. Rough hands gripped Wilt's shoulders and pulled him to his feet and out of the room. As he struggled to open his eyes, he felt the darkness clinging to the world around him, dripping from its every surface, as if an infection had spread that only he could see. A sickness to which there was no cure.

Lights and shapes began to blur into focus as he struggled to catch his feet. His boots dragged across the stone floor, bouncing and scraping the leather on stone in a series of jumps, as though he were a stone skipping across the surface of a troubled pond.

Wilt.

The voice was inside his mind, speaking directly to him. Trying to pin down the whirlwind.

Wilt. Wake up.

He raised his head slowly, trying to hold the image of the world in one place as he was pulled across the floor.

Focus, Wilt. It is almost time.

The voice was familiar, like the spark that had led him from the darkness, that had left him here. Like that voice, but different. Delco.

Wilt rolled his head to one side and was rewarded with a glimpse of another body being dragged beside him. Delco, his eyes closed, his face a mask of concentration.

'He's awake.'

The guard shook Wilt and the world jumped and swam out of focus, the lights stretching into long snakes that twisted and curled around his mind.

'Good enough. He'll want them conscious.'

Wilt tried to speak, his lips moving vaguely against each other and a low groan escaping his throat. He was rewarded with a heavy clap over the back of his head that sent the world into a grey blur.

'Not a word from either of you. You'll speak soon enough, I'll wager.'

Focus, Wilt. Find the centre.

The clear voice in his mind gave him something to cling onto as the world lurched nauseatingly past. He closed his eyes and found the darkness waiting for him. Watching him.

Wilt looked calmly at it, his mind suddenly still. The depths called to him, the strange currents twisting and pulling at his mind.

The centre.

In the centre of the darkness, Wilt saw a circle of stones falling one into the other, never-ending. A series of faces toppling backward to tumble upright again.

'The prisoners, Cantor, as you requested.'

Wilt fell against the cold stone floor, smelling dust and sweat in the air, and something else. Blood? Fear?

'Good. Leave that one. Him. Bring him to me.'

Wilt was pulled up again and dragged across the room, then tossed onto the floor. He heard the shuffle of feet and the low growl of a wolf not more than a few feet from his head.

'Has he woken?'

'He just began to stir, Cantor.'

Wilt felt the light brush across his mind, as though someone were ruffling his hair.

'Yes, he is awake. Good. Leave us.'

Wilt heard heels snap together in a salute then march out of the room. There were other noises here, shufflings and heavy breaths.

'Open your eyes, boy.'

Wilt opened his eyes to see Cantor Cortis sitting above him on stone steps leading up to the raised platform where his throne sat. Two enormous wolves stood at attention with him, one on either side, their eyes red and hungry, their teeth bared. The walls around the room were lined with guards. Cortis fingered the weld blade, all black now, a sword-shaped hole in the world.

'Yes. You see, you are quite trapped. But then you weren't going to try and escape, were you?' Cortis leaned over his knees, peering eagerly at Wilt's face, his eyes crazed.

Wilt stared directly into them and recognised the madness and fury that danced there. For a moment he almost pitied them.

Cortis's face twisted into a mask of anger as if he read Wilt's thoughts. 'Save it. You and I know it will not matter. Not now. Stand up.'

Wilt slowly got to his feet, concentrating on holding the world still as it tried to lurch and shake out of frame. As he did so, he felt Cortis's mind push against him again, stronger this time, as though testing his barriers.

'Yes. Yes, they have weakened you. Good. Very good.' Cortis's voice dropped into a distracted whisper. 'I never wanted it to be this way, you know. I was only to show the way. Open the door. But the dark, it wouldn't let me go. They held me there, used me. Those serpents. You know them.'

Wilt felt the touch again, as though Cortis were leaning on his mind, pushing the protective membrane, stretching it as his fingers probed the surface.

'So instead I found you. A key. A window into the dark, so easily tapped that your friends did it without their knowledge.'

The fingers against Wilt's mind writhed and twisted, as though curling against themselves. He closed his eyes and saw the darkness beneath, its pools filled with hungry serpents, just waiting for him to float within reach.

'You will help me.'

Again Cortis struck, pushing against his barriers, stretching him, threatening to break through. He held his mind still and separate, and ignored the panic that rushed up inside him.

'Ah, you still resist.' Cortis's voice was a whisper of regret. 'Very well.' He raised his voice and called to his guards. 'Bring the other one forward.'

Wilt heard more shuffling feet and the rough slap of a body thrown on the ground next to him. The sound finally forced his eyes open, and he saw Delco lying next to him, his eyes closed and face blank.

'We will have to see whether your friend here can provide an easier way in.'

Wilt looked up at Cortis, who was peering hungrily at Delco's prone form.

'You realise how it works, don't you? The connections you form with others, the pathways between your minds. Welds without colour, connections without conscious thought. Each road goes two ways, and anyone at all can use them if they know the key.'

Cortis gripped the weld blade and closed his eyes, lifting his head as if listening to some distant sound.

A low groan escaped Delco's lips, and his face twitched and spasmed as Cortis began to invade his mind. Wilt moved beneath the surface world and saw the thick black weld snaking from Cortis's mind directly into Delco's.

The next moment, a deep coldness surrounded his own mind as something slipped behind his barriers, eating into him. The sea of serpents danced and thrashed in hungry joy as they slithered toward his unprotected mind.

This way.

Wilt heard the voice and blinked his eyes open, sure he had heard it from Delco's lips. But it was in his mind, a spark of light resisting the darkness. He suddenly knew what he needed to do.

The weld twisted above them and he sent his mind into it, diving into the surging flow. The world became a black rush of movement; Cortis's twisted weld burrowed into Delco's mind and filled the space with darkness, infecting it and bleeding through its surface, eating away at everything it touched as it sought the way from Delco's mind to Wilt's. The unprotected pathway.

Wilt let the flow take him, spiralling through collapsing walls and hidden chambers in Delco's mind, sinking toward the target.

There.

Thin black serpents slid down a narrow tunnel, a strange translucent weld that linked Wilt's and Delco's minds. Its surface seemed to resist the stain of Cortis's thoughts, and they slid through quickly, unable to cling to anything. Slid through and came out hungry, ready to attack.

Wilt slid through with them and pushed to the head of the flow, redirecting it from the wide open spaces of his mind toward the weld he had created with Cortis, back into the loop.

The darkness recognised him and snapped at his heels, pursuing him down the tunnels, heedless of the direction.

Wilt broke out into the thick black weld Cortis had formed with Delco, rejoining the flow, losing the serpents that bit at his heels in the wash and chaos of the thick black tide.

'No! What is happening?'

Wilt opened his eyes to see Cortis sitting forward on his throne, his eyes closed and face strained, fingers clawed and digging into the arms of his chair as he struggled to make sense of the rush inside their minds. The weld blade had clattered to the floor and now lay on the stone by the doorway, as though it had flung itself free.

Wilt looked at Delco, still unconscious, his face blank and untroubled. His mind on the brink. Wilt closed his eyes again and dived back into the flow.

The feedback loop he had created between the three of them was whirling ever faster, the black serpents indistinguishable now, the darkness just a liquid rush of speed and movement. He saw the edges fray and burn away, the weld eating at itself. He let it pass by him, pulling himself from its urgent song, pushing into Delco's damaged mind, trying to see what he could salvage.

The wasn't much to save. The walls and chambers of Delco's mind had melted away into a large open space, a swamp of inky darkness, pools of black bubbling here and there on its surface. Cortis had not been gentle; he had blasted everything in his path, trying to find the way into Wilt's mind.

Wilt pushed on, away from the blasted landscape, his mind's eye searching out the spark he knew had to be there.

There.

It floated above him, a flickering light of thought dancing in the currents, staying always out of reach of the darkness below.

And there again.

Two of them now, dancing in time with each other, circling around and around.

'There you are.'

Wilt spun around to see a great black serpent rearing behind him, Cortis's features moulded into its face.

'You sought to use the darkness against me? To redirect the power back into my servant's mind? Foolish boy. You cannot hope to defeat the dark. Our numbers swell with every passing night. You only delay the inevitable.'

The voice was Cortis's, but deeper, strained, as though another was controlling his speech.

'The time of man has come to an end. You do not yet see, but you will. You will.'

The serpent swelled in size, its head flaring out into a saucer shape, the inky blackness of its skin blotting out the world.

'There is nothing left for you here. Nothing left for any of you.'

Wilt was aware of a sudden warmth on his back as the sparks pushed against him.

'We are aware of the others. The ones who try to hide down here, in the dark. They will not escape.'

The blackness became the world as the serpent's head sucked up into a crashing wave, ready to break over everything.

'There can be nothing beyond the darkness. Nothing beneath

death. Your prophecies are useless here. The blood within the stone. The true master of that power sends his greetings.'

The wave broke over Wilt, knocking all thought and sense from him as it dumped over his mind. He opened his eyes and all the welds shattered.

Cortis was sitting above him, his eyes still closed, his face covered in sweat. Whatever had attacked Wilt was not done with Cortis.

Wilt pulled himself to his feet and looked at Delco's body. His face was empty of life. His body was dead, but there was more to it than that. Somehow he was sure Delco had escaped.

The two enormous wolves stared hungrily at him from their seats on either side of Cortis's throne. But Wilt felt stronger than he had in days, as though all weakness had been blasted away in the black tide. He took a step toward the throne and was rewarded with two low warning growls. He smiled at them and took another step.

A crash from the other side of the room almost cost him his life then, as he turned his head automatically. One of the wolves took that opportunity to launch at him, and Wilt's peripheral vision and heightened reflexes were all that saved him. He fell backward and rolled as the weight of the wolf's body slammed into him, its jaws snapping at the air where his neck had been moments before.

As he rolled, clutching the wolf's body close to him now to avoid it rearing back and sinking its jaws into his shoulder, he saw the commotion at the far end of the room. Guards were amassing around the doorway, crowding each other in their eagerness to get their sword arms free, getting in each other's way and paying the penalty for it. Wilt caught a glimpse of short dark hair as two guards fell back from the fray, blood spurting from their chests.

The wolf in his arms took his full attention then, pushing its paws against his thighs and springing away, its long claws leaving deep, warm pocks of red in Wilt's legs. As soon as it was free from his grasp it turned and leaped at him again, keeping its front legs high to swat any resistance away and clear the path for its jaws to sink home. It had performed the move hundreds of times, against hundreds of victims, human and animal, and it hadn't failed once.

Until now.

Once the wolf had pushed free, Wilt had rolled to his feet and leaped, his back legs changing momentarily into the long, elastic muscles of a cat, sending him high toward the ceiling. His hands had shot out, claws digging into the wooden beam above as he flipped over the wolf, landing directly behind it just as it jumped to attack empty air.

Wilt sprang again, landing on the wolf's back, his hand reaching around to the front of its throat, fingers elongated into long claws. The wolf seemed confused for a moment, wondering where its victim had gone, before the claws slashed across its throat, emptying it of life.

As soon as the first wolf fell, the second paused and sniffed the air uncertainly, as if recognising that even without a cold stinging blade in his hand, this human was dangerous. A deep growl curled its lips.

Wilt held his palm out toward it. 'Not as dumb as you look, huh, boy?'

The wolf took a step back, its growl deepening.

'Here. Let me help make up your mind.'

Wilt sent a weld straight into the animal's mind, a black cloud of fear and panic flowering instantly as it struck. Images of fire and blood and pain swamped the wolf's consciousness.

The wolf yelped and sprang away, sprinting past the guards that still crowded the door in its single-minded flight.

Two guards were just getting to their feet as the wolf crashed past, sending them sprawling, and they were soon joined by another heavily bleeding comrade as Daemi's lighting-fast blade struck home.

Wilt was mesmerised as she danced between the guards, her arms and legs a whirl of movement.

'She's not bad, is she?'

Wilt pulled his eyes away from Daemi to see Higgs beside him, having snuck his way somehow past the fight. He clapped Wilt's shoulder, a gleeful smile on his face.

Wilt clasped Higgs's arm in return, then turned back to watch the fight. There were still at least five or six guards trying to take Daemi down. 'Do you think we should help her?'

As he said the words, two more guards fell away and a third stumbled over their bodies, Daemi's blade darting into him before he could regain his feet.

'Nah.' Higgs shook his head. 'She looks like she can handle things.' He turned to examine Cortis, an eager curiosity on his face. 'Been busy here, have you?'

Wilt followed his gaze to where Cortis sat, his face a grey mask. He felt a flash of pity as he thought of the black wave that had blasted him clear, and of what that power was now doing to what was left of Cortis's mind.

A final cry and clatter of armour hitting the floor told them Daemi had finished her work. She strode quickly across the chamber toward them, her long knife still clasped in her hand.

'And where have you been?'

Wilt tried to keep his features blank, knowing the slightest smile would bring trouble. 'Um.'

'Oh no.' Higgs had just noticed Delco's body sprawled on the floor. He hurried over and placed his hands gently on his exposed throat.

Daemi softened her tone. 'Is he?'

Higgs nodded silently and closed Delco's eyes.

'No, he's still there.'

They both looked at Wilt, and Higgs shook his head. 'There's no—'

'I know his body is dead, but it's—' Wilt stuttered to a halt, wondering how to begin explaining the bright sparks in the darkness, the warmth of shared thought. 'He is still within the welds. Outside of time.'

Petron shuffled into the room then, his body hunched and favouring his right side.

'Petron!' Higgs jumped to his feet and hurried over to him, but Petron shooed him away before he could get too close. 'What's the matter with you? Why are you limping?'

'I'm old, boy, old and weary, that's all.' Petron continued toward where Cortis sat, his left foot dragging across the stone floor. It was more than just age and a few bumps and bruises.

'Cantor Wrexley?' Daemi's voice betrayed her hope, and Petron stopped his shuffle to take her in with gentle eyes. He opened his mouth to speak, but seemed unable to form the words, eventually just shaking his head and moving on, quicker now, to where his enemy sat.

Daemi dropped her head and Wilt saw her shoulders shake.

Petron stopped at the base of the stage that held Cortis's throne and glared up at him, his eyes burning with a hatred Wilt had never seen before. It only lasted for a moment, then Petron took control of himself.

'Well, Cortis. It seems someone else got to you first.' Petron stared at Cortis, at his grey dead face, at the cold sweat that still trickled down his forehead, at his fingers digging into the stone arms of his throne, fingers raw and bleeding. 'Perhaps it is for the best,' he whispered, and reached tentatively out to touch him. His fingers paused inches from his skin.

'What's happening to him?' Higgs couldn't disguise his fascination. He skipped around the back of the throne, and was about to jump up to where Cortis sat when Petron waved him away.

'No, boy! Leave him be. The power he used, that used him, it … it has lost patience, I think. Don't touch him!'

He shouted the last words as Higgs began to reach out, and Higgs snatched his hand back quickly.

'The darkness, the depths beneath the welds. It spoke to me,' Wilt said calmly, knowing how mad he sounded.

Petron simply nodded, a sympathetic frown on his face. 'Yes.

Cortis was the servant of something far below the surface. Something that should never have been awoken.' He dropped his eyes. 'But perhaps the fault lies with all of us, all who try to use that power for our own ends. We know the risks, the lure of it. It cannot come without consequence.'

'Why me, though? Why did it speak to me?'

Petron looked hard at Wilt, as if judging whether he was ready to hear the truth. 'You have a special affinity with the weld. You become part of it, much easier than most. Surely Biore showed you this. The darkness lures you, but does not consume you. You can move between the planes.'

'Biore was the same.'

'No.' Petron shook his head. 'No, the darkness had hold of him long before you came to Redmondis. Biore was much weaker than you.'

'But you and Wrexley, you were against using that power.'

'Except when we needed it. Then we were only too happy to use you, to use any advantage we had. We were so blinded by revenge we didn't even see where we were draining our power from.' Petron shook his head again and looked up at Cortis, his eyes red and cold. 'No. We were no better than Cortis. Less blinded by greed perhaps, but just as weak. We would have fallen just as readily.'

Higgs jumped down from the platform and stood with his hands on his hips. 'But he's dead now, isn't he? He looks dead. Do you understand what he was on about, Wilt?'

'A little.' Wilt reached out to clasp Higgs by the shoulder again, then froze as something moved at the edge of his vision.

'Well, I'm not sure even he knows what he was talking about. Welds and darkness, all too high-blown for me. You should try crafting some time, much simp—'

Higgs's body shuddered forward and Wilt felt something hot spray across his face.

They both looked down and stared at the black weld blade protruding from the centre of Higgs's chest.

Wilt heard a voice deep inside him begin to scream, but couldn't seem to do anything but stare at his friend, at the bemused smile on Higgs's face, as if he were trying to understand what practical joke had just been played on him.

'Huh.' Higgs tried to speak but just coughed up blood, and his eyes locked onto Wilt's as the life inside them faded.

'Seems I'm not quite the shot I used to be, Meat.' Red Charley stood in the doorway, his head bandaged and bleeding, one eye completely covered, the other bloodshot and weeping, but looking straight at Wilt. 'I was aiming for you. Still. He was next on my list anyway.'

'No!'

Wilt heard the cry from Daemi just as he saw more guards swarm through the doorway behind Red Charley. He looked at Higgs, at his lifeless eyes, and a cold rush of fury erupted inside his mind. Doors swung open as it flooded through him, a deep laugh of triumph echoing at its edges.

Wilt stared the black weld blade sticking out of Higgs's chest, at the inky darkness that swam across its surface. At the power that it promised. An image of the circle of stones tried to push its way into his mind, forever falling in turn, spinning in a never-ending circle, a whirlpool that sucked into the darkness, creating a point of focus. Wilt's instincts were trying to gain control, but control was the last thing he wanted right now. He consciously wiped the image from his mind, opening himself completely.

The sounds of the world died, and he was suddenly in a dark, silent tunnel. At the far end a grey shape moved against the darkness, four legged, its curling tail trailing behind it. He moved toward it and it skipped further into the tunnel, further into the dark.

Wilt hesitated, only just able to see the shape against the darkness.

Higgs.

His lips formed the word, but no sound came out. The shape turned toward him, however, answering his call.

Higgs. It's me.

The dark walls of the tunnel pulsed with power. A cold rush of air from outside the tunnel pushed against his face, as though death itself was calling to him. He took another step, slower now, bending down and holding his hand in front of him.

Higgs. Stay here. Stay with me.

The cat trotted silently toward him, head cocked as though listening, as though trying to understand his words. It stopped ten feet from him, and Wilt stopped as well, knowing any further movement would send it scurrying away again, into the nothingness that waited for it. Wilt dropped to his knees.

Higgs. Please.

The cat sat on its haunches and studied him, unwilling to come any closer.

Wilt finally understood what he needed to do. He slunk forward on four padded feet, and the smaller cat sprang toward him, twisting himself playfully around his friend.

Another breath sighed out of the tunnel, and both cats raised their heads, sniffing the air. It called to them.

The smaller cat rolled to his feet, ready to move into the dark. He was distracted by two dancing sparks, tumbling over each other in the air, dancing above their heads. The small cat sprang up at one, almost swatting it from the sky but only pushing it higher, and both sparks curled into a spin, as though laughing at the two cats below.

The breath pushed out again, calling them, but the sparks above their heads danced away from the tunnel, leading them out, away from the darkness. The cats followed them, eyes locked on their dance, forgetting the silent call.

Wilt felt a rush of noise and movement; guards swarmed through the door behind Red Charley as Daemi rushed toward them, her long knife drawn. He saw her rush past him, saw the nearest guards fall, watched as others pushed through toward where Wilt waited for them.

Wilt reached out to the closest one, his arm a dark mist of cold shadow. A flare of power surged into him as he reached through the guard's body, clasping his beating heart and holding it, feeling it struggle and die. The body dropped where it stood, eyes wide and staring, horror carved into its face. Wilt turned to the next one, eager to continue.

The guards fell as quickly as they came through the room. To Petron's eyes, where Wilt had stood was now a black, writhing mist, as though thousands of tiny welds were working in concert, snakes swimming in a school of human form. He fed on the guards that stumbled into his path, draining them quickly and mercilessly, leaving them suddenly alone in cold death. The darkness that waited inside him was free, and it was a terrible sight to behold.

To Daemi, Wilt had simply disappeared. She had pushed past him to fight off the approaching guards, but as she cut through them they seemed to put up less and less resistance, almost eager to fall on her blade. It was as though they were running from something much worse. She would have been overwhelmed by sheer numbers within moments, but those guards she had let get in behind her never struck again, and soon enough there were only a few left standing in front of her, their arms shaking, their eyes wide. A shadow moved across her vision, and they too suddenly fell.

To Red Charley, the scene looked very different. Where Wilt had been, a creature of darkness had suddenly reared up, its eyes burning, its touch instant death to any who came near. Red Charley knew death was coming for him.

Power roared in Wilt's mind, blocking out everything but hunger and the howl of victory. Each guard he touched instantly emptied their story into him, a lifetime's worth of images and intrigues, the twisting paths that had led them to this spot. He watched them all without feeling, that part of his mind hidden far below now, curled up and warm and uncaring.

Soon there were only three left standing. Three left for him to feed on.

'Daemi!' Petron kept his gaze fixed on where Wilt had been,

where the black form now hovered in the air. 'Daemi, we must flee. He's—'

Daemi spun around to see Petron stumbling toward her. She caught his shoulder and pulled him to his feet. 'Where is Wilt?'

She shook his shoulder as she spoke, but he didn't seem to understand her words. He merely gestured toward the centre of the room.

'It's too late.'

He wasn't making any sense. She grabbed his chin and turned his face toward her. For a moment she saw it, in the reflection of his eyes, a looming form of shadow, ready to consume them.

Wilt hesitated as the last guard fell at his feet. The dark rush called to him, urged him on, but he held it back and tried to make sense of where he was. Each guard he had drained had filled his world, their lives collapsing into single remembered moments that flooded Wilt's mind. The weld ignored them, but he could not. He experienced it as a fall through time, a rush of feeling that knocked him senseless, yet left no impression before he moved to the next victim.

Red Charley. The one he hated. The one who had taken everything from him. This one he would remember. With this one he would take his time. He blinked across the room and reached into Red Charley's mind.

'Get up, Meat. It's time.'

A sharp kick to his ribs knocked the dreams from his mind. Dreams of sunshine. Dreams of his mother. He shook them off and scrambled to his feet before the man got any angrier and kicked him again.

The man grunted and walked out of the room, out into the cold night. He pulled his ragged boots on and hurried after, not wanting to be left behind in the dark. These alleyways were no place for a child to be alone.

The man strode confidently down the middle of the alley, daring any to challenge him. He scurried behind, watching for movement in the shadows. Eyes peered at him from the shadows, eyes that were hungry and fearful and willing to do almost anything.

The bright moon shone down over the tall man's broad, muscled shoulders, his red hair grey in its light. His hammer swung easily at his side, a fact that still amazed the boy, who was unable to even lift it from the ground. He'd suffered more than one beating after being caught trying.

The twisted alleys opened into a neighbourhood the boy had never explored. The streets were wider, the houses more lavish. There was money here, and the boy was clever enough now to know that money meant power. And power was something to be feared.

'Here, Meat. The third floor window should be open. Hurry up now.'

Without another word the man reached down and boosted him up to the first floor, and the boy found himself clinging onto a thin window ledge, high above the street, his body frozen in sudden fear, not wanting to move an inch in case he fell.

'Move, Meat. We don't have long before the guild rats come round.'

A small rock shot into the small of his back, and he almost lost his footing as the sudden pain washed through him. He forced his hands to unclench and shuffled along the ledge to where a long drain pipe stuck out from the wall and offered him a path upward. He swung himself around it and scurried up the pipe, eager now to show his skill, his ability to climb anything. He was the fastest, the best climber in all of Greystone. He'd show them.

The third floor window was unlatched just as the man had promised, and he dropped silently onto the floor inside, his boots sinking into the thick rug. He bent down and stroked it, for a moment imagining the beast that must have worn this skin at one time. Something even bigger than the man. The thought brought him back to the moment and he hurried on.

He moved through the building, past rows of riches he'd never dreamed of—silver goblets and golden statues—his fingers trailing over each item as he passed, imagining what each could bring on the street, and what that money could mean.

Finally he reached the front door and shot the bolt back, almost falling backward as the man shoved the door open and charged into the room, grabbing him roughly by the shoulder and shaking him, his eyes burning.

'What did you take, Meat? Show me now or by the gods—'

The boy shook his head quickly, showing his empty hands, and the man finally pushed him away, hurrying on to begin taking what he could. The boy rubbed his bruised shoulder and watched him pile all the treasure into his sack, disappearing from his view. He rubbed his shoulder and waited to be noticed again.

Another night, much later. The man lies drunk on the ground in his corner of the room, and the boy, a teenager now, is huddled in another corner, staring at him, fingering the knife. He'd won it from one of the other rats, won it fair too. Climbed faster and higher than any of them and now had this knife to show for it. Except he couldn't show it, not to the man. The man would take it and sell it and drink the profits, then lash out in anger when the boy complained of an aching stomach. No. He couldn't show the man. Not that way. Maybe another way though; maybe he could show the man that he wasn't just a boy anymore.

He leaned forward, the knife clenched in his hand now, and began to crawl across the room, not thinking about what he was going to do, not allowing any of the thoughts screaming up at him from deep inside to register. Then the man stirred and rolled over with a groan and he leaped back into the shadows, the knife hidden inside his tunic, his eyes wide and wary.

Another night, another time. He has power now, undisputed. A patch of the night highway all his own. The best, the fastest. The most silent. He sees the younger ones look up to him and he pushes his shoulders back, unaware of how much it makes him look like his father. The man no longer strides through the alleys like that though. He hides now, hides and crawls and just survives. The boy makes sure of that. He could end him any night he chose, but he finds it better to keep him there, on the ground, among the whispers and scurrying conceits, where he can watch him suffer.

The whispers have gotten louder recently. They have told of a task, a guild task, the first since his own, almost a year before. His night of failure. He pushes the black thought from his mind. He knows that if he can make this prize his own, they will finally welcome him. To where the real power lay.

He won't have to scrap among the rats anymore.

He crouches in the dark, in the sudden cold, waiting for it to fall into his web.

Wilt would have liked to enjoy this moment, the moment of Red Charley's death. Giving him exactly what he deserved. But what Wilt had become, the black void that he existed within, had no feelings about the matter. He simply reached out and took the life from his victim, felt it flare briefly in the rush of the weld, then dropped the drained body to the ground and moved on to his next target.

'He's lost. We must flee,' Petron whispered, straining to form the words through his terrified lips. In his eyes the black shape loomed toward them.

Daemi didn't question him. She pushed through the door, feeling the deep cold reach out to her, its searing touch tearing down her back as she tried to pull them both out of the room.

Wilt hesitated, a sudden pause throbbing through the rush. Something was wrong. Wilt could still feel what he'd touched. It wasn't death. The power inside him screamed in anger as he watched the two forms flee. Leaving him as all others had. But the warmth on his fingertips told him otherwise. He had felt something there, something other than fear. A connection.

Why he was just a child, really.

He was back in the dark alley, looking down from on high at the young Red Charley, his breath misting in the dark, his eyes wide and alert. Eager.

He was just like us.

He looked down at another scene now, two young boys skimming rocks across the surface of a river. Laughing and teasing each other in the shadows of the high town wall.

He was just like any of us.

A third scene, a high bonfire lighting up the night as two brothers sit in its light and dry themselves in its heat. The younger boy shivers in the wind that throws sparks high across the night sky as he listens and learns from his older brother.

Just like me.

Another place and time, a lone black-robed boy watches out a high tower window as his schoolmates practise their newly honed powers in the courtyard below. Birds shoot high into the sky and other animals leap and scuffle on the stones. The boy smiles with them, but then turns back to the small mirror on his bed, stares at it and watches as his eyes fill with black.

Wilt's mind was a whirlwind, yet he felt something clear and silent at its centre.

The wind howled and ripped at his mind as it surged around him, screaming at him to ignore the voices, ignore everything but the power and the darkness. Become what he was meant to be. A shadow on the world. Unstoppable.

Wilt stepped into the silence and found himself back in the world.

The floor was scattered with bodies, eyes wide and empty, faces twisted into masks of pain and despair. He moved his eyes quickly across them, not wanting to remember the faces.

In his hand he clasped the silver weld blade. He raised it up and peered at its mirrored surface; the darkness that had tainted it had drained away, lost in the whirlwind he'd unleashed. Wilt stared at his reflection, his face drawn and grey, his eyes filled with black ink.

We're going to have to do something about that.

Higgs. That was Higgs's voice.

Of course it's my voice. You really should try and understand what you're doing before you do it, you know.

Take it easy on the boy now, it can be a little confusing.

'Biore?' Wilt's voice echoed across the room.

Yes, I'm here too. You don't need to shout.

And us, of course. Couldn't just let you go out and make a mess of things all on your own.

'Delco. So that means …'

Yes, Rawick is here too. But he hasn't spoken in some years now and I'm not entirely sure he remembers how. I'll have to work at it.

'But how?'

The blade of course. Honestly, I don't know how anyone ever thought you were the clever one.

'The weld blade. You're in the blade?'

Not inside the blade, Wilt, Biore answered. *Inside the weld. The blade is just a gateway, much like you yourself.*

Higgs took over again. *It was something I wanted to show you. When you change, you can take certain things with you, like the heartstone, and the weld blade. Take them and use them in a new form. So when it hit me—*

'You changed into your other form, taking the blade with you.'

Delco spoke up. *That's not strictly correct. At least, that's not how Rawick explained it to me, but if it helps you get your head around things then—*

There isn't one way to explain it, Wilt. The welds are deep, far deeper than most realise. It is their great power and their great threat. And that threat still remains. You know of what I speak.

Wilt saw the whirlwind again, the darkness, the presence that filled them both and whispered his name. 'I know.'

First things first though, we really need to do something about those eyes. Lucky for you I happen to be a particularly skilled crafter. Oh, that reminds me, did I get to tell you about how I freed Daemi from Cortis's dungeon? I had to form a key …

Wilt let the weld blade drop to his side as he walked from the room, listening to Higgs's eager voice in his mind. The howl inside his heart was quiet. He was no longer alone.

Epilogue

The cat ran easily up the stone wall, his silver claws leaving a strange scattered pattern of divots in the rock. The sun was warm on his back, and he thought about finding a mantle or ledge to stretch out on and enjoy its heat, but another, deeper instinct urged him onwards, up the wall of the tower, toward the high window above.

Surely there's plenty of time for a few adventures.

Not now, Higgs.

But when are we going to have this kind of opportunity again, Biore? We're in the driver's seat. Let's take this body for a spin.

Time is one thing we won't be short of. Behave yourself.

The cat jumped up onto the window ledge and peered into the room. The window was open and the warm scent of the deep forest far below filled the air. A single occupied bed stood in the far corner of the room, and a small table and chair were pulled up by the fireplace. An old man sat there, fingering a glass of something strong smelling, staring at a vision only he could see.

'I suppose I should have expected a visit.' Petron didn't turn around, his gaze moving back to his glass.

'You—you left the window open for me then?' Wilt found it strange to speak aloud at first, his voice rough and dry in his throat.

'No, not you.' Petron placed the glass carefully on the table and turned around.

He looks so old.

Be gentle with him, Wilt, he has lost—

'We sent patrols down, you know, to clear out the bodies. At first I protested, worried that anyone we sent wouldn't come back. But I was overruled—just a worried old man you know—and the first patrols found nothing so they went deeper. All the way through the tunnels. Didn't find any sign of you.'

'I was careful to keep my distance.'

'So you think you can control it then? Look at me.'

Wilt raised his head, following the order in Petron's tone automatically.

'Your eyes look almost normal.'

Wilt smiled sheepishly and lifted his hand to his face, slipping the green lenses free. When he looked back up at Petron, he saw him flinch.

'Ah.'

Wilt placed the lenses back, and his eyes were green again. 'Something I came up with. Black eyes tend to make people nervous.'

'Very clever. Any crafter would be proud.'

Wilt pushed himself to his feet and walked slowly across the room. He could see Petron's muscles clench as he approached and stopped halfway across the room. He held his hand out and placed a small carved wooden figure on the table. 'He is proud.'

Petron glared at the figure, his eyes watering as he recognised the piece his own hands had carved, the piece he had given Higgs at the start of his training. 'So.'

'So.'

Petron's hand reached out for his glass, then hesitated and moved to the figurine instead. His fingers touched it, then pulled back in pain. 'Argh! The cold burns.'

'Sorry. It'll warm up soon enough.'

Petron juggled the figurine back and forth between his hands until he could hold it, then held it in front of his face, studying the lines he had carved into it months before. 'And ... and the others?' His voice was a hoarse whisper.

'Biore. And Delco, and his brother Rawick. At least, part of

Rawick. He's been in there a long time.'

'But not—'

Wilt saw the hope break across Petron's face and dropped his eyes, unable to answer. He simply shook his head.

Petron placed the figurine on the table and grabbed the glass again. 'No. I didn't think so.'

A low groan sounded from the bed and Petron got to his feet to tend to his patient. His breath misted in the unnatural cold.

Wilt stayed by the window, not wanting to let the effects of his power fill the room completely. 'And Daemi?'

Petron bent down to change the cloth on his patient's forehead. He whispered strange words as he set it in place, and the body in the bed eased its troubled groans. Finally he stood up wiping his hands. 'In a few hours you can ask her yourself.'

Wilt stared at the body in the bed, saw the dark hair sprawled across the pillow, and had to stop himself from running over to her. 'Is she—'

'She has deep burns down her back, burns that did more than physical damage. But she will survive.'

Wilt rubbed the tips of his fingers, recalling a dark vision of a black hand reaching out toward her, dragging its claws down her spine. His hand.

'She'll be okay, Wilt.'

'Tell her I'm sorry.'

'You can tell her yourself.'

'No,' Wilt whispered, his head bowed. 'I can't.'

Petron nodded at the long silver knife hanging at Wilt's side. It looked just like a guard's blade now, except for its colour, the silver light gleaming unnaturally in the dim room. 'The weld blade. You've changed it.'

Wilt pulled his cloak closed to hide the blade from sight. 'Another thing Higgs showed me.'

'Yes. Quite resourceful, that one. Has a true sense of the life within things.'

'The blood within the stone.'

Petron grunted and nodded in reply. 'I shall miss him.'

Tell him I'll miss him too.

'He says—'

'Never mind what he says.' Petron looked at the carved figure again, then slid it into his pocket. 'Foolish boy.' He picked up his glass again to stare at the liquid pooled inside it, then reached for the bottle and poured the contents of the glass back into it. 'Foolish boy.'

Petron's fingers shook as he stoppered the bottle and placed it back onto the table. 'What will you do now?'

'Hmm? Now? There's plenty of work here. Get this place back up and running. Plenty of wielders and crafters that need teaching. Not all the Masters were completely useless. I suppose some of them are still around.'

'You'll stay then?'

Petron chewed his lip as if pondering the deeper question in Wilt's words. 'Yes. I'll stay. You, however—'

'I must leave.'

'You must leave.'

The mist from Petron's breath was stronger now, whiter. The temperature of the room had dropped again. Wilt pulled himself onto the ledge, to try to minimise the discomfort he was causing.

'You're too dangerous.'

Wilt nodded and looked out the window, out over the deep green sea of trees. 'I'm going to find it. Whatever it is. The … the voice in the darkness. It's something I should have realised earlier. The Tangle, there's something there that knows more. Some awareness. I'm going to seek it out.'

Petron hesitated before answering, weighing up his words. 'Be careful, Wilt. The welds are deep. Far deeper than—'

'I know. Believe me, I know.' Wilt raised his head moments before the sound of hurried footsteps could be heard outside the door.

'Goodbye, Petron.'

'Goodbye, Wilt. I ... we will—'

The door burst open then and strange music filled the room as Heather barged in, holding out the sounding bowl, the music emanating from its hollow.

'Petron! Look!' She stopped when she saw Petron sitting alone at his table, his patient fast asleep in his bed, the window flung open.

'Heather. What a nice surprise.'

Wilt could hear the heartstone song fade as he left them, the cat running down the wall of the tower, headed toward the walls and the wide open forest beyond.

So the spark blooms into a flame, a wraith, a true weapon to wield against the darkness. Even now it approaches, drawn by the currents that surge deep below the surface world. Drawn by the very depths themselves.

The trees welcome it into their dominion, acknowledging its power. They shift and mutter amongst themselves, hoping to be heard, hoping to draw out its true potential, much as they once whispered to me. Much as they have whispered to all the wild ones. The ones who delved too deeply. The ones who left the human world behind.

Still the prophecy has not yet been fulfilled. The blood within the stone has awoken. The spark has begun to harness the full power of the welds, the connections that link all life. Connections so many mistreated, not recognising their true potential. But darkness still stains the land, feeding on the petty fears and intrigues of those who walk its surface. I taste its corruption on the wind.

The trees murmur patience, they have known such threats before. They know their nature. They have more faith in the prospect of salvation than I.

Or perhaps they simply tire of this world. Of the ants that scurry about its surface. Perhaps they too welcome a return to the depths of oblivion.

The leaves skitter and dance in the wind, reproaching my fear, mocking my all too human misgivings. My doubt. The time fast approaches when all such thoughts will become meaningless.

I feel it coming, approaching ever closer. I wait and watch and try to accept my fate.

About the Author

T.R. Thompson is an Australian speculative fiction author. He lives in Belgrave on the outskirts of Melbourne with his wife and two young sons.

When not writing or reading, he spends too much time gaming and taking long meandering walks through the forest that always seem to end up at a tavern.

The Blood Within The Stone is his first novel.

Lightning Source UK Ltd.
Milton Keynes UK
UKHW010802150822
407319UK00002B/417

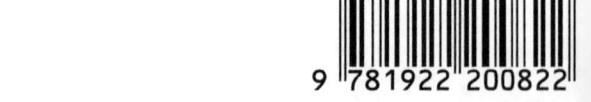